❶ Mansion
❷ Freeman Avenue
❸ Paradise Green
❹ Stratford High School
❺ The Dusty Corner Bookshop
❻ First Congregational Church
❼ United Aircraft plant

An Ellen Anderson Mystery

CONSPIRACY ON THE HOUSATONIC

A Novel Approach to SAT Preparation

Kendall Svengalis

Duneland Press

Guilford, Connecticut, 2014

While this is a work of fiction, it draws upon people
living and dead, real and imagined, for its inspiration.
The story is a creative window into the world of
Stratford, Connecticut, in the year 1942.

Published in the United States by Duneland Press,
Guilford, CT

www.dunelandpress.com

Library of Congress Cataloging-in-Publication Data

Svengalis, Kendall, 1947-
Conspiracy on the Housatonic / Kendall Svengalis
p. cm.

Summary: Swedish-American girl detective, Ellen Anderson, discovers
Nazi agents operating in her hometown of Stratford, Connecticut.
An SAT vocabulary-building novel. Includes SAT word glossary.

ISBN: 978-0-9819995-6-2 (paperback)
ISBN: 978-0-9819995-7-9 (eBook)

Interior design by Ellen Haffling Svengalis

Printed in the United States of America
First Edition

For Ellen, Queen of my heart

Preface

This novel was conceived more than twenty years ago, when my children, Hillary and Andrew Svengalis, were students in the Barrington, Rhode Island Public Schools. As they **grappled** with vocabulary lessons, and later studied for the SAT exams, it struck me that a better approach to learning vocabulary would be to place these words in a narrative context that would better **facilitate** their mastery. *Conspiracy on the Housatonic* represents this novel approach to the SATs. Each of the nearly 1,500 SAT words appearing in this text is drawn from a variety of SAT word lists, representing the words most commonly used in the Critical Reading section of the SAT tests. Each of these words is highlighted in **boldface**, and is defined in a glossary at the back of the book. This list is supplemented by a list of 50 names of leading political figures, historical events, concepts, and terms significant to the era and story line.

Mastering vocabulary is much more than an exercise in test preparation, however, but an essential path to a higher level of reading comprehension that can **facilitate** both academic achievement and professional advancement. The author is of the firm belief that "higher order thinking skills" can only be achieved through rigorous mastery of vocabulary and subject matter content, rather than through formal reading comprehension skills which devote insufficient attention to the broad vocabulary and world knowledge that children need to **extract** meaning from texts. To do otherwise is to put the cart before the horse. As E.D. Hirsch **elucidates** in his **estimable** books *Cultural Literacy: What Every American Needs to Know* (1988) and *The Knowledge Deficit: Closing the Shocking Education Gap for American Children* (2007), educational success is highly dependent on the **acquisition** of world knowledge to advance effective reading comprehension. The Core Knowledge Sequence* developed by his Core Knowledge Foundation, is a **coherent**, **cumulative**, and content-specific course of study for grades Preschool-8 that is designed to help children establish strong foundations of knowledge, grade by grade. This knowledge deficit is one of the primary reasons why American students, particularly those from minority or underprivileged backgrounds, fail to achieve the level of educational success which is their birthright.

This novel is intended to serve as a means of addressing this knowledge and vocabulary deficit. While designed primarily for high school students preparing for the SAT tests, high school English teachers, and SAT instructors, this book can be read by anyone desirous of increasing his or her vocabulary, and doing so in way that is both entertaining and educational.

Conspiracy on the Housatonic is set in 1942 Stratford, Connecticut, shortly after the attack on Pearl Harbor, and at a time when Stratford was a center of Allied war production, specifically the Vought F4U Corsair fighter aircraft. While the story is fictitious, it draws upon real world people and places of the time to add an aura of historical **verisimilitude** to the narrative. It also utilizes a variety of 1942-era postcards, photographs and other images to **augment** the historical **milieu**.

The author wishes to thank Melissa A. Benson for her cover design and interior illustrations, the Stratford Historical Society for representative postcards and photographs of the era, the Library of Congress, Prints and Photographs Division, for the World War II posters and graphics, the Worcester Historical Museum, Winifred Ingram for the photograph of her father, the Reverend F. Stanley Sellick, and my wife, Ellen Haffling Svengalis for serving as the inspiration for the book's heroine, for her photographs, and for her superb layout.

* Core Knowledge is not to be confused with the Common Core, a top-down attempt by federal and state officials to impose national standards on local communities.

Chapter 1

Theatre of the Mind

It was a Sunday evening not unlike many others for Ellen Anderson and her Stratford High School chums. Ellen had invited Betsy Dalrymple and Linnea Matthews to the Anderson home on Freeman Avenue to listen to another episode of *Inner Sanctum* on the family's Crosley **console** radio. Sitting on the **davenport** in the darkened living room with their eyes fixated on the glowing dials, the girls listened intently as the eerie sound of the studio organ heralded the opening of another blood-curdling tale:

> *Lipton tea and Lipton soup present...Inner...Sanctum...Mysteries*
> *Good evening friends, this is Raymond, your host of the Inner Sanctum,*
> *inviting you in through the squeaking door.*
> *Come on in, and be prepared to be scared out of your wits...*

In carefully **modulated** and **ominous** tones, host Raymond Johnson set the atmospheric mood of the *Inner Sanctum* mysteries. Ellen had been to several New York plays with her parents, but there was nothing like this theatre of the mind to drive the imagination of a bright and **precocious** girl of seventeen. The stories were almost guaranteed to send chills up and down her spine. Since its debut in January of 1941, Ellen had almost never missed an episode.

Inner Sanctum wasn't the only program to which Ellen listened after finishing her homework. She could rattle off a **profuse litany** of programs, including *Edgar Bergen and Charlie McCarthy*, *Fibber McGee and Molly*, *Burns and Allen*, *Baby Snooks* with Fanny Brice, the *Jack Benny* program, and two programs that appealed to the teen set—*The Aldrich Family*, with its slightly dizzy hero, Henry Aldrich, and *The Hardy Family*, featuring the ever-popular Mickey Rooney as Andy Hardy, and a variety of mystery and suspense thrillers.

Ellen wasn't totally dependent on the Crosley **console** radio around which her family and friends frequently gathered in the living room of her Freeman Avenue home. She had received a Crosley Model 517 Bakelite table radio for Christmas from her parents. It was her most treasured **acquisition** that Christmas of 1941, and one she kept on the nightstand next to her bed. Not infrequently, her

mother had to remind her to turn it off, or she wouldn't be fit for school the next day. The weekends were another story. Ellen often fell asleep listening to some of her favorite shows on Friday and Saturday evenings, a cup of hot Ovaltine resting on her nightstand.

Ellen had collected her share of radio premiums since becoming addicted to the medium as a child. She had a Little Orphan Annie birthstone ring which she obtained by sending in ten cents and a seal from under the lid of a jar of Ovaltine. She was a member of the Dick Tracy Secret Service Patrol and received a code book, badge, and pledge for mailing in two Quaker Puffed Wheat box tops. She had a Lone Ranger silver bullet ring with a secret compartment for storing messages, an autographed photograph of Captain Midnight, a Jack Armstrong **pedometer**, and many other items **endorsed** by famous radio stars.

It was the mystery and detective programs that appealed most to Ellen's **fervent** imagination, however—shows like *Suspense*, *The Shadow*, *Nick Carter: Master Detective*, *Gangbusters*, based on real life police stories, and, most of all, *Inner Sanctum*. Ellen imagined herself as the heroine of these mysteries, the one with the **keen** mental **faculties** and **trenchant** determination to solve the most complex cases.

Hers was not a **transient** obsession, however. Stratford had already taken note of Ellen's **aptitude** as an amateur detective, an **aptitude** driven by her passion for mystery novels. At the age of fourteen, she succeeded in recovering her neighbor Jim Ellerby's brand new blue Ford roadster, which had been stolen from a parking space right in front of Hamilton Pharmacy in the Paradise Green business block. In fact, the car disappeared while Ellen was inside enjoying a delicious chocolate malted with some members of her softball team.

Ellen **surmised**, quite **ingeniously** as it turned out, that it would be taken to one of the local body shops and dismantled for its parts, the total value of which would exceed that of the car as a whole. Using the local telephone directory as her guide, she spent every evening after school patrolling every lane and byway around town looking for signs of the **purloined** automobile. Then, one evening, as the **dappled** glow of twilight settled upon this charming coastal community, Ellen's **intuition** seemed to draw her to the Sutton Body Shop on Barnum Avenue. Suddenly, she had a **presage**, an almost **clairvoyant** sense, that something illegal was going on inside the walls of this small automotive establishment. Leaving her Schwinn bicycle in the tall grass at the rear of the shop, she crept up to one of the windows and peered in.

There it was! The Ellerby's Ford roadster—license number HB733—being dismantled by two **nondescript** men in dark blue overalls. Rather than run the risk of being detected, however, Ellen quickly grabbed her bicycle, sped off to the Stratford Police Station on Main Street, and alerted the desk sergeant of her discovery. Before long, the car was recovered, and the **miscreants apprehended** and brought to justice. Indeed, the prosecutor argued against any form of **clemency** in light of the seriousness of the crime, which was the **culmination** of a wave of **larceny** that had **afflicted** Stratford for many months. For her **meritorious** actions, Ellen received a **commendation** from the police department, and was the proud recipient of a generous $100 reward from her grateful neighbors.

It was an **auspicious** start for Ellen's still **inchoate** career, but certainly not **orthodox** behavior for a girl of fourteen. Naturally, the case garnered her glowing **accolades** in *The Stratford News*, the **adulation** of her parents, and the **plaudits** of her neighbors, teachers and classmates. Although she **aspired** to a career in the field of criminal investigation, her ambitions were nevertheless subjected to periodic cold doses of reality from her cautious parents. Her father, Eric, in particular, was a **pragmatic** sort inclined to **admonish** her that detective work was a dangerous occupation, particularly for a woman, and that things might have turned out quite differently if she had been detected by the thieves. Ellen respected his sense of **prudence**, but hers was an **indefatigable** spirit, with a **dogged** commitment to a goal once her mind was made up.

"I know, Dad," she was prompted to say. "But there are many occupations that a woman can do just as well as a man. I don't see why I can't have the same opportunities, if that's what I want to do."

"Your mother and I just don't want anything to happen to you," her father cautioned.

Ellen had just turned seventeen on her last birthday—October 4, 1941. A junior at Stratford High School, she was possessed of a **vivacious** personality, and had blossomed into a real beauty. Her bright face and sparkling eyes were accompanied by a delicate mouth and chin. Standing five foot, six inches tall, with shoulder-length blond hair, she maintained a slim build thanks to her high school athletic activities, and despite her love of chocolate in its various **manifestations**. Her physical appearance had undergone a genuine **metamorphosis** since her awkward early teenage years. She was a stylish dresser with an **impeccable** eye for the latest fashion trends. She was also an excellent student and exhibited **uncanny** powers of judgment and observation far beyond her **chronological** age. Among her many friends at Stratford High, Betsy and Linnea were the kind of close **confidants** with whom she could exchange secrets.

Boys were another matter entirely, and still on the **periphery** of her life, however. She occasionally went to the movies with Ken Swenson, sometimes as far away as the **opulent** Majestic or Bijou theaters in Bridgeport. But their relationship was more friendship than **ardor**. A member of her family's Swedish social circle, Ken was **seemingly** too interested in books and his studies to take girls too seriously at this stage in his life. While college was one of his **preoccupations**, he figured, like most of his male classmates, that he'd be in the service shortly after graduation. After all, many of the young men in town had either enlisted or were drafted after war was declared against Japan and Nazi Germany. Ellen was thrilled when he asked her to the Stratford High junior prom, however, an event which was only six weeks away.

The Anderson family lived in an attractive two-story colonial-style home on Freeman Avenue in the Paradise Green section of Stratford. Eric and Edna Anderson, Ellen's father and mother, usually left the girls alone to enjoy their radio dramas. In fact, this evening, they were out dancing with some of their Swedish friends at the Norden Club in the

Black Rock section of Bridgeport. The Andersons were **avid** participants in the local Swedish-American cultural scene. Eric was a charter member of the North

Star Singers, a Swedish male chorus based in Bridgeport, with whom he sang second tenor. He enjoyed performing the songs of Hugo Alfvén, Wilhelm Stenhammar, Gunnar Wennerberg, and the **parodies** of 18th century **troubadour** Carl Michael Bellman. Both Eric and Edna were also members of a local Swedish folk dance group, for which Edna had sewn the costumes. It was a way of carrying on the rich cultural traditions Ellen's grandparents had brought over from Sweden around the turn of the century before settling in the Bridgeport area.

Ellen, too, embraced her Swedish heritage. Most of all, she enjoyed the picnics and dances held at the farm in Monroe owned by the Good Templars, a Swedish-American fraternal lodge and **temperance** society which **abstained** from the use of

alcohol and promoted **sobriety**. The North Star Singers often gathered at the farm for picnics, singing and dancing. Interestingly, the farm was just a stone's throw from the rural retreat of American opera singer Grace Moore, who once sent a note to the president of the chorus telling him how much she enjoyed the **consonant** voices of the Swedish songsters **wafting** through the valley.

Ellen's father, Eric, was a tool designer by **vocation** with the E.V. Anderson Company, a Bridgeport tool and die works founded by his father in 1922, as the economy was coming out of the economic recession of 1920-21. The success of the business was due, in no small part, to Eric's **fastidious** design work which met the most exacting **criteria** and was widely admired in the industry. Among his designs were molds for **precision** engine parts, both automobile and marine, and the American Flyer model trains manufactured by the A. C. Gilbert Company of New Haven, which also manufactured the popular Erector Set. Many of the toolmakers with whom Eric worked were also Swedish.

With the start of World War II, Eric was now designing complex parts for the Corsair fighter aircraft under contract with the Vought-Sikorsky plant in Stratford, now officially called the United Aircraft & Transportation Corporation. Most of the Corsairs were to be based on United States aircraft carriers or islands in the Pacific. Others were being shipped to the British and French allies who, at that moment, were caught in a life and death struggle with Nazi Germany. With the United States' entry into the war, these parts would be a critical ingredient in the Allied war effort.

Unlike some of its **impecunious** competitors, the E.V. Anderson Company was so successful that Ellen's grandfather was able to purchase not only a home in rural Easton, but a lakeside cottage on Candlewood Lake, north of Danbury. While not excessively **parsimonious**, Ellen's grandfather had a **proclivity** for **frugality** and was not given to **extravagant** tastes or **profligate** spending habits. One of Ellen's greatest pleasures was going to the Candlewood Lake cottage with her parents, or with Betsy and Linnea, and swimming or boating off her grandparents' dock.

Eric possessed a **whimsical** sense of humor and enjoyed amusing Edna and his friends with his latest **witticisms**, including a whole **panoply** of Ole and Lena jokes popular among those of Scandinavian **extraction**. He also enjoyed telling ethnic jokes about the Norwegians. They were the same jokes the Norwegians told about the Swedes, as Ellen later learned. Rather than being **pejorative** in tone, however, they reflected the good-natured **camaraderie** shared by these neighbors on the Scandinavian **peninsula**.

Theirs was a close-knit family whose activities were **circumscribed** by work, church, and Swedish clubs and organizations. The Andersons were also **inveterate** coffee lovers, like most Swedes. As far as Ellen was concerned, her grandmother Holmgren made the best coffee. Typically, when offered a

second cup, her grandmother was fond of asking for *femton droppar*—that's Swedish for fifteen drops. Whenever she said this, Ellen's father humorously offered to get out the eyedropper and measure out fifteen drops of coffee. Coffee was an **integral** part of life in the Anderson household and, to hear the Swedes tell it, a virtual **panacea** for all ailments.

Ellen was also involved in a variety of **extracurricular** activities at Stratford High School, including the school choir, and the softball and volleyball teams, reflecting not only an **exceptional** soprano voice, but an **innate** talent for athletics. She also sang in the junior choir at the First Congregational Church, and enjoyed bird-watching and gardening with her mother. Indeed, the backyard garden they tended was **replete** with a large variety of flowers, both annual and **perennial**. With her grandfather Victor's encouragement, she even taught herself to play the guitar and performed folksongs and **ballads** at some of the Swedish gatherings that she and her parents attended.

~~~~~~~~~~~~~~~~~

When the *Inner Sanctum* mystery was over, Ellen turned to Betsy:
"How would you like to take us for a ride in that convertible of yours, Betsy?"
"I'll second that," replied Linnea. "We could go up River Road to Putney."
River Road ran along the shore of the Housatonic River, which separated Stratford from the neighboring town of Milford to the east. Beginning its 149-mile journey in western Massachusetts, the Housatonic **meandered** through the **primeval** forests of northwestern Connecticut before making its way south to Long Island Sound. Ellen's favorite spot along the river was actually in the scenic village of West Cornwall in the northwest corner of the state, where an historic covered bridge spanned

a beautiful stretch of water frequented by trout fisherman, including her father. She had often imagined owning a little cottage on one of the charming hillsides overlooking the river and its **picturesque** covered bridge.

The girls took the car Betsy had borrowed from her parents—a 1934 LaSalle coupe convertible, with **rumble seat**. The trio had no difficulty squeezing their **lithe** frames into the front seat, however, while Betsy drove. Ellen was not a **novice** when it came to driving. Since obtaining her driver's license shortly after her sixteenth birthday, she occasionally drove her parents' 1941 blue Hudson convertible on those rare occasions when it was not in use. Ellen's father was not normally the type to buy a convertible, generally **oscillating** between various **utilitarian**, family-friendly sedans. But Ellen pleaded and **cajoled** long enough that he finally **capitulated**, purchasing one that was **palatable** to his own tastes. Ellen learned to drive after some patient instruction from her father, who helped her master the gear shift and clutch. On rare occasions, he had to **chide** her for being a little too heavy on the gas pedal, however. Not that she was as bad as Molly Jankowsky, across the street, who had her driver's license **revoked** after receiving three speeding tickets in a month.

It was a cool April evening, with a full moon and a **smattering** of stars poking out from the cloud-laced canopy overhead. The glow from the moon was bright enough to cast a bright reflection on the **tranquil** waters of the Housatonic. Leaving Freeman Avenue, they proceeded through the Paradise Green business district, and followed Main Street north until River Road split off to the right, just beyond the popular Housatonic Lodge. Heading north on River Road, with their hair blowing in the cool night air, the girls began singing some of their favorite radio jingles.

Oh, the big red letters stand for the Jell-O family;
Oh, the big red letters stand for the Jell-O family;

Jell-O pudding, yum, yum, yum,
Jell-O pudding, yum, yum, yum.
Jell-O tap-i-oca pudding yes-siree!

"Hey, how about this one?" suggested Betsy:

Have you tried Wheaties?
They're whole wheat with all of the bran.
Won't you try Wheaties?
For wheat is the best food of man.
They're crispy and crunchy the whole year through,
The kiddies never tire of them, and neither will you.
So just try Wheaties, the best breakfast food in the land.

"And don't forget Tom Mix," added Linnea. "That's my favorite."

Shredded Ralston for your breakfast
Starts your day out shining bright.
Gives you lots of cowboy energy
With a flavor that's just right.
It's delicious and nutritious,
Bite-size and ready to eat.
Take a tip from Tom,
Go and tell your Mom:
Shredded Ralston can't be beat!

"Say, maybe we should go into broadcasting," laughed Linnea. "We could form a vocal trio and sing advertising jingles—you know, like the Andrews Sisters."

"Not so fast," replied Betsy. "I'm trying to lose weight, and if we don't stop this I'll have to go home and eat a bowl of Shredded Ralston."

Finally, on a **secluded** stretch of road near the village of Putney, the girls pulled over to admire the **quiescent** view from the shoreline. They traversed a **circuitous** path to the river, just north of the Chandler mansion, a **forbidding** old weather-beaten **Victorian** structure that hadn't seen life for over three years, since the death of old man Roderick Chandler and his **eccentric** wife, Hortense.

"From what I understand, Mrs. Chandler was a strange bird," Betsy observed.

"I still recall the newspaper headlines following her death," said Ellen. "It read: 'Local woman dies with forty-seven cats in residence,' or something like that."

"I understand she acquired most of them after Mr. Chandler died," Linnea added.

"I'll bet they did a number on the old place. I'm not surprised nobody has purchased it," replied Betsy. "It probably needs a thorough **fumigating** to **mitigate** the odors."

"Who would want to own forty-seven cats? Just think of the cat food bills," added Ellen.

The girls passed a small **stagnant** pond and continued down the short path to the river to admire the **serene** view from the narrow beach. A lone canoe plied the waters on the Milford side, then put into shore.

Scene on Housatonic River, Putney, Conn.

After absorbing the calm and beautiful evening on the river for several minutes, and skipping rocks across its **placid** surface, the girls began the brief walk back to the car. Suddenly, through the trees, a **luminous** glow came from the **weathered** and abandoned old house, now **shrouded** in mystery.

"Did you see that, Betsy?" Ellen exclaimed.

"See what?"

"That light in the window."

"No, I didn't. Are you sure it wasn't the moon reflecting off one of the windows?"

"No, I saw an **evanescent** glow in one of the upstairs windows. There it is, again."

"Yes, you're right. I can see it now," whispered Betsy, with Linnea nodding in agreement.

"I wonder what could be going on in there. There are no automobiles parked in the driveway, or any other evidence that it's inhabited," Ellen added.

"Do you suppose some homeless people have taken up residence there?" said Linnea.

"It's certainly possible, but, whatever it is, we can't worry about it now," Ellen reminded her friends. "We have to be getting back to town. It's almost 11:00, and we've got school tomorrow."

With their **nocturnal excursion** concluded, the girls climbed back into the LaSalle and headed for home, now driving south on River Road. Betsy and Linnea were already thinking about other things, including securing dates for the prom. But Ellen couldn't help thinking about what those mysterious lights signified.

Chapter 2

Latin Roots and Probate Courts

Although she was born at Bridgeport's St. Vincent's Hospital in 1924, Ellen had lived her entire life in Stratford, where her parents built a two-story colonial on Freeman Avenue in 1921. Founded by New England Puritans in 1639, Stratford was one of the oldest **municipalities** in the United States, named for Shakespeare's Stratford-upon-Avon in England. Along its tree-lined streets stood many stately homes and other **venerable** structures of historic significance, including the Judson House on Academy Hill, built in 1723, the Lovejoy Tavern, the Perry House, and the First Congregational Church in Stratford

Center, whose **congregation** was formed the same year the town was founded. There were other **vestiges** of its colonial past. The **hallowed** Congregational Burying Ground and Christ Episcopal Church Burying Ground, **venerated** by local residents, contain ancient tombstones where many of Stratford's earliest residents are **interred**.

Largely a residential community of single-family homes, Stratford was also a **burgeoning** manufacturing center and home to a variety of industrial and commercial enterprises, mostly at its south and west ends, including the Stratford Army Engine Plant, **adjacent** to the Stratford-Bridgeport Airport which had just opened in 1939, and Sikorsky Aircraft which moved to Stratford from Bridgeport in 1929. In 1939, Chance Vought joined with Igor Sikorsky to form the Vought-Sikorsky Division of the United Aircraft and Transportation Corporation. Its work force swelled to more than 12,000 employees when it began manufacturing the Vought F4U Corsair fighter aircraft. By 1942, Stratford's **latent** industrial potential had been unleashed and the town had become a leading center of Allied wartime production.

For residents of Bridgeport, who lived in double- or triple-decker apartment houses, Stratford was a step up to suburban living and a private backyard. By 1940, more than 19,000 souls called it home. The Stratford Center business district occupied the block immediately south of the New York, New Haven & Hartford Railroad overpass, a block which included the Stratford Theatre, the Lovell Building and Hardware Store, and the Dusty Corner Bookshop. The north end

of town contained the largest **expanse** of **arable** land, which continued to support a variety of **agricultural** activities, including small scale truck and dairy farming. South of the airport, the coastal district of Lordship, on Long Island Sound, **beckoned** those drawn to sea and sand.

Stratford, like most cities and towns across America, was forced to **jettison** its former sense of **insularity** and direct its unified efforts to war **mobilization** and military production. Many of her sons, and some of her daughters, had enlisted in the various branches of the military, or were employed in defense plants whose **acrid** smoke now polluted the once **pristine** air of the community. Pursuant to **President Roosevelt's** creation of the Office of Civilian Defense, Stratford civilians were recruited for service in the local chapter of the **Civil Air Patrol**, which took on the responsibility of patrolling the town's coastline and urging their fellow citizens to remain **vigilant** in the face of enemy attacks or **espionage**. Such activities soon came to be performed with a **quotidian** regularity. Not wanting to be **remiss**

in performing his patriotic duty, Ellen's father, Eric, responded to the call from the Council of Defense and volunteered to serve as the air raid warden for his Freeman Avenue neighborhood. It was his duty to ensure that local residents observed blackouts and kept their shades pulled at night. A steam-powered air-raid siren was installed above the Tilo Roofing Company to warn residents in the event of enemy attack.

Scrap drives enlisted the aid of the town's young people who collected iron, steel, aluminum, rubber, paper, cloth and chicken fat for recycling. While adults bought United States Defense Savings Bonds, young people purchased war savings stamps which could later be redeemed for bonds. Bond drive rallies to **galvanize** public support for the war effort were major events, but no more so than when promoted by the generous and **magnanimous** efforts of a Hollywood star or national celebrity.

BUY WAR BONDS

~~~~~~~~~~~~~~~~

Monday mornings usually came all too soon for Ellen who usually enjoyed weekend activities with friends.

"Ellen, time to get up for school," her mother shouted from the bottom of the stairs as the sunlight filtered in through her **diaphanous** bedroom curtains.

Ellen's mother was always up before everyone else, first to get Ellen's father off to the shop, and then to prepare Ellen's breakfast. Finally yielding to the **inevitable**, Ellen rubbed her sleepy eyelids and popped out of bed. After a few minutes in the bathroom, where she washed her face and hands and combed her hair, Ellen donned her new blue tweed pleated skirt and matching sweater, and hurried downstairs. A bowl of hot Cream of Wheat and a glass of orange juice awaited her in the kitchen. Her mother joined her at the kitchen table, a hot cup of coffee and a Swedish cinnamon bun in front of her.

"Any tests this week, Ellen?"

"Yes, I have a test of Latin roots on Wednesday and an English test on

Friday. It's on *A Tale of Two Cities*. I finished reading it last week. It was the **unabridged** edition, not the **abridged** edition many schools use. Besides, I still vividly remember the film adaptation with Ronald Colman which played at the Stratford Theater a few years ago. I've always **revered** Ronald Colman. He's so romantic and has the most **mellifluous** voice. Right now, though, 'tis a far, far better thing that I get an 'A' on this test," she said, with a laugh.

Once she had finished her breakfast, Ellen went to the front closet and grabbed her spring coat and put on her shoes. Her books were already resting on the end table near the front door.

"I'll see you about 5:00, Mom." She kissed her mother on the cheek and headed out the front door.

Stratford High School was eight blocks from the Anderson's home. Occasionally, Ellen got a ride with Betsy, or one of her other friends lucky

enough to have access to an automobile, but mostly she walked. Although, school opened at 8:00 a.m., Ellen hated to **procrastinate** and usually arrived about fifteen minutes before the start of her first class, a habit she **attributed** to her sense of **punctuality**, one of the most important Swedish social **mores** she had learned from her parents. **Tardiness** was not a part of her vocabulary.

As she ambled along Main Street this morning, Ellen reflected, again, on the mysterious lights she and her friends had observed in the old Chandler mansion on River Road. She hoped that she could convince Ken Swenson to drive her up there on Saturday to do a little investigation.

Ellen had a full class schedule this year. In addition to Latin and English, her classes included calculus, American history, physical education, and chorus. She was a **diligent** student and had an excellent **rapport** with all the members of the faculty, but was particularly fond of her Latin teacher, Mr. DeLeurere, her English teacher, the **genteel** Mrs. Carmichael, and Miss Satterfield, who taught American history.

Mr. DeLeurere was what one might call a "character." He was passionate about Latin and **eloquent** in its defense. He used his classes as a **forum** to **expound** upon its value in everyday life. Some of the students may have found his classes rather **abstruse** and **unorthodox**, but Ellen seemed to thrive on the complexities of the language and found his lectures most **enlightening**.

"Latin is very much a living language, despite what some people say," he said on the first day of class. He stressed its value in vocabulary building and never missed an opportunity to break English words down to their Latin roots. For Ellen, it was like learning a secret code. Today, they were reviewing Latin prefixes and suffixes:

"What is an aquarium?" Mr. DeLeurere asked Ellen's first period class.

"Literally, a place where there is water," answered Christine Applegate.

"Good. Now, how about an auditorium?" he continued.

"That's a place where you hear," replied Harold Baxter.

"Very good. Now, let's try some prefixes. How about the word *contradiction*?"

Raising her hand in the front row, Ellen answered: "That's when you say something against what has been said—literally to speak against. It can also refer to two incompatible ideas."

"Very good, Ellen. And there are many **derivatives** of the verb *dico*, like *diction, malediction, benediction, valedictorian*, to name just a few. A **valedictory** is a farewell speech; a **valedictorian** is one who delivers it at a graduation ceremony."

Before they knew it, the 8:55 bell rang, and it was time to head upstairs for English. On her way out the door, however, Ellen posed a question to Mr. DeLeurere:

"Mr. DeLeurere, you live in Putney, don't you, not far from the old Chandler mansion?"

"Why, yes, I do, Ellen, why do you ask?"

"Oh, I was curious about the Chandler place. It's a charming old house and I wondered if anyone's living there now."

"Not that I know of. I think it's tied up in **probate**. There's a word with a Latin **etymology** for you—*probatus*—literally, "a thing proved." It's the legal process by which the will of a **deceased** person is proven in court. In other words, the Chandlers' heirs are probably fighting over who gets the property. Who knows? It may sit there unoccupied for years before the case is settled, like something out of *Bleak House* by Charles Dickens."

"*Bleak House*? I don't know that one. We're reading *A Tale of Two Cities* in Mrs. Carmichael's English class."

"*Bleak House* is Dickens' **exposé** of the **probate** courts of England," Mr. DeLeurere explained. "But, in England, they call them **chancery** courts. It was possible for cases to drag on so long that the value of the estates could be completely eaten up by legal fees."

"Thanks, Mr. DeLeurere, that's why your class is so **edifying**."

"Oh, you're quite welcome, my dear. I'm always pleased to have another Latin convert. In fact there's another example for you—*convert*—to change or transform someone or something. But you need to get to class. I could keep this up all day."

Despite his literary **circumlocutions**, Ellen enjoyed Mr. DeLeurere's class and admired his **cosmopolitan** and scholarly **erudition**. Learning classical mythology was one of the **collateral** benefits of studying Latin with Mr. DeLeurere, who had spent the previous summer on the Greek island of Rhodes, famous for the **Colossus** which once dominated its ancient harbor. A world traveler, he also entertained his students with stories of his adventures in a variety of **exotic** locales.

~~~~~~~~~~~~~~~~

By the time Friday came around, Ellen didn't know where the week had gone. She was sure she had gotten *A*s on both of her tests. But now, she had something else on her mind—convincing Ken Swensen to drive her up to Putney on Saturday morning. She found him at his locker on Friday after school. She walked up and put her hand on his arm.

"Hi, Ken, what are you doing on Saturday?"

"What did you have in mind? I was planning on going to the library and finding out what they have on **cryptology**."

"Say, that's right up my alley, too, but I had something else in mind. I need your help, and your car."

"O.K. I can always go to the library afterwards."

"But first, I'd like you to accompany me to town hall. I have a little bit of research to do in the town clerk's office," Ellen suggested.

Stratford Town Hall was a short walk across the street from the high school. The clerk's office was centrally located on the first floor. Ellen and Ken approached Mr. Wilcoxson, the town clerk.

"Good afternoon, Ellen, what can I do for you?"

"We're looking for some information on the old Chandler mansion on River Road. We want to find out the name of the current owner," Ellen explained.

"Let's see," muttered Mr. Wilcoxson, "that would be 5278 River Road, as I recall." Ellen marveled at his **encyclopedic** knowledge of town facts and figures. She watched as he pulled a large bound volume off one of the hundreds of shelves at the back of the office, and proceeded to open it on the counter in front of her and Ken.

"According to our records, that property's tied up in the **probate** court. The **litigants** are Mrs. Chandler's niece and her tax accountant who had **power of attorney** at the time of her death."

"Do you happen to know where either of them lives?"

"I'm pretty sure that the niece lives in Ohio. The accountant practices in New Haven, but you can confirm that with the **probate** court, if you like. Their office is next door."

"Thank you so much. You've been a big help, Mr. Wilcoxson."

Ellen thought it best to **verify** the facts while they were in the building, so she took the opportunity to consult with the **probate** clerk.

"Yes, Mrs. Chandler's niece lives in Ohio—Dayton, to be exact," the clerk informed them. "That's near Columbus. Her name is Shirley Kepler. The accountant is John R. Schlechter. The address given here is in New Haven—36 Crown Street."

"Thank you. That tells us what we wanted to know."

Once outside, Ken paused a moment before the two walked to his car. "All right, Ellen, you want to tell me what this is all about?"

Ellen grabbed Ken by the arm, smiled, and said: "Sure, but why don't we do it over a malt at Hamilton's?"

Climbing into Ken's 1934 Ford roadster, they drove north on Main Street to the popular pharmacy and malt shop on Paradise Green. They sat in an unoccupied booth at the front of the store.

"O.K., so what's this all about, Ellen?" Ken rested his elbows on the table while Ellen began telling him about her experience of the previous Sunday evening.

"I just have this gut feeling that there's something odd going on in that old house, and I'm determined to **ascertain** what it is."

Sipping on his chocolate malt, Ken rolled his eyes with an expression that she had seen before when she floated one of her "interesting" ideas.

"What makes you think there's anything strange going on there?" he inquired. "There may be many logical explanations for what you saw. I mean, even if you did see lights, it strains **credulity** to believe that anything strange, or illegal, is going on there."

"Well, for one thing, we now know that Mrs. Chandler's niece lives in Ohio. That eliminates her. I'm inclined to **impute** blame to the accountant. Perhaps he's taking advantage of the fact that the niece is out of state and is taking the opportunity of cleaning out the valuables before the estate is settled. I'm sure he comprehends their **intrinsic** value. After all, the Chandlers were an **affluent** family, with an **acquisitive** passion for antiques. But there's another thing. There were no vehicles parked in the driveway. If the accountant, who comes from New Haven, was in there, where was his automobile? That's why this case needs some investigation, and where you come in. It's still in an **amorphous** state and needs to be fleshed out. Like most mysteries, this case may fit no established **paradigm**, so I expect we may learn bits and pieces by a process of **serendipity**. And, if at any point you think I'm being **impetuous**, you can try to **debunk** my theories and bring me back to reality. One reason I hesitate to hazard an opinion is that I don't want to **foreclose** any possibilities."

"I'll tell you what, Ellen, why don't I swing by and pick you up tomorrow morning at 10:00 and we'll drive up there and 'case the joint.'"

Ellen laughed. "You sound like a character in a Humphrey Bogart movie."

"You bet–*The Maltese Falcon*."

"Sounds great. Then, I'll see you at 10:00–sharp."

Chapter 3

Mansion on the Housatonic

True to his word, Ken was at Ellen's house at 10:00 the next morning. Having just roused herself from a **somnolent repose**, Ellen was pacing about in her **bandeau** and matching pink rayon **step-ins** trying to decide what clothes to wear on her morning adventure. Peaking through the curtains from the privacy of her bedroom, she observed him walking up to the front door and ringing the bell.

"Mom! I'm not dressed. Tell Ken I'll be down in a minute."

Donning a light brown woolen skirt and pink blouse, she slipped into her brown loafers.

"Come in, Ken. Can I offer you a nice hot bowl of Cream of Wheat?" Ellen's mother inquired.

"No, thank you, Mrs. Anderson, my mother fed me before I left home. But I will have half a glass of orange juice, if you don't mind."

"Of course," she said. "I just squeezed it fresh this morning. Have a seat. Now, tell me, what are you and Ellen up to?"

"Oh, Ellen wants me to help her investigate the old Chandler mansion on River Road. She's convinced that something strange is going on over there. If it was anybody else, I probably wouldn't have gotten myself involved, but Ellen's quite **perspicacious** and **cunning** and has **acute** powers of observation, so I'm inclined to trust her judgment," Ken explained.

At that moment, Ellen came bounding down the stairs, and promptly sat down at the kitchen table. She drank a glass of orange juice, and consumed half a grapefruit and a bowl of Wheaties while Ken continued talking with her mother.

"I suppose you're thinking about college, Ken," suggested Ellen's mother.

"Yes, I plan on applying to Yale and the University of Connecticut, but I expect I'll be drafted before that. My brother Carl is already in the Air Force. He's making training flights in the Hawaiian Islands and I expect he'll be assigned to an aircraft carrier in the Pacific before long. I don't know if I have the intestinal **fortitude** to land an airplane on an aircraft carrier, so I think I'll enlist in the

Navy before I'm drafted. But I have another year to worry about that."

"Carl entrusted his Ford roadster to Ken while he's in the service," Ellen explained. "That's what we're taking up to Putney this morning."

Ellen quickly stuck her head out the back door to check the temperature, then grabbed a sweater and draped it over her shoulders.

"I'm ready, Ken. Shall we go?"

Ken opened the passenger side of the car for Ellen. Then, running around to the other side, he jumped behind the wheel. He started the engine and backed the convertible out of the Anderson driveway. A moment later, the car was cruising down Freeman Avenue, and making a left turn onto Main Street at Paradise Green.

It was a perfect day for a drive. Ken had **retracted** the roadster's convertible top before they set out, so the two young people were quickly **invigorated** by the fresh spring air blowing in their faces. Ellen admired how **adroitly** Ken handled the car, but mostly, she admired Ken. She was resigned to the fact that he kept his **amorous propensities** in check, however, and was not the type to become  even mildly **infatuated** with girls at this stage in his life. But she could hope, anyway. Ken was a **winsome** young man, with an engaging personality and a ready smile. Not **overtly** emotional, he generally maintained a calm and **pacific countenance**. Ellen couldn't help but stare **wistfully** at his handsome features and curly blond hair as he drove. His **prepossessing** appearance made it difficult for her to concentrate on anything else. Whenever she looked into his green eyes, she couldn't help thinking of the Helen O'Connell and Bob Eberly hit *Green Eyes* with the Tommy Dorsey Orchestra. But she was careful to turn away when he looked in her direction, so he wouldn't catch her staring at him.

Ellen had known Ken for as long as she could remember. The first time they met was at one of the Swedish picnics in Monroe. He and his parents and sister, Astrid, lived in a **quaint** little Cape Cod style house on Brewster's Pond, just two blocks east of Paradise Green. In addition to attending the same church, their families attended many of the same Swedish social functions. In fact, there was a strong **congruity** between them on many levels. Ken and Ellen had attended Garden School together and, now, Stratford High. She also knew that Ken was sufficiently **pliable** that he could be coaxed into assisting her when requested.

Ken was a **conscientious** student and a **bibliophile** with an **insatiable** thirst for knowledge of all sorts. He was also an **assiduous** worker at whatever task he undertook. In his spare time, he was employed at the Dusty Corner Bookshop in Stratford Center, near the First Congregational Church. The owner, Mr. Mueller, kept him busy stocking the shelves, making deliveries, arranging the window displays, and sweeping up. Mr. Mueller and his wife, Helge, specialized in **antiquarian** and rare books, including first editions, as well as more **prosaic** fare. Mr. Mueller had an **idiosyncratic** personality with a **prodigious** and **encyclopedic** knowledge of books and authors. He was also the **exclusive** New England agent for several European publishing houses, including those in Paris, Frankfurt, and Berlin, but shipments from those sources slowed to a crawl after war was declared.

It was of some concern to Ken, however, that Mr. Mueller also stocked German National **Socialist** literature, some of which, he later learned, had been shipped to the two **German-American Bund** camps in New York and New Jersey. These were views with which he could not **abide**. On rare occasions, Bund members also came to the shop for this literature; but, mostly, they had copies shipped to their homes. From Ken's observations, most of these buyers lived in the greater New York metropolitan area. Others lived in nearby New Jersey, Connecticut and Pennsylvania.

Ken learned that, until the late 30s, Bund members were far more transparent about their activities and held **conventions** in the New York metropolitan area. The Bund claimed more than 50,000 members nationwide, with a presence in 47 states, including more than two dozen youth camps. In 1937, the Bund had even proposed building a camp in Southbury, Connecticut, but a public outcry resulted in the passage of a **zoning** law outlawing **paramilitary** training. After war was declared, a number of Bund leaders were arrested or placed in **internment** camps, and other group members generally kept a low profile, preferring to have their books sent by U.S. mail. One of Ken's responsibilities was taking these shipments to the Main Street post office. **Cognizant** of the **incendiary** and **malevolent** content of much of this literature, however, particularly those which directed their **calumnies** against President Roosevelt and the **Jews**, he decided to keep a record of the addresses to which the shipments were being mailed in a personal log he kept under the front seat of his roadster. He had a feeling that this information might come in handy some day.

Ken also shared Ellen's love of music, playing violin in the Stratford High concert orchestra. However, it was when he asked her to the junior prom that Ellen's romantic impulses were **kindled**, and she began looking at Ken with a fresh pair of eyes. Those feelings were heightened as she sat next to him in the front seat of his roadster.

"I want you to stop at that country store on River Road," said Ellen. "You can see the Chandler mansion from there."

"At your service, Miss Anderson," he replied.

The old country store stood on River Road on a narrow slice of land between the pavement and the Housatonic River and opposite the north end of Fowler Island. Its white clapboard siding had recently been treated to a fresh coat of paint. A sign over the entrance read: "Wexler's News and Sundries."

As they climbed out of the car and walked up the steps, Ellen and Ken could not escape the headlines which seemed to leap off the front pages of both the *New York Times* and the *Daily News* for April 18, 1942 announcing Doolittle's

bombing of Tokyo. The **concise** articles reported the daring raid by General Jimmy Doolittle and his squadron of flyers from an aircraft carrier in the Pacific.

"At last – we've **avenged** the attack on Pearl Harbor!" Ken exclaimed. "And to think, my brother Carl may soon be flying similar missions."

Ellen thought back to that dark day—December 7th—when the Japanese had bombed Pearl Harbor. It was a Sunday afternoon. She and her parents were on their way home from visiting her grandparents in Easton when they heard the news bulletin on their car radio. When they got home, they remained glued to the **console** radio in their living room for the remainder of the day, as the **grisly** details of the **horrific** attack were reported to a shocked nation. The following day, students assembled in the high school auditorium to hear President Roosevelt's address to Congress. She could still remember his words, almost **verbatim**:

*Yesterday, December 7th, 1941 — a date which will live in **infamy** — the United States of America was suddenly and **deliberately** attacked by naval and air forces of the Empire of Japan...*

It was an event that would change the lives of every American, not only those enlisting or being drafted into the armed services, but millions of civilians who were being called upon to do their part on the **domestic** front. What Pearl Harbor proved was how **resilient** the American people were, and how responsive to the deadly challenge. Those young men about to graduate anticipated being immediately drawn into the conflict.

Stratford had been on a wartime footing ever since September, 1939, when Germany invaded Poland. Both industrial production and housing starts had mushroomed, eliminating Depression-era unemployment. When the Selective Service Act was signed into law on September 16, 1940, every man from the age of 21 to 36 was required to register for the draft. After the attack on Pearl Harbor, the law was amended to require the registration of all men from 18 to 64. Many enlisted as soon as they graduated from high school. Many of the boys Ellen knew who had graduated the previous June were either in boot camp or were being shipped overseas. Others left school **prematurely** in order to enlist, or had sufficient credits in order to graduate mid-year. In February, 1942, the first seventeen of Stratford's wartime draftees were inducted into the service.

"Ken, let's just sit on the porch for a minute so we can **assess** the landscape and study the Chandler mansion a little more closely. How about buying me a Moxie from the cooler there?"

Ken lifted the lid of the cooler and pulled out two Moxies. He took them to the counter inside and paid Mrs. Wexler, the wife of the **proprietor**. He returned to the front steps, but not before popping the caps on the bottle opener at the side of the cooler.

"Ellen, did you know that Moxie was President Coolidge's favorite beverage?"

"No kidding? Well, then I guess we're in good company."

Ellen had been staring intently at the old structure which stood in **arboreal** splendor on the embankment, not more than fifty feet from shore and about a hundred yards from the store.

"Ken, doesn't it look as if the Chandler place and this store were built by the same person? I mean, look at the architectural **adornments** around the porch and the roof."

The Chandler house, an **elegant Queen Anne Victorian**, was highlighted by a wraparound porch which extended around three sides of its lower level, a portion

of which offered a **panoramic** view of the Housatonic. A second-floor balcony occupied the same **expanse**, with large windows providing similar views from the interior. The attic level, with an **intricately** carved gable roof and **spire** fit the house like an old hat. The **soffits** were **embellished** by **Victorian** gingerbread detailing.

"It's very possible," he replied. "Not only is the **filigree** on both porches strikingly similar, but these are the only two buildings along this stretch of River Road. In fact, the store is close enough to have been a carriage house, or **annex** of some sort."

"Why don't we go inside and ask the **proprietress**?" suggested Ellen.

"Great idea," said Ken.

"Good morning. Is it Mrs. Wexler? My name is Ellen Anderson and this is my friend, Ken Swensen."

"Pleased to meet you. By any chance are you the Ellen Anderson I've read about in the *Stratford News* a while back?"

"Yes, that's me," Ellen replied, with a hint of pride. "But that was three years ago. I'm flattered you remembered."

"Yes, I'm Mrs. Wexler, but you can call me Abby."

"Abby, do you mind if we ask you a couple of questions?"

"No, not at all. What would you like to know?"

Mrs. Wexler was a **corpulent** woman of medium height, **presumably** in her mid-fifties. Her medium-length black hair, laced with streaks of gray, was piled on top of her head. She had brown eyes, an engaging smile, and an **amiable** and **cordial** manner about her. She stood behind the counter with a white apron tied around her waist, the **archetypal personification** of a female grocery store clerk. A variety of enticing **confections** was prominently displayed on the counter in front of her, including pies, cakes and doughnuts. They were just the sort of **culinary** delights to which a **gourmand** like Mrs. Wexler was probably **enamored**. Indeed, it looked as though she frequently sampled the wares.

"Well, we couldn't help but notice that your store and the old Chandler mansion next door appear to have been built by the same people. What can you tell us about them?"

"Well, Ellen, you're right on that score. When the Chandler mansion was built in the 1840s, I believe, this building was used as a boathouse. It's my understanding that the original owner was a sea captain, and later, a local fisherman, so the house is somewhat an **artifact** of the town's **maritime** history. The original owner hired a number of local **artisans** to build it. He stored his boats in the lower level of this building. It fell into **disrepute** after that, having been used by smugglers to avoid **excise taxes**. My husband bought the building from the Chandlers in 1918 and began operating it as a store the following year. He figured it could **augment** our income and give me something to do in his absence. My husband's a traveling salesman for a Bridgeport **dry goods** company called East Coast Drygoods—perhaps you've heard of it? His territory covers all of New England. He's got a rather **astute** business sense and saw the potential in **renovating** this property. He likes to say that running the store keeps me out of trouble while he's engaged in his **nomadic** profession."

"How long did the Chandlers own the house next door?" Ellen continued.

"As far as I know, they bought it around 1900, give or take a year. The Chandlers were an **atypical** and **eccentric** couple, rather **ascetic** by nature, and pretty much kept to themselves. But they did **patronize** the store until they both died. I often made deliveries to the house, particularly after Mrs. Chandler's health began to **atrophy** and she became a virtual **recluse**. When I first met her, she was quite **loquacious**. But as she aged, her comments were **pithier** and less long-winded."

"I remember reading that the house was **inundated** with cats when she died," Ellen added.

"Oh, my word, yes! They were crawling all over the place. And I should know. I sold Mrs. Chandler the cat food. The Chandlers were usually in **concord** on most things, but Mr. Chandler would never have **acquiesced** to her having so many animals around the house. When he died, however, his wife adopted every stray in the neighborhood. And, my goodness, did they have kittens! I couldn't bring myself to cast any **aspersions** on Mrs. Chandler because she was a sweet old lady. I **ascribed** her behavior to a sincere love for animals, perhaps what one might describe as a **mawkish sentimentality**. But there's no question that she was **idiosyncratic**. The town animal warden had to take all the cats away when she died. I doubt that he was able to dispose of them all. They were **dispersed** all over Stratford and neighboring towns. Sadly, some had to be put to sleep."

"Have you noticed anybody in the house since she died?" Ellen inquired.

"Funny you should ask. For several years after Mrs. Chandler's death—I believe it was 1939. Yes, that's right, 1939. I remember because that's the year my mother died up in New Hampshire. Anyway, I went to the funeral and offered my **condolences** to her niece, who was the only surviving relative, as well as the **putative** heir. Her niece collected some family memorabilia right after she died—you know, photographs and letters, and things like that. But, mostly, it was her accountant who hung around. He's the one who got **power of attorney**. I once saw him hauling out some of her furniture with a truck. I've always been **skeptical** of that man. I'm sure he **coveted** her property and took advantage of the old lady to get her to change her will in his favor. I have a particular **aversion** to vultures like that," she explained. "No doubt motivated by his **cupidity**, he also tried to put her in an **asylum**, but she refused. I mean, she was 91 when she died and, if she were a light bulb, didn't exactly have all her filaments burning, if you know what I mean. What we need is somebody to **advocate** on behalf of old folks like that who have lost their marbles, so to speak. Not to speak ill of the **deceased**, mind you."

"I heartily agree. We had a similar situation in our family," Ellen **interjected**.

"Anyway, after Mrs. Chandler died, there was a **dearth** of activity around the place for several years and the exterior became increasingly **unkempt**. I'm not normally a busybody, but both the accountant and the niece made **nominal** visits to the store. After all, we're the only establishment within a mile. So, I've learned a few things just by being here, minding the store. The niece gave me her address and telephone number during her last visit. We have a **tacit** understanding that I should keep an eye on the place. That was about eight months ago. She's called me a few times, and asked if I had observed anything. I told her that the accountant—his name is Schlechter—was hauling furniture out of the house. The Chandlers had antiques, and the house is probably **bereft** of those by now. That's probably what he was after, in addition to the property itself. I wouldn't be surprised if he's **embezzled** her available cash and securities, having **arrogated** to himself control over her property. I've been **wary** of him from the first time I set eyes on him. I think the niece expected that her aunt would have **bequeathed** the property to her, instead of the **pittance** left to her under the will. I think it was shortly after that that she got a lawyer and took Mr. Schlechter to **probate** court. That's probably where it is now. Those cases can take years to settle, or so I understand."

"Mrs. Wexler—I mean Abby—may we have the name and phone number of the niece?"

"Of course. Maybe you can help expose that **skullduggerist**. I don't normally go around **disparaging** other people, but he's a **pernicious** individual. What he's doing is **tantamount** to theft. It would be a crime if he succeeds in **bilking** her out of what should be family property. After all, if Mrs. Chandler had died **intestate**, her niece would have been the sole **beneficiary** of her aunt's estate. But, as I was saying, there wasn't much activity in the house until the past few months. That's when I started noticing lights in the house, and at all hours of the night. And I don't think it was that accountant in every instance because I rarely saw his car or truck in the driveway. It's all very curious."

"I'll say," Ellen countered.

"There's something else that may explain the lack of cars or trucks in the driveway when the house appears to be occupied. Mrs. Chandler once told me that there is a cave entrance on the river which provides a water inlet to the basement of the mansion. From what she told me, it was a natural cave that was further **excavated** years ago to connect it to the basement of the house. She told me that her husband once used it to tie up his small motorboat. The entrance is hidden by the tall marsh grass. We also had a small channel that once connected the back of our place to the river, but it has since silted up. Anyway, it's just possible that someone is again using that cave to enter the mansion from the river."

"Very interesting," Ken **interjected**. "We'll have to check it out."

"By the way, did you ever think of calling the police?" Ellen inquired.

"Well, I've been rather **dilatory** on that score and **ambivalent** about speaking to the authorities. I considered it, but thought there might be some logical explanation and then I'd wind up **reproving** myself for behaving like a foolish busybody."

"To tell you the truth, Mrs. Wexler, we're suspicious, too, but we think it would be more **expedient** not to say anything to the police just yet, at least until after Ken and I have had a chance to do our own investigation. First, we want to contact the niece. For the time being, however, we don't want Mr. Schlechter, or anyone else, to get the idea that he's being watched. The police would only gum up the works. And, in the meantime, we'll check in with you to see what you may have observed."

"I'd be happy to help you, Ellen. In fact, it's right up my alley. I have a definite **affinity** for mysteries. I have dozens of mystery novels scattered around our apartment upstairs. Raymond Chandler, Dashell Hammett, Mickey Spillane—I've read 'em all. *The Maltese Falcon*—now, there's a mystery novel. And I loved the movie with Humphrey Bogart and Mary Aster. But this may be the real thing. Oh, and by the way, that Mr. Schlechter has a trace of a European accent. Probably a German **dialect**, but I couldn't swear to it."

"Thanks, Abby. That could prove to be very helpful if we ever run into him," Ellen replied. "I'm sure we'll be in touch."

Ken helped Ellen into his roadster and the two headed back down River Road.

"Ken, I think we're on to something. Perhaps now you can appreciate why I had my suspicions about that old place. Mrs. Wexler confirmed those suspicions."

"I agree. What would you say to our coming back this evening after it's dark and putting the house under **surveillance**?"

"Great idea, Mr. Watson, but not before I call Mrs. Chandler's niece in Ohio. I'm very anxious to find out what she knows. Why don't you call me later this afternoon after you're finished at the library?"

Chapter 4

A Call to Ohio

After Ken dropped her off at home, Ellen found her mother in the kitchen, decorating a chocolate layer cake.

"Now, keep your fingers off of that cake, young lady. That's for the party at the Swedish Athletic Club this evening. Here's a spoon. You're welcome to what's left of the icing in the bowl."

"Mother, do you mind if I place a long-distance call to Ohio? It's very important to the case I'm working on. I promise not to take too long."

"Well, I suppose it'll be all right. But don't mention it to your father. You know how **frugal** he is."

Ellen went into the living room and sat in the Queen Anne wing chair next to the end table where the telephone rested. She picked up the receiver and dialed for the operator.

"Hello, operator? I would like to place a person-to-person call to a Miss Shirley Kepler in Dayton, Ohio. The number is Yellowstone 83953."

"I have your party on the line," the operator replied.

"Hello, Mrs. Shirley Kepler, please?"

"Yes, this is Shirley Kepler. Who's calling?"

"My name is Ellen Anderson, and I'm calling from Stratford, Connecticut."

"That's a coincidence. I was born in Stratford. What can I do for you?"

"I'm calling about your aunt's home on River Road. I have some information which may be of interest to you."

"Really? Perhaps, you know that my aunt's property is tied up in **probate**. I wouldn't want to say anything that would **jeopardize** the court case in which I'm a **litigant**."

"Yes, I'm aware of your **probate** matter, but this is something else. I have reason to believe that someone is living in your aunt's home illegally. I've noticed lights on in the house at late hours. And there are no vehicles in the driveway. Mrs. Wexler, who runs the country store next door, has observed the same things. She's the one who gave me your name and phone number. I learned from the town **probate** clerk about your court case and thought you would like to know about these developments."

"Yes, I appreciate your taking the time to contact me. This is very troubling."

"Mrs. Wexler doesn't trust your aunt's accountant, and, frankly, neither do I. She thinks he may be **absconding** with the contents of the house. But I think there's something else going on."

"Well, she's right about the accountant. I'm convinced that **avarice** drove him to use **undue influence** to take advantage of my aunt's advanced age and mental condition. You have to understand that, after doing her tax returns for a number of years, he was well aware of her financial **assets**. After **insinuating** himself into her affairs through his **fiduciary** relationship, he got her to **accede** to having himself written into her will."

"That's disgusting. What a **despicable** person. He's obviously **unscrupulous** and has no conscience."

"I'm hoping the **probate** court will agree with you and throw the book at him. But, in the meantime, do you think I should call the police?"

"Mrs. Wexler and I had a similar discussion, but we decided that it would be best to wait until I've had a chance to investigate the matter a bit further."

"Say, are you a detective, or something?"

"Well, you could say I'm an amateur investigator. What I'm doing is completely off the record. And that's the reason for my call. What can you tell me about the old house? Mrs. Wexler believes that there is a **subterranean** entrance from the river."

"That's right, Ellen. The house is very old and, from what I remember, was built over a natural tunnel in the rock. Maybe the original owner used it for smuggling. I don't know. I do know that, as kids, we used to explore the tunnel that led into my aunt and uncle's basement. You could actually float a small boat into the tunnel at high tide and then make your way up a stairway to the basement. From the basement, there's a hidden passageway behind the walls that leads to several rooms on the lower level, and to the master bedroom on the upper level. One of the passages leads into the library on the first floor, through a swinging bookcase. If you were standing in the library, you would never know it's there. The other entrance leads through a cleverly concealed section of paneling into the living room. It's something right out of one of those

Nancy Drew mysteries, or the movies with Bonita Granville. Now, there's a spunky actress. Perhaps you've seen them?"

"Yes, I've seen all four. And I'm a big Nancy Drew fan. Well, I think you've told me what I wanted to know, Mrs. Kepler. We plan to do some further investigation to find out who may have gained access to the house. When we do, I promise to inform you of our findings. I wish you all the best in your case against the accountant."

"Thank you ever so much. I appreciate your taking an interest in the old place. I would like to have your phone number in case I need to get in contact with you, Ellen."

"Sure. My phone number here is Edison 71635."

"Got it. Thank you. Let's keep in touch."

Ellen's mother walked into the living room with a cake knife in one hand and a towel in the other just as her daughter was replacing the receiver.

"Ohio? So who do you know in Ohio?"

"Mrs. Chandler's niece, Shirley Kepler. She's involved in a **probate** case against her aunt's accountant who **finagled** himself into her aunt's will. I told her about the strange goings-on at the Chandler mansion and she gave me some very important information."

"I suppose you know what you're doing. You're certainly not one of those **frivolous** girls like that Sally Turner down the street."

"Well, thank you, Mom, I'm pleased to have earned your **approbation**."

"There you go again, with more of your fancy words. See what happens when I send you to school?"

"It's from the Latin, Mom: *approbare*. It means *your approval*."

"Then, why didn't you just say *approval*?"

"Because I'm trying to improve my vocabulary, and I can't do that using just **monosyllabic** words. Oh, I almost forgot. I promised to call Ken. He should be back from the library by now."

Ellen picked up the receiver and dialed the Swenson residence.

"Hi, Astrid, is Ken home?"

"Yes, Ellen, he's right here."

"Ken? How did you make out at the library?"

"Great! I found three books on **cryptology**. Miss Russell, the librarian, knows about all kinds of **arcane** subjects, even the most **obscure**. So, what did you learn from Mrs. Chandler's niece?"

"Well, that Mrs. Wexler was right about the hidden entrance to the house. She also told me about the passageway that leads to various rooms in the house. I would love to get inside. I love the idea of secret passageways."

"You may get your wish, Ellen. But, for now, I have good news. Tommy McCauley is letting us borrow his motorboat. It's moored at Bailey's Boatyard

on the Milford side of the river, just north of the Washington Bridge. He knows the river pretty well and said there's a duck blind on the east side of Fowler Island with a great view of the Chandler mansion. It's a fairly **desolate** spot. I tell you what. I'll pick you up at 7:00 this evening. It should be sufficiently dark by then that we won't be detected."

"I'll be waiting. See you then. Oh, and don't forget your binoculars. I'll bring along my camera."

Ellen had no idea what a few hours of **surveillance** might accomplish, but she wanted to give it a try. Besides, she couldn't think of anything she'd rather do than sit quietly in a motorboat with Ken.

Ken was prompt, as usual. Ellen had changed into some khakis and one of her father's plaid shirts. She wore deck shoes. Approaching the pending adventure with a **modicum** of **trepidation**, she also brought along two life preservers, a **precaution** about which her mother and father were **adamant**.

"I see that you're all prepared. My father insisted that I bring life preservers, too. I would never be **foolhardy** enough to **circumvent** that **mandate**. By the way, you look pretty snazzy in those duds."

Ellen was used to Ken seeing her in dresses and skirts, but was pleased that he took note of how she was dressed. His **compliments** were a good sign. He was paying attention. Before she knew it, the two were off down Main Street and turning east onto Barnum Avenue. The Washington Bridge lay just about a mile ahead. The Bailey Boatyard was located on the Milford side of the river, just north of the bridge.

Tommy's Chris-Craft runabout was moored about twenty yards from the boathouse. He was obviously very **meticulous** about the manner in which he maintained his small craft. Ellen couldn't help but notice how its highly polished wood frame gleamed in the moonlight.

"Tommy said he filled the gas tank this morning and left us a full can of gas in the storage compartment, just in case we run out."

Ken stepped into the boat first and took a seat. Ellen handed him the picnic basket, their life preservers, Ken's binoculars, and her box camera. Then, as she extended her right foot into the boat, she caught her deck shoe on an exposed nailhead and fell helplessly forward. Ken barely had time to rise and catch her in his arms. Their faces pressed against each other, their lips and noses lightly touching. Ken was **nonplused** by the unexpected encounter and tried his best to make light of it. Though unintentional, the incident gave Ellen a sudden rush of **exhilaration**. She turned her head away **demurely**, certain that he could read her mind.

"I'm so sorry, Ken. That was clumsy of me. I caught my shoe on something."

"That's O.K. You have to be **wary** of these old docks. Do we have everything?"

"Yes, I think so."

Ken placed his binoculars around his neck. Ellen positioned her camera within easy reach on the floor and the lunch basket on the back seat.

"My mother packed us some egg salad sandwiches, baby gherkins, and chocolate brownies. And here's a thermos of Swedish petrol."

Ken knew **instinctively** that she was talking about coffee—the brew that powered Swedes.

Ken pushed off from the dock with one of the oars and gave a yank on the starter cord. The engine started up without hesitation.

"Tommy keeps this baby well tuned," Ken observed.

Making their way up the east side of the river, they managed to **navigate** the three miles to Putney in about twenty minutes.

"I would suggest we motor by the house for a closer look, take some photos, and then position ourselves behind the duck blind on our way back," suggested Ken.

"Good idea. I would like to get some closer snapshots than we can get from behind the duck blind."

"But don't be too obvious about taking the photos, in case we're being observed from the house," Ken cautioned.

As the craft approached the riverside mansion, they could clearly observe the cave's location, although it was partially concealed by the tall marsh grasses, and what remained of a **derelict** fishing vessel. There were no signs of life in the house, however.

"Ken, if we're going to explore the cave, I think we're going to have to be more **circumspect** in our approach and leave our boat around that bend in the river and then wade in. We can't risk having our boat being observed from the house. But that will have to wait for another visit."

Grabbing her camera from the floor of the boat, Ellen held it at waist level, looked in the viewfinder, and took a half dozen quick snapshots before returning it to its resting place.

"There, that should do it for now. Let's get on to the duck blind."

Ken swung the boat around the north end of the **desolate** island and cruised slowly behind the duck blind, before turning off the engine. He tied the boat to the side of the duck blind and the two made themselves comfortable. For what seemed like an **interminable** length of time, they sat quietly and waited for any signs of activity from the mansion or its nearby shoreline. Ellen passed out the sandwiches and poured coffee for the two of them. They talked of school, mostly, of their favorite teachers, and of the Swedish activities that had first brought them together. Although they had observed a few boats plying the waters near the Washington Bridge when they departed, they hadn't observed a single craft this far north.

"Well, Ken, don't you think it's about time we **aborted** this adventure and headed back to the boatyard. It's a pity our efforts have been **fruitless**, but it will be nearly 10:00 by the time we get back."

"You're right. We should be getting back."

Just as Ken was getting ready to pull on the starter cord, Ellen observed a small craft on the other side of the island and detected the sound of its engine.

"Wait!" she whispered. "Do you hear that, Ken?"

The two watched intently as a small motor boat with two men aboard approached the cliff from the south. The man at the **prow** used an oar to push the marsh grasses from the cave's entrance. A few seconds later, the boat entered the cave and disappeared from view.

"I wouldn't have believed it if I hadn't seen it with my own eyes," exclaimed Ken. "I confess that I had my doubts when you first explained this case to me at Hamilton's, but now I'm convinced that you're on to something."

"Let's wait a few minutes more and see if any lights appear in the house," suggested Ellen.

"Of course," Ken replied.

The two didn't have to wait long before what appeared to be the light of lanterns **refracted** through the windows on the first floor of the mansion, then the second floor.

"Well, do you believe me now?"

"I have to confess that I initially thought your imagination had gotten the better of you. I promise not to doubt you again. It is odd that the house is being occupied while still in legal **limbo**," Ken observed.

"This has to be the accountant's doing. Why else would strangers be using the house?" observed Ellen.

"Exactly. I suppose there's nothing else we can learn tonight. I say we **curtail** our adventure and head back to the boatyard," Ken suggested.

Ken untied the boat and used the oars to guide it away from the duck blind until they were clear of Fowler Island. Then he started the motor, switched on the headlights, and steered the boat swiftly down the Housatonic's eastern shore. It was just shy of 10:30 when he brought the boat into its slip at the boatyard.

By the time Ken had driven Ellen home, their **speculations** had become even more intense. Ellen periodically suffered from **insomnia** when her mind was **preoccupied**. Her experience on the river just **exacerbated** the problem. It was after 2:00 in the morning before she finally drifted off.

Chapter 5

Questions without Answers

When Ellen awoke on Sunday morning, her mind was still racing with thoughts of the previous night's adventure. But right now, it was time to get ready for church. Ellen taught a third grade Sunday School class at the First Congregational Church on Main Street at 9:30, and she tried to get there by 9:00 to review the lesson for the day. Her students were a **precocious** bunch and always full of challenging questions, **eschatological** and otherwise. Her parents typically joined her for church at 10:30.

This morning, her mother made bacon and Swedish pancakes topped with **lingonberries**. Ellen barely had a chance to finish her orange juice when her father asked about her expedition of the night before.

"Your mother tells me you've been cruising the river at night, with Ken. Sounds romantic."

"Oh, Dad, it's nothing like that. I do like Ken, but he's not much interested in girls right now. It's more of a **platonic** relationship. We've been friends since our first Swedish picnic. I think he views me as a safe date—not too threatening. I think that's why he asked me to the prom. He hasn't the nerve to ask anyone else. But that's O.K. He'll come around one of these days and I plan to be there with my butterfly net," Ellen explained, with a chuckle.

"I guess your mother and I are to blame for taking you to those Swedish picnics," her father replied. "But seriously, Ken is a good boy from what his mother tells me, very **conscientious** and an excellent student. She says he may even be in the running for class **valedictorian**."

"That's right, but don't count me out, yet. We both have straight As, at least so far."

"Yes, I know. And I won't **reproach** you for going out on the river at night because your mother informed me you wore your life jacket," he added.

"Oh, I wouldn't be without one. I know how **treacherous** those currents can be, particularly near the sound."

Coincidentally, both the Sunday School lesson and text of the sermon for that Sunday related the story of Moses and the Israelites wandering in the wilderness. Ellen couldn't help but be reminded of her own mental wanderings as she **pondered** the mystery posed by the Chandler mansion.

Reverend Sellick, a **paragon** of Christian virtue, was in rare form that morning. His **erudite explication** of the Biblical text and **animated** delivery were enough to **captivate** the most jaded **agnostic**. As he **railed** against **iniquity** and **intolerance**, and urged his **congregation** to **repudiate** sin and **debauchery,** many in the pews were **discomfited**. **Pondering** the substance of his sermon forced Ellen to **grapple** with the evils with which the world was now confronted. As she sat in the pew in a state of deep **contemplation**, she was reminded of Rev. Sellick's **profound** concern for all of the young men and women from the church who were currently serving in the

armed forces. Like most members of the **congregation**, both in and out of uniform, Ellen and her parents eagerly awaited each issue of *The Log with a Few Splinters,* the informative monthly newsletter Pastor Sellick **compiled** from the letters and postcards he received from servicemen and women. It quickly became an **indispensable** source of news around town regarding the activities of the brave men and women from the church who were now scattered across the country, and the world.

When services were over, Ellen found Ken and his parents at coffee hour, in the church basement. While their parents chatted with other members of the **congregation**, Ellen and Ken **recapitulated** what they had learned, and discussed the next step in their investigation.

"I'm going to be pretty busy at the bookshop this week," said Ken, "but I will be free on Friday evening and all day Saturday. Why don't we meet up after school on Friday and **weigh** our options?"

"Fine. We need to give some thought to our next move," Ellen replied.

~~~~~~~~~~~~~~~~

Business at the Dusty Corner Book Shop was brisk that week. Most of it was the normal walk-in trade: people looking for particular books or authors, others browsing the shelves and finding their own special treasures by a process of **serendipity**. One of Ken's chores was receiving and unpacking shipments at the small loading dock located at the shop's alley entrance. On Wednesday, a large shipment of National **Socialist** literature arrived from a mysterious Brooklyn publishing house with which he was unfamiliar. Although such materials were **anathema** to Ken's **libertarian** political sensibilities, he decided to keep his own private counsel for the time being and see what he could learn about the level of Mr. Mueller's involvement. Was he an innocent **intermediary**, or did the **empirical** evidence suggest that his views **transgressed** the boundaries of **legitimate** political opinion, mirroring the views expressed in these **vile tracts**?

One of Ken's responsibilities was taking mail orders to the post office on Main Street. While most of the packages were **legitimate**—usually rare or foreign language books, others were of a more questionable nature. Ken knew which ones they were because Mr. Mueller packed them **surreptitiously** in the backroom.

On Wednesday, Mr. Mueller called Ken into his office.

"Ken, I have several packages that I'd like you to take to the post office today before it closes. They're on the table in the back room."

"Sure, Mr. Mueller. Do you want me to pay the postage by check, or cash?"

"Here's a blank check. Just make it out to "Postmaster Stratford." And I have one large package that I want you to deliver personally to a Stratford address."

Ken loaded the collection of smaller packages into a large cardboard box and carried them to his **rumble seat**. The large box was as big as all the others combined. Pulling out of the alley and onto Main Street, he drove to a side street near the high school. Then, taking his log from under the front seat, he began recording the addresses to which the packages were addressed:

> 1501 Amwell Road, Somerset, New Jersey
> 578 West 125th Street, New York, New York
> 695 West 107th Street, New York, New York
> 124 Benham Avenue, Bridgeport, Conn.
> 536 Third Avenue, Stroudsburg, Penn.

The address on the large box read:
5278 River Road
Stratford, Conn.

Ken froze in his tracks. *Wasn't that the address of the Chandler mansion? There were no other houses in that vicinity, except the Wexler's country store. What else could it be?* The possibility **conjured** up all sorts of imaginative prospects to his mind. He immediately thought of contacting Ellen. But first he had to get the other packages to the post office before closing. Once these were safely on their way, he immediately drove over to Ellen's house. He was in luck. Ellen was home from softball practice and promptly came to the door when he rang the bell.

"You're not going to believe our good fortune. I want you to take a look in my **rumble seat**."

Ellen rushed out the front door to Ken's roadster parked in the driveway.

"Say, that's the address of the Chandler mansion. So, what does this mean?"

"Well, I should explain that this package contains German language books, specifically National **Socialist** literature, in other words, Nazi books and pamphlets. While I don't wish to **insinuate** that Mr. Mueller is sympathetic to these views, he has been a **conduit** for this literature to Nazi sympathizers in the United States for a number of years. Many of them are undoubtedly members of the German-American Bund, a pro-Nazi political organization. I did some research on the group at the Stratford Public Library last week. Since American entry into the war, many of its members have been placed in **internment** camps. The remainder have gone underground. They're obviously no longer a **viable** political organization, but they do pose the threat of various types of **clandestine** activity, including **espionage** and **sabotage**. You can be certain that the Nazi spies who were put ashore on Long Island earlier this year had help from Bund members. These people are fully committed to the violent overthrow of the United States government. And they would think nothing of **abrogating** the freedoms of Americans as they have done to those in Europe. The fact that some of Mr. Mueller's customers are living in the Chandler mansion indicates that he must have some knowledge of their activities. Why don't you come with me to make the delivery. I think this could be very interesting."

"Sure thing. Let me get a sweater."

Ellen climbed in the front seat and Ken quickly backed out of the driveway. A few minutes later, they were pulling into the circular driveway in front of the Chandler mansion.

"Wait here while I ring the bell," Ken suggested.

Taking the package from the **rumble seat**, Ken carried it to the front door. There was no bell, just an antique brass knocker, which he knocked twice. There was no answer. He tried again. No response. Just as he reached for the knocker a third time, the door opened and a balding gentleman with a moustache appeared.

"May I help you?"

"Yes, I have a delivery here from the Dusty Corner Book Shop for a Mr. Helmut Kuhn. Do I have the correct address?" Ken inquired.

"Yes, you do. I will see that Mr. Kuhn receives the package. Thank you."

Taking the box from Ken's hands, he closed the door rather **brusquely**, before Ken had an opportunity to prolong the conversation. When he returned to the car, Ellen was waiting anxiously to hear his description of what had transpired.

"So, what did he say to you?"

"Not much. I was attempting to **instigate** a more prolonged conversation, but he was rather **curt** with me. He just said that he would see that Mr. Kuhn received the package, and then closed the door. I wanted to engage him in a conversation about his home, but he didn't give me the chance."

"What did he look like?" Ellen inquired, as Ken climbed back into the car and eased it to the edge of the roadway.

"He appeared to be about sixty-five years of age, and perhaps five foot eight

inches tall. I'd say he weighed about 160 pounds. He had a **receding** hairline, and an aristocratic, yet **sinister mien**. He nose was long and thin, almost beaklike. To tell you the truth, he reminded me of Conrad Veidt."

"Who?"

"You know, that actor who plays Nazis in the movies. He was the **proprietor** of the auction house in *All Through the Night*, the Humphrey Bogart movie we saw at the Majestic before Christmas. He also played Jaffar in *Thief of Baghdad*. His characters are always the **epitome** of evil."

"Oh, yes, I remember them both. He gave me the creeps."

"At least the bookshop provided me with a **pretense** for knocking on the door."

"Did he have an accent?" Ellen inquired.

"Definitely," Ken replied. "I can't say conclusively that it was German, but it was certainly European."

Ken looked both ways, then pulled out of the circular driveway. The fresh air off the river had the unmistakable aroma of spring.

"What I'd like to know is who gave him permission to be in the house?" said Ellen.

"The accountant, no doubt. What was his name?"

"Schlechter. That's what Mr. Wilcoxson said. After all, he appears to have temporary control of the property, pending the resolution of the **probate** case. He may very well be part of the same **insidious** fraternity—in other words, a Nazi sympathizer. But I wouldn't be surprised if they're using it for more than a National **Socialist** reading room," Ellen continued.

"All the more reason why we need to get inside the house if we're going to learn anything more."

"Ken, have you thought of confronting Mr. Mueller and asking him why he's selling Nazi **propaganda**? He may not be **culpable**, but he can probably give us a lead on what this group is up to."

"Yes, I've thought about it a lot over the last few days, but I think I'd prefer to avoid the subject a bit longer. I want to keep gathering information. After all, we don't know his true sympathies. As long as he thinks I'm **oblivious** to the **nefarious** side of his otherwise **legitimate** business, and the people with whom he associates, he'll continue to give me opportunities to learn more. If I tip my hand, I'm afraid he'll clam up."

"You're right. I'll **defer** to your judgment. You know him best. It's good we can talk these things out before we do something foolish or counter-productive. I can be **impulsive** at times."

As Ken pulled into the Anderson driveway, he handed Ellen a book of matches. "Take a look at this. I found it lying in the flower bed at the bottom of the front stairs."

Ellen read the cover aloud: "Elm City Diner, 34 Crown Street, New Haven,

Conn. Why that's where Mr. Schlechter has his office. But I believe his address is 36 Crown Street. At least, that's what Mr. Wilcoxson said."

"Yes, I believe you're right. I think we need to pay Mr. Schlechter a little visit. I want to get a look at the man. Perhaps, that will help put things into perspective."

Chapter 6

On the Train to New Haven

Saturday morning came early to the Anderson home. Father Eric was up early to go fly fishing with Herb Sandstrom. Ellen could hear the sound of voices in the kitchen as her mother prepared his breakfast. By the time she came downstairs, he had already pulled the car out of the garage and was on his way to his favorite fishing spot on the Housatonic in West Cornwall.

"Ellen, before you go off **gallivanting** today, I'd like you to go to the grocery store for me," Ellen's mother said, as she stood at the kitchen sink. Ellen drank a glass of orange juice and poured herself a bowl of Kellogg's Pep.

"Sure, Mom, what did you want me to get?"

"There's a list there on the counter."

Reaching across the table to the counter, Ellen examined the grocery list while lifting a spoon of Kellogg's Pep to her mouth.

"Your Dad's already taken the car, so you'll have to use the red wagon. There's a five dollar bill there on the counter. That should cover it. Oh, and don't forget the ration book. You'll need it to buy the coffee."

Once she had finished her breakfast, Ellen took a sweater out of the front hall closet, opened the double doors to the garage, and found the red wagon in the back. She started off down Freeman Avenue on her way to the First National supermarket at Paradise Green. Flowers in the small wedge-shaped park on Main Street were emerging from their winter **hibernation**. The tulip trees were budding, as were the beech. Squirrels scampered across the lawn, feasting on what was left of the prior season's beechnuts.

She crossed Main Street in the vicinity of the popular Clough's Variety Store at 3618 Main Street. Ben Clough, its **avuncular proprietor**, was outside cranking up the green awnings that shielded the front of the store from the glare of the sun's rays. Wearing a blue work apron, he **cordially** greeted passersby. Clough's, a combination hardware and variety store, had been an institution on the Green since Ellen was a little girl. Ellen recalled that Mr. Clough's wife was of Swedish ancestry.

"Good morning, Ellen. And how are you this morning?"

"I'm just fine, Mr. Clough. Did you have a good time at the Swedish picnic last week?"

"You betcha! The family always enjoys going up to the farm in Monroe. The wife's fond of the Swedish music and dancing in the barn. Her parents were born in Sweden, you know. She wishes I could do those Swedish folk dances like your Mom and Dad. Please say 'hello' to them for me."

"I sure will."

"Say, Mr. Clough. Did you ever sell anything to the people living in the old Chandler mansion on River Road?"

"Funny, you should ask. I sold a half dozen sawhorses and several large sheets of plywood to a gentleman living there. I wouldn't have remembered except that he had them delivered. That, and three or four kerosene lanterns. He paid cash. Why do you ask?"

"Oh, I'm doing a little investigation for a friend. It's a **probate** matter. Thanks for the information."

"You bet. Anytime, Ellen."

Leaving her wagon on the sidewalk outside the First National, Ellen grabbed a grocery cart and proceeded down the first **aisle**. Just as she rounded the corner, she spotted her friend, Betsy Dalrymple, standing in front of the cereal boxes.

"Hey, little girl, can I trade you a Little Orphan Annie decoder ring for your Tom Mix Straight Shooters badge?" Ellen shouted.

"Not on your life," Betsy laughed. "They'd kick me out of the Tom Mix Fan Club."

"So, what brings you here?" Ellen replied.

"I was trying to decide if I wanted to eat the 'Breakfast of Champions' or the cereal that gives you lots of cowboy energy."

"I'd go for the Shredded Ralston, myself, although I have nothing against Wheaties."

"Say, are you interested in a couple of tickets to see **Ozzie Nelson** at the Ritz Ballroom tonight? My brother was planning to go, but he can't make it, and I don't have a date. The tickets are yours, if you want them."

"Gee, thanks, Betsy, that's swell. I'll bet I can convince Ken to take me."

"Great. Here take them. They're all yours. Any news about the old Chandler mansion on River Road?"

Ellen lowered her voice. "Funny you should ask. Ken and I are following up on some clues today. Nothing concrete to report yet, however. I'll let you know when we learn something."

When Ellen returned home, her mother was standing at the back door, waving her in.

"It's Ken, on the telephone. He has some news for you." Ellen put down the groceries and ran into the living room.

"Hi, Ken. What's up?"

"Remember what I said about driving to New Haven. I'm afraid we can't use my car. Dad says that gas rationing begins next month and I'll have to stop all my non-essential driving because we'll only be allowed three gallons a week. He intends to siphon all the gas currently in our cars and store it in the garage for emergencies. He insists that I confine my driving to Stratford and Bridgeport, if that."

"Then, why don't we take the train," Ellen suggested. The New Haven train station isn't far from Crown Street and we can park your car at the Stratford Station."

"That's a great idea. Would you be ready to go in about ten minutes?"

"Sure. I'm ready now."

"Great! Be sure to bring enough for your fare. I don't get paid until next Friday."

Ellen had barely finished helping her mother put away the groceries when Ken pulled into the Anderson driveway, and was knocking at the back door.

"Ready to go, Miss Anderson?"

"Just let me get grab my coat and hat," Ellen replied.

The Stratford train station was less than a mile down Main Street from Freeman Avenue, in Stratford Center, and just a stone's throw from the Dusty Corner Book Shop. Ken parked his roadster in the **adjacent** parking lot and the two scurried up the stairs to the platform.

"We're in luck. The next eastbound train's at 10:30," Ellen reported, scanning the schedule board.

Within a few minutes, the New York, New Haven & Hartford Railroad pulled into Stratford Station. Ken reached for Ellen's hand and guided her into the closest car. Ellen felt a surge of excitement as he clasped her hand in his. While they had danced before, largely at the urging of their parents, this was the first time he had held her hand of his own **volition**. Quickly taking the first open seat of the crowded passenger car, they soon felt the car jerk forward.

"Tickets, please," shouted the conductor.

Ken and Ellen each handed the conductor a dollar bill and received change in return. The ride to New Haven was only twenty minutes, passing through the towns of Milford, Orange, and West Haven. As they neared New Haven, they spotted the stately **Gothic spire** of Harkness Chapel on the Yale University

campus just before the train pulled into Union Station.

Ellen had been to New Haven many times. Generally, it was in the company of her parents for joint concerts or social events between her father's North Star Singers and the Apollo Singing Society, New Haven's own Swedish male chorus. Apollo, founded in 1905, was just one of many Swedish male choruses that dotted the American landscape from Boston to Seattle. When they weren't performing at one of the local churches, or in Battell Chapel on the Yale University campus, they congregated at Apollo's clubhouse for refreshments. On a few other memorable occasions, Ellen accompanied her father to the

A.C. Gilbert Company, where the famous American Flyer toy trains were manufactured, and for which he designed various **component** parts. Ellen recalled being **mesmerized** by the sights and sounds of the **elaborate** model railroad layouts where the trains were tested. She envied the jobs of those who did the testing

and could not imagine being paid to play with trains all day. At the time, it seemed to her like the dream job.

Crown Street was located a third of a mile from Union Station, a distance Ellen and Ken walked in less than five minutes. The Elm City Diner was located in a three-story office building at 34 Crown Street in the middle of a large red brick business block, and across the street from the Acme Office Furniture Company. An **archaic** gas street lamp stood on the sidewalk in front of the diner. Entering the lobby of the five-story office building at 36 Crown Street, they quickly scanned the directory.

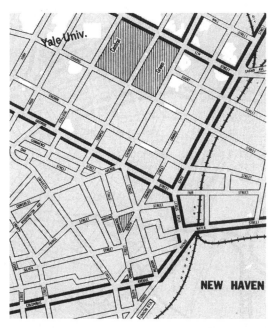

NEW HAVEN

"There he is—John Schlechter—Accountant — Room 364," Ellen exclaimed.

"Why don't we investigate his office?" said Ken. "We can do it on the **pretext** that we're looking for a doctor. Here, let's look in the phone book." Ken reached for the telephone directory resting on a shelf in the lobby, next to a phone booth.

"Here's a dentist at 88 Crown—Dr. Ernest Jackman. We'll pretend we're looking for him. That way, we can find out what this Schlechter looks like."

Ellen pushed the elevator button and the two friends watched the arrow descend to the first floor. An elderly male operator in uniform stepped out. "Going up?"

"Third floor, please," Ellen replied.

Mr. Schlechter's office was at the far end of a narrow corridor. Ellen turned the knob and the two entered. A **demure**, gray-haired woman about sixty years of age sat behind a desk, typing. She looked up, pleasantly.

"Excuse me, I think we're lost. We're looking for Dr. Jackman's office, the dentist. I was sure he was in this building. At least he used to be here," said Ellen.

"There's no Dr. Jackman on this floor, or in this building, as far as I know," the woman replied. "Perhaps Mr. Schlechter's heard of him."

At that moment, a tall, dark-haired man emerged from an inner office, his face **accentuated** by a pencil thin mustache.

"Dr. Jackman? I've never heard of him. He must be in another building downtown, Cora. Why don't you check the phone book for these people."

Cora reached for the phone book sitting on her desk. "Let's see—dentists—Jackman—here he is. He's at 88 Crown. That's further up the block."

While Ken engaged the secretary, Ellen cast her eyes around the office and at Mr. Schlechter. The office was rather **austere**, with a **paucity** of furniture, and showed signs of neglect. Even the potted plants were **flaccid** from lack of proper watering. Beyond the secretary's desk, there were four chairs for clients and a few copies of *Life, Time, Liberty*, and the *Saturday Evening Post* scattered across a small coffee table.

Mr. Schlechter wore a double-breasted gray suit with vest. His thinning dark hair was combed over his balding scalp. His **fabricated** smile appeared to mask a more serious **demeanor**. A gold tooth was visible when he opened his mouth to speak.

"Sorry to have troubled you," Ellen said.

"Oh, no problem," replied the secretary.

Ellen and Ken watched Mr. Schlechter return to his office as they passed outside into the hall.

The pair waited until they were at the elevator before speaking.

"Well, now at least we know what he looks like. He looked a bit **sinister** to me," Ken observed. Ellen echoed his sentiments.

"Well, we already know that he cheated an old lady out of her estate," Ellen replied.

At that moment, a short man in a brown leather jacket stepped out of the elevator and began walking in the direction of Schlechter's office.

"I could swear I've seen that man before," Ken observed, as they entered the elevator.

"I think he's also a client of Mr. Schlechter. He was in the office the last time I was here."

"Oh, they're old friends," replied the elevator operator. "He pops in on a regular basis. They often have lunch in the diner downstairs."

"You don't happen to remember his name, do you?" Ken inquired.

"Yes, it's Gerard Koch. I think he works at Shoreline Blueprint."

"That's right. Now I remember." Ken replied. "He introduced himself while we were waiting to see Mr. Schlechter."

It was almost noon, and Ellen and Ken decided to have a bite to eat at the Elm Street Diner, a rather **garish** dive that served the local population. Entering through an interior entrance right off the lobby, they took a booth in the far corner. They were soon approached by a **genial** middle-aged waitress in a starched white uniform and apron, a waitress cap perched on top of her head, like a **proletarian tiara.**

"What can I get you folks?"

"We'd like to see a menu, please," Ellen replied.

"Sure thing, missy. Here you are."

Glancing over the menu, Ellen ordered a tuna salad sandwich on wheat toast and a coke. Ken asked for a hamburger with onions and a chocolate malt.

"Coming right up."

"Say, Ken, that was pretty crafty of you, pretending that you knew that man, and had been here before. I figured you were pumping the elevator operator for information."

"Well, I do know him, in a way. That's the man who accepted the books from me when we drove up to the mansion the other day."

"Really!" Ellen whispered. "Don't look now, but Mr. Schlechter and his buddy just entered the diner. I hope they don't sit too close to us."

The two older gentlemen sat two booths away. A mother with three children sat in the booth between them, providing a bit of cover. But the **petulant** children were so **garrulous** that it was difficult to detect what the men were saying. To avoid being recognized, Ellen switched sides and sat next to Ken, with both their backs now facing the men.

"I wish those kids would pipe down so we can eavesdrop on their conversation," Ellen whispered.

"Here you go. Tuna salad on wheat toast, and, for the gentleman, a hamburger with onions. You're not planning to kiss her anytime soon, are you?"

Ken and Ellen both smiled and tried to make light of the remark, chalking it up to typical waitress **banter**.

No sooner had she deposited the plates on their table, than the mother rounded up her three children, picked up her check and walked to the cash register.

"I can't believe our good luck," Ellen whispered. "Now, let's eat quietly and see if we can learn something."

As luck would have it, the two men's voices were sufficiently **audible** that Ken and Ellen could grasp significant portions of their conversation.

"I tell you, we've got to have those plans completed in three weeks. Heinrich is afraid that our men at the plant will be detected before the job is completed. If that happens, all our work will be for **naught**," Schlechter **vehemently** insisted. "The closer we get to completing our work, the more I fear something will go wrong. That's why we can't have anyone **usurping** Heinrich's authority. He understands full well how important these plans are to our war efforts."

At that moment, the waitress approached the men.

"I'll have the Bratwurst with sauerkraut, and a glass of beer."

"I'll have the chicken sandwich and a black coffee," said Schlechter.

"Coming right up, gentlemen."

"So, it's **imperative** that we get the job done quickly. If any of our **agents** are detected, it could trigger an investigation and threaten the entire operation," he continued.

"Here you go gentlemen, Bratwurst with sauerkraut and chicken sandwich. I'll be right back with your drinks."

"Danke schön—I mean, thank you."

"You fool!" Schlechter whispered. "How many times have I told you that speaking German is out. You're just asking for trouble."

The two men spent the next ten minutes eating, without much further conversation. Ellen and Ken strained **furtively** to hear more, but were disappointed by the ensuing silence and by the periodic **obsequious** and **officious** interruptions of their waitress.

"Ken, we have to follow that little man when he leaves the restaurant, if possible."

"Sit still. They're getting up," Ken whispered.

Ellen cautiously turned around to see the two men approaching the cashier.

"Wait until they leave the diner. Then we'll follow him," he suggested.

As they walked up to the cashier, Ellen observed the two men shaking hands, after which Schlechter walked back into the lobby of the **adjacent** office building. As Ken and Ellen left through the front door of the diner, they saw Koch walking in the direction of the Yale campus. Continuing west on Crown Street, he made a right turn at Church Street. **Endeavoring** to follow at a healthy distance, they passed two business blocks and a variety of commercial establishments: a dressmaker's shop, a tobacconist, a dry cleaners, and Caruthers' Department Store. Then, suddenly, they observed the man enter a book store at the corner of Church and Chapel. The sign over the door read "Between the Covers."

"Dare we follow him?" Ellen suggested.

"I don't see why not. The store is busy enough with this large university **clientele** to allow us to be **inconspicuous**," Ken replied.

Ken was quickly drawn to the books on **cryptology** and took particular note of the **seminal** work on the subject which Miss Russell at the Stratford Public Library had just recommended to him.

Ellen was **awestruck** by the **plenitude** of books on shelf after shelf. The two began with a **cursory** look at the best sellers at the front of the store. Then, Ellen wandered far enough back to observe the area in which the Koch was browsing. He pulled one book after another from the shelves and skimmed their contents. He must have looked for more than twenty minutes. Finally, settling on one particular book, he made his way to the sales counter.

"Keep an eye on him, Ken, while I check out the section where he was browsing."

Ellen walked quickly to the rear of the store and eyed the shelves at which Koch had spent all his time. The books were all on the subject of aviation and aircraft, its history, design, and air warfare. By the time she returned to the front of the store, the man had left with his purchase.

"Quick, he's heading back to Crown Street," Ken observed. "We'd better hurry or we'll lose him."

Again, they followed at a distance, stopping occasionally to look in store windows so as to appear **inconspicuous**. Pausing in front of the Caruthers' Department Store, Ellen took note of a particularly attractive dress in the window. It was a lovely combination of midnight blue taffeta and matching velvet, an embroidered bolero jacket over a floor length taffeta skirt, with velvet waistband.

"Oh, Ken, isn't it stunning? I would love to wear that to the prom. It's not only elegant, but **complements** my hair. It is $7.50, but perhaps I can convince Dad to buy it for me. I don't have that much in my savings account."

"Yes, it's very nice, but we're losing sight of Mr. Koch. We'd better hurry along."

Ellen and Ken picked up their pace as Koch continued walking south on Church, to George Street, where he turned west and continued for another block and a half. Then, they observed him dart into an alleyway in the middle the block between College and High Streets. When they arrived at the alley, it was deserted.

"Look, Ken: Shoreline Blueprint, just as the elevator operator indicated."

There, fronting at 312 George Street was Shoreline Blueprint. Mr. Koch had obviously entered through the back door, off the alley.

"Well, what do we do now?" Ellen exclaimed. "He could be in there all afternoon."

"This is too good an opportunity to neglect. We'll just have to wait and follow him when he comes out. Why don't we wait in the lobby of that apartment house across the street?

Ken and Ellen waited patiently for more than an hour in the apartment house lobby, trying to act **unobtrusive** when residents entered and departed. Finally, their subject emerged from the alley and began walking back down George Street.

"There he goes, Ken." Ellen shouted, anxiously.

They let him get a half block ahead when they stepped out on the sidewalk and began following. When he got to Church Street, he turned south in what appeared to be the direction of Union Station.

"I wonder if he's going our way?" Ken **pondered**.

"Apparently so."

By the time they reached the train station, they observed Koch sitting on one of the benches near the door to the tracks. The overhead train schedule indicated the next train to Stratford leaving at 2:15. They had only ten minutes to wait for the Boston to New York line.

"Keep your eye on him, Ellen. I want to browse at the magazines."

"I won't let him out of my sight."

Ken looked over the magazines at
the newsstand, his eyes periodically
glancing over to observe the object
of their scrutiny. He scanned the
variety of magazines for sale: *Time*,
Newsweek, *Saturday Evening Post*,
Colliers, the movie magazines with
sensual photos of the current crop

of Hollywood starlets, the outdoor magazines, the pulps, and the comic books. He
was drawn to the latest issue of *Life*, with a story on General Jimmy Doolittle's
daring raid on Tokyo. On the cover was a photograph of Nelson Rockefeller,
President Roosevelt's Coordinator of Inter-American Affairs. But the story of
the Doolittle raid was what intrigued him. After all, his brother was now in the
Pacific and would soon be flying missions against the Japanese.

He was only halfway through the article when an announcement was heard
over the public address system:

"Train now arriving on track number 2 for Milford, Stratford, Bridgeport,
Fairfield, Stamford, Greenwich, New Rochelle, and Grand Central Station, New
York City. All aboard!"

Ken placed the *Life* magazine back on the rack and joined Ellen on the way
to the exit.

"Make sure we get on the same car, but not too close," Ellen whispered.

They watched as Mr. Koch made his way to the far end of the car. Ellen
took a window seat. Ken picked up a discarded copy of the *Hartford Courant*
on the **adjacent** seat and began scanning the headlines. Ellen was content to
enjoy the view of the countryside. About twenty minutes later, the conductor
entered the car.

"Stratford, Stratford next."

As the train eased into Stratford Station, Ellen and Ken rose and made their
way to the nearest door, while Koch exited at the opposite end. Stepping down
from the platform with **alacrity**, he quickly hailed a Yellow Cab which had
been idling in the parking lot.

"Quick, Ellen, he's getting into that cab. We'll have to make a run for my car or we'll lose him."

By the time Ken pulled his roadster out of the parking lot, the Yellow Cab had gotten as far as the high school.

"Give it some gas, Ken, or he'll get away."

They were in luck. The cab was forced to stop for a light at Barnum Avenue. The only question now was keeping at a distance to avoid possible detection. The cab continued north on Main Street, past Paradise Green, and onto River Road. Ken hovered at a distance as the cab approached the Chandler mansion and pulled into the circular drive. A few seconds later, it sped off in the opposite direction, passing Ken and Ellen in the process. Ken slowed a bit as he passed the mansion and the two observed Koch walking around to the side of the house, a package in his left hand. At the junction with Main Street, Ken swung up the hill to Putney. As he drove, they both had a lot on their minds. What did this all mean? What was the nature of Koch's meeting with Schlechter? What was he doing at Shoreline Blueprint? And what was he doing at the Chandler mansion?

"Ken, I almost forget. Betsy Dalrymple gave me two tickets to see Ozzie Nelson at the Ritz Ballroom tonight. Are you interested?"

"Why sure," said Ken, as he pulled into the Anderson driveway. "It will give me a chance to perfect my swing dancing technique before the prom. What time shall I pick you up?"

"7:00. The dance starts at 7:30 and we don't want to be late."

"Don't worry about me. Haven't you ever heard of Swedish **punctuality**?"

"Of course, silly," she replied. "I just want to be sure. I've never heard Ozzie Nelson before and I don't want to miss any of the excitement."

Chapter 7

Ozzie Nelson at the Ritz Ballroom

Ellen was a bundle of excitement as Ken dropped her off in front of her Freeman Avenue home. She hurried in through the front door, with the screen door banging closed after her.

Her mother called out from kitchen: "Is that you, Ellen? I was wondering when you were coming home."

"Yes, it's me. Ken and I had an interesting trip to New Haven on the train."

"New Haven? What were you doing in New Haven?"

"We went to check up on that shady accountant, Mr. Schlechter, the one who's trying to steal Mrs. Chandler's estate."

"So, did you learn anything? That **scoundrel** should be run out of town on a rail."

"Well, we got a good look at him, and one of his associates. They're both German, that's for sure. I could detect it by their accents and conversation. Ken and I are convinced that they're up to no good, but we haven't nailed down anything specific yet."

"I hope you're not getting yourself into any potentially dangerous situations," her mother warned.

"No, nothing like that. We're both being very careful," Ellen replied.

"So what's in store for this evening? Are Betsy and Linnea coming over to listen to the radio?"

"No. As a matter of fact, Betsy gave me two tickets for tonight's USO dance at the Ritz Ballroom. Ozzie Nelson and his orchestra are playing."

"Ozzie Nelson! Your father and I saw him in New York a couple of years ago. A bunch of us from the Swedish Athletic Club went to see him perform at the New Yorker Hotel. He plays a lot of that swing music these days. You'll find some of his records in one of our albums: *Over Somebody Else's Shoulder* was one of his big hits. *Jersey Jive* and *Central Avenue Shuffle* are two of my favorites."

"Boy, Mom, I didn't realize that you were so hip."

"Say, just because your father and I are over forty doesn't mean we can't swing with the best of them. So, what are you planning to wear tonight?"

"I thought I'd wear that orchid rose dress, but I think it needs ironing."

"You go right ahead, honey, while I put this cake in the oven. We're playing bridge at the Peterson's this evening—that is, if your father gets back at a reasonable hour from his fishing expedition. If he comes home with any fish, he'll have to put 'em on ice until tomorrow."

Ellen went to her second floor bedroom and laid her favorite dancing dress out on the bed. Then, she pulled the ironing board out of the hall closet and ironed out the wrinkles.

"Ellen, I hope you're going to have a bite to eat before going out," her mother shouted from the bottom of the stairs.

"Yes, I think that's a good idea. The dance will probably go on until after 11:00 and I want to stay to the bitter end."

She laid out her best set of **lingerie** and new black **patent** leather shoes, before hopping in the shower. Then she dressed, fixed her hair, and dabbed some of that Blue Waltz perfume that she got for Christmas behind her ears. She looked herself over in the mirror and joined her mother in the kitchen. A turkey sandwich and a glass of milk awaited her on the kitchen table.

"You go ahead and eat, honey. I'll wait for your father to get home."

At that moment, they could hear the sound of the Anderson's car pulling into the driveway. Ellen's father opened the doors to the garage and put away his fishing pole, hip waders, and tackle box. Then, he walked in the back door with a string of trout.

"Put them in the basement ice box, dear. You can clean them tomorrow," Ellen's mother advised.

After placing the fish on ice, he took a seat at the kitchen table and proceeded to **regale** Ellen and her mother about his trip to West Cornwall.

"The day couldn't have been better. The air was fresh and **invigorating** and the fish were very cooperative. Herb caught nine trout. I landed six. So, what have you been up to, young lady?"

Ellen related her day's escapade to New Haven, as her father listened intently.

"Sounds like you might be dealing with a bunch of **fifth columnists**," her father suggested.

"**Fifth columnists**?"

"Yes, spies, working for a foreign government," her father explained. "It's a term first used in Spain during their civil war. The Brits use it to describe German nationals suspected of **espionage**. **Fifth columnists** are operating in this country, too. Some are of the **National Socialist** variety, operating under the umbrella of the German-American Bund movement. Others are American communists, under the direction of the Soviet Union. It's only due to military necessity that we are now allied with the Soviet Union, as you probably know. In point of fact, they are just as evil as the Nazis, and just as dangerous. Hitler and Stalin are really just twin **manifestations** of the same **totalitarian** impulses. Mark my words, when we're done with the Nazis we'll be dealing with the Soviet threat."

"You're right about the **fifth columnists**," Ellen replied. "That's what Ken and I think. But we're withholding judgment until we can gather more proof. After all, we don't want to make false accusations against innocent people when the facts are still a bit **nebulous**. That would be a **fiasco**."

"That's a very wise way to approach it, Ellen. You don't want to be too hasty and then bungle the case. If that happens, you'll only damage your **credibility**."

"Ken and I have other plans tonight. We're going to see Ozzie Nelson and his orchestra at the Ritz Ballroom in Bridgeport. Even detectives need a little relaxation now and then," Ellen said, with a smile.

"I thought you looked a little too spiffy to be sitting around listening to the radio," her father replied. "And what's that perfume you have on?"

"It's what you and Mom bought me for Christmas—Blue Waltz. Don't you remember?"

"Well, no, but the name sounds appropriate."

A few minutes later, they heard a knock at the front door.

"It's probably Ken," Ellen exclaimed. "I told him to be prompt."

"He's such a good boy. Always comes to the door like a gentleman. Not like that Ferguson boy who takes your friend Barbara out next door. He just pulls up in his jalopy and honks that **ludicrous** and irritating horn of his. She's just too **submissive**. I'm **stupefied** that any self-respecting girl should put up with that kind of **puerile** behavior," Ellen's mother lamented. "After all, it's the role of the female sex to civilize men," she added.

"Hey, I heard that," shouted Ellen's father, now sitting behind his newspaper. "Did you have to civilize me, Edna?"

"No, dear, you were already civilized."

"What can I say, Mom. Some girls are so **superficial** and **fickle** and others are so boy crazy they'll put up with almost anything. And some boys can be so **obtuse**, without regard for proper **decorum**. I've got more self-respect than that. And, besides, Ken comes from a good home. His parents have him well trained."

Ellen went to the front door and invited Ken in.

"Good evening, Mr. and Mrs. Anderson."

"Hello, Ken. I hear you have an exciting evening planned—Ozzie Nelson no less."

"Yes, Mr. Anderson, thanks to Ellen. Or I should say, thanks to Betsy Dalrymple, who gave her the free tickets."

"My, Ellen, you look most **beguiling**. Here, I brought you a carnation for your dress."

"Oh, how thoughtful."

At that moment, Ellen's mother stood at the door to the dining room, wiping her hands with a dish towel.

"You kids have a good time, but don't stay out too late."

"Don't worry, Mrs. Anderson. I'll have her back by midnight before my roadster turns into a pumpkin."

"Oh, wait just a minute. Let me take a picture. My camera's in the kitchen."

"Mom's the shutterbug in the family," Ellen explained.

"O.K. Smile, you two."

Ellen draped her white beaded sweater over her shoulders as Ken opened the car door for her.

"Your coach, M'lady."

"Thank you, kind sir."

Ken took Barnum Avenue, then Route 1 to the Black Rock section of Bridgeport. As they neared the Bridgeport line, Ellen pointed out the former home of the movie star and tap dancing wonder, Eleanor Powell, who grew up in Stratford and learned to dance at Quilty's Ballroom in Bridgeport.

The Ritz Ballroom, a popular venue for big bands and other musical events, was located on Fairfield Avenue near Davidson Street and Courtland Avenue. It opened on March 23, 1923 under the management of Joe Berry and George McCormack. Its wooden dance floor was originally part of the ice skating rink at the Parlor Rock Amusement Park in Trumbull, which had been moved to the Brooklawn Pavilion, also owned by Barry and McCormack. Among the big names playing the Ritz were Glenn Miller, Guy Lombardo, Artie Shaw, Bing Crosby, and trumpet sensation, Bunny Berigan, famous for *I Can't Get Started With You*, a number he first recorded in 1937.

As they pulled into the parking lot, Ellen could see the crowd lined up at the front entrance.

"Looks like they've got a big crowd tonight," Ellen exclaimed.

"I'll say. The last time I was here, there weren't nearly so many people. But that was for Stella Kowalski and Her Polka Hot Shots."

"Stella Kowalski? And who did you take to that dance, may I ask?"

"No one. I was eight and went with my parents because they couldn't get a baby sitter. One little girl asked me to dance, but we mostly just jumped up and down with the music, that is when we weren't gorging ourselves on punch and cookies."

As the line neared the entrance, Ellen spotted Crystal Harris and Bob Neary, two of her Stratford High classmates. Crystal was a sweet girl, but almost too **saccharine** for some tastes.

"Hi Crystal. Hi Bob. Have you seen anyone else from Stratford High?"

"Hi, Ellen. Yes, Robert Straight and Sally Reynolds are already inside."

Ellen knew all about Sally Reynolds. She was the most **egotistical** girl in her class. A **mercurial** personality, she was **ostentatious** in her dress, excessively **preoccupied** with her hair and makeup, and **flirtatious** with all the boys, Ken included. With a **capricious** personality and **pert demeanor**, she took only a passing interest in her studies. Lacking any sense of **fidelity**, she was also **notorious** for going after boys who already had girlfriends and, without an ounce of **penitence**, seemed to take particular delight in luring them away and wrapping them around her little finger. With **salient** features like these, she wasn't very popular with many of the girls at school who often **derided** her for her behavior and **ostracized** her from the most popular **cliques**. Indeed, the **consensus** around school, **apocryphal** perhaps, was that she has caused the breakup of numerous relationships.

The **capacious** Ritz Ballroom was beautifully decorated for the **propitious** occasion. With the efforts of the local **USO**, the walls were **festooned** with patriotic streamers and the ceiling was **rife** with glittering paper stars in red, white and blue.

The **United Service Organization**—popularly known as the USO—was founded in 1941 in response to a request from President Roosevelt to provide morale and entertainment to American servicemen and women and their families. It served as an umbrella organization for six civilian groups: the Salvation Army, the YMCA, the YWCA, the National Catholic Community Service, the National Travelers Aid Association, and the National Jewish Welfare Board. The USO centers and clubs were known around the world as "A Home Away from Home" to millions of those in the armed services. Its camp shows brought Hollywood and big name entertainment to those stationed around the world. Whether on the home front,

or overseas, the USO gave a much needed lift to servicemen and women, many of whom were going into harm's way.

The theme of the dance—*Celebrating Our Boys in Uniform*—was Bridgeport's way of lifting the spirits of Connecticut servicemen before they were shipped overseas. Local personalities who supported various **philanthropic** activities were serving in the canteen and dancing with the men in uniform. Katherine Hepburn, a Connecticut native who arrived by train from New York for the event, was pouring coffee at the canteen and signing autographs. Ellen estimated that there must have been over three hundred servicemen in attendance. She also

ruminated about the sacrifices of the servicemen they were there to support, and the **abnegation** which they were willing to endure for the sake of their country.

Suddenly, the crowd quieted as the master of ceremonies stepped up to the ribbon microphone on the bandstand.

"Good evening, ladies and gentlemen. I am pleased to welcome so many of our servicemen to tonight's dance. We want you all to know that, no matter where you may be stationed across the globe, our hearts will always be with you. And now, without further ado, I give you Ozzie Nelson and his orchestra!"

With a burst of applause, the celebrated bandleader walked out on stage, and, with a quick downbeat, brought his magical orchestra to life with the strains of *You Made Me Love You*, a melody made popular by Harry James. For Ellen, it immediately brought back the **lyrics** that Judy Garland sang to her heartthrob, Clark Gable, in *Broadway Melody of 1938*. Ken took Ellen by the hand and led her onto the crowded dance floor, then took her in his arms. As they glided across the floor in time with the music, Ellen couldn't help wondering what her future with Ken might hold. Perhaps she was being silly. In another year, he would be in the service, and sent to God knows where. But for now, she wanted to savor the moment. And Ken, for his part, reflected on how **alluring** Ellen looked that evening. That attraction was heightened by the **intoxicating** perfume she wore.

It was a wonderful evening. The orchestra played in 45-minute sets alternating between romantic slow numbers and the pulsating **cadences** of the swing tunes for which it was famous. They also played **medleys** of other big band hits and Ozzie Nelson's own compositions, including *Night Ride*, *Never In A Million Years*, *Sophisticated Swing*, *Head Over Heels In Love*, *They Can't Take That Away From Me*, *Whirligig*, and *Whoa Babe!* The crowd was **captivated** by the sounds of the orchestra. During the swing numbers, the floor was transformed into a maze of intricate **choreography**, twirling skirts and musical gymnastics. Boys and girls **cavorted** across the dance floor. Girls were tossed, flipped, pulled and dragged across the floor by their athletic partners, all to the delight of the less adventurous and more **sedentary** onlookers.

Ellen was pleasantly surprised by Ken's **prowess** as a swing dancer.

"Where did you learn to dance like this, Ken? You've certainly kept it a secret."

"Well, my sister Astrid's been helping me in the gym, after school. I knew

I needed some coaching before the prom, and this has been a great dress rehearsal."

Just as the couple was headed back to one of the couches on the perimeter of the dance floor, Sally Reynolds gave Ellen a **perfunctory** glance and approached Ken.

"Hi, Ken, would you please dance with me?"

"Well, O.K. You don't mind, do you, Ellen?"

"No, Ken, you two go right ahead."

"Bob will be happy to dance with you, Ellen," Sally suggested.

"Sure, Ellen, would you like to dance?"

As the couples glided across the dance floor, Ellen was unable to take her eyes off Ken.

She knew how **solipsistic** Sally was and wanted Ken back in her arms.

"Ken, you know, I've had my eye on you for some time. Did you know that I lived on the other side of Brewster Pond from you?"

"Really?"

"Yes, since we were in the sixth grade. Don't you think it's about time we got better acquainted? I sat behind you in freshman English, but you probably didn't pay me any mind. You could make up for it by taking me to the movies next Saturday? There's a swell Andy Hardy picture playing at the Majestic."

"But what about Bob?"

"Oh, I'm not serious about Bob. He's so ... so ... 1941. A real square. He's the kind of boy a girl can tire of rather quickly. Not much upstairs, if you know what I mean. I'd drop him like a hot potato for you." She looked Ken in the eyes, inviting a response.

"I'm sorry, Sally, but Ellen and I already made plans. But thanks for asking."

"Well, you can't blame a girl for trying."

Ellen was relieved when Ken was back at her side.

"You won't believe the nerve of that girl, Ellen. Despite being **intellectually vacuous**, she has this **supercilious** manner of looking down on other people. She even had the nerve to put down her date. What a **flagrant** display of bad manners. Then, she asked me to take her to the movies next Saturday."

"I'm not surprised. She is very **brazen**. I mean, a girl asking a boy for a date. I find her behavior rather **appalling**. She has this particularly **cloying** way of getting what she wants. I hope you **rebuked** her?"

"Well, I told her that we already had plans," Ken replied.

"That's nice to hear, particularly since we didn't make any plans." Ellen looked into his eyes and he into hers. At that moment, words would have been **superfluous**.

Ozzie Nelson, again, stepped to the microphone and announced the band's closing number. He was joined by his wife, the lovely Harriet Hilliard, for a duet of *Two Sleepy People*. It was the perfect ending for an evening that passed much too quickly. As they drove back to Stratford, Ellen's mind was consumed with thoughts of Ken, as well as the mystery which engulfed them both.

Chapter 8

Visiting an Aircraft Factory

As usual, Ellen was the last one in her family to awaken on Sunday morning. Her mother and father had already finished their breakfast and her father was in the living room engaged in one his favorite Sunday morning pleasures—reading the funnies in the *New York Journal American.*

There they were, in full glorious color—*Bringing Up Father, Flash Gordon, Barney Google and Snuffy Smith, Prince Valiant, Blondie, Tim Tyler's Luck, Mickey Mouse, Tillie the Toiler, The Lone Ranger, Skippy,* and *The Phantom.*

"And can you beat those *Katzenjammer Kids*? Hans and Fritz are always trying to put one over on the Captain and the Inspector. But they always get their **comeuppance**. And how about that *Dingle-Hoofer und His Dog*? But isn't it **ironic** that we are at war with Nazi Germany and the *New York American* has two German **dialect** cartoons on the same page? Which reminds me, Ellen, how would you like to visit the United Aircraft Plant with me this afternoon, after we get back from church? I promised Rex Beisel I'd bring him my drawings for one of the airplane parts we're tooling. Maybe he'll let us take a look inside the plant."

"That would be great, Dad! I've been eager to get a look inside that plant for as long as I can remember, but particularly since they began building the Corsairs. Why, it's one of the most important aircraft plants in the country. I'm always hearing about it from my classmates, many of whom have fathers and mothers who work there. I know I've **alluded** to the prospect of touring the plant, but never thought my hopes would become reality."

"O.K., I'll tell you what. When, we get back from church, we'll drive over to the shop and pick up the plans. Then we'll head over to the factory."

"I'll bring my history book and notebook. I'll want you to drop me off at the library on our way home."

The E. V. Anderson Company was located on Connecticut Avenue in Bridgeport. Ellen had been there many times, of course. She had played with the typewriters in her grandfather's office and walked among the lathes, drills, and other machines, observing the workmen. Her father's office was in the design department on the second floor of the two-story brick building. Rulers and pencils were scattered about his drafting table. Ellen often admired the **intricacy** of his drawings, which were **conspicuous** for their exactness and **precision**.

"Let's see, I need these three drawings," her father said, as he rolled them up and secured them with a rubber band.

Climbing back into the family's Hudson convertible, Ellen and her father drove back to town by way of Stratford Avenue. In a few minutes, they came to Main Street in Stratford where they turned south in the direction of the aircraft plant.

Igor Sikorsky had been making airplanes in Stratford since 1929, when he moved his operations to an **expanse** of farmland on the Housatonic River. The complex consisted of an office building on Main Street, and several enormous factory and engineering buildings on Sniffens Lane. Another feature of the complex was an airplane launching ramp extending out into the river. Sikorsky's most famous products during the ensuing decade were the **behemoth** trans-Pacific Clipper ships that were crossing the Pacific Ocean, and the S-42 flying boats that linked many remote locations around the world. When Chance Vought joined Sikorsky in 1939, the operation was converted to the production of the Corsair fighter planes.

Ellen's father pulled his car into the visitor parking lot situated across Main Street from the main office. Entering through the front door, they were greeted by a uniformed security guard.

"I have an appointment with Rex Beisel of the engineering department. Please tell him that Eric Anderson is here."

"Yes, Mr. Anderson, I'll get him on the intercom."

A few minutes later, a tall, slightly built man with glasses came through the swinging doors that led to the factory.

"Hello, Eric. Good to see you. Why don't we go to my office and have a look at your plans. You couldn't have come at a better time. We'll be entering that phase of production in a few weeks."

"Rex, this is my daughter, Ellen. Any chance she could get a look inside the plant?"

"Why, of course. I'll have my assistant give her the cook's tour. By the way, you're probably aware that the factory's going **full bore**. For the past six months, we've been operating 24-hours a day, seven days a week. Most of our employees are working 48-hour weeks, many getting lots of overtime in addition to their regular **compensation**. Would you believe we've expanded the company parking lot three times already since the plant was converted to wartime production? And we'll be adding thousands of additional employees once the Corsair goes into full production in June. The government's even built 400 new apartments at Success Park to accommodate the influx of additional workers. Many Stratford families are taking in boarders."

"Yes, I've heard. In fact, one of our neighbors took in a boarder last week."

"Oh, here's my assistant, Joel Johnson. He'll be glad to show Ellen around the plant. You two can join us in my office when you're finished."

"Good afternoon, Ellen. I understand you want to see how airplanes are built?"

"Yes, I would enjoy that very much."

"Then, why don't we start in the engineering department?" Joel guided Ellen up a flight of stairs to a series of offices overlooking Main Street.

"This is where the plans for the Vought Corsair are drawn up. We have some of the top aircraft designers in the country working in these offices. In fact, it was Mr. Beisel and his engineering staff who designed the Corsair using Pratt and Whitney's new 2000 horsepower Double Wasp Engine."

In one of those offices, Ellen's father and Mr. Beisel were intently examining the drawings Ellen's father had brought with him.

"From engineering, the designs are broken down into hundreds of **constituent** parts by our **requisition** department. They deal with dozens of sub-contractors to whom production of those parts is **consigned**. All of this must be highly coordinated so that the production will proceed without any delays. Our work is also supervised by the **War Production Board**, a **federal** agency that coordinates the production of all manner of aircraft and other weapons."

"So, the E.V. Anderson Company is one of those sub-contractors?" Ellen observed.

"That's right. Now I'll take you to the factory to observe the assembly process."

From a third floor hallway, Joel led Ellen onto the balcony of a huge factory building where several **prototype** Corsairs were being assembled **simultaneously**. Ellen was struck by the deafening **cacophony** of all the activity on the assembly room floor. A half-dozen overhead cranes, suspended on tracks running on both sides of the work floor, traveled back and forth, delivering heavy **components**

to individual workstations along the track assembly line.

"This is where the Vought Corsairs will be assembled, beginning in June. The engines are built by our Pratt & Whitney division in East Hartford and shipped here for final installation. They are finely **calibrated** before they even reach us, but will be re-tested before they leave the plant."

Ellen observed hundreds of **industrious** employees engaged in all phases of assembly. Some were welding the structural bones of the **fuselage**, others riveting the aluminum sidewalls.

Ellen noticed many women among the workers. She thought to herself that,

perhaps, one of these was the **stereotypical** *Rosie the Riveter* she had heard so much about.

"Here you can observe one of the Pratt & Whitney engines being lowered into the nose of the aircraft. And over there, our workers are bolting the machine guns in the wings before they receive their aluminum coverings."

"This is fascinating, Mr. Johnson. I must **concede** I had no idea that all this activity was going on in my home town."

"Yes, the first F4U Corsair was assembled in our experimental hanger right here in Stratford. Lyman Bullard, our chief test pilot, made the first flight on May 26, 1940. By October, it had achieved a speed of 405 miles per hour—the fastest fighter aircraft in the world. We are now experimenting with an even faster **prototype** that we expect will exceed 450 miles per hour, with improved **maneuverability**."

"Why are the wings bent like that?" Ellen inquired.

"That's part of its special design, so the wings can be folded for use on aircraft carriers. It has a wing-span of 41 feet and a folded width of 17 feet. It's a **lethal** fighting machine, with six machine guns and racks for bombs. We expect the Corsair will be used quite successfully against the Japanese, but we have some bugs to work out. Landing is still a bit of a problem because of the long nose. And, unless corrected, the undercarriage bounce will make it difficult to land on the flight decks of the aircraft carriers, which is dangerous for both pilots and deck crew. In fact, one of the parts your father is working on is a bleed valve to be installed in the legs that will allow the **hydraulic** pressure to be released more gradually as the planes are landed. It's a critical **innovation** which will help save the lives of our pilots."

"It sounds like there are literally thousands of individual engineering problems with a plane like this that have to be **allocated** to hundreds of employees."

"You're absolutely right. And all this activity must be **compressed** into a tight production schedule to keep up with wartime demand. The government has already **requisitioned** 6,000 planes from this facility alone. Labor **disputes** are also tightly controlled. The National Labor Relations Board is **mandated** to employ **arbitration** to get workers back on the job as soon as possible in the unlikely event of a labor **dispute**. Unless, for some reason, the government **rescinds** its order, we'll be busy making Corsairs for some time to come. But it's very satisfying knowing that the Corsair is going to help us win the war in the Pacific. Well, I think I'd better get you back to your father. I expect he and Mr. Beisel should be finished by now."

By the time Mr. Johnson had escorted Ellen back to the engineering department, her father and Mr. Beisel were concluding their meeting.

"Here's that pretty young lady. So, what do you think of our operation now?"

"Oh, it's fascinating, Mr. Beisel. I want to thank you for letting me have a look. It gives me a much better idea of the work my father is doing, and how it's helping the war effort."

"That's quite a daughter you've got there, Eric. And I understand she's quite the amateur detective."

"Yes, her mother and I are very proud of her. Well, thank you very much. I'm sure we'll be able to finalize these designs by early next week and be in production shortly after that. We don't want the lack of parts to **inhibit** the start of production when your June assembly schedule gets underway."

"Mr. Beisel? I have one more question for you," said Ellen. "What do you do to prevent **sabotage** and **espionage**? I mean, with 12,000 employees, how can you guarantee that some of them might not be stealing the secrets of the Corsair? I'm sure the Nazis would love to get their hands on the design, and share it with the Japanese air force."

"Well, young lady, we have a very **formidable** employee screening program to root out spies and **saboteurs**. The name of every applicant is tracked back to every place they've ever lived, with security investigations conducted by the local police forces. Our security force is never **dormant**, keeping a close watch on plant operations to prevent **incursions** by our **adversaries**. I think you can be pretty confident that there aren't any Nazi spies running around inside the plant. We are quite **vigilant** about plant security. I hope that **allays** your concerns."

"Yes, thank you, Mr. Beisel."

"You know, Eric, I think you daughter has quite a **fecund** imagination."

Ellen quietly took **umbrage** at Mr. Beisel's remark and felt a little **indignation** at the way he appeared to **deprecate** her concerns about **espionage**. It made her realize that she would need some solid evidence in order to be taken seriously.

As Mr. Beisel walked Ellen and her father downstairs to the main entrance, Ellen couldn't help but think that the Germans and Japanese would love to learn the details of how these planes are designed and built. She also had a suspicion that the people living in the old Chandler mansion were somehow involved in such an effort.

"Dad, don't forget to drop me off at the public library on your way home. I have a little research to do."

"Research on Nazi spies?" said Ellen's father, with a laugh.

"No, nothing like that, at least this time. I have a report due for my American history class on the origins of the First World War. I have my history book and notebook in the backseat."

Two minutes later, Ellen's father dropped her off in front of the library on Main Street.

"I'll be home by 6:00 for dinner," Ellen promised.

Built of St. Lawrence marble in the **Romanesque** style, the **venerable** Stratford Public Library had been a local landmark since 1896. Indeed, it stood like an **immutable** presence on Main Street, a symbol of learning and **intellectual** curiosity. Ellen walked up the front steps and  passed through the arched entryway. The librarian, Miss Fanny Russell, stood behind the reference desk.

"Good afternoon, Miss Russell."

"Hello, Ellen. Working on a school project, or just doing homework?"

"I have to write a five-page paper on the origins of World War I."

"Try the 327s in the back alcove. If you don't find what you want there, you can look in the card **catalog**. I hope there are some books left. There are several others with that same assignment."

Ellen walked to the rear of the library and began **perusing** the shelves. Luckily, there were still a few books on the subject available. She selected an armful and took them to the nearest table where a classmate was doing algebra homework. Selecting one of the books, she began reading and taking notes. On occasion, her eyes strayed to the **ornate** woodwork of the library's interior, the polished wood floors, the oak bookcases, and the brass chandeliers that hung suspended by chains from the vaulted ceiling. Suddenly, another patron entered the alcove and began scanning the bookshelf on the opposite wall.

When he turned to face her, Ellen's almost dropped the book she was holding. It was Gerard Koch...

A Chance Encounter at the Library

What was Gerard Koch doing at the Stratford Public Library? His presence was a little unnerving, particularly after Saturday's events. Trying to maintain a **nonchalant** pose, Ellen continued her reading, pausing now and then to observe his movements. When her heart slowed to a normal beat, she took closer note of his **swarthy** complexion and **diminutive** stature. But what she really wanted to do was to get a closer look at the books to which he was drawn. Rising from her chair, she **feigned** interest in the shelves from which he had removed several large **folio** volumes. They were atlases and books of **nautical** maps, including maps of the Connecticut shoreline and Housatonic River. Before returning to her seat, she made a quick pass behind his chair to **ascertain** what he was reading. There, opened before him, was a map showing the mouth of the Housatonic River and Long Island Sound. The book remained open to that page for more than five minutes, his fingers carefully tracing the contours of the river.

Ellen tried to **construe** the intent of his **cogitations**. *Was he interested in the United Aircraft Plant and its production? Or was he coordinating a **rendezvous** with a German submarine off the Stratford shoreline?* The possibilities were many. Whatever it was, the Housatonic River undoubtedly figured prominently in his **deliberations**. As the 5:00 closing time approached, Miss Russell passed through the various reading areas to notify the patrons who were still in the library.

"We'll be closing in fifteen minutes. If you have any books to check out, please bring them to the circulation desk."

Ellen chose two of the books she was reading and brought them to Miss Russell who removed the circulation card and inserted a date-stamped card in the rear pocket. Ellen observed Gerard Koch leave by way of the rear door and retrieve a bicycle he had left in the library's bicycle rack. Walking it to the sidewalk on Main Street, he climbed on and set off north, toward Paradise Green and, no doubt, the Chandler mansion.

Ellen walked home along Main Street, passing Sterling House and the First Congregational Church before crossing Church Street to the Stratford Center business block. She enjoyed looking in the store windows. There was Kelman's grocery store, Main Street **Cobblers**, the Stratford Department Store and, in the Tuttle Building, the Great A & P Tea Company. At the three-story Lovell Building, she glanced in the windows of Ann's Beauty Shop and Lovell's Hardware, long a **reputable** source of tools, building supplies, and housewares. She had been on the Lovell Building's second floor many times to see Dr. Smith, her family physician, who had recently **inoculated** her for smallpox.

Then she crossed the little alleyway between it and the Dusty Corner Book Shop, a two-story wood-frame structure which, in earlier days, had served as the headquarters of the old Stratford Volunteer Fire Company. The windows displayed a variety of books, both old and new. To the left were the old and rare books, the first editions. To the right, the current bestsellers and children's books—among them the *Nancy Drew* books, the *Hardy Boys*, the *Rover Boys*, the *Bobbsey Twins*, the *Girl Scouts*, the *Radio Boys*, *Tom Swift,* and the *Judy Bolton* mysteries. There were also the children's classics, like *Little Women*, *Tom Sawyer*, and *The Adventures of Huckleberry Finn*, and even some **lurid** murder mysteries. It was a display Ken had enjoyed arranging, under Mr. Mueller's watchful guidance.

Ellen also reflected on Mr. Mueller's **covert** operations—the National **Socialist** literature that he had Ken mail to customers in New York and New Jersey, and deliver to one particular house in Stratford. According to Ken, he kept those books in a back room, **accessible** only to those with whom he had special relationships. She also **ruminated** about how **ironic** it was that this man who sold young people, or their parents, the Bobbsey Twins also sold literature in support of an **odious** political movement that now threatened the world.

But enough window-shopping. It was time to get home for dinner. Ellen continued on past the former Stratford Town Hall and Newton Reed's building before walking under the New York, New Haven & Hartford Railroad overpass. Up ahead, Ellen surveyed the stately **façade** of the new town hall whose dedication she and her fellow Garden School classmates attended in 1937 and, next to it, her own Stratford High School. From nearby Barnum Avenue it was just six more blocks to Freeman Avenue, and home.

Ellen's mother was just putting dinner on the dining room table when she walked up the front steps and into the living room.

"I'm home, Mom. Is dinner ready?"

"Yes, as soon as your father comes downstairs," her mother replied.

Her mother had prepared a delicious pot roast, with steamed carrots and mashed potatoes.

Ellen loved her mother's gravy which she poured out generously from the gravy boat. Her meals were a **sensuous culinary** experience guaranteed to satisfy her **voracious palate**.

"Dad, guess who I saw at the library?"

"Who's that?"

"Gerard Koch—the same man Ken and I trailed from Mr. Schlechter's office in New Haven."

"What was he doing at the library?"

"He was looking at nautical atlases of coastal Connecticut. I had a chance to look over his shoulder when I passed behind him."

"So, what do you think it means?"

"I don't know, yet. I mean, there are so many **disparate** pieces to this puzzle that I haven't been able to assemble them in any **coherent** order yet. I can only **surmise** that he's **contemplating** some sort of **rendezvous** on the river or nearby coastline."

"Well, that's not an unreasonable assumption. If he only knew you were wise to him."

"Are Betsy and Linnea coming over this evening, Ellen?" Ellen's mother inquired.

"Yes, I expect them by 7:00, just in time for the *Jack Benny* program. After that we're going to listen to the *Chase and Sanborn Hour* with Edgar Bergen and Charlie McCarthy."

"And, don't tell, me—*Inner Sanctum* at 8:30."

"How did you ever guess, Mom?"

"Well, you've only listened to *Inner Sanctum* for eight months straight. I would be **flabbergasted** if you missed it tonight. Say, I almost forgot. There's some strawberry jell-O with bananas in the refrigerator. Would you see if it has **congealed** yet?"

"Sure. You know how much I love strawberry JELL-O. Shall I sing you the JELL-O jingle?"

"No, that won't be necessary, dear. I hear it every time *Henry Aldrich* and *Jack Benny* are on the radio."

After dinner was concluded, Ellen and her mother were washing up the dinner dishes when the front doorbell rang. It was Betsy and Linnea.

"Good evening girls, please step into our inner sanctum," Ellen's mother said, with a sly grin on her face.

"We brought our math books, Ellen. We thought we could do some problems while we listen," Linnea suggested.

"Good idea. I'll get my calculus textbook. I still have a few problems to complete for Monday."

The girls positioned themselves on the living room's **commodious davenport** while Ellen turned on the radio.

…We interrupt this program for a minute with an important Washington bulletin. The OPA announces its point value ratings upon canned and processed foods under the new ration system, effective May 1st. The schedule is more severe than anticipated. These point ration values will cut canned food **consumption** *to at least one-half less than last year's levels. Each person gets 48 ration points a month. This ration allows, as one example, the purchase of one medium-sized can of peas, a medium can of tomatoes, a large can of peaches—three cans a month. A pound and a quarter can of peas is valued at 16 points. Fruits and fruit juices cost more heavily in ration points, canned soups the least. Canned baby foods are rated the lowest, at one point, and some at two points. We encourage you to eat lots of fresh fruits and vegetables which are not rationed. Stay tuned to this station for further bulletins from the Office of Price Administration.*

"Mom, did you hear that? Three canned goods per person per month. The

implicit message of that announcement is that we'd better start **cultivating** our **Victory Garden** and **propagating** our own fruits and vegetables if we're going to **ameliorate** the coming food shortage. We could go hungry on such **meager** rations. Dad, I hope you're ready to dig up the back yard and turn it into a **fertile** source of **agricultural** bounty?"

"You betcha! I'll hitch up the mule to the plow in the morning," he said with a wink.

The Anderson family had already gotten their first taste of rationing in January, when the first war ration books were issued for sugar and coffee. In fact, Ellen and her mother rushed to the local First National supermarket at Paradise Green in 1941, when news of upcoming rationing was first announced. In a matter of hours, local housewives had cleaned the shelves of both items. Meat was the next item to be rationed, and anyone eating fourteen or more meals in a restaurant per month had to surrender his ration book to the manager to guarantee compliance with the law.

They all listened as Ellen tuned the radio to WTIC, the NBC affiliate in Hartford:

> *... J-E-L-L-O... The Jack Benny program with Mary Livingston and Phil Harris and his orchestra. The orchestra opens the program with Boo-Hoo.*

About five minutes into the program, the telephone rang. Jumping off the **davenport**, Ellen grabbed the receiver and carried it in the direction of the kitchen.

"Hello, Anderson residence."

"Hello, Ellen, this is Abby Wexler. I thought you'd like to know that there has been a lot of activity going on at the old Chandler place over the past few days. Two cars pulled in the driveway about an hour ago and four men entered the house. Also, I've noticed a small motorboat approach the house from the river the last three evenings, with two men aboard. I couldn't see it very well after it disappeared into the weeds, but I thought you should know. Who knows what they're **concocting**?"

"I really appreciate your keeping me posted. I don't think there's much I can do this evening, particularly with the old house so full of visitors, but I think I'll drive up there and have a look, anyway. Thanks for calling. I'll be in touch."

Returning to the **davenport**, Ellen joined her chums for the remainder of the Jack Benny program.

"What was that all about, Ellen? We couldn't help but overhear your conversation," Linnea inquired.

"That was Abby Wexler, the **proprietress** of the country store next to the Chandler mansion. She's been keeping an eye on the place for me and wanted to report some increased activity at the house this evening. When *Inner Sanctum's* over, would you mind if we took a drive up there to investigate what's going on.

"I've been waiting for you to ask me, Ellen," Betsy exclaimed.

"Great! We can park your car on Main Street and walk through the woods to a spot overlooking River Road."

At the conclusion of *Inner Sanctum*, Ellen grabbed her father's binoculars and the three girls climbed into Betsy's LaSalle coupe. A few minutes later they were in Putney, where they parked on Main Street, just north of Putney Chapel. The girls followed a narrow path into the woods until the river came into view. They walked until they had a virtually unobstructed view of the Chandler mansion, just north of where Main Street met River Road. Quickly, they took positions behind of a clump of oak trees.

The two automobiles Abby mentioned were still parked in the circular driveway. The house was a blaze of light, punctuated by the passing shadows of the multiple occupants. Ellen recognized one of the cars as a 1938 Studebaker, just like the one her next door neighbor owned, but she couldn't identify the other one, which had a futuristic design. *"Oh, where was Ken when she needed him?"* she thought to herself.

"Linnea, hand me my binoculars. I want to get a look at those license plates," Ellen said.

"GT657—that's the blue Studebaker. It's a New York plate."

Ellen recorded the number in her notebook.

"The other one's a Connecticut plate—JL243. I'd better sketch the car. I'll bet Ken can identify it," she added.

After Ellen did her best to sketch the design of the automobile, the girls maintained their **surveillance** for nearly an hour. About 10:45, the front door of the house opened and a half dozen men emerged.

"Quick, let's get back to the car. I want to be **poised** to follow them when they pull out of the driveway," Ellen urged.

Running back to Betsy's coupe, they drove to the intersection of Main Street and River Road. From that **vantage point**, they could see the cars in front of the mansion.

"Here comes the Studebaker. If it gets on the Merritt Parkway, we'll just let it go. I'm more interested in the one with the Connecticut plate," Ellen cautioned.

"The other car's heading south. Let's follow it," shouted Betsy.

Pulling onto River Road, the girls followed the car of unknown make, maintaining a safe distance to avoid detection.

"Careful, Betsy. We don't want them to think they're being followed."

The car continued south on River Road until it merged with Main Street. Betsy was able to keep the car in sight through Paradise Green, past Barnum Avenue and after it made a right turn at Broadbridge Avenue, which ran parallel to the railroad overpass. Finally, the car came to a stop in front of a house near the intersection of Broadbridge and King Street, near the railroad **viaduct**.

"Stay on Broadbridge, Betsy, then double back. Wait for them to get inside the house." Ellen urged. "Then, we'll drive past and get the address."

Betsy crept along to give the car's occupants enough time to get inside the residence, then reversed direction and drove slowly back.

"It's 18 King," Ellen exclaimed. "That's all the information I need to trace the names of the owners in the city directory. You can take me home now."

As Betsy dropped her off at her Freeman Avenue home, Ellen thanked her chums for the timely assistance.

"You've both been a big help. Now, I just need to find out who lives at 18 King and what the men were doing there. Thanks so much, Betsy, Linnea. See you at school tomorrow."

By the time Ellen brushed her teeth and climbed into bed, it was nearly 11:30. A full day of classes awaited her in the morning. She couldn't wait to tell Ken that her adventure had led back to the heart of Stratford.

Chapter 10

Strange Happenings at the Bookshop

Ellen had become so **preoccupied** with the goings on at the Chandler mansion that she found it difficult to keep completely focused on her schoolwork. Nevertheless, she was relieved when Mr. DeLeurere returned the test on Latin roots to the anxious students in her Monday morning Latin class.

"*An 'A'—what a relief*," Ellen thought to herself as Mr. DeLeurere walked down the **aisle** between the desks, passing out the graded exams.

Fortunately, Ellen was one of those students who could earn high marks just by paying close attention in class. She absorbed knowledge like a sponge. She also **attributed** her success to being genuinely interested in all her subjects. In Latin, she had no trouble learning all the noun **declensions** and verb **conjugations**. What would have been **daunting** for many students, was a **facile** task for her.

"Christine, would you please **conjugate** the present indicative of the verb *voco* for the class," said Mr. DeLeurere.

"Yes: voco, vocas, vocat, vocamus, vocatis, vocant."

"Very good, Christine. Now, Ellen, how about the future indicative of the verb *laudo*?"

"Let's see, laudabo, laudabis, laudabat, laudabimus, laudabitis, laudabunt."

"Excellent."

Mr. DeLeurere had an effective way of keeping the **listless** students in his classes on their toes. A **vacuous** look or wayward expression was bound to get his attention. His classes were always **scintillating**, never **banal. Conscientious** students were never **afflicted** with **ennui.** His "Latin scholars" never knew when they would be called upon to recite, and failure to respond correctly could earn a swift **chastisement**. Although they were generally not the recipients of empty **platitudes**, **conscientious** students could receive hearty **kudos** for correct responses. For the unprepared, however, Mr. DeLeurere could be the **bane** of their existence. Unlike Ellen, who thought his **pedagogical** style appropriate to the subject matter, some students thought he employed old-fashioned, almost **antediluvian**, academic standards. And the bell signifying the end of class came none too soon for these less than **punctilious** and **torpid** slackers.

As class came to an end, Ellen suddenly recalled that her classmate, Christine Applegate, lived near King Street. She approached her in the hall outside their second floor classroom:

"Christine, you live near King Street, don't you?"

"Actually, we live on Broadbridge Avenue, about a block from the train station. Why do you ask?"

"I'm trying to find out who lives in a house near yours."

"What's the address?"

"18 King Street."

"I don't know, but my brother delivers the *Stratford News* to most of the houses on our street. If you want to walk me home after school, we can ask him about the people who live there. Say, what's this all about?"

"Christine, I'm afraid I can't tell you right now. It's connected with a case I'm working on. I'll have to ask you to trust me for the time being."

"That's all right, Ellen, I understand. Why don't I meet you at the back entrance when school is over."

Ellen ran into Ken, briefly, during her afternoon physical education class. The girls, dressed in their regulation blue one-piece rompers, were running from the gym to the field across King Street they used for field hockey. At the same moment, Coach Lambert's 1:00 boys' gym class, which had just completed a **tedious** round of **calisthenics**, was already choosing up sides on the **adjacent** softball field. When the procession of girls appeared, however, their eyes were **uniformly** diverted in their direction until Coach Lambert promptly called them to attention.

"This sport is called softball, gentleman, not bird watching. Choose up sides," he barked.

Ellen jumped out of the procession and ran over to where Ken was standing.

"I've got a lot to tell you. Can we meet somewhere after school?"

"I'm working at the bookshop until 6:00. Why don't you drop by after 5:00. I think Mr. Mueller's out of town, but his wife will be there. We can talk then."

"Great. I'll be there."

Field hockey was not Ellen's favorite sport. She much preferred softball or volleyball. But she was usually chosen to play goalie because of her quick reflexes. That afternoon, she was **gratified** because her team held the opposition scoreless. In fact, she only had two saves because her teammates kept the ball at the other end of the field for most of the period.

When her last period chorus class was over, she quickly made her way to the school's rear entrance where Christine was already waiting for her.

"I'm so glad you asked for my help, Ellen. I mean, I know about your reputation as a crime solver."

"I'm glad you can help me, too, Christine," Ellen responded, as they started walking south on King Street.

"You know, Ellen, I don't have many friends. I think it's because I'm so shy. I have trouble fitting in. Most of the popular girls just ignore me and the less popular girls probably think I'm **aloof**. Most of the girls are more interested in their makeup, clothes, and boys than in having me for a friend. And we're just too **impoverished** to afford such things as makeup or fine clothes. I guess that's why I enjoy reading those **maudlin** romances from the library so much. I can get lost in a book and don't have to experience rejection. I hope we can be friends."

Christine's request **evinced** in Ellen a combination of **pathos, altruism**, and embarrassment. **Pathos** because it was unusual for a young person to have to ask another to be a friend. Such relationships usually came about naturally, and without being verbalized. And embarrassment because Ellen regretted not having made an effort to get to know Christine before now. And now that she had made the effort, it was primarily for more **mundane** reasons. She was determined to **reciprocate**, however, and make up for past omissions.

"I'd love to be your friend, Christine. You're a swell kid. I would **attribute** your shyness to a lack of self confidence. You can't expect other people to like you if you don't feel good about yourself."

"Perhaps you're right, Ellen. I just need to get out of the dumps. I'd love to go to the prom, but no one has asked me. I'm so **bashful**. And even if someone asked me, I couldn't afford to buy a nice dress. In fact, I haven't had a new dress in over two years, since my father died. Some of them are **threadbare**, even **tattered** beyond mending. Mom works at the A & P, but we also depend on what my brother makes on his paper route and the little I make working Saturdays at Clough's Hardware on the Green. I offered to quit school and get a job in a defense plant, but Mom will hear none of it. She insists that I graduate from high school and go to college. Not that I know where we'd get the money."

"I don't mean to hurt your feelings, Christine, but you could use a good makeover. I would be happy to come over and help you fix your hair and show you about makeup and clothes. I don't think it's good to be too **preoccupied** with those things, but one should certainly try to make a nice appearance. And you can be sure one of the nice boys will take notice. And not one of the **sophomoric** types, mind you. Besides, I should be able to help you find some nice dresses, too. They might not be new, but they'll be attractive and stylish."

Ellen could not help but feel a **profound empathy** for Christine considering the tragedy that had overtaken the Applegate family and the emotional **anguish** which it must have **engendered**. Although she was somewhat **diffident** by nature, even **laconic** on first impression, Christine was quite **loquacious** once Ellen got her to open up. And she was a pretty girl, too, though a bit **unkempt**.

"Oh, would you, Ellen? I would be so grateful. I'm **amenable** to just about anything."

"As a matter of fact, I have a lovely new flowered print dress that my grandmother bought me for my birthday, but it's too small. It should fit you quite well."

"If not, I can alter it in Miss Nilsson's sewing class," Christine suggested.

"You're a really pretty girl, Christine. We'll get those boys to take notice."

"Here's my house, Ellen."

When the girls had reached Christine's modest Broadbridge Avenue home, Ellen realized that, although the family was not **destitute**, it lacked the financial resources to repair the house's

KING STREET, LOOKING NORTH, STRATFORD, CONN.

dilapidated exterior and **refurbish** the interior. It also lacked many of the **amenities** Ellen took for granted in her own home, like an automatic dishwasher. And, the **antiquated** washing machine the Applegates owned was somewhat **anachronistic** for 1942.

"Billy must be home from delivering papers. His bicycle is in the garage. Come on in. Mom won't be home from the A & P until after 5:00."

"Billy, I'd like you to meet my good friend, Ellen Anderson. She's in my Latin and American history classes. Billy's ten, Ellen, and in the fourth grade at Garden School. He's also quite **precocious** for his age."

"**Precocious**? Is that good?" Billy inquired.

"Yes, it means that you're very bright for your age," Christine explained.

Billy was stretched out on the living room floor of the family's small bungalow reading comic books.

"Pleased to meet you, Ellen. Do you like Captain Marvel?"

"Sure, but I don't have much time to read comic books these days. Mostly, I read the Sunday funnies in the *New York Journal American.*"

"What's your favorite?" Billy inquired.

"I like the adventure serials the best, like *Flash Gordon, Prince Valiant* and *Tim Tyler's Luck.*"

"Me, too!" Billy exclaimed. "But my favorite comic books are *Captain Marvel, Superman,* and *Batman.* Did you know that Captain Marvel is really a radio news reporter? His name is Billy, just like mine—Billy Batson. He says the magic word *SHAZAM* and he turns into Captain Marvel. And do you know what *SHAZAM* stands for?"

"Why, no," Ellen replied.

"Solomon, Hercules, Atlas, Zeus, Achilles and Mercury. That spells *SHAZAM.* He has the wisdom of Solomon, the strength of Hercules, the stamina of Atlas, the power of Zeus, the courage of Achilles, and the speed of Mercury."

"Say, Christine, your brother's quite **verbose** for a ten-year old. I wonder if Mr. DeLeurere knows about Captain Marvel. With all those characters from

Greek mythology, it's right up his alley."

"And did you see the *Adventures of Captain Marvel* serial last year at the Stratford Theatre? I saw all fifteen episodes. It was great!"

"No, but I did see some of them. I wasn't able to go every Saturday. That's the whole point of serials. The idea is to get you to come back every Saturday. By the way, Billy, I want to ask you a question about one of your newspaper customers. They live at 18 King Street."

"18 King Street? Just a minute, let me check my collection book... Here it is: Klaus Mueller. Oh, yea, I know him. He owns the bookstore in Stratford Center where I get my used Hardy Boys books. I just collected from him today. He's a nice old man, but something must have happened to him because his head was bandaged and he had bruises on his face. He told me he fell down his basement stairs. Sometimes, he gives me used comic books he picks up from people who are selling him books. He sells them in his store, too."

Ellen was **dumbfounded** to learn that the home in question was, **coincidentally**, owned by the Muellers. She also suspected that Ken was already aware of this.

Ellen turned to Christine, who was quietly taking in the conversation.

"Christine, you and Billy could be a big help to me by keeping an eye on the Mueller house. I have a suspicion that his injuries were a **deliberate** case of **assault** and **battery**. If possible, I'd like to know who comes to the house and their license plate numbers. This could be very important. I need you to be my **confidants**, so please don't tell anyone about this, at least for the time being. Think of yourselves as undercover agents."

"Gee, me an undercover agent," exclaimed Billy.

"Well, I've got to get going. I'm meeting my boyfriend, Ken, this afternoon," Ellen explained.

"I'm **ecstatic** that you want to help me, Ellen. I only wish we had become better acquainted before now."

Leaving the Applegate home, Ellen felt **ebullient** as she walked to Main Street, then turned south in the direction of the business block. When she arrived at the Dusty Corner Bookshop, Mrs. Mueller was standing behind the counter helping a customer. She found Ken busy in the back room, opening boxes of books from publishers and distributors. Boxes of used books covered the floor, ready to be sorted by subject and placed on the shelves.

"Hi, Ellen. Did you happen to notice Mrs. Mueller when you arrived?"

"Yes, I saw her helping a customer."

"No, did you notice her face? She's visibly upset about something, almost **morose**. On several occasions, I've seen tears in her eyes. She told me that Mr. Mueller's sick, but I think it's worse than that."

"That's what I want to tell you. I think he was **assailed** by some of his associates. The brother of one of my classmates, Billy Applegate, delivers newspapers to the Mueller home. He told me that Mr. Mueller's face is bandaged and that he has bruises on his face. I think it happened last night. Betsy and Linnea and I followed a car from the Chandler mansion to Mr. Mueller's home. I didn't realize at the time that he lived there. I just wrote down the address and figured I'd go to the library today and look it up in the city directory."

"That's very troubling, but also encouraging. Perhaps, he isn't a Nazi sympathizer after all. I hope he'll be all right. Say, I want to show you something. Mrs. Mueller's been so busy out front that she left the door to the rare book room unlocked. Follow me."

Ken led Ellen into a small room connected to the storeroom. There, on floor-to-ceiling shelves were hundreds of rare and out-of-print **tomes**, as well as books in German and French.

"Look over here. This is where Mr. Mueller keeps the German language books. There's Goethe, Schiller, Nietzsche, Thomas Mann, Hoffmann, Kafka, Brecht, both in German and English translations, as well as **anthologies** of German poetry. And here's the National **Socialist** literature: Hitler's *Mein Kampf*, the *Protocols of the Elders of Zion*, and other **illicit propaganda** pamphlets of all sorts. I've seen him bring customers in here and close the door if I'm around. He always handles the transactions at the cash register for these books, so I won't see what he's selling. He also personally wraps the packages mailed to customers. He doesn't think I know what they contain."

"Do you think he's being pressured into selling this kind of literature because of his German heritage and because of his contacts with German publishing houses?" Ellen inquired.

"I think that's right. They need a middleman, and he's perfectly suited to serve their needs. On the surface, he operates a perfectly respectable bookstore in a small town. But underneath, he serves as a clearinghouse for **noxious** National **Socialist** literature and activities."

"But, perhaps, he's now becoming **intransigent** and his associates are using physical **intimidation** to bring him back into line," Ellen suggested.

"That seems to be the most likely **scenario**. Quick! I hear Mrs. Mueller calling. Let's get out of here."

Ken closed the door to the rare book room as best he could, then went back to the task of unpacking books.

"Ken, can you come help me up here. I need a strong pair of hands."

"Sure thing, Mrs. Mueller."

"Would you please carry this box of books to Mrs. Stewart's automobile? It's much too **strenuous** a job for me."

"Certainly, Mrs. Mueller."

Ken lifted the heavy box of used books and carried it to Mrs. Stewart's Plymouth coupe parked on Main Street.

Ellen, who followed Ken to the front of the store, had a better opportunity to observe Mrs. Mueller more closely now. She could not avoid noticing the redness of her eyes and the signs of **distress** in her face.

"Is everything all right, Mrs. Mueller? You look upset."

"It's my husband. He fell down the basement stairs and injured himself. I'll have to manage the store by myself until he's well enough to work again."

"I'm sorry to hear it. I'm sure Ken can help you out until he's back on his feet."

As Ken returned to his duties in the backroom, Ellen perused the shelves in one of the alcoves near the front door. She particularly enjoyed looking over the large selection of mystery novels. As she returned one of the books to its place on the shelf, she heard car doors slamming on the street outside. Two men, projecting a **stolid** and **intimidating demeanor**, entered the front door and approached Mrs. Mueller.

"We'd like to see your German literature section," said the taller of the two men.

"Yes. Please follow me," Mrs. Mueller responded.

"Ken, please watch the front counter while I help these gentlemen."

"Certainly, Mrs. Mueller."

Leading the **unsavory** looking men into the rare book room, she promptly closed the door after them. Ken, anxious to hear any conversation, moved to a nearby worktable, then noiselessly pressed his ear to the door.

"Mrs. Mueller, we've tried to be reasonable, but your husband refuses to cooperate. You'd better convince him to do as he's told, or things will get worse for him and his relatives in the **fatherland**. What he got last night was just a sample."

Ken had heard enough. He quickly bolted to the front of the store and resumed his position behind the counter. He motioned for Ellen to follow him.

"Ellen, take a good look at the two men when they come out of the back room."

"First, let me get the make and model of their car and their license plate number" she suggested. "I'll be right back."

Ken perused the books on the front counter, while Mrs. Mueller continued to deal with the visitors. A few seconds later, Ellen returned to the counter.

"It's a black 1937 Ford Model 74 with a Connecticut registration—PF745. It's different than the car we followed last night. I didn't recognize the make and model of that car, but it was definitely not a Ford. That reminds me, I drew a sketch of it. I thought that, perhaps, you could identify it."

Pulling a notebook out of her purse, she showed Ken the drawing she made on Sunday evening.

"I'd recognize that car anywhere. That's a DeSoto Airflow. They called it

the car of the future, but it's probably a 1934 model. Put it away, quickly. I hear Mrs. Mueller and her visitors."

Ellen slid over to one of the front display tables while Mrs.

Mueller and the two men walked to the front of the store. Ken puttered around the front counter with an air of **nonchalance**.

Ellen took careful notice of the two men as they walked to the front door. One was of medium build and height, about 5 foot 10 inches tall, with jet black hair combed straight back. She couldn't help but notice his rather pronounced earlobes which seemed to dangle on each side of his head. The other man was of considerable **girth**, probably weighing 300 pounds, with brown wavy hair. Both looked **intimidating**, particularly to a girl of seventeen.

"We'll get back to you about the books, Mrs. Mueller. I think our offer is quite generous," said the larger of the two men. They left the store and climbed into their automobile.

Mrs. Mueller was visibly shaken by the encounter and had trouble concealing her **anxiety**.

"Is anything wrong, Mrs. Mueller?" Ken inquired, after the men had driven away.

"Nothing I can talk about, but I appreciate your concern. This is something Mr. Mueller and I have to work out for ourselves. Oh, I see it's closing time. Would you please lock the front door, Ken, while I empty the cash register."

"Sure thing, Mrs. Mueller."

Ken grabbed his sport coat from the rack in the back room and Ellen retrieved the school books she had left on a rear table.

"I still have a few things to tend to, so I'll wish you two young people a good evening. I'll need you after school again tomorrow, Ken. No telling when Mr. Mueller will be healthy enough to return to the store."

Mrs. Mueller escorted them out through the back, locking the door after them.

Climbing into the waiting roadster, Ken edged the car out onto Main Street between the bookstore and the old town hall.

"Ken, we need to bring the police into this. We can't let these men **perpetrate** continued violence against the Muellers. You could see that Mrs. Mueller's in **distress**."

"I know what you're saying, but we don't want to be **rash**. There are other considerations involved here. I learned something very important by eavesdropping on their conversation. Mr. Mueller has relatives in Germany who are in danger if he **balks** at their demands and fails to **placate** them. That's something he's **grappling** with. It would be **presumptuous** of us to **intervene** under such circumstances. That's a decision the Muellers will have to work out for themselves. After all, the Mueller's could **denounce** these characters to the police whenever they choose to do so."

"I see what you mean. But we can't let it go on indefinitely."

"I suggest we keep a close watch on the situation and see what develops. If Mr. Mueller remains **intransigent,** and continued violence **manifests** itself, we always have the option of involving the police. In the meantime, we should continue with our **surveillance**. After all, I'm in a perfect position to monitor the situation."

By the time Ken dropped Ellen off at her front door, it was a few minutes after 6:00 and Ellen's mother was putting dinner on the table. She realized that her mother was always **punctilious** about starting dinner on time.

"It's about time you got home, young lady. You've got two minutes to freshen up. Your father's as hungry as a Viking, **figuratively** speaking of course."

Chapter 11

A Trip to Manhattan

When Tuesday morning arrived, Ellen was up at the first sign of daybreak, and at least an hour before her alarm clock signaled it was time to get up. Sitting up in bed, she took the time to review her class notes and read a chapter in her American history textbook before heading downstairs for breakfast. By the time she approached the front entrance to Stratford High School, Ken was already waiting for her.

"Well, aren't you the prompt one, Mr. Swenson!"

"I couldn't wait to speak to you. I got a call from Mrs. Mueller last night. Since Mr. Mueller's still **recuperating** from his injuries, she's **delegated** me to deliver some books to a bookstore in New York City on Saturday. I have reason to believe that the **proprietors** are involved in the same **clandestine** activity."

"What makes you say that, Ken?"

"Because it's a bookstore with which Mr. Mueller has often exchanged inventory, including National **Socialist** literature. It's also an address I've recorded in my notebook when I took packages to the post office."

"Where in New York?"

"It's on 122nd Street, not far from Grant's Tomb and Riverside Drive. I've never driven into the city before, but I suppose I can find my way there without too much difficulty. But what I wanted to ask is if you'd like to accompany me. If there is a connection, you can help me look for clues."

"Sure, I'd love to. I'll have to get permission from my parents first, but I think they trust you behind the wheel. I won't say anything about the Nazi connection. I don't want to alarm them."

~~~~~~~~~~~~~~~~

By the time Saturday morning arrived, Ellen and Ken were anxious to be off on their assignment. Mrs. Mueller was behind the counter at the bookstore when Ken arrived to pick up the delivery van, which he had already loaded with eight cartons of books on Friday afternoon.

"Ken, you'll find three more sealed cardboard boxes in the storeroom which need to be loaded," Mrs. Mueller advised. "That makes a total of eleven boxes. Here's the address and a road map. The store's called Central European Books and Imports at 502 West 122nd Street. You've mailed things there before. Let's see, it's 9:30. It should take you about two hours to get to the city and make your delivery and another two hours to get back here. Barring any **unforeseen** complications, you should be back here no later than 3:00. You drive safely now," Mrs. Mueller cautioned. "I wouldn't want anything to happen to you."

"Don't you worry, Mrs. Mueller. I'm a very cautious driver."

The Mueller's brown delivery van was parked out back, next to Ken's Ford roadster. Ken had already decided that it was best not to tell Mrs. Mueller that Ellen would be accompanying him in the van. When he arrived at Ellen's home, she was standing at the front door waiting for him.

"We'll be back this afternoon, Mom," Ellen shouted as she ran down the front steps and climbed into the front seat next to Ken.

"Mom packed us some ham sandwiches and a thermos of coffee. Oh, and some of Vivian's cinnamon buns you like so much. I also brought an umbrella. It looks like we could get a downpour."

"Here's the map. I'll let you serve as my **navigator**, but it shouldn't be too difficult. We just follow the Merritt Parkway to Pelham where we merge with Route 1 into the city until it intersects with Riverside Drive at 178th Street. Then down Riverside Drive about four miles to 122nd Street. It's right near Grant's Tomb."

The Merritt Parkway was an engineering and **aesthetic** gem, its gentle contours lined with a canopy of trees and punctuated with dozens of **Art Deco**-style bridges, many **adorned** with classical and modern design elements. Built to relieve congestion on the

heavily traveled Boston Post Road, its initial segment from Greenwich to Norwalk was opened in 1938. In 1939, the segment from Norwalk to the Housatonic River in Stratford was opened to traffic. Four Mobil gas stations lined the 37-mile route, and a lone toll booth was located in Greenwich.

It was an overcast day, with an **intermittent** drizzle. Traffic was light most of the way as they made their way through Stratford, Trumbull, Fairfield, Westport, Norwalk, New Canaan, Stamford, and Greenwich, before entering New York at Rye Brook. From there, they drove to the Bronx, crossing the Harlem River at 178th Street. Many of the streets in that part of the city exhibited signs of urban **blight**, a consequence of the Depression that left many of the city's residents **indigent**. Ellen also noticed that a number of the buildings were the victims of **vandalism**, their exteriors **defaced** by **graffiti**, much of it directed at Hitler, Tojo, and Mussolini.

"Ellen, I'm going to drop you off a few blocks from the store so you can play the part of a **bibliophile** while I make my delivery," Ken suggested. "I'll pick you up in front of Grant's Tomb when I'm finished."

"That sounds like a good plan. I'm anxious to get a look at the types of books they stock. I can ask if they have a copy of the *Protocols of the Elders of Zion.* That should be a tip-off to what kind of establishment it is."

"Exactly what is the *Protocols of the Elders of Zion?*" Ken inquired. "The Mueller's carry it in their store, but I really have no idea what it's about."

"The *Protocols of the Elders of Zion* is a clever **forgery** and **hoax** which **alleges** that there is Jewish and Masonic **conspiracy** to dominate the world. It was **allegedly** written by a secret **cabal** of European Jews known as the Elders of Zion. It's been used for years to **propagate** the myth of a Jewish **conspiracy** and **foment prejudice**

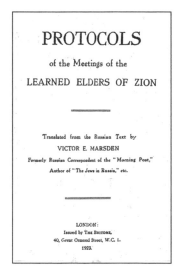

and hatred of the Jews. In reality, it was a clever **forgery** by an agent of the Russian czar to make the Jews **scapegoats** for Russia's defeat in the Russo-Japanese War. Its **provenance** is actually much older than that. It was originally written by a Frenchman named Maurice Joly in 1864 and titled *The*

Dialogue in Hell between Machiavelli and Montesquieu. But in 1894, Mathieu Golovinski, a clever **plagiarist**, rewrote the text to prove to Tsar Nicholas II that the revolt in Russia was a Jewish plot. By 1917, it was being used to blame the Jews for the **Russian Revolution**, on the **pretense** that the **Bolsheviks** were largely Jewish. In 1921, Philip Graves, a correspondent for *The Times* of London exposed the **forgery**. However, that didn't stop it from becoming a **staple** of Nazi **propaganda**. Miss Tyler discussed it last year in my world history class as a case study of mass **deception**, and I've done a bit of research about it on my own."

It was just past 11:30 when Ken reached 122nd Street and let Ellen out behind the imposing **Gothic edifice** of Riverside Church. Ellen paused momentarily to appreciate its architectural **grandeur**.

Riverside Church and Grant's Tomb, Riverside Drive, New York.

"I think a half hour should be enough time for me to make my delivery and for you to investigate the book shop. I'll watch for you in front of Grant's Tomb about noon. If I don't see you right away, I'll just keep circling."

The overcast skies had given way to a light drizzle. Ellen buttoned up her trench coat, pulled a blue beret over her hair, and opened her umbrella as she began to make her way down 122nd Street. A stiff wind off the Hudson River blew across her face and caught the exposed hem of her dress as she struggled to keep her umbrella from being blown inside-out.

Morningside Heights was a **dynamic** neighborhood that encompassed a varied blend of local residents and students at the **confluence** of Columbia University and the Jewish Theological Seminary. The architecture of the street was an **eclectic amalgamation** of academic buildings, massive apartment houses and older **brownstones**, some with commercial establishments in their lower levels. About a block and a half east of Riverside Church, she spied Central European Books and Imports, situated in a worn **brownstone** on the south side of the street. The bookstore occupied the lower level of the building, down a short flight of stairs and behind a black wrought-iron fence. Above the bookstore was what appeared to be an **adjunct** antique store, **accessible** by another flight of stairs, its windows revealing a rich and varied assortment of porcelain vases, lamps, furniture, statuary, paintings, and other **objets d'art**.

As Ellen descended the stairs to the bookstore, she observed Ken pulling the Mueller's delivery van up on the curb. A bell attached to the door rang as she entered, but it was barely **audible** above the **din** of the voices inside. Several dozen patrons busily occupied themselves at bookshelves and book-covered tables, some in **animated discourse**, much of it **discreet**. Ellen noted that most spoke in English, but she also detected a **smattering** of foreign tongues, mostly French, Spanish and German, and others she could not identify. A poster mounted on an easel at the front of the store announced an upcoming poetry reading by a **renowned** local **bard** at the **Roerich Museum**. An elderly woman standing at the cash register gave Ellen a **cordial salutation** as she entered. Ellen's eyes were almost immediately drawn to the new books and bestsellers neatly arranged on several large wooden tables at the front of the store. There she saw *For Whom the Bell Tolls*, a new novel by Ernest Hemingway, *Saratoga Trunk* by Edna Ferber, and *Random Harvest* by James Hilton. Among the nonfiction titles, she took note of William Shirer's *Berlin Diary*, and examined Alice Duer Miller's **poignant** novel in verse, *The White Cliffs*.

Gradually, she worked her way though a virtual **labyrinth** of alcoves, where she **discerned** one **esoteric** specialty after another, from popular fare to scholarly **tomes**, including titles in what appeared to be a dozen European languages.

"May I help you, miss," said a **diminutive** man with horn-rimmed spectacles who approached Ellen from behind, startling her.

"Well, I was looking for one book in particular: *The Protocols of the Elders of Zion*. But I'd be interested in any other titles you have in that **genre**," Ellen replied. "I have a particular interest in the origins of the Jewish **conspiracy**."

"Yes, I believe we have a copy of that in stock. We also have *The International Jew* by Henry Ford. I can show you all four volumes, if you like?"

"Yes, please," Ellen responded.

"If you'd like to keep browsing, I'll bring them out for you."

Ellen detected a trace of a German accent despite the clerk's efforts to conceal it. Disappearing behind one of the alcoves, he emerged several minutes later with a **plethora** of books and pamphlets.

"Here are a number of items in which you may be interested. Let me know if I can be of any further assistance. We don't believe in **censorship**, but, for obvious reasons, we don't keep these things on the open shelves."

"I understand. Thank you very much."

As Ellen pored over these **anti-Semitic tracts**, she **pondered** where in the store they might be stored. She also reflected on the **irony** of the **juxtaposition** of a bookstore stocking this type of **insidious** literature and a **predominantly** Jewish neighborhood. But New York was a city of many contrasts, many mysteries and cultures, often in close **proximity**. Looking for a chair, she peered around the corner, only to catch the clerk disappearing behind a hinged bookcase in a wall of the German language alcove. When it closed, its existence was completely disguised by a wall of books. Finding an empty chair in a neighboring alcove, she began examining the *Protocols*. Choosing a page at random, she read:

> ... *Loans hang like the sword of* **Damocles** *over the heads of rulers, who, instead of taking from their subjects by a temporary tax, come begging with outstretched palm of our bankers... the* **Goy** *states go on in persisting in putting more on to themselves so that they must* **inevitably** *perish, drained by voluntary bloodletting ...*

Ellen didn't grasp the full import of the passage, but **surmised** that it had something to do with the Jews as money lenders and their power over non-Jews who are forced to borrow from them as a result of fiscal mismanagement. She wondered what similar **tracts** might be stored behind that concealed bookcase. Suddenly, curiosity got the better of her, and, **jettisoning** concern for the potential **liabilities** of her actions, she approached the bookcase behind which the clerk had disappeared. Placing her books on a vacant space on one of the shelves, her fingers explored the sides of each shelf searching for some mechanism which might activate the rotating bookcase. Then, she found it–a button on the underside of a chest-high shelf. She pressed it, then had to quickly step aside as the bookshelf swung out, barely scraping the tip of her shoe. Then, with some **trepidation**, she stepped inside the barely illuminated space, pulling the moving bookcase behind her so as not to arouse suspicion. It took a few moments before her eyes could adjust to the encompassing darkness, and she felt confident moving about. The only light she could **discern** was coming from across the darkened space, filtering out from the perimeter of a doorway that was slightly ajar.

There was just enough light to read the titles of the books on the shelves, some of which were more obvious than others. But it was just what she had suspected. Shelf after shelf was filled with National **Socialist** and **anti-Semitic** books, pamphlets and **propaganda tracts**, in both German and English, from one end of the room to the other, much of it written, from what she could hastily **discern**, in the most **turgid** and **ideologically** tortured prose. There were also Marxist **tracts** of various sizes and descriptions—a **veritable** treasure-trove of the kind of **radical left-wing** literature which provided the **spurious** philosophical **underpinnings** of the **reprehensible ideologies** that drove the current **conflagration** across the globe. From what she could **glean**, much of it was less than **pellucid**, **promulgating** the kind of **theoretical** and **abstract** analysis comprehensible primarily to those with a **propensity** for **abstruse** and **radical** political thought.

Suddenly, Ellen stopped in her tracks. The sound of voices, which appeared to be coming from behind the revolving bookcase at the other end of the room, increased in volume. It was clearly impossible to escape by the way she had come. She had to find a hiding place quickly, lest her presence be detected. Several feet away, an empty wooden crate offered the only hope of concealment. Quickly, she crouched behind it and crawled inside, pulling the flimsy lid after her. She found herself lying on a bed of **canvas** which provided some comfort from the crate's sharp edges. Narrow cracks between the slats allowed her to observe four men emerge from the now opened bookcase.

"Schroeder, how soon can you get your hands on the **detonators**?" said one of the men in a **strident** tone.

"This evening. I'm meeting our contact at the auto warehouse at 63 Flushing Avenue, near the Brooklyn Navy Yard. He also supplies us with the dynamite."

"Excellent! There are two destroyers scheduled to dock shortly for repairs, and I don't want them returning to service. Do you understand?"

"Yes, we can take care of them. It will be months before they will be able to repair the damage."

Ellen struggled to remain perfectly still, but a splinter from inside the crate penetrated her trench coat, causing her to jump and brush against the side of the crate. Her heart pounded furiously inside her chest, as she prayed that her movements were not detected. She felt fortunate that she was not **claustrophobic**.

"What was that?" shouted one of the men.

"I didn't hear anything. Probably your imagination. These old buildings make all sorts of noises."

"I could have sworn I heard something coming from those bookshelves over there. Miller, take a look."

One of the men walked over to the shelves **adjacent** to the crate and began pushing against the books. Suddenly, a rat scurried across the open floor.

"See, it was nothing. Just one of the **feral** rodents that love to gnaw on books."

"Then, we need to set some traps. I hate rats."

Ellen could detect one of the men making notations in a small notebook, then place it in the inside pocket of his suit jacket.

"We'll meet back here on Tuesday evening, at 8:00. I want to hear a progress report from each one of you. Do you understand? You know your assignments. The Fuehrer is counting on you to carry out your assignments."

Ellen remained motionless as the four men exited through the revolving bookshelf.

Breathing a sigh of relief, she wiped the perspiration from her brow while waiting a few moments to emerge from the cramped confines of the book crate. Finally, convinced that they were not returning, she backed out, stood up, and stretched her **lithe** frame. The door on the other side of the room was ajar, the lights still on. She walked **tremulously** across the open floor and stepped inside. Suddenly, a chill coursed though her body. Her eyes were immediately drawn to a world map indicating countries under Nazi or **Axis** occupation. A portrait of **Adolf Hitler** hung **audaciously** on the opposite wall. There was nothing **ambiguous** about these physical indications of the Nazi political movement. She opened several of the file cabinet drawers and surveyed **copious** correspondence, all neatly arranged in labeled files. Among them were letters and communiqués from Germany. Stuffing several of the files inside her trench coat, she looked hastily for another means of **egress**. Around a corner, in a small **anteroom**, she found a bolted door and reached for it, just as voices were **audible** from the storeroom.

"Miller, that **canvas** wasn't lying there earlier, was it?"

"No."

"Someone was hiding in that crate. Quick! Get the others and search the entire floor. I'll search outdoors."

Ellen, in the meantime, had managed to unbolt the door and had stepped into the narrow passageway which separated the bookstore from the **adjacent brownstone**. Running into the rear courtyard, she managed to drop to the ground behind a large concrete planter as she heard footsteps echoing in the courtyard's open **expanse**. Suddenly, they stopped. Ellen sized up the **predicament** in which she now found herself. *Should she make a run for the back door of one of the townhouses on the other side of the courtyard, and risk being spotted, or wait to see if her pursuer gave up the chase? And what if the door she chose was locked? She would be trapped in the courtyard.* Hearing footsteps on the concrete sidewalk, she froze in place.

Suddenly, her pursuer ran in the direction of 122nd Street, giving her the opportunity to bolt for the nearest doorway. To her good fortune, the door was unlocked, and she scurried inside. Walking straight through the dimly lit hallway, she emerged at the other end and exited on 121st Street. The rain had largely **abated** by this time, reminding her that she had abandoned her umbrella in the bookstore. With her heart still pounding, she walked west to Broadway, then hurriedly in the direction of Grant's Tomb. By the time

she crossed Riverside Drive, Ken was already there, idling at the curbside on the east side of the massive **mausoleum**.

"Whew! Am I glad to see you! I had a close call. It's probably my own fault for being so **inquisitive**. But I couldn't let the opportunity go to waste."

"Slow down and tell me all about it," Ken exclaimed.

Ellen proceeded to relate the story of how she found her way into the secret storeroom and into what appeared to be the party headquarters.

"You took quite a chance," Ken suggested. "What if they had detected you in that crate? Do you think they would have let you go? I think not. These people are **ruthless**. After all, they're prepared to blow up a couple of destroyers. They wouldn't have allowed you to stand in their way."

"I know. I took quite a risk. Let's not say anything to my parents. They would be worried sick. So, did you learn anything?"

"Not much, I'm afraid. I made my deliveries at the front of the store. They had me stack the boxes near the front counter. I didn't see anything suspicious. They did ask me where old man Mueller was. I told them he had an accident and I was filling in. I gave the packing slip to a rather **staid** little man in an office near the cash register, and left. I'd been circling Grant's Tomb for about ten minutes when you arrived."

"By the way, I brought along a few souvenirs." Ellen reached inside her trench coat and pulled out several manila files containing party correspondence. She began flipping through the letters as Ken drove north on Riverside Drive.

"They're all in German. I'm afraid my Latin language skills won't help me much in **deciphering** them. Best we turn these over to the F.B.I."

"Tell you what. I'll pull over at the next drug store and we'll find out where the closest F.B.I. office is located," said Ken. "After all, it's critical that we report the planned **sabotage** at the Brooklyn Naval Shipyard."

After driving more than a mile north on Riverside Drive, they spotted a Rexall Drugs on the corner of 135th Street.

"Pull over here, Ken, I'll make the call."

Ellen hopped out of the van and ran into the drug store. She promptly spotted a phone booth in the rear of the store with a large city directory suspended from a chain. Flipping through the pages, she located the address of the local F.B.I. office.

"*Here it is,*" she thought out loud, "*181 Canal Street. Why that's miles in the opposite direction.*" Making a mental note of the address, she exited the drug store and climbed back in the van.

"I'm afraid we're going in the wrong direction. The F.B.I. office is located at 181 Canal Street. According to the map, it's in the Chinatown section of SoHo, that's the neighborhood south of Houston Street, near Columbus Park."

"Well, we've got to do it. I just hope Mrs. Mueller won't get too worried when we don't return on schedule," Ken cautioned.

Circling back on Riverside Drive, Ken and Ellen made their way through light traffic to the Henry Hudson Parkway, which became the West Street Express Highway south of 72nd Street. Fifteen minutes later, they turned left onto Canal Street. After another mile and a half, they pulled up to a red brick **edifice** in the middle of a short block. Leaving the van parked out front, they climbed a short flight of stairs and passed through a glass doorway to an interior hallway. The first office on the right read: "Federal Bureau of Investigation—Manhattan Office." They stepped inside and approached a **pulchritudinous** dark-haired woman at the reception desk.

"May I help you?"

"Yes, we'd like to speak to one of your investigators," said Ellen.

"May I ask what this concerns?"

"Well, you might say that it concerns potential **sabotage**."

"Please have a seat. I'll get Chief Inspector Conrad."

Ellen fumbled nervously with the files of letters, while Ken flipped through a copy of *Life* magazine resting on the coffee table. A few minutes later, a tall gentleman with a mustache approached the two young sleuths.

"I understand you have some information about **sabotage**. Would you please come into my office?"

Ken and Ellen followed Inspector Conrad down a narrow corridor. He ushered them into his compact office, closing the door behind them.

"Please have a seat and tell me what this is all about."

"Well, to begin at the beginning, we have been on the trail of some **fifth columnists** who are operating out of a house in Stratford, Connecticut, where we live. My friend Ken here works for the **proprietor** of a bookstore that, **surreptitiously**, stocks **National Socialist** literature. Today, he was asked to make a delivery to a bookstore on West 122nd Street, not far from Riverside Church. While he made his delivery, I poked around inside the store and asked if they had a copy of the *Protocols of the Elders of Zion*, which they did. But I also made my way into a hidden storeroom where they kept all their **radical socialist** and **communist** literature. Luckily, I was able to escape detection by hiding in a book crate when several men entered the storeroom. When they left, I explored an office which contained a portrait of Adolf Hitler and a map of Nazi-occupied Europe. And to **corroborate** my story, I removed several files from one their cabinets. The letters are all in German."

"But what's this about **sabotage**?" inquired the inspector.

"While I was hiding inside the book crate, the men were discussing plans to blow up two destroyers at the Brooklyn Naval Yard. Apparently, they plan to attach explosive devices to the ships soon after they arrive in port. One of the men said that they were getting the dynamite and **detonators** from a contact at an automobile warehouse at 63 Flushing Avenue in Brooklyn."

"Did you hear any names mentioned?"

"I heard three names: Heinrich, Miller, and Schroeder. Heinrich was the one who gave the orders. The others were **deferential** to him, so I assume they were **subordinates**. Oh, and one other thing: they mentioned that they were using divers to plant the explosive devices."

"So tell me, how did you get yourselves involved in this operation in the first place?"

Ellen explained the story of the mansion on the river and its connection to the **proprietor** of the store where Ken worked. She also explained that Mr. Mueller had relations in Nazi Germany whose safety was being **exploited** to keep him in line. She also reported that they were not hesitant to employ violence when the threats to family members were insufficient to **induce** their cooperation.

"Mr. Mueller's a **congenial** old man, rather **docile** in fact. I'm sure he's not sympathetic to Nazism, but is being used because of his involvement in the book import business," Ken explained. "They need a source for Nazi **propaganda** and he's been forced into that role. We haven't said anything to the Stratford police yet, in **deference** to Mr. Mueller's relatives in Germany, and despite the fact that they beat him up last week to force his continued cooperation. But if things get much worse, we are prepared to tell them."

"I appreciate you young people coming to us. But, while I can't issue any official **injunction** for you to **cease and desist** from this dangerous activity, I must **beseech** you to leave this matter to the professionals. You're dealing with **ruthless** people who have become a **corrosive** influence within the city. If this is the Robert Heinrich I think it is, he's one the leaders of the Nazi **hierarchy** in the United States. In fact, he reports directly to Colonel Hans Pieckenbrock, head of the Foreign Intelligence Collection division of Abwehr, the German spy network. More importantly, he's been involved in the murders of several F.B.I. informants in the city. We had him tracked to the Bowery several weeks ago, then to a townhouse in Gramercy Park, then to a **defunct** antique store in Greenwich Village, but he's **eluded** us repeatedly. His whereabouts have been a **conundrum** to my men for many weeks now.

The plot you've **delineated** may allow us to take him into custody and **counteract** a potentially **catastrophic** explosion at the Brooklyn Naval Yard. Without your timely **intervention**, that could have turned into a genuine **debacle**. And the Stratford connection you've related reveals that this is a far more **convoluted** and widespread operation than we had originally **surmised**. It sounds to me like you have an opportunity to uncover something significant in Stratford, so we'll keep out of it for the present, provided you confine your activities to what you can **glean** from working at Mr. Mueller's bookstore. But let me give you my card in case anything further turns up. I want you to call me if you learn anything significant in Stratford. We're also very anxious to discover where their organization **convenes**. Do you understand? Here's my card. Please call me if you learn anything further, or have any questions about how to proceed."

"I won't hesitate to call you if we learn anything." said Ken. "Of course, we would have no reason to return to the city anytime soon. Mr. Mueller made deliveries only three or fours times a year, even when he was well. And once he's recovered from his injuries, he'll be making them himself."

"In the meantime," the inspector continued, "I'll have to **defer** to our translator to examine these letters for additional clues. I can't thank you enough for bringing this **documentation** to us promptly. You've performed a genuine service to your country. But, as I said before, please be careful and don't take any chances. We have plenty of agents who get paid to take these risks."

Chief Inspector Conrad walked Ken and Ellen back to the front door and stood on the top step of the landing as they got back into the delivery van. Retracing the route up the Hudson River Parkway to Riverside Drive, they made their way back to the Merritt Parkway, and home. Both were emotionally exhausted by the time they pulled into the alley behind the Dusty Corner Book Shop.

"Wait here, while I let Mrs. Mueller know I've returned."

Several minutes later, Ken emerged from the back entrance to the bookshop and hopped into the front seat of his roadster, where Ellen was already waiting.

"Would you look at that? Five dollars, on top of my weekly pay. Finally, I'm **solvent**. Mrs. Mueller was so pleased that I successfully made the delivery that she wanted to pay me a bonus in addition to my hourly wages. This is cause for celebration. What do you say we head over to Hamilton's for a chocolate malt? My treat!"

Steering his roadster through the narrow alleyway between the book shop and the old town hall, he quickly pulled onto Main Street and headed in the direction of the malt shop at Paradise Green. The two had much to discuss.

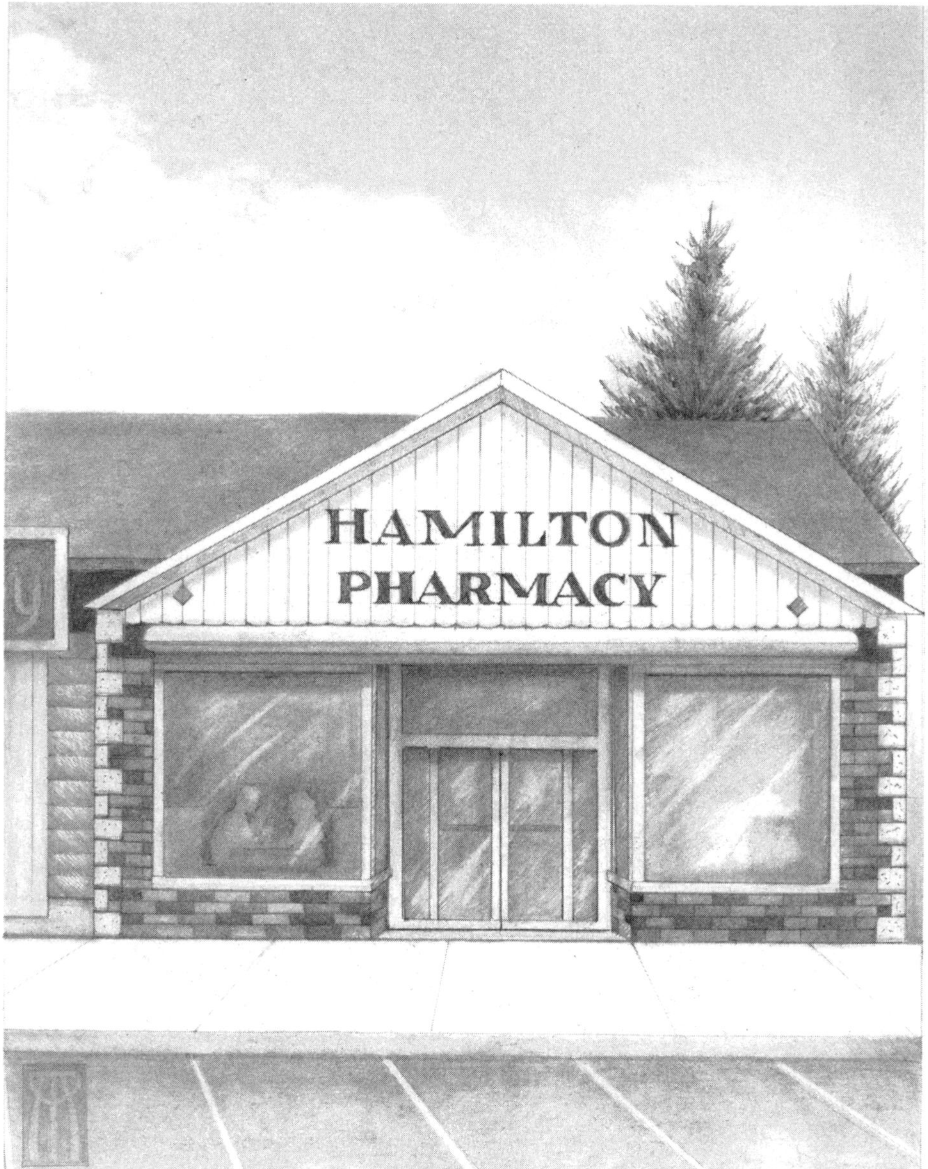
HAMILTON
PHARMACY
©MMXIV

Chapter 12

Developments on the River

No sooner had Ken pulled his roadster up to the curb in front of Hamilton's than he spotted Tommy McCauley ready to climb into his father's green Packard coupe. Ellen thought it a **putrid** shade of green, but refrained from expressing her opinion in front of Tommy. It certainly wasn't a color she would have selected.

Tommy was one of Ken's best friends. **Gregarious** and **genial** by nature, he was a bit of a **maverick**, however, who spent most of his time tinkering with his father's Packard and the Chris-Craft runabout he managed to salvage from Bailey's Boatyard where he was employed part-time. He was not particularly **enthralled** with school work, preferring the industrial arts and auto mechanics with which he was most **proficient,** to his academic subjects. He seemed to have a mind of his own, despite being periodically **berated** by his father for **lackluster** grades and a **lethargic** attitude about his homework. In light of his **recalcitrance**, Tommy hung out at the boatyard to avoid the **rancor** which **ensued** whenever his father became **querulous**. Ellen recalled his being placed in some **remedial** classes his freshman year, a consequence of his inability to **regurgitate** facts and figures from his textbooks. But, now, he seems to have found his **niche** in the industrial arts department where he became **engrossed** in the subject matter and **reveled** in its hands-on activities, particularly auto repair.

"Am I glad to see you," exclaimed Tommy. "I was just over to your house, Ken, but your mother said you were working."

"Yea, we've been in New York making deliveries for Mr. Mueller, but we ran into a little more excitement than we anticipated," explained Ken. "I'll tell you more about that later. What's your news?"

"I've got some information that you will find very interesting. I couldn't forget about that day you borrowed my boat to do some **sleuthing** upriver. As you know, I spend a fair amount of time in my boat or working around Bailey's Boatyard. Well, lately I've noticed a boat cruising around Nells Island and making its way through the marsh grass. Although I see them with fishing equipment, that's really not much of a place for casting. And they're certainly not oystermen. I know practically all the oystermen in the area and none of them can identify the men in the boat. I can't help wondering what they're doing there, day after day, if they're not fishing. That made me think of the suspicious boat you spotted approaching the old Chandler place on River Road a couple of weeks ago. I thought the two of them might be one and the same."

"You say they have fishing equipment, but are probably not fishing?" Ken inquired.

"That's right. I mean, I really can't be sure, since I couldn't very well go in after them. A better course would be to stake out a **secluded** position in advance and wait for them to approach."

"You say they do this practically every day?"

"Well, most days I've been at the boatyard," Tommy replied. "Usually about 3:00 in the afternoon."

"I have a suggestion. What do you say Ellen and I come over tomorrow at 2:00 and you guide us to an appropriate place where we can observe their activities. From there, we'll see if anything develops."

"Sure thing! I know a perfect observation spot. My Dad and I have used it on several occasions for duck hunting. And if we spot anything significant, you can buy me a chocolate malt."

"That makes two. I just promised Ellen a malt. We'll see you then."

As Tommy fired up his Dad's Packard, Ken escorted Ellen into Hamilton's, where the two made their way to their favorite booth in front of the store's picture window overlooking Main Street.

"So, what can I get for you two?"

It was "Pop" Gagnon, a local fixture at Hamilton's, at least since Ellen's father had been in school. Pop was a **benevolent** old **codger** who had a **penchant** for using Connecticut **colloquialisms,** like *shots* for those little sprinkles they put on your ice cream**,** or *grinder* for that foot long sandwich on a submarine roll. **Convivial** by nature, "Pop" knew all the students by name. And, although he lived in Trumbull, he had a decided **bias** for the Stratford High School sports teams and was often heard **railing** against Stratford's opponents on the gridiron or basketball court.

"For a change, I'd like a hot fudge sundae. And don't spare the hot fudge.

I've had a hard day," exclaimed Ellen.

"And for you, Ken?"

"I'll have the usual."

"One hot fudge sundae and one chocolate malt coming right up!" said Pop.

As Ken gazed out the front window at the passing cars and bicycles, Ellen trained her eyes on his gentle features and green eyes. Suddenly, her emotions got the better of her and she began to imagine herself in his arms, an emotional rush to which she did not often **succumb**. She knew it was a **quixotic** fantasy. Ken wasn't ready for romance yet, particularly with military service or college staring him in the face in another year. Then, suddenly, he turned his head and looked right at her. Their eyes met. Ellen smiled and Ken returned the expression, then looked away again, shyly.

"So, what do think about these mysterious boatmen prowling around Nells Island," Ellen inquired.

"After what we've seen so far, I believe they're observing the test flights coming out of the United Aircraft plant. After all, the south end of the marsh is a perfect place to monitor the planes taking off from the airport," Ken suggested.

"I agree. But now we have to confirm our suspicions."

"Say, doesn't your father have a movie camera? I thought I saw him with one up at the Good Templar's Farm in Monroe at the last Swedish Midsummer picnic."

"Yes, he does, do you think I should bring it?" Ellen replied.

"Sure! That is, if he has no objection."

"No, I don't think so, but we'll need to **procure** a roll of 8mm film first."

"No problem. You're speaking to a tycoon. I have more than six dollars in my wallet."

Once they had finished their ice cream, they bought a roll of film for the movie camera. By the time she and Ken arrived at her Freeman Avenue residence, Edna was just putting dinner on the table.

"It's about time, young lady. Would Ken like to stay and have dinner with us? I'm serving pork roast, with my delicious gravy?"

"No, thank you, Mrs. Anderson. My mother's expecting me home just about now. But I'll take a rain check on it. I'll see you tomorrow, Ellen. Shall I pick you up about 1:30?"

"Perfect. I'll be dressed and ready for action."

As Ken bounded down the front steps, Ellen's father was just emerging from the basement.

"Hi, Dad. What have you been up to?"

"I've been in the darkroom, developing the film in your camera."

"You know, I almost forgot about those photographs. What do they show?"

"Well, nothing just yet. They're hanging up to dry. We can have a look after dinner."

The three took their seats at the dining room table and began passing around the warm dishes—roast pork, boiled potatoes, gravy, green beans almandine. Ellen poured herself a glass of milk from the porcelain pitcher.

"Mother says you've been in New York City today?"

"Yes, Ken asked me to **navigate** while he drove a load of books to a bookstore on the Upper West Side. Mr. Mueller was a little under the weather."

"You know, it's been more than a year since we were last in the city. It was a year ago January when we heard **Jussi Björling**, that fabulous Swedish tenor, at the Metropolitan Opera. Isn't that right, Edna?"

"Yes, it was Verdi's *Il Trovatore*. I've never heard such a voice—so radiant. It gave me goosebumps."

"We'll have to take you to New York to hear him sometime, Ellen. But I'm afraid it will have to wait until the war's over. He's gone back to Sweden, and you know how dangerous it is to travel these days, what with all those German submarines prowling the Atlantic. They say that **aerial reconnaissance** has even spotted some **U-boats** in Long Island Sound. In the meantime, you'll have to settle for the phonograph records."

"Isn't he the one who sings *Sverige* and *Ack Värmeland du sköna* so beautifully? I love those recordings. I've been meaning to play them for Miss Porter, our choral director. Sometimes, she lets us bring in music of our own to play for music appreciation days. And it can't be swing. She says she likes swing, too, but that we have to listen to that

on our own. She's trying to raise our **aesthetic** standards."

"Well, I have to agree with her," Ellen's father responded. "When I was in school, it was ragtime my teachers didn't approve of, particularly during school hours. They had a **demarcation** line between the classics and the popular music of the day. They wanted us to hear Franz Schubert and Beethoven. It wasn't their aim to **demean** the music we listened to. They simply wanted to **nurture** in us an appreciation for something more **sublime**. It certainly raised my **aesthetic** standards. I grew up without a record player at home, and I didn't even have a **crystal set** until 1922. But they had a Victrola **gramophone** at school, and that's how I developed an **affinity** for classical music, and playing the violin. And now, your mother and I genuinely enjoy going to the symphony, and taking you with us. And, besides, there's plenty of classical music on the radio these days, as well as music to satisfy the most **eclectic** tastes. We certainly couldn't dial up whatever music we wanted when I was your age."

"I know the Swedes really enjoy hearing your father and Vern Hanson play their fiddles for the barn dances up at the farm," Ellen's mother **interjected**. "They perform it so **zealously** that sometimes I have an awful time getting him to put down his violin and get up on the dance floor with me. While your father isn't a **virtuoso**, he had a Swedish neighbor who taught him all sorts of Swedish fiddle tunes. With a lot of **assiduous** practice, he's gotten pretty **adept** at playing those melodies."

"That reminds me. Mr. Clough told me how much he and his wife enjoy the Swedish music up at the farm."

"When did you see Mr. Clough, Ellen?"

"The day you sent me to the First National for groceries."

With their hunger nearly **assuaged**, Ellen and her father saved a little room for a slice of that warm strawberry rhubarb pie Edna had just pulled from the oven. Edna, who was trying to **adhere** to an **abstemious** dietary **regimen**, decided she would refrain from desert. Indeed, none of the Andersons had a weight problem because they were **resolved** to avoid the kind of **gluttony** that affected some families.

"That was fabulous, Edna. You certainly do make a fine pie," Eric exclaimed.

Cleaning off the dining room table, Ellen and her father **alleviated** Edna of some of the **domestic** chores by washing and drying the dinner dishes. Indeed, unlike some husbands, Eric never **balked** at helping Edna in the kitchen, even after a **strenuous** day at the shop. Perhaps, it was the affect of Edna's **succulent** cooking that **mollified** whatever **aversions** he may have had towards helping in the kitchen. As they washed and wiped the dishes, Ellen's father was always good for a bit of **levity**, including the humorous **anecdotes** or Swedish **maxims** he regularly picked up at the shop.

After the dinner dishes were put away, Ellen and her father retreated to the basement darkroom to have a look at the photographs she had taken the week before. In light of the adventure she and Ken had planned for Sunday afternoon, the results would be even more **compelling**. Opening the clothespins which suspended the photographs on a string across the room, Eric laid seven photographs across his workbench.

"Well, there they are. Do you see anything of **ominous import**?"

"I'm mainly concerned about this motorboat, and there are only three photographs in which it appears, two of them from an angle which doesn't allow me to read its markings. Perhaps if I use your magnifying glass?"

Ellen held the magnifying glass close to the photograph and strained her eyes to read the numbers and letters which appeared on the boat's **prow**.

"It says CT 4-2-6-4-7. Here, you take a look."

"Yes, that's right. I agree. So what does it all mean?"

"Ken and I are going over to Nells Island tomorrow to see if we can catch the men in this boat filming the Corsair experimental flights. We think they're trying to steal defense secrets. Tommy McCauley, who knows the island well, is going to guide us to a place where we can **surreptitiously** observe their activities. With what I've learned from this photograph, we should be able to match up the boat to the one which is operating out of the cave at the old mansion on River Road."

"But have you considered the risks involved?"

"Of course, Dad! Tommy's no **neophyte**, and not nearly as **fatuous** as most boys his age. And, besides, we'll be there ahead of time, safely positioned to avoid detection. Mom's packing us a nice lunch."

"I'm not sure a baloney sandwich will save you if you get into difficulty," Ellen's father said with a chuckle.

"No, I thought we could loft some exploding cinnamon buns in their direction,"

Ellen retorted, with a smile.

"O.K., but you should have a backup plan in case anything goes wrong. How much time do you think you're going to need?"

"I would say about three hours, based on what Tommy's told us about their previous movements on the river."

"Then, why don't we say this: If you're not back here by 6:30, I'll call the harbor police and have them look for you. Here's a map of Stratford. Where will you be?"

"Right here, on the southernmost tip of Nells Island, where it looks like a lobster's claw."

"Got it. 6:30. Remember, if you're not back by then, I'll call the harbor police."

"Right, Dad."

"We won't tell your mother. Just say you're going boating on the river. No sense in getting her all worked up. You know how excitable those Holmgrens are."

By the time Ellen and her father had emerged from the basement, Edna was sitting comfortably in the living room, listening to WQXR's *Symphony Hall*, doing some Swedish embroidery, and **oblivious** to the plans being cooked up by her husband and daughter.

"Mom. *Gangbusters* will be on in a few minutes."

"Don't touch that dial, young lady, I'm listening to Dvorak, and Tchaikovsky's *Symphony Number Four* is up next. I want a little peace and quiet for a change. You've got your radio upstairs."

"You're right, Mom. I should have been more **conciliatory**, particularly after that fabulous dinner and pie."

"That's all right, dear. Now, let me listen to the rest of the *Roman Carnival Overture*."

Ellen made her way up the center stairs and laid down on her twin bed next to the Crosley Bakelite radio she had received for Christmas. She quickly turned the dial to WABC and heard the opening theme of *Gangbusters*. This was followed by *Radio Guild*, the *Lucky Strike Hit Parade*, *Truth or Consequences*, and *Bob Crosby's Orchestra*. By 10:45, she was fast asleep, fully dressed, on top of her bed.

Chapter 13

Sunday in the Tidal Marsh

It was Sunday morning, and Ellen was up at the first sign of daylight, still in the clothes she had worn the previous day. The sounds of Bob Crosby's orchestra playing *In a Little Gypsy Tea Room* were still **wafting** through her head from the night before. Hearing her parents already downstairs, she quickly took a shower and put on her Sunday dress for church.

When she came downstairs, her father was **perusing** the sports pages of the Sunday paper.

"So, how did the Yankees do yesterday, Dad?" Ellen inquired.

"They lost 4-3 to the Chicago White Sox, in ten innings. But, I've been reading the war news. Things are not going well for the Brits. The German bombing has caused a lot of **wanton** destruction and **razed** whole neighborhoods in some cities, particularly London. They've even destroyed some of their beautiful cathedrals, including St. Michael's Cathedral in Coventry. So far, Westminster Abbey has been spared. You remember, that's where the **coronation** of King George VI was held in 1937. The **Wehrmacht** is also advancing in the Soviet Union and the **Crimean Peninsula**, which some commentators believe could become a real **quagmire** for them. I'm afraid the Allies are in for a lot more bad news before things get better. I think we waited too long to join the fight. A lot of innocent people have already died and **indigenous** populations **devastated**."

"I think you can blame that **timorous** Prime Minister, **Neville Chamberlain**, who thought Hitler was going to give us *peace in our time*, and **conceded** Czechoslovakia to the Germans," Ellen observed. "Instead of **abjuring** from such a **patently absurd** agreement, he thought he could negotiate with a madman. He helped lead the world into this political **maelstrom**. In fact, all of Western Europe, and the United States, **dithered** while Hitler was rearming Germany and engaging in the most **virulent** and hate-filled **rhetoric**. Democracy is **waning** in Western Europe. Even the French thought they were **impregnable** behind their Maginot line, an attitude we now know was **inane**. From the outset, I knew that a bully like Hitler wasn't **malleable** and was **impervious** to reason—and I was only thirteen years old at the time. You can't **appease** a man like that. There's no way he will be **dissuaded** from his **ravenous** designs on Europe. I **abhor** bullies, whether in the schoolyard or across the ocean. Evil must be **confronted**. The last thing we need are political **moderates** who lack a moral compass."

"Of course, the Swedes haven't helped things by clinging to their **vaunted neutrality** and letting the rest of Europe fight their battles for them," Ellen's father replied. "Hitler certainly won't spare them once he has conquered and **pillaged** the rest of Europe, and brought all its previously **sovereign** nations under his control. It's a **paradox**, isn't it? Here's a man who should have been a **pariah** in a country like Germany, which had reached the **pinnacle** of cultural and scientific achievement. But, instead, he's convinced millions to blindly follow his **pernicious doctrines**. Look what he's doing to **quell** the **insurgents** in Germany and defeat the **partisans** in France. And now he's using the **servile** populations of the occupied countries as virtual slaves to advance his ambitions. He is not at all **scrupulous** about who lives or dies. I don't think we've ever faced a more **implacable** and **dastardly** foe."

"Breakfast is ready, you two," Edna called. "You'll have to bring your political **deliberations** to the dining room table for now."

As Ellen and her parents gathered around the dining room table, the smell of bacon and warm French toast **pervaded** the room. Sprinkling her French toast with cinnamon and sugar, Ellen looked out at the rapidly darkening sky.

"You look **perplexed**," Ellen's mother observed.

"I'm wondering if the weather will hold or if we'll be forced to abandon our **excursion** on the river this afternoon."

"I wouldn't worry just yet. You know how quickly these storm clouds can

dissipate."

Ellen's father asked her to pass the maple syrup they had purchased in Vermont, then allowed the **viscous** substance to flow from the bottle.

Fifteen minutes later, with her hunger **satiated**, Ellen was up and off to the First Congregational Church for her 9:30 Sunday School class.

"See you at church" she remarked, as she headed out the front door and walked in the direction of Church Street.

There was no lesson to prepare this morning. Mrs. Foster, the Sunday School superintendent, asked Ellen and the other teachers to have their students make posters for the annual church bazaar and ice cream social next Saturday. Poster boards, construction paper, crayons, scissors and glue were soon scattered across the tables of her classroom.

"Miss Ellen, my Dad says that the war is not going well in Europe."

"You're right, Charlene, but the Allies are getting stronger every day. And America is building lots of tanks, planes, and ships."

"My father works at the United Aircraft plant," said Billy O'Brien.

"Mine, too," said Jennifer Santos.

"Yes, a lot of your fathers, and some of your mothers, are helping the war effort. But you can do your part, too, by taking part in the scrap and rubber drives, and by buying war stamps and bonds. And by not complaining when you don't have sugar for your cereal, or all the canned goods you're used to. We all have to share in the sacrifice. And if

you're inclined to complain about what you don't have, think about the millions of helpless civilians in Europe who are suffering death and destruction at the hands of the **fanatical** German military machine. And, remember, the church is doing its part as well. The proceeds of our bazaar are going to European war relief."

It was nearly time for church as Ellen quickly gathered up the children's artistic efforts and brought them to Mrs. Foster's office. By the time she got upstairs, her parents were already seated in their favorite pew. Ellen took her seat as organist Louise Miller began playing the processional hymn: *Onward Christian Soldiers.*

Reverend Sellick's sermon was laced with biblical passages, but his focus, like that of most **clergy** these days, was on the situation in Europe and the **abject** plight of the unfortunates who were caught in the crossfire and suffering extreme **privation**. He called for **divine** guidance and upon the **congregation** to do its part through both prayer and relief efforts. He **exhorted** the members of the **congregation** to come to God with open and **contrite** hearts, to **consecrate** their lives to His service, and to **shun prurient** influences. As a man of considerable **probity** and moral **rectitude**, Reverend Sellick commanded great respect within the church, and did so without a trace of **sanctimoniousness**. Under the circumstances, when the collection plates were passed around, the **congregants** were not inclined to be **penurious**, even the **stingiest** among them. Ken and his parents were sitting across the **aisle** from Ellen and her parents, prompting occasional glances between the two young people. As the service concluded, the senior choir processed out to the strains of *Joyful, Joyful, We Adore Thee.* Ken and Ellen and their parents filed out of the sanctuary with the rest of the **congregants**. The two chatted briefly in the front **vestibule** and confirmed that Ken would pick her up at 1:30.

It was just past noon when Ellen's father pulled the family's Hudson into the driveway. Ellen beat her parents to the front door, then headed upstairs to her bedroom. She changed out of her Sunday dress into some of the casual clothes she had purchased from the L.L. Bean **catalog**, including a pair of dark green slacks and a green plaid flannel shirt, the perfect **camouflage** to avoid detection in the marsh. Then, she pulled her hair back into a ponytail, a move which **accentuated** her strikingly beautiful facial features.

Ellen found her father in the basement, typing an article for *Musiktidning (Music News)*, the national newspaper of the American Union of Swedish Singers to which the North Star Singers belonged.

"So, what's the article about, Dad?" Ellen inquired.

"It's about the last Eastern Division **convention** the North Star Singers hosted in Bridgeport."

"Oh, yes, the one where I got to be an usherette for your Grand Concert at the Klein Auditorium. It was a beautiful concert. Say, by the way, may I borrow your movie camera? We plan to do some filming on the river today."

"Of course. It's over there on the second shelf, next to the movie reels."

Removing the camera from its leather case, Ellen loaded the roll of 8mm film Ken had purchased for her the day before, then snapped it shut.

"And don't forget your life preserver, young lady."

"Dad, let me **allay** your concerns. I wouldn't think of neglecting my life preserver. You've got me well trained. I also have a strap for the camera, so I don't drop it in the river."

Giving her father a kiss on the cheek, she ran up the basement stairs to the kitchen where her mother was wrapping some sandwiches and putting them in a wicker picnic basket.

"There's also a thermos of hot coffee, some cinnamon buns, and few tollhouse cookies."

"Thanks, Mom. I think I hear Ken pulling in the driveway. Yep, there he is."

"Remember, we're having dinner at 6:00, as usual."

"I know, Mom, I'll be home before that."

Clad in her father's dark green windbreaker, Ellen placed the wicker basket and life preservers in the **rumble seat** of Ken's roadster. Her father's movie camera and binoculars were slung over her shoulder by their leather straps. Then, she climbed into the front seat next to Ken.

"I'm glad Tommy's joining us today," said Ken. "He knows the area much better than I do, having gone duck hunting there many times with his father. I'm sure he'll spare us from any **calamity**."

As they crossed Washington Bridge, Ellen could observe Tommy McCauley standing on the dock of Bailey's Boatyard, next to his Chris-Craft runabout which was moored a few yards south of the boathouse. A few minutes later, Ken pulled his roadster into the parking lot, and the two amateur sleuths walked briskly to the dock.

"Hi, Tommy," said Ken. "I'm so glad you offered to help us. I hope we're not **impinging** on any of your plans."

"Of course not. You don't have to **goad** me into going out on the river."

Taking her by the hand, Tommy guided Ellen into the boat's backseat, then handed her the wicker picnic basket. As he did so, Ellen noted the image of Betty Grable prominently displayed on top of the boat's shiny wood **veneer**.

"I see that you've added Betty Grable to your battleship, Tommy."

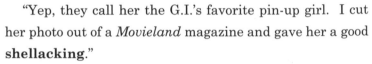

"Yep, they call her the G.I.'s favorite pin-up girl. I cut her photo out of a *Movieland* magazine and gave her a good **shellacking**."

"I hope you weren't too rough on her. I hear that 20th Century Fox has insured her legs for $1 million with Lloyds of London."

"No, I treated her with the utmost respect. By the way, there's a container of **potable** water under the back seat, in case we get thirsty," Tommy advised.

"Say, Tommy, what are those oil slicks on the water. Is there a leak somewhere?" asked Ellen.

"Nothing major, but because gasoline is not **soluble** with water, it's **transmuted** slowly and tends to remain on the surface for a time."

Ellen placed the camera case and binoculars on the seat next to her. Tommy pulled on the starter cord, and then climbed into the driver's seat next to Ken.

Though it was midday, the sky had turned an **ominous** shade of dark gray. Winds from the west were churning the waters as their boat glided southward, toward the mouth of the Housatonic.

"I wish I'd brought an umbrella. I don't want to get caught in a downpour," Ellen exclaimed.

"According to the harbormaster, the **adverse** weather's still a hundred miles west of here," replied Tommy. "I just hope he's right."

As Tommy **deftly** guided his runabout down the east bank of the Housatonic, Ellen cast her eyes into its **limpid** and shallow depths. The most prominent feature of Nells Island was the **ubiquitous** marsh grass, an **aquatic** plant that grew along the Housatonic, particularly at the approach to Long Island Sound. Once inside the area designated as Nells Island, the marsh grass was too tall for the **intrepid** adventurers to see over.

"Are you sure you know where you're going?" Ellen inquired.

"Have no fear. I've been through here many times with my father," Tommy explained.

Sure enough, a few minutes later, their boat emerged on the opposite side of the island, with the open waters of Long Island Sound looming in the distance, and the **undulating** waves lapping against the craft. More importantly, the Vought-Sikorsky Plant was clearly visible from this **vantage point**.

"There's a very narrow passageway over to the left, right around that bend," Tommy explained. "I suggest we conceal ourselves in there. There's a little sandbar we can use as our base."

Once the runabout was safely inside the narrow passage, Tommy turned off the engine and handed Ken one of the auxiliary oars. With the oars barely touching river bottom, the boys managed to maneuver the boat to a small sandbar about five feet from the outward ring of marsh grass which provided them with cover. The **fetid** odor of the **brackish** water **assaulted** their nostrils.

"Now, we simply have to be patient and see what develops. I just hope our friends haven't been using this same spot as their observation point," Ken cautioned. "We don't want a confrontation."

"Don't worry, I can outrun them in open water," Tommy boasted.

"I hope it doesn't come to that. They might be armed, and I don't see a machine gun mounted on your deck. *Frank Winslow of the Navy* you are not."

"While you two warriors are planning military strategy, why don't we have a sandwich?" Ellen suggested.

"What have you got?" Tommy inquired.

"Let's see, I've got a ham on rye, egg salad on wheat, and sill on crisp bread."

"Sill? What's that?" Tommy inquired.

"Sill is herring. It's a Swedish delicacy. It will be a new experience for you."

Tommy's response was **phlegmatic**, at best.

"Uh, I'll pass. The **pungent** aroma is sufficient experience for me. Are you sure it isn't **rancid**?

"No, silly, that's the way herring smells."

"May I have the ham on rye, please."

"I understand," Ellen replied. "Sill is sort of an acquired taste, particularly if you're not Scandinavian."

"I know what you mean," Tommy replied. "My Irish grandparents are always serving corned beef and cabbage, and I hate cabbage. I think these ethnic dishes remind the old folks of the days when they were **impoverished** peasants back in the old country and were forced to eat that stuff. Give me a good cheeseburger and an order of fries."

Suddenly, without warning, the light-hearted **camaraderie** was interrupted by a Corsair lifting off from the airport on the west side of Main Street. The sound of the engines reached a noisy **crescendo** as the plane rose rapidly into the air, made a sharp banking movement, accelerated, and then began making a number of acrobatic **maneuvers**, before heading east over the Sound. A few minutes later, a second aircraft lifted off, heading in the same direction. Reaching for her binoculars, Ellen scanned the horizon for the planes, picking them up several miles over the Sound where they were practicing what appeared to be **evasive maneuvers**.

"Shhhh!" whispered Ken. "I hear a motor coming this way."

The three young people lowered their heads and listened as the sounds of an outboard motor increased in volume. Between the marsh grasses, they were able to **discern** the outline of a small motor boat of unknown make.

"I told you that they **adhere** to a regular schedule," Tommy observed.

"I see fishing poles," Ellen whispered, looking intently through her binoculars. "But they may be just a **ruse**."

"They're a bit earlier than normal. We're lucky we got here ahead of them," observed Tommy.

"That's it! The boat in the photographs. License number CT 4-2-6-4-7," Ellen whispered, excitedly.

Gradually, the two men maneuvered their boat to a position just inside the claw-like projection that formed the southernmost extent of Nells Island, then tossed out a small anchor. Gazing through her binoculars, Ellen observed them reach for their fishing poles and begin casting in the inlet's shallow waters. But strangely, she never saw them bait their hooks. If they were fishermen, they exhibited an **inept** and peculiarly **nonchalant** attitude about their sport.

This went on for the better part of an hour. Then, one of the fishermen reached for a pair of binoculars and began looking in the direction of the aircraft plant. Again, he reached into the boat, this time emerging with a movie camera. This was Ellen's cue. She opened her camera case and pulled out her father's movie camera. Then, zooming in as best she could on the cameraman in the other boat, she **poised** herself to begin filming at the first sign of movement.

Then it happened. The sound of an airplane engine on the opposite side of the river caused the mysterious cameraman to begin filming, raising his camera as the next Corsair lifted off from the runway into the darkened afternoon sky. Ellen followed his every movement with her own camera, then

followed the flight of the Corsair herself to place the activity in **context**. It was obvious that this mysterious cameraman was following the Corsair's every acrobatic move as it circled the skies above the river.

Less than ten minutes later, a second Corsair lifted off the runway, its movements **emulating** those of the first plane. Clearly, the pilots were putting their aircraft to the test, measuring speed, **acceleration**, engine performance, **maneuverability**, and structural **integrity**, and whatever else test pilots did. When their tests were completed, the planes flew off in the direction of the airport on the west side of Main Street.

For the next several minutes, the air was **devoid** of sound, save the ripples of the waves among the grasses and the minor rustlings of the men in the other boat. Through her binoculars, Ellen could see the cameraman fiddling with his equipment and apparently loading a fresh roll of film. The sound of the men's hushed voices was barely **audible** through the grasses. Without the sound of the aircraft to muffle their voices, Ellen and her companions maintained absolute silence, awaiting further activity from the nearby airport.

It was nearly 4:00 before another pair of Corsairs took off from the runway and were put through their paces. Again, the cameraman followed their every movement, both over the river, and out over the Sound. Ellen, who had used her film sparingly, captured representative close-ups of the cameraman's activities as well as some of the Corsair's **maneuvers**. Once the two aircraft headed off in the direction of the airport, and her film was exhausted, Ellen stowed her camera in the back seat and retrieved her binoculars to monitor the further movements of the unknown men.

Ken, who had taken up a **prone** position on the sandbar next to the runabout, waved a hand in Ellen's direction and motioned for her to hand him the binoculars. Intently, he followed the men's movements and strained to hear what they were saying to one another.

Finally, after about a half hour without further activity from the airport, one of the men started up the small outboard motor and eased their craft out of the protective cover of the marsh grass and out into the Housatonic's main channel.

"I think they've decided to call it a day," observed Tommy.

"Yes, and I think we've accomplished what we set out to do," replied Ken. "What say we wait five more minutes, then head back to the boatyard?"

"Right, but we don't want them to hear our engine. We'd better let them get up as far as the Washington Bridge where the automobile traffic will muffle the sounds of our motor."

Once the **allotted** time had passed, Tommy gave a yank on the starter cord and eased the runabout out of the small cove and into the narrow channel which divided Nell's Island. Ten minutes later, they were safely back at Bailey's Boatyard.

Suddenly, without warning, the heavens opened up. The clouds, already **pregnant** with moisture, released a torrent of rain on the **intrepid** adventurers.

"We'll catch up with you later, Tommy," Ellen shouted, as she and Ken ran for the parking lot and his parked roadster. Quickly tossing a tarp over his runabout, Tommy headed for the boathouse to wait out the storm.

Ellen and Ken jumped into the front seat of the roadster with such velocity that they almost bumped heads. When their eyes met, however, Ellen gave Ken a quick kiss on the cheek, startling both herself and her companion. All she could say was "Thanks for a wonderful day!"

"You're welcome," said Ken, almost embarrassed by the touch of affection. "But I should get you home as quickly as possible. You're almost soaked clear through. I can't have you catching anything, what with the junior prom just around the corner."

"I agree, but let me drop this roll of film off at Hamilton's first. It's our first piece of concrete evidence, and I can't wait to get a look at the results."

"you buy 'em we'll fly 'em!"

DEFENSE
BONDS
STAMPS

THE MORE BONDS YOU BUY · THE MORE PLANES WILL FLY

Chapter 14

The Fate of Nations

The war in the Pacific was taking on a new sense of urgency as American forces began challenging Japan's previously **inexorable** advances across Asia and the

islands of the South Pacific. The Battle of the Coral Sea was the chief topic of discussion at school on Monday. The morning editions reported details of a five-day **epic** naval and air battle between the American and Japanese naval **armadas**, in which bombers and fighter aircraft inflicted heavy losses on each other. Although the Japanese air force sank more American tonnage,

it lost so many fighter pilots that it was forced to abandon its planned invasion of the Solomon Islands. **Ironically**, the two fleets never made contact with each other.

~~~~~~~~~~~~~~~~

On Wednesday evening, after dinner, Ken joined Ellen and her father in the Anderson basement to screen the freshly developed film of their escapade

on the river. The two **intrepid** detectives stared at the small projection screen that Ellen's father had mounted on the wall at the end of the darkroom worktable where he did his film editing. The film, which she had picked up at Hamilton's Pharmacy, provided **incontrovertible** evidence of the **espionage** being carried out by this **clandestine** spy ring.

"That's him, that's Gerard Koch," exclaimed Ellen, jumping off her seat. "I should have recognized him earlier."

"You're right," added Ken. "He's the one who had lunch

with Mr. Schlechter the day we went to New Haven, and the man to whom I delivered the box of books at the Chandler mansion."

"And the man I encountered at the Stratford Public Library, examining the nautical atlases," added Ellen. "I think the **preponderance** of the evidence suggests that they're trying to steal military secrets. The filming of the test flights proves it. They're undoubtedly interested in the new **prototype** of the Corsair, the one that Joel Johnson told me will exceed 450 miles per hour. Think what an impact that will have on the war in the Pacific, as well as the European front."

"So, what do you suggest we do now?" Ken inquired.

"Although I'm still in a bit of a **quandary** at this **juncture**, I think we should now confront Mr. Mueller. It's **imperative** that we tell him what we know, and **induce** him to confess his involvement. We have to convince him that there's no future in knuckling under to these threats to his family in Germany, particularly if the authorities can capture the entire gang, and lock them up. While he certainly hasn't been purposefully **mendacious**, he has been **complicit** in **abetting** enemy **espionage**. He's simply got to **reconcile** himself to the **propriety** of **extricating** himself from their **domination**."

"I tell you what. I'm working at the bookstore on Thursday after school. Why don't you join me about 3:00 and we'll confront him together? I think it will have a greater impact if he knows that we're both aware of his involvement. If he continues to be **intractable**, we'll just have to tell him that we'll be forced to go to the police. It will be difficult for him to **refute** what we have to say. While I understand the **predicament** he's in, I hate to see him continue to **debase** himself in the face of these bullies."

"So, we're in **accord** then. We'll meet at the bookstore at 3:00."

~~~~~~~~~~~~~~~~

Ellen, who normally had no **compunctions** about expressing herself, was uncharacteristically **taciturn** during her Thursday classes, her mind consumed by the **manifold** possibilities of her and Ken's upcoming confrontation with Mr. Mueller, and its **concomitant** impact on the case they were pursuing. For Mr. DeLeurere, Ellen's classroom **demeanor** was a peculiar **aberration**, particularly in light of her normal **diligence** and **effervescence**. Similarly, Mrs. Carmichael found her **restive** and particularly **enigmatic** in English class, almost **eschewing** the class discussion of *A Tale of Two Cities*.

By 11:00, however, during the discussion in Miss Satterfield's American history class, Ellen's powers of concentration reasserted themselves. Although some members of the class found Miss Satterfield's lectures a little **arid** and too **cerebral** for their liking, Ellen appreciated all the **nuances** of political theory she **elucidated**, and **cherished** the **intellectual** challenges presented by her **coherent** and **comprehensive** review of current events.

"Class, I want you to **fathom** the moment in history in which we find ourselves," explained Miss Satterfield. "These are not the random **vicissitudes** of political fortune, but the calculated consequences of political **ideology**. We are living in an age **buffeted** by the forces of **totalitarianism** which are in the **ascendancy**. These **totalitarian** movements—**National Socialism** or **Soviet Communism**—are now **belligerents** pitted against one another. But, they are, in reality, twin **manifestations** of the same **collectivist** philosophy. These are both **fallacious** philosophies of the left, in which the state—in other words, the government—is **paramount** and the citizen exists only to serve the needs of the collective or, in reality, the ruling class. And they are **regimes** in which the **arbitrary** acts of the rulers have replaced the rule of law.

"I want you to think of political philosophies as being points on a **continuum**, with **national socialism** and **communism**, as we have today, on the far left, and **anarchy** on the far right. In other words, on one side we have total government **regimentation** and, on the other, the absence of formal government control, which may lead to societal **chaos**.

"The challenge," she continued, "is to find the proper role of government somewhere between these two extremes, but as close to maximum freedom as reasonably possible. This was the challenge our founding fathers faced. They correctly recognized the threat posed by an absolute or **oppressive** government, having just defeated Great Britain in the American Revolution. And remember that the countries of Europe were almost universally governed by **monarchies** and **despots** at that time, not to mention the **potentates** of the Middle East and Orient. By **enfranchising** the people, the United States was a political **anomaly** for its time. There were no **antecedents** of the kind of democratic republic which the founding fathers established. Despite a variety of **discordant** voices representing thirteen **disparate** colonies, the fifty-five men who met in Philadelphia in 1787 were united in the belief that a free people

needed to be protected from an overreaching national government. They **espoused** a government of limited powers, **constrained** by the language of the Constitution.

"This explains why our Constitution is largely a document of negative liberties, designed to keep government in check and protect us from its excesses. This **entailed** creating an **elaborate** constitutional mechanism which assigned certain limited powers to the national government, while leaving the balance to the states, or to the people. This is the very **essence** of **federalism**. From a technical point of view, it is incorrect to call the government in Washington, DC the **federal** government. It is, in fact, the national government, operating within a **federal** system that balances the powers of the national government, the state governments, and the people. In their **sagacity**, the founding fathers were **resolved** that we should hold the Constitution **sacrosanct.** In other words, they did not intend for their creation to be an **ephemeral** experiment.

"The founding fathers were also united in the belief that the rights of the people were bestowed upon them by God. Therefore, what God had given them could not be taken away by man, or by government. These God-given rights which we

venerate will never become **obsolete**. Furthermore, the national government they created was structured in such a way that no individual or group could gain a monopoly on power. The three branches—Executive, Legislative and Judicial—were established to provide a system of checks and balances. The Legislative Branch enacts the laws, the Executive Branch carries out the laws, and the courts—the Supreme Court in particular—interprets the laws to ensure that they do not conflict with the Constitution."

"Miss Satterfield?"

"Yes, Ellen."

"A few years ago, President Roosevelt **connived** to pack the Supreme Court with additional Justices because the Court was declaring some of his New Deal legislation **unconstitutional**. It seems to me that this was a direct violation of the **essence** of checks and balances that our founding fathers established."

"That's correct, Ellen. That episode **elicited** considerable outrage and was a **contentious** issue with members of both parties. It was one of the most significant **blemishes** on President Roosevelt's record. The President believed that the Depression gave him the justification for an extraordinary increase in the power of the Executive Branch. Remember that the President already had the power to appoint all **federal** judges, with the advice and consent of the Senate. But instead of waiting for the court to change over time with his new appointments, he tried to **accelerate** the process by increasing the size of the court. Naturally, it would have been a **boon** to executive power had he gotten away with this. However, George Washington, James Madison, and Benjamin Franklin would never have **condoned** such actions. President Roosevelt was subjected to some **scathing** criticism from both Republican and Democratic politicians who **decried** his actions. **Contemporaneous** newspaper columnists were quick to aim their **caustic** and **vitriolic** commentary in his direction. Although he did abandon the effort, he made no attempt to **expiate** his **hubristic** actions.

"But you also have to view his action in the broader context of developments in Europe, where **totalitarian** governments were on the rise. There was a growing **consensus** that government's role should be **buttressed** to deal with the world-wide economic crisis from which we were suffering. Hitler came to power in 1933. His **ascendancy** was ultimately a consequence of the Treaty of Versailles, which ended World War I, and the **onerous** economic crisis that **ensued** for the German people, including **hyper-inflation** that **rendered** the currency virtually worthless, coupled with widespread unemployment. You must remember that Hitler and his supporters harbored a deep-seated **vindictiveness** over Germany's defeat in the First World War. Many of the German people believed that the situation cried out for the leadership of a **Nietzchean** Superman, in other words, a supreme and all-powerful leader who could lead Germany out of its economic **morass**. In this political environment, power, strength, dominance, and control were considered to be the highest values. Hitler's **fascist** and **racist** views were **disseminated** in the form of his book *Mein Kampf*, or, in English, *My Struggle*, which he wrote while in prison. Many of Hitler's **authoritarian** ideas were drawn from the philosophy of **Friedrich Nietzsche** whose concept of the Superman provided the foundation for Hitler's conception of the Master Race.

"That **combustive** political mood was **exacerbated** by the **onerous reparations** imposed by the Allies. **Exhorting** the **wrath** of a **raucous** and **disgruntled** populace with his **bombastic orations**, his **edicts annulled** the laws which protected civil liberties. He also effectively **censured** political **dissent**. And his **defamatory polemics** against the Jews and other minorities aroused the worst instincts of the German people. This social **pathology** is **replete** with examples of **divisive** political **discourse** and acts of violence. Mobs of **brownshirts defiled** synagogues and **desecrated** Jewish cemeteries. Even decent people refrained from **deploring** the actions of the **fascists** for fear of being subjected to the same **harangues**, hoping that the

fractious political mood would eventually **dissipate**. This political movement is known as **fascism**, a governmental system where all political and economic power is centralized in the state and no **dissent** is tolerated. Nothing can **deter** the **fascists** from their evil and **nefarious** actions. Hitler is a **demagogue** of the worst sort who must be **eradicated** from the face of the earth.

"The Soviet Union," she continued, "which came to power in 1917, is driven by an economic and political philosophy called **communism** which divides the world into two classes of people: the **bourgeoisie**, or middle or property-owning class, and the **proletariat**, or working class. According to Karl Marx's *Communist Manifesto*, power should **emanate** from the **disaffected** working class. The communists' **purported** goal was to create a workers' **utopia** and **subvert** the governments of other nations. But this was blatant **hypocrisy** because the country is, in fact, controlled by a political **elite**, not by the workers. This gang of **ruthless** thugs, led first by **Vladimir Lenin**, and, now, Joseph Stalin, have ruled like supreme **dictators** and have **mercilessly** crushed any potential **coup** that might attempt to **oust** them from power. Their **ideology** is simply a **smoke screen** to mask their ultimate quest for power.

"Their **regimes** have reflected a distinct **antagonism** to the democratic ideals of the West. Millions among the vast **heterogeneous** populations under Soviet rule have either been killed by the **imperious regime**, or died as a result of the **deleterious agricultural** policies designed to centralize more power in the hands of the state. Even before the onset of the war, this forced **collectivization** of privately owned farms drove millions of **hapless** peasants to **forage** for food to keep themselves alive. And the country's literature has been **expurgated** to remove all references hostile to the **regime**. By 1939, any churches still **extant** in the Soviet Union were closed and their **clergy** killed, exiled or imprisoned.

"There are reporters, like Walter Duranty of the *New York Times*, who attempted to **expunge** the record of this murderous **regime** and to **dispel** the rumors of its **infamous** acts. His articles were the very **antithesis** of honest reporting and an **affront** to responsible journalism. They amounted to a form of **cognitive dissonance** which **exonerated** the Soviet Union of its crimes against humanity. Although these articles were designed to **aggrandize** his stature in both the United States and the Soviet Union, their falsehoods are now leaking out. **Ironically**, the United States now finds itself in a position of forging a temporary alliance with one **totalitarian regime** for the purpose of defeating another **totalitarian regime**. At this very moment, those two **regimes** are waging an **epic** battle on the Eastern Front which will have a decisive impact on the war.

"The point I've tried to **elucidate** today is that, despite our democratic **republic** of constitutionally limited powers, those foreign influences have been **pervasive** here as well. Since the onset of the stock market crash in 1929, and the ensuing Depression, the national government, under both Presidents Hoover and Roosevelt, has achieved a significant **accretion** of power to the point that it would be barely recognizable to our founding fathers. President Roosevelt has **burnished** his reputation as a champion of the common man, but he has **concomitantly** exhibited a **predilection** for the **acquisition** of power over our economic affairs, which **contravenes** constitutional and **free market** principles. Sadly, most people have been swept up in the **euphoria** which has accompanied the New Deal, and have **exalted** its leaders. There are few **iconoclasts** around willing to challenge the prevailing **ethos**, and only a handful **obstreperous** enough to challenge this **assault** on our liberties.

"Finally, I want to leave with you two quotations whose origins are **obscured** by time, but which ring particularly true today in this age of expanding government power across the globe. Please write them in your notebooks for future discussion:

> *A democracy cannot exist as a permanent form of government. It can only exist until the voters discover that they can vote themselves **largesse** from the public treasury. From that moment on, the majority always votes for the candidates promising the most benefits from the public treasury with the result that a democracy always collapses over loose **fiscal** policy, always followed by a **dictatorship**. The average age of the world's greatest civilizations has been 200 years.*

"And also this **adage**:

> *Great nations rise and fall. The people go from **bondage** to spiritual*

truth, to great courage, from courage to liberty, from liberty to **abundance**, *from* **abundance** *to selfishness, from selfishness to* **complacency**, *from* **complacency** *to* **apathy**, *from* **apathy** *to dependence, from dependence back again to* **bondage**.

"I leave you to **ponder** those thoughts over the next few days. Might they be a **portent** of America's future? I want to know where you think we are on that sliding slope to **bondage**. Will the United States be around for its two hundredth birthday? And, if so, what will it look like? Class dismissed!"

Chapter 15

Confrontation

As Ellen left her second floor classroom, her mind was consumed by Miss Satterfield's **cogent chronicle** of recent history, and **catalyzed** by those two quotations. *Where, indeed, was America headed? She had significant challenges abroad, but also at home.* Miss Satterfield's **didacticism** was particularly **poignant** at this moment in time. And for Ellen, these **incisive** quotations were more than **hypothetical musings** because she was totally **immersed** in a case of **espionage** involving one of those **totalitarian** powers.

As the school day ended, Ellen retrieved her books from her locker and began the short walk to the Dusty Corner Book Shop for the 3:00 **interrogation** of Mr. Mueller. As she entered the store, the small bell hanging on the door announced her arrival. She hoped they could **extract** some valuable information or concessions from the kindly old man.

"Good afternoon, Mrs. Mueller, is Ken available?"

"Hello, Ellen. Yes, he's in the back room with Mr. Mueller."

Ken and Mr. Mueller were in the back room removing **extraneous** books from the shelves to be placed in the bargain bins, and boxing **superfluous** stock for sale to other book stores. Several bandages on Mr. Mueller's head were a visible reminder of the beating Ellen knew he had recently received from the members of the **espionage** ring.

"Hello, Ellen, what brings you here?"

"Ken and I have something we'd like to discuss with you, Mr. Mueller, if you don't mind."

"Not at all. Please have a seat. Now, what is it that's on your mind?"

"I trust you won't **upbraid** us for being **impertinent**, Mr. Mueller, because Ken and I have **vacillated** for some time about bringing these matters to your attention. But, based on what we have observed these past several weeks, we feel we have no choice but to be **forthright** with you. Frankly, we are well aware of the Nazi spy ring that is operating in Stratford and pressuring you to do their bidding. Independently of you and your bookstore, I became aware that they are operating out of the old Chandler mansion on the Housatonic, in Putney. Perhaps you know the place?"

Mr. Mueller sat **glum** and motionless, his elbows resting on his knees and his head in his hands. He appeared **transfixed** by the import of Ellen's surprising **revelations**. She continued:

"As a result of our investigations, we've learned that they are attempting to steal secrets of the Corsair aircraft from United Aircraft and **consummate** their transfer to their agents in Germany. We also know that they are forcing you to act as a **conduit** for **National Socialist** literature by threatening harm to your **vulnerable** relatives in Germany, and that the bruises you have are a result of a beating you received at their hands. And a week ago Saturday, I joined Ken in making that delivery to Central European Books and Imports in New York. While Ken made his delivery, I hid in a back room and discovered a plot by Nazi **saboteurs** to blow up ships at the Brooklyn Naval Yard."

"I had no idea you were aware of all these goings-on," replied Mr. Mueller. "This is incredible! You should know at the outset that I had no idea about the plans to blow up ships at the Brooklyn Naval Yard."

"Yes, and it's **incumbent** upon us to inform the authorities of what we have learned. But we're waiting for the right time, and don't want to put you or your wife in harm's way. Not only that, but we don't want to be the cause of harm to your family members in Germany."

"While I appreciate your **candor,** and hesitate to **chastise** you for involving yourselves in this dangerous business, I must impress upon you the risks involved if you continue to meddle in their affairs. As you have observed, Helge and I have relatives in Germany who are at risk for their lives, but you do not. You have no reason to become involved."

"Oh, but you're wrong, Mr. Mueller," replied Ken. "This is our country and these men can potentially do her great injury. We cannot **abdicate** our responsibilities. It is **imperative** that we stop them. Why don't you tell us what you know about this spy ring so we'll have a better understanding of what we're up against."

"I suppose it doesn't matter now, since you know so much already. Certainly, I can **validate** everything you have said. My participation has followed a rather **tortuous** path. I got involved back in 1936, following the rise of the Nazi movement in Germany and during the height of the German-American Bund movement in the United States. It started out on an **amicable** basis. Some of the German **expatriates**, who had been **patronizing** my store for German language literature, asked me to import some **National Socialist** materials. It started slowly and **incrementally**, and then expanded to larger quantities for groups, **caucuses**, and other **fascist** political organizations. Before I knew it, I had become one of the leading East Coast sources for Nazi material. Central European Books and Imports in New York City is the other major dealer. In 1938, after **Kristallnacht**, I knew that **accommodating** these people wasn't morally **tenable**, and it was my **inclination** to sever my relationship with them. But, to my shame, I didn't do anything about it. By that time, it was clear that the German people and many of their supporters in this country had developed an **idolatrous** admiration for Adolf Hitler. Finally, after the Germans invaded Poland in September 1939, I **resolved** to stop importing or dealing in this literature. I didn't go out my way to **denigrate** their activities, but I refused to order any more of these books. Believe me, I regret having cooperated with them and seek **exculpation** for my guilt. Indeed, I seek **absolution** from God for my **complicity**."

"And what happened next?" Ellen inquired.

"I was **accosted** by three men one evening just before closing time who **coerced** me into cooperating. They informed me that they knew all about my relatives in Bavaria, and, by **innuendo**, **intimated** that they would be **abducted** and sent to concentration camps unless I continued to be **compliant** with their wishes. They have been able to **exploit** that knowledge to force me to comply with their demands. In an **erratic** fit of anger, laced with **vulgar** language, they **wreaked** havoc in the bookstore and smashed one of my display cases to make their point. Much of their violence was simply **gratuitous**. Helge wasn't in the shop that night, but I wanted to avoid further **acrimony** over this issue, and feared for her safety, too."

"And you told them what?" Ken inquired.

"There wasn't much I could do. After all, I'm not as **hardy** and **agile** as I was in my youth, and not nearly as **pugnacious**. No doubt I would suffer in any **altercation** with these **incorrigible brutes**. So, when I came to grips with my inability to **disavow** them, I agreed to **abet** their activities and follow their instructions."

"Did you ever think about going to the authorities?"

"No, Ellen, they warned me about that too. They said that if I went to the police and **renounced** them, my brother and his family would never live long enough to see a concentration camp. They even threatened harm to Helge. What was I to do?"

"What about the bandages on your head? How did you get those?" Ken inquired.

"These same three men unexpectedly visited me at home two weeks ago and gave me a good working over. Helge was visiting her sister in Waterbury, so she escaped the ordeal. I had to go to the emergency room at Bridgeport Hospital where they treated my **abrasions** and **contusions** with **antiseptic** and put me on an **analgesic** to reduce the pain and swelling. But it took several hours before they could completely stop the bleeding and get my blood to **coagulate**. Although I have been applying an **emollient** to my bruises, there's little anyone can do to **salve** my ego."

"Mr. Mueller, we understand your plight, believe us," Ellen **consoled** him. "But you can't continue to **wallow** in self pity, or **rationalize** your **complicity**. Things have simply gotten out of hand and more lives are now at risk than simply your family. Our goal is to catch these people and **confound** their plans, but to do so in a manner which minimizes the risk to you, your wife, and your relatives in Germany. What else can you tell us about their activities?"

"I can tell you that they have several **surrogates** working inside the aircraft plant, including a number of draftsmen. Naturally, they are extremely interested in the design of the Corsair and its potential value to the German and Japanese military. I also know that they have extensive film footage of the test flights. I don't know if they have **explicit** plans developed yet to transfer the information they have gathered to their contacts, but it could be either by submarine in Long Island Sound, through agents at the German Consulate in New York City, or through Central European Books and Imports. My guess is that, if they use the land route, the plans will either be secreted in a shipment of books and antiques, or transferred by diplomatic courier to the German Consulate."

"What about the mansion on the river? How many are living there?" Ellen continued.

"The last time I was there, there were two men living on the premises. There are five others who work at the United Aircraft plant, but who live in town."

"How many of these men can you **enumerate** for us?" Ken inquired.

"Let me see. There's Otto Reisling, Kurt Janning, Eric Miller, Fred Weisfogle and Leo Geyer. They've all lived in Stratford, or Bridgeport, for years, but are secretly sympathetic to the **genocidal** Nazi **regime**. These **toadies** are, by and large, **conformists** who are **tractable** to the party line. Even if they wanted to **extricate** themselves from involvement, they're in too deep to back out now. Afraid to incur the **wrath** and **vituperation** of their leadership, they've become **vapid sycophants**."

"What about the ones who live at the mansion? We know one of them is named Gerard Koch," Ken added.

"Yes, he's the local head man. Despite what appears to be a **benign** and **affable** exterior, he is **boisterous** and **dogmatic** in his opinions and **acerbic** in his speech, with a **callous penchant** for **profanity**. He's the one in charge of the Stratford operations. He has a **doctorate** in aeronautical engineering from the University of Freiburg and worked for a time at Shoreline Blueprint in New Haven, where he developed an **expertise** with American design standards and blueprint production. The other is Helmut Kuhn, an **unctuous** and most **irascible** personality who frequently goes into **vociferous tirades** when things don't go as planned. He's an aircraft designer by trade, whose scientific **acumen** is **commensurate** with his political **sophistication**. But he would never get security clearance because he's been in the United States less than a year. He has a **canny** sense of the overall **strategic** mission, however. That's why he was put in charge of coordinating the work of the designers who are inside the plant. Koch was a cameraman back in the old country, which is why he's taken charge of filming the test flights. He's also the chief **interlocutor** with the group's German contacts. In the **aggregate**, these are men **aggrieved** by Germany's defeat in the last war, with a strong **antipathy** to our democratic ideals. They're a **variegated** lot, but **analogous** to a den of **vipers**."

"What about the thugs who beat you up?" Ellen inquired.

"Oh, they're imported muscle from New York who are in **collusion** with the local gang. They have a more **tenuous** connection to Stratford than the others. I don't know their names, but they probably use **aliases** or **pseudonyms**, like many **fifth columnists**. I can't tell you the depth of the **enmity** I feel towards them."

"What I don't understand is how you know so much in light of the fact that they've had to use violence to keep you in line. Wouldn't they be **reticent** about telling you much?" Ken asked.

"They don't share a lot with me, but enough that I've been able to piece it all together. The rest I've picked up through my German book import contacts. Koch and Kuhn simply don't comprehend the depth of my knowledge."

"And what about John Schlechter? How does he figure in all this?"

"Schlechter is an accountant and the **alleged** bookkeeper of the German-American Bund who acquired the river mansion from one of his former clients. He engages in the most **licentious** behavior and hurls bitter **invective** against anyone who dares cross him. I have such a **profound disdain** for the man. Frankly, he's a crook who violated his **fiduciary** duties to an old woman for whom he worked. As she began to lose her **mental capacity**, he employed a variety of **blandishments** to **induce** her to leave her property to him. I know there's a **probate** contest over the woman's will because Schlechter's been **carping** about it. While the case has been pending, he's made the mansion available to the spy ring. I've heard that the property's been **appraised** at over a hundred thousand dollars, although I think that may be a bit **exorbitant**."

"Mr. Mueller, I wouldn't be **disheartened**. From what you've told us, I think we're on the verge of breaking this case wide open," Ellen explained. "But we'd like to keep all this close to our vests for now, waiting for the time when they decide to move the plans and film out of the country. That's where your help can be **invaluable**. We'd like to **apprehend** the entire gang **simultaneously**. Will you work with us?"

"Yes, I will help you. But you must tell the authorities not to let any of them escape so they can cause harm to my family."

"Of course. We're in **accord** on that score and will use the utmost **discretion**," said Ellen. "And, besides, you should be **inviolable** from physical attack as long as Ken is working at the store."

"This is good. But let us not tell Helge. I have become **inured** to their threats of violence, but my fears have been **compounded** because of the great emotional strain placed on her. She's under a lot of **duress** and has been particularly

despondent in recent weeks. She fears that they will soon be playing a **dirge** over my lifeless body."

"Of course. We understand," Ellen replied. "Finally, we would like your advice about getting inside the house. What do you suggest? When is it occupied?"

"From what I've been able to **discern**, there are just a few people living in the house at any one time. Sometimes, they're out on the river in the afternoon or early evening photographing the test flights. Periodically, they have group meetings involving agents from Connecticut and New York, after which they may **carouse** into the early hours of the morning. Your best opportunity is to time their movements and then gain access by way of the cave entrance at the base of the cliff. And, above all, be careful. These are **ruthless** men who will stop at nothing to achieve their mission."

"We can't thank you enough for all your help, Mr. Mueller."

"You should also be aware that Hitler has even more **grandiose** plans for striking the United States directly. Since at least 1937, he has been obsessed with developing the **prototype** of a four-engine long-range bomber, the Messerschmidt Me 264, with the ability to reach the East Coast from Europe.

He would like nothing better than to reduce New York City to rubble, just as he has much of London. I don't even think the F.B.I. is aware of this."

"That's simply incredible, Mr. Mueller," Ken exclaimed. "We'll be sure to pass along the information to the F.B.I. office in New York City."

With that, Ellen said 'goodbye' and left by way of the back door. As she made her way home along Main Street, she **contemplated** how the **cumulative** bits of evidence were beginning to **coalesce**. When she arrived home in time for dinner, her mother informed her that Shirley Kepler, Mrs. Chandler's niece, had called from Ohio with important news.

Chapter 16

The Secret Passageway

Although she was anxious to tell her parents what Mr. Mueller had **disclosed** at the Dusty Corner Book Shop, Ellen **forestalled** her **revelations** for the time being. What most concerned her right now was returning Shirley Kepler's telephone call after dinner.

"Hello, is this Shirley?"

"Yes, it is. Who's calling?"

"It's Ellen Anderson, in Stratford."

"Yes, Ellen, thanks for returning my call. I have some exciting news for you. We are on the verge of settling the **probate** matter with Mr. Schlechter. We concluded the last of our **depositions** last week. The witnesses were **unanimous** in their opinion that my aunt did not have the **testamentary capacity** to change her will, including my aunt's doctor, who is an **eminent** general practitioner, her social worker, and the attending nurse who cared for her during her last days when the will was drawn up. And just to show you how **devious** Schlechter is, the social worker who witnessed the will **divulged** that she was told by both Schlechter and his attorney that she was witnessing the updating of a **power of attorney** in order to access funds to pay her medical bills, when it was, in fact, an entirely new will leaving everything to Schlechter. They had the **effrontery** to show her only the page on which her signature was required, rather than the complete document. We're also prepared to **emend** our complaint to report the lawyer to the State Attorney General for an **egregious** violation of his **fiduciary** responsibilities. As for Mr. Schlechter, the man is evil **incarnate** and deserves no **reprieve**. And since he's shown no signs of **repentance**, his **depravity** and **execrable** actions will probably cost him his accountant's license. Our attorneys are still negotiating, but I think the handwriting is on the wall. We may bring in an impartial **arbiter** to avoid a **protracted** court battle. From a legal perspective, however, we've got him cornered, and not a moment too soon. I've been suffering **incessant** headaches that I'm sure are related to this seemingly **intractable** case."

"This is great news! It must be reassuring to finally see justice being done."

"Thank you. But the reason for my call was to ask if you've detected any activity in the house? The last time we spoke, you told me that some strange people were living there."

"That's right. They're still there, but we have them under **surveillance**. I have a feeling that they'll be vacating soon for reasons that have nothing to do with your **probate** case. To tell you the truth, we've discovered that they're **fifth columnists** working on behalf of the **Third Reich**."

"I don't believe it. You mean Nazis?"

"Yes! And we're close to breaking the case wide open if we can get inside the house to gather some physical evidence. You once told me about a secret passageway leading to the first floor library and the master bedroom on the second floor."

"That's right. If you enter the house by way of the cave on the riverside, there's a steep series of stone steps on the right side leading to the basement. From the basement, you can gain access to the house through a secret passageway located behind a corner bookcase that is opened by means of a trip lever located underneath the bottom shelf. Just make sure you pull the bookcase closed behind you. Once on the first floor, you can observe the library through a couple of cleverly disguised peepholes behind the books. There's a similar arrangement in the second floor master bedroom. It's highly unlikely that the occupants are aware of these passageways. It's my guess that they have simply used the basement stairs to get to the first floor. If you want to avoid detection, however, tread lightly on the stairs. They're old and creaky and might give you away."

"Thanks for the advice. And good luck in concluding your court case. I hope they put that **reprobate** behind bars. I'll let you know what happens at this end."

"Thanks, Ellen. I do appreciate all your efforts on my behalf. This whole case has been rather **enervating** from an emotional standpoint, and **exasperating**, to say the least. I've been **encumbered** by it for more than two years now. But, now, I'm **exulted** by the **imminent** prospect of receiving **restitution** as a result of our legal proceedings. I'll be talking to you soon."

After hanging up the receiver, Ellen joined her father in the living room, while her mother puttered around in the kitchen.

"Well, I'll be a monkey's uncle!" exclaimed Ellen's father. "Did you see what Congress did yesterday? They voted to create the Women's Auxiliary Army Corps. What's this world coming to? Pretty soon they'll have women driving tanks and flying bombers over Nazi Germany! Who's going to cook my dinner, then?"

"Oh, Dad, don't you think that's a little bit **hyperbolic**? I think most of the women will be serving in support roles, like nursing and office work. That can be dangerous enough as it is, particularly when it's in a combat zone. But I don't think the President or members of Congress expect women to serve on the front lines. They're just making **judicious** use of the manpower they have. Besides, Mom's not planning to enlist."

"Well, maybe so, but it won't be long before they'll **chafe** at being **relegated** to secondary roles when they may **relish** doing all the things men do. Look at that Rosie gal who's doing all the riveting. She should be sewing buttons on uniforms, not working in a defense plant."

"But, Dad, Miss Satterfield said the factories don't have enough men to perform the factory jobs, what with so many in uniform. So we have to be **mutable** and not **deprecate** the willingness of women to do what has traditionally been considered a man's work. And what's happening today is certainly not **irrevocable**. After the war is over, I'm sure things will pretty much get back to normal."

"Ellen, I hope you realize that your father is being **facetious**? He gets a kick out of seeing if people will take him seriously," Ellen's mother observed. "But I suppose it's much better than

some of that **ribald** humor he hears when the men get together at the Swedish Athletic Club."

"Oh, Dad, you had me going there for a while."

"Well, I'll be **jubilant** when they ring the death **knell** over Adolf Hitler and his **stormtroopers**. I'm not used to all this **chaos**. Why, just the other day I heard that the Stratford Coastal Watch Battery has spotted German submarines in Long Island Sound."

"No kidding? Where did they spot them?"

"About a mile east of Stratford Point Lighthouse."

In light of this **revelation**, Ellen **ruminated** about the potential of transferring the plans of the Corsair to a German submarine at the mouth of the Housatonic.

"Say, Ellen," shouted Ellen's mother from the kitchen, "Spike Jones and His City Slickers are on *The Kraft Music Hall* this evening. Why don't you turn the radio on?"

Reaching for the dial, Ellen turned to WEAF, the flagship station of the NBC Red network in New York City.

...Good evening ladies and gentlemen. This is Ken Carpenter speaking for the Kraft Music Hall, starring Bing Crosby and our special guests— Spike Jones and His City Slickers.

Following some lighthearted **banter** with Bing Crosby, Spike Jones stepped to the microphone and introduced the band's first number:

Good evening music lovers. We would like to start this show off with a special greeting to Uncle Adolf in Berlin.

"I wonder if Hitler has actually heard *Der Fuehrer's Face* in Germany?" Ellen inquired.

"Well, if he hasn't, I'm sure he will soon. It's already on the *Hit Parade* and has had a big impact in **fostering** Allied morale," her father replied.

"You know, the **satirists**, comedians and cartoonists are having a field day holding

Hitler up to **ridicule**, not to mention Charlie Chaplain who did a great job impersonating Hitler in *The Great Dictator* a couple of years ago. And every man with a face and a comb is doing the same."

Suddenly, the telephone rang and Ellen heard her mother answer it.

"Yes, Ken, she's right here."

"Hi, Ken, what's up?"

"I just got a call from Mr. Mueller. He told me that a special meeting has been called for this evening at the Chandler place. He said the **operatives** from New York are attending, as well as the local members of the network. It seems like the perfect time to drive over there and eavesdrop. We may not get another chance like this."

"All right. Pick me up at 7:00. And don't forget to bring a flashlight. I'll see you in a few minutes."

"Dad—Ken and I have a little investigating to do. We'll be back in a couple of hours."

"You be careful now. I don't get any **vicarious** thrills from your engaging in risky behavior. And I hope you're not neglecting your homework."

"Don't worry about that. I did most of it right after school."

It was just two minutes before 7:00 when Ken pulled his roadster up in front of the Anderson residence and rang the front doorbell. Although the fresh scent of spring was in the air, Ellen felt obliged to bring along a warm jacket to block the cool breezes which often blew across the river. They took the now familiar route up River Road. A few minutes later, Ken pulled his car into a patch of woods about a hundred yards north of the mansion, then turned off his headlights.

"Save your flashlight for later. We'll have to find our way through the woods by moonlight," Ken suggested.

Making their way through the thicket of trees and underbrush, the pair came upon a narrow path leading toward the mansion. From their **oblique** angle, they could observe the first floor of the dwelling ablaze with the light of kerosene lanterns. A lone automobile was parked in front.

"Here's where it's going to get a bit tricky. Luckily, I wore my clam diggers and **canvas** tennis shoes," Ellen explained.

Winding their way along the base of the cliff, with the mansion looming above, they found themselves mired in moist and soggy ground.

"We'd better take off our shoes and socks and wade in from here," cautioned Ken, who rolled up his pants to his knees.

By the time they neared the entrance to the cave, the water was knee deep and Ellen's clam diggers were taking on water. Their feet sank in the **morass** of the muddy river bottom.

"Where's your flashlight, Ellen?"

"Right here."

Before she could turn it on, they were startled by a floodlight from a motorboat approaching the cave from the south. They were trapped. There was nowhere to go but wade further in. Soon, the water was chest high and they were swimming into the cave.

"What'll we do now?" whispered Ellen.

"Quick, plaster yourself to the wall behind those stone steps and hope they don't see us."

As the motorboat glided into the cave's narrow slip, Ellen and Ken had no choice but to lower themselves into the frigid water, with only their heads exposed. Concealed in the shadows, and with their hearts pounding, they kept perfectly still and listened as the occupants tied the boat to a ring set into the stone on the side of the stairway.

"Hand me your camera, Gerard."

"Here it is. Don't drop it. These are the last films I expect to take on this mission."

Suddenly, however, Ellen felt the urge to sneeze. To **suppress** it, she lowered her head under the water and waited until the urge **subsided**, then waited for Ken to tap her on the shoulder when the coast was clear. When she emerged from the watery darkness, the two men had climbed the steep flight of stairs with the aid of a lantern, and opened the doorway above. Ken and Ellen remained motionless in the frigid water.

"Don't move," Ken cautioned. "Give them time to make their way to the first floor. Who knows? They may have forgotten something." They waited a minute longer before moving.

"Now, let's get out of this water before we catch a death. Do you still have your flashlight?"

"Right here," Ellen pointed, as she reached to a small **niche** in the rock where she had saved it from water damage.

"We can take some **consolation** for that because I'm afraid mine's drenched. I suppose it won't be much use until it's dried out."

Working their way around to the front of the stone staircase, they stopped on the landing where they tried to squeeze the water out of their clothes.

"Eeeww! I did not enjoy that one bit. I'm soaked clear through," Ellen whispered."

"We could always build a fire and dry our clothes," Ken suggested.

"Not on your life, Mr. Swenson. This isn't Girl Scout camp. There are boys present. Besides, we don't have time. We need to get upstairs—now!"

Once they were at least partially dried out, Ken and Ellen put on their socks and shoes and began the steep ascent up the stone steps, their path interrupted by the **desiccated** remains of dead sea gulls that had used the cave as a nesting place. Opening the large wooden door at the top of the stairs, they were startled by the creak of its rusty hinges.

"Stop! Don't open it any further. Just slip through the way it is. I'm afraid it could give us away," Ellen cautioned.

The basement was pitch black as Ellen turned on her flashlight, exposing the contours of the room and its dirt floor to the light's glow.

"Shirley Kepler told me that there is a passageway behind that bookcase. She said we need to find the trip lever near the bottom shelf to open it. You feel on that side and I'll feel on this side."

"I can't find anything here," said Ken. "Here, let me try your side."

Running his fingers along the bottom shelf, Ken finally detected a steel catch which, when pressed, allowed him to pull it away from the wall. Once they were both inside, Ellen pulled it closed.

"Now, be very quiet. Shirley told me that the stairs are creaky. Take them one at a time."

At that moment, Ken and Ellen heard what sounded like visitors entering the front door. The ensuing commotion gave them opportunity to make their way to the top of the stairs despite the occasionally unwanted sounds from the aged stairway.

"Turn off your flashlight, Ellen. I can see light coming in through those cracks in the wall."

"It's just as Shirley described it. Those are the peepholes behind the bookshelves."

Within the next few minutes, more than a dozen men had assembled in the mansion's **ornate** library, a relic of Roderick Chandler's passion for old and rare books. They spoke informally for several minutes, before one of the men called the meeting to order.

"All right, comrades. Let's get down to business. Helmut, I want to see what progress you've made in reproducing the plans of the Corsair."

"Yes, Herr Heinrich, we have been able to duplicate this aircraft down to the last wingnut. As you can see, our men inside the plant have carefully reconstructed the plans by **methodically** memorizing the technical dimensions and specifications and duplicating them here. The plans are faithful in every way to the originals."

Both Ellen and Ken were able to observe Helmut Kuhn unroll the blueprints on a makeshift trestle table which had been placed in the center of the library. The others gathered around to examine the results of their painstaking work.

"The plans have all been photographed upstairs and reduced to microfilm," reported Geyer, the group's expert in the use of the miniature Minox camera, a popular tool of intelligence services worldwide. He held the small film container in the palm of his hand. "And as an added precaution, I've concealed the microfilm in the lid of my shaving kit, which I won't let out of my possession until we are back on German soil. So, even if the blueprints are discovered in the book shipments, we'll still have both the film and microfilm as backups."

"Our thanks go to Reisling, Janning, Miller, Weisfogle and Geyer for months of painstaking work," Heinrich continued. "Once these are delivered to the **fatherland** and our comrades in Japan, we can duplicate the best features of this aircraft and take steps to defeat it in the air. And what of the filmmaking, Herr Koch?"

"We have **compiled** more than two hours of footage taken from observation points in the Housatonic River. These have been carefully edited in **chronological** sequence to reflect the plane's development and testing."

"Excellent, gentlemen. The Fuehrer's **munificence** will be amply bestowed upon you for your **myriad** contributions to the **fatherland**. The only question that remains is how we convey the plans and film footage to Germany. It is my recommendation that we use one of our submarines in Long Island Sound, and that Koch, Kuhn and Geyer accompany them to Bremen, as technical advisors."

"But, Herr Heinrich, there are great dangers with this plan. The State of Connecticut and the coastal defense batteries are on high alert for our submarines. Just the other day, I observed shore patrols communicating by means of **semaphore** signals. And their efforts are being supported by a heightened **aerial surveillance** by the Army Air Corps. With all due respect, we would be grossly **negligent** if we attempted to run this **gauntlet**. All our months of **espionage** and careful engineering work could be lost in a matter of minutes. I recommend that we employ our diplomatic channels at the German Consulate in New York City and convey the materials to Hamburg by way of **neutral** shipping."

"Yes, Biermann, but how shall we transport the materials to New York City?" inquired Gerard Koch.

"We'll use Herr Mueller. He makes periodic trips to the city to transport books in his delivery van. Three or four of our men can accompany him to see that he reaches the German Consulate safely. He gives us an **innocuous** cover. After that, we can dispose of him to cover our tracks, and abandon the truck. Our New York agents can get the job done. We'll pay Herr Mueller a visit in the morning and tell him that he's going on a little errand."

Again, Ellen recognized Heinrich's voice:

"Hearing no objections, I instruct Biermann, Kuhn, Koch and Geyer to accompany Herr Mueller to New York. The rest can follow by train and meet them at the Hudson River docks. You are to confront Herr Mueller first thing in the morning and tell him that he's driving you to the city. Should he harbor any reservations, he won't have the opportunity to communicate them to anyone. You can place the film and blueprints in these two briefcases. Geyer will retain possession of the microfilm, and Biermann the photographic negatives. There must be no **hiatus** in our activity until we have **attained** our goal."

Chapter 17

In Pursuit

As the men filed out of the library, Ellen stood shivering in her wet clothes. Turning on her flashlight to illuminate the darkness, she put her hand on Ken's shoulder and whispered in his ear.

"We've got to get out of here quickly and call Chief Inspector Conrad. Not only are they ready to secret these plans out of the country, but Mr. Mueller's life is in jeopardy."

Although Ellen proceeded slowly down the wooden stairway to avoid any possibility of detection, she almost lost her balance and had to grab on to Ken to prevent herself from taking a tumble. Once at the bottom, Ken reached down and released the catch that secured the swinging bookcase. Shining her flashlight on the dirt floor, Ellen looked across the basement to the large wooden door and the stone steps which would lead them to the cave below. The motorboat was still secured at the base of the steps.

"What do you say we take the boat out of here, using the oars?" Ken suggested.

"Not a good idea. While I'm not anxious to get into the cold and clammy water again, we dare not risk alerting our "friends" that someone has been here. I'm afraid we're going to have to swim out of here."

Ken and Ellen lowered themselves into the water again and used a gentle breaststroke to make their way upstream along the shoreline to the vicinity of the woodland path.

"That's about where we parked the car," Ellen suggested. They continued to swim until their feet touched bottom and they had emerged onto dry land. A few moments later, they found Ken's roadster just where they had parked it.

"There's a blanket in the **rumble seat**. You'd better wrap it around yourself," Ken advised. After the last car had driven away from the mansion, Ken turned on his ignition and guided his roadster onto River Road.

~~~~~~~~~~~~~~~

Ellen's parents were sitting in their living room listening to the radio when she and Ken entered by way of the back door.

"Nice to see that you people are home safe and sound," Ellen's father remarked from the comfort of his favorite Queen Anne wingchair as he lowered the *Stratford News* to his lap.

"Ken, talk to my parents for a few minutes while I run upstairs and change my clothes," Ellen whispered.

"But, how will I explain my wet clothes?"

"Oh, just tell them you fell off the dock at the boatyard and I fished you out." Ellen hurried through the dining room to avoid their seeing her **disheveled** state.

Ken stepped **timorously** into the living room and stood in front of the family's Crosley **console** radio.

"Ken, my word, what happened to you?" exclaimed Ellen's mother. "It looks like you fell in the river."

"It was an accident. I caught my shoe on the dock at Bailey's Boatyard and took an accidental tumble into the water. Ellen fished me out and got a little wet herself. After my ego recovered, we both had a good laugh over it."

"You should get out of those wet clothes, Ken. I'm sure Eric's got a sweater you can wear."

"Thanks, Mrs. Anderson."

By the time Ellen came down the stairs and entered the living room, her parents were engaged in a lively conversation with Ken who was wearing a Stratford High sweater from an earlier era.

"You'll have to excuse us," Ellen said. "We have an important phone call to make."

Darting into the kitchen, Ken retrieved Chief Inspector Conrad's card from his **sodden** wallet and dialed the New York number.

"Hello? May I speak to Chief Inspector Conrad? It's an emergency."

"Yes, this is Inspector Conrad. Who's calling?"

"It's Ken Swenson, from Stratford, Connecticut. Ellen Anderson and I spoke with you last week in your office. I have some important news to report."

"Oh, yes, I remember you very well. The information you supplied allowed us to **apprehend** two divers at the Brooklyn Naval Yard who were preparing to blow up one or both of the battleships. You're lucky I was still in the office. So, what can you tell me about the movements of the Nazi agents in Stratford?"

"That they've now completed their work and are prepared to deliver plans of the Corsair aircraft to Germany via the German Consulate or on a ship docked on the Hudson River. They plan to use Mr. Mueller's delivery van, forcing Mr. Mueller to drive them there. Then they plan to kill him and dispose of his body. It's **imperative** that your men be posted outside the Consulate to intercept the van when it arrives."

"What does the van look like?"

"It's a plain brown panel truck, Connecticut license number MV424. I expect that three or four of their agents will be in the truck with Mr. Mueller."

"Have you spoken to Mr. Mueller?"

"No, we haven't."

"Please, say nothing to him. We will protect him once the van arrives. But I want you to do one more thing. I want you to follow the van to the city just in case they attempt some alternate **maneuver**. But keep far enough back so that you're not detected. The consulate is at 17 Battery Place, where the West Street Express Highway meets Battery Park. I'll have my agents stationed at strategic locations on the street. Get yourself a detailed street map of the city in case you have trouble finding it. And don't hesitate to abandon your car once you get close. But my main concern is for you to keep them in your sights. If, for some reason, they change their plans, call me at your earliest opportunity. Also, I must **prescribe** one more thing. Do not confront these men directly. Leave that to my men. Your role is limited to **surveillance** only. That is my firm **directive**."

"You have our word. We'll keep our distance. And one more thing. Mr. Mueller is concerned about his relatives in Germany. It's **imperative** that you pick up the rest of the members of this gang before anyone can give the order to have his relatives arrested. I have a list of all the Stratford agents and the last names of some of the New York contingent, which I will turn over to you tomorrow."

"We'll certainly do our best to **apprehend** the lot of them," replied Inspector Conrad.

~~~~~~~~~~~~~~~

Friday morning came quickly as Ellen dressed for what her mother thought was just a typical day at school. She wore a dark blue corduroy jumper and pale blue blouse. Following a hearty breakfast of bacon, eggs, toast and orange juice, she waited for Ken to pick her up. At 7:45, Ken's roadster pulled up in front of the Anderson home.

"Good morning, Ellen. I drove by the store already and Mr. Mueller's van is still parked out back. I suggest we park alongside the Stratford Theater and wait for them to leave."

For more than an hour, the two sat patiently in the front seat of Ken's roadster. Ken had an unobstructed view of the front of the bookstore through his rearview mirror. A few minutes before 10:00, a black Buick sedan pulled up in front of the bookstore. Four men emerged, two with briefcases, and went inside. About ten minutes later, the van, with Mr. Mueller driving, pulled out of the narrow driveway between the bookstore and the old town hall and turned south onto Main Street. Ken waited a few seconds and allowed another car to pass before initiating the pursuit. They followed the van south on Main Street until it made a right turn at Brodie's Drug Store at the intersection of Main Street and Route 1.

Following the van on Route 1 was a nerve wracking experience. Between the periodic traffic lights and a host of cars and trucks, it was a challenge trying to keep the van in view while, at the same time, avoiding detection. On several occasions, Ken observed faces peering out from the van's rear windows, but he could never be sure if his car was the object of their observations. Their route took them through Stratford, Bridgeport, Fairfield, Westport, Norwalk, Stamford, Darien, Greenwich, Port Chester, Rye, Mamaroneck, Larchmont, New Rochelle, Pelham, and the Bronx. After crossing the Harlem River at 178th Street, they drove south on the Henry Hudson Parkway until it turned into the West Street Express Highway. Finally, as they neared the southern tip of Manhattan Island, Ken reduced speed and drove into a parking space at the north side of Battery Park. The brown delivery van was in clear sight as it pulled up in front of the German Consulate at 17 Battery Place.

For several minutes, the van sat quietly in front of the consulate. Then, suddenly, before anyone emerged from the vehicle, a shot rang out and the van accelerated, making a sharp left turn onto Broadway. Something had obviously

gone terribly wrong. Perhaps the
occupants of the van became aware
of the **surveillance** and beat a
hasty retreat before they could be
apprehended. It was all a muddle.
Obviously, a swift resolution of the
plot was **precluded**. Fortunately,
Ken had not turned off his engine
and was able to swing back into
pursuit, but not without running

the traffic light at the intersection of Battery Place and Broadway. By that time,
the van was already several blocks ahead, in front of Trinity Church, at Wall
Street. Ken and Ellen passed several New York landmarks as the van made its
way north on Broadway—the Woolworth Building, City Hall, the Singer Building
at Prince Street, the campus of New York University, the Flatiron Building at
East 23rd Street, the Gimbel's and Macy's Department Stores at 34th Street,
Times Square, and Columbus Circle at the southwest corner of Central Park.

With all the cars, buses,
trolleys, trucks, and taxis, it
was a major challenge to keep
the van in sight.

Ken had no idea if any
F.B.I. agents had joined the
hunt, or if he and Ellen were
the van's lone pursuers.
Ellen had a **prescient** notion
that they might be headed to
Central European Books and Imports on West 122nd Street, part of a hastily
conceived backup plan. This was the only **scenario** that made sense to her
since the planned **rendezvous** at the German consulate had been **aborted** and
she knew that Central European Books was part of the operation.

At West 86th Street, the van turned left in the direction of Riverside Park,
and then north on Riverside Drive. At 116th Street, the campus of Columbia
University loomed to the east, and the stately **spire** of the Riverside Church

lay a few blocks ahead.

"I think we have to assume they're headed back to Central European Books and Imports," Ken suggested. "I'm going to drop you off behind Riverside Church, like I did before, and let you make your way over there. In the meantime, I'll telephone Chief Inspector Conrad. I hope I'm right. If they switch vans, however, we're sunk, unless we're able to follow it. Otherwise, we'll never find them in this city. Wait, here's the church office. I'm going to run in and use their telephone while you wait here. Hopefully, Chief Inspector Conrad can radio some of his men to meet us there."

Leaping from the roadster, Ken entered the church office and confronted an elderly woman at the reception desk.

"Pardon me, but may I use your telephone? It's an emergency."

"Why certainly, young man. I trust it's not long distance?"

"No, it's a local call to the F.B.I."

"Well, then, by all means. Here you are."

Ken dialed the local F.B.I. office. The receptionist picked up on the second ring.

"May I speak with Inspector Conrad, please?"

"I'm sorry. He's not here at the moment. May I take a message?"

"This is Ken Swenson. Tell him that we have followed the brown van to Central European Books and Imports at 502 West 122nd Street. I'm in the Riverside Church office at the moment, but we'll be driving over to the bookstore when I hang up. If they abandon the brown van to cover their trail, we'll be forced to follow whatever vehicle they use. If that's the case, I have no idea when I'll be able to call next. Have you got all that?"

"I understand. I'll get in touch with him immediately."

With that, Ken exited the office onto Claremont Avenue where Ellen sat patiently in the waiting roadster.

"So, were you able to reach him?"

"No, but I left a message with his secretary. She said she'll radio him immediately and tell him where we are. I just hope we'll be there when they arrive."

As Ken drove east on 122nd Street, he saw the brown van in the distance, parked partially on the sidewalk.

"I'll tell you what. I'm going to let you off a block west of the bookstore, then circle the block. You need to get inside the bookstore and find out what's going on. But don't go exploring in any back rooms. Stay in the public areas. I'll keep hovering to see if our friends leave by some other means."

When Ken let Ellen off at the corner of Broadway and 122nd Street, the bright sunlight was punctuated by a few darkening clouds. As she approached the bookstore, only a few passersby occupied the street. But she was startled to observe the 1934 DeSoto Airflow she had seen at the old mansion on the Housatonic. Once inside, she saw no immediate signs of the men they had followed, and **surmised** that they were probably in the back room. Ellen occupied herself by looking at books in one of the fiction alcoves, while **simultaneously** keeping her eyes on the front door. Unfortunately, the store was nearly empty— not a good omen to have no witnesses about. Moving around the store, she tried to appear as **nonchalant** as possible. Indeed, the store was so quiet that she was startled when Mr. Mueller and two men in dark overcoats passed through the room in which she was browsing. And, as if to **forestall** any urge that he might have had to say anything, Ellen **surreptitiously** raised her finger to her lips, then lowered her eyes again to the books on the table.

"May I help you, miss?"

Ellen was startled by this man who appeared, seemingly, from out of nowhere. She had seen that face before, the last time she was in the store. Yes, it was the man who had helped her find the *Protocols* and other books on the **alleged** "Jewish **conspiracy**."

"No. Thank you. I'm just browsing today."

"Very well. Just ask if you need anything."

Ellen was suddenly enveloped by a sense of foreboding. What if the clerk remembered her from her previous visit, and **implicated** her in the escape from the backroom?

Her worst fears were realized when, suddenly, she was **accosted** by one of the two men who had accompanied Mr. Mueller. Out of the corner of her eye, she observed one of the store clerks pulling down the shade over the front door and locking it. Save Ellen, there was not a customer in the store.

"Excuse me, miss, would you please come with me?"

CENTRAL EUROPEAN
BOOKS & IMPORTS

↓ BOOKS

©MMXIV

Chapter 18

Cornered

Ellen was now cornered in one of the store's rear alcoves. Surveying her surroundings for a possible escape route, she found her path blocked by a brute of a man who now hovered over her, and the clerk who had locked the front door. Moreover, there didn't appear to be anyone else in the store who might come to her aid. Any **inclination** on her part to bolt was **forestalled**.

"Bring her into the back room," shouted another man, who emerged from the swinging bookcase.

Ellen was grabbed roughly from behind and a hand clapped over her mouth before she had an opportunity to scream, not that it would have done any good under the circumstances. Then, she was forcibly dragged to the storeroom where she had hidden away just a few weeks before.

"Now, sit down and tell us what you are doing here."

Ellen recognized the voice of her **inquisitor** as that of Rupert Heinrich, whom Inspector Conrad had described as **ruthless**, the man responsible for the death of several F.B.I. agents in the city, and the ringleader she had heard ordering the bombing of the ships at the Brooklyn Naval Yard.

"I'm a student at Columbia University. I often come here. What's this all about? You have no right to hold me. I've done nothing wrong."

"Spare us your **insipid fabrications**. According to Dollmeier, you were here two weeks ago asking for books on the Jewish **conspiracy**, and then you disappeared, we believe, into this very room. Then you escaped out that door," pointing to the **anteroom** through which she had once escaped.

"I don't know what you're talking about."

"Kruger, have you searched her purse?"

"She wasn't carrying one. Just this small change purse with a few dollars in it."

"Don't you have any identification? Driver's license, student identification?"

"No, I left them in my dorm room," Ellen replied.

"Where do you live?"

"In a dormitory on the Columbia campus."

"What's the name of the dormitory?"

"McAllister Hall," said Ellen, without missing a beat.

"And what are you studying?"

"Anthropology."

"Kruger, bring Herr Mueller in here. I don't trust her **veracity** in the least. I'm sure she's being **obstinate**."

A few moments later, Mr. Mueller was brought into the room. Kruger had wrenched Mueller's arm behind his back and was applying sufficient force to cause him to wince with pain.

"Now, Herr Mueller, tell us what you know about this young woman," Heinrich ordered.

"I've never seen her before."

"Don't try being **evasive**. We have other ways of **eliciting** a response."

"I told you. I've never seen her before."

"If you're going to be **obdurate**, I'll have Kruger here break your arm." Kruger proceeded to bend the old man's arm behind his back until he began to **writhe** in pain.

"No! Stop! I'll tell you what you want to know," Ellen exclaimed. "But don't hurt him."

"Ellen, please, I don't care what they do to me," pleaded Mr. Mueller.

"Ah, so now we'll get some truth from the young lady," said Heinrich. "Get Mueller out of here. He's served his purpose."

Still smarting from the **grievous** abuse his captors had **meted** out, Mueller was dragged from the room, and Ellen was left alone to face her captors.

"All right, let's start from the beginning. Tell us your name. No **obfuscating**."

"Ellen Anderson."

"And where do you live?"

"Stratford, Connecticut."

"How long have you known Herr Mueller?"

"Since I was a little girl. His book shop has been in Stratford for as long as I can remember."

"Why are you here?"

"I followed Mr. Mueller's delivery van from Stratford because I discovered he was in danger."

"What kind of danger?"

"Bad associates."

"I suppose that means us?"

"I think that's obvious."

"What do you know about us?"

"I know that you're Nazis and enemies of our country, just like Adolf Hitler. I also know you're involved in the selling of **Nazi** literature and you're forcing Mr. Mueller to sell it also."

Ellen hoped that they would be **mollified** with her explanation of the National **Socialist** literature as the **rationale** for her involvement. If they suspected anything more, she would expose herself to even more significant risk.

"You've got some **temerity** for a young woman. But you obviously know too much. You will regret **disparaging** and **vilifying** the Fuehrer. Once the Third Reich and its allies have established complete **hegemony** over Europe and the Pacific, and have brought England under their **punitive yoke**, the United States will have to bow to our demands as well."

Ellen was **repulsed** by Heinrich's **haughty** and **imperious demeanor**, as well as by his complete lack of moral **turpitude**. And while she feared for her safety, she remained **sanguine** about her ultimate **liberation**.

"It's clear that we can't afford to release you to bring the authorities down upon our heads. Tie her up and lock her in the furnace room. We'll return for her later when it's time to load the truck. We can pack her in one of those wooden book crates we're transporting to the docks, then throw her and Mueller overboard once our ship gets out to sea."

Judging by Heinrich's **insolent** tone, she knew they were serious. Now, she was worried. Her only hope was that Ken and the F.B.I. would find her before that **harrowing** prospect materialized. Ellen's heart was pounding so hard when she heard of their **insidious** plans that she found herself **hyperventilating**. Feeling that she might faint at any moment, she struggled to maintain consciousness. In **retrospect**, she wished she had never put herself in such peril.

One of the men she recognized from Thursday evening's gathering at the river mansion tied her hands behind her back and placed a gag around her mouth. He also tied her ankles together. Then, dragging her to the basement and into the furnace room, he **tethered** her to one of the supporting columns, and locked the door. Ellen struggled **futilely** with her **restraints** to see if they offered hope of escape, but her **predicamen**t appeared **dire**. In this seemingly **inextricable dilemma**, she might have lost hope, but for her religious faith. Sufficient light **permeated** the room from a lone basement window, however, that she was able to **appraise** her surroundings. Then she remembered. She always kept a small Swiss Army knife in her jacket pocket for just this kind of **adversity**. But could she reach it? She knew she had to do it without delay. Once they had her packed away in a book crate, her situation would be hopeless.

She struggled in **torrid** fashion for nearly twenty minutes. Finally, after much **forbearance**, she was able to **distend** her shoulders far enough to pull her jacket pocket within reach of her tied hands, and reach inside. Once inside, she managed to grasp the knife with her fingers. With her arms and fingers aching from the strain, she finally removed the knife from her pocket and dropped it on the floor behind her. Her next task was opening the blade. Suddenly, she heard a key in the door and moved quickly to conceal the knife beneath her outstretched frame. She could only hope that they had no plans to move her at the present time, and that she would have more time to **effectuate** her escape.

"You're a quiet one, you are," said her captor, **mockingly**. "I just came to make sure you're no female Harry Houdini."

Not wanting to delay his departure, Ellen made no sound. Nor could she have uttered anything **intelligible**, as her gag **foreclosed** that possibility. A few seconds later, after examining her bonds, he was gone, locking the door behind him.

It took less than a minute to grasp the knife in her fingers. Although it had **multifarious** uses, Ellen's only task was to pry open the small knife blade, which she accomplished after some effort. She had even greater difficulty getting it into a position to **exert** sufficient **leverage** to run the blade against the ropes. But with a little **perseverance**, she began to **frenetically** saw away at the ropes which secured her hands. One by one, the strands of the rope began to pop and she was soon removing them from her aching wrists. After that, her ankles were easily cut free, and the gag removed from around her mouth. Now, to open that transom window.

Fortunately, the furnace room was also used for storage. A collection of wooden crates, when stacked one on top of another, offered sufficient height to reach the window and release the latch. The window was narrow, but easily navigable for someone of Ellen's **lithe** and **sinuous** frame. Except for ripping the hem of her jumper, and suffering a small **laceration** on her ankle, she escaped relatively **unscathed**.

Once outside, she soon recognized where she was. She was in a window well on the same side of the building from which she had escaped the last time, its narrow corridor leading either to 122nd Street or to the rear courtyard. Feeling emboldened after her brush with death, she decided to walk straight out to 122nd Street and freedom. Surprisingly, there was not a soul on the street, only a few parked cars on the other side, and the brown van still parked in front of the bookstore. She hurriedly ran across and up the street, crouched behind a green sedan, and waited for Ken to reappear. **Fortuitously**, she didn't have to wait long. When his car approached her concealed position, she leaped out and flagged him down.

"Where have you been? I've been terribly worried about you," Ken exclaimed, as Ellen climbed into his roadster.

"It's a long story. One of the clerks recognized me from my previous visit and Heinrich subjected me to the third degree in the back room. Then, they tied me up in the basement."

"Good God! How did you escape?"

"Haven't you ever heard of a Swiss Army knife?"

"Of course, but having a knife and being able to use it when your hands are tied is another. I'm amazed both by your **guile** and your emotional **fortitude**. I should have never let you go in there alone."

"I wonder how long it will take before they realize I've **eluded** their grasp."

"Not long, I expect."

As their car approached Amsterdam Avenue, Ken looked into his rearview mirror to see a large black delivery truck pull up in front of the bookstore.

"Don't turn around, but there's a truck stopping in front of the bookstore. I knew they didn't dare use Mr. Mueller's van at this point. It would be a dead giveaway."

"I didn't tell you. They're headed for the docks, but which one I don't know."

"I wish Inspector Conrad or one of his men would get here. It's been nearly an hour since I called them. We'll have no choice but to follow that truck ourselves and hope that we can alert the authorities or flag down a policeman along the way."

"Ken, why don't you keep circling the block until they pull away? I'll slouch down so they don't see me."

A few minutes later, Ken observed four men carrying several large wooden crates to the back of the **nondescript** black truck. He recognized several of the men from Thursday night's gathering at the mansion in Stratford. They gave him only a passing glance as his roadster passed the bookstore for the third time.

"Write down this license number: We may need it to track down the truck if we lose it in traffic," Ken instructed. "It's a New York plate: FSX1278."

"I'll bet Mr. Mueller is in one of those crates. What nerve they have to be **flouting** the law in broad daylight. We're the only ones who can save him and **foil** their plans," Ellen exclaimed.

"I'd feel a lot better if the F.B.I. would show up. Inspector Conrad should have **dispatched** some of his men by now. In the meantime, why don't we park on Amsterdam Avenue and wait for the truck to pull out."

The bright morning sky had given way to a dark and **ominous** cloud cover and high winds. What little sunlight remained was **diffused** across a blackened sky. Distant thunder from across the Hudson River offered a **portent** of a coming thunderstorm. As Ken and Ellen sat parked on the east side of the street, they **contemplated** how **fraught** with danger the next few hours would be for Mr. Mueller, and how **forlorn** he must feel in light of the **ignominious** end they had planned for him. They found it difficult to even imagine that those men could **contemplate** an act so **heinous**.

"If only we could let Mr. Mueller know that we haven't **forsaken** him," Ellen suggested.

"Well, F.B.I or not, there's the truck. We have no choice but to follow it."

The large black truck wasted no time in leaving the bookstore, even driving through the stop sign at Amsterdam Avenue, and continuing south on Morningside Drive at a high rate of speed. With few other cars on the road, the presence of Ken's roadster must have been obvious to the truck's occupants. South of 113th Street, as it approached the Cathedral of St. John the Divine, it slowed to a crawl, all the better to gauge the intentions of its pursuers. Ken was forced to break abruptly so as not to pass the truck and put himself and Ellen in danger of being run off the road. Suddenly, gunshots rang out and a bullet ricocheted off of Ken's hood.

"Good grief!" exclaimed Ken. "These guys mean business! That was a little too close for my taste."

"I think we'd better back off," Ellen cautioned. "Hopefully, we can catch them when they hit heavier traffic. No sense in getting ourselves killed in the meantime while no one else is around."

Ken and Ellen were **undaunted** and continued to keep the truck in their sights, but at a distance of several blocks. At 86th Street, the truck made a hard left turn, before being brought to a halt by the light at Central Park West. Then, catching a green light, it took the 86th Street Transverse Road through Central Park, just south of the **reservoir**. Ellen noted that the trees and plantings in Central Park were at their most **verdant**. At the underpass, however, the truck again slowed to a crawl, forcing Ken to hit his brakes. Only as other vehicles filled the road behind Ken's roadster was it obliged to continue on its way. When it ran the red light at Fifth Avenue, however, Ken was forced to stop for oncoming traffic.

"Where are they going? I thought they'd be heading for the Hudson River docks," Ellen shouted.

"Your guess is as good as mine. I think they're trying to lose us before they commit to their ultimate destination," Ken suggested, as the light turned green. "Don't worry. I can still see them. Look, they're turning to the right up ahead. That must be about First Avenue. I hope I'm right or we're going to lose them."

Chapter 19

A Warehouse in Brooklyn

By the time Ken made the same turn onto First Avenue, the truck was blocks ahead and barely visible. Eventually, he was able to close to within a few blocks. The chase continued south on First Avenue for three more miles until the truck turned into Allen Street south of Houston Street. From there, the route became a virtual maze of intersecting streets and boulevards, until the Brooklyn Bridge loomed ahead to the left. Then, without warning, they observed two men jump from the rear of the truck and run toward the subway station at City Hall, **adjacent** to the entrance to the Brooklyn Bridge. One carried a briefcase. They could only watch helplessly as the men disappeared into a **subterranean** tunnel and a sea of humanity.

"What do we do now?" Ellen exclaimed.

"There's nothing we can do but follow the truck and try to save Mr. Mueller," Ken replied.

"My guess is they're heading for the auto warehouse on Flushing Avenue near the Brooklyn Naval Yard," Ellen suggested.

"How did you know that?"

"Heinrich mentioned it in the backroom of the bookstore two weeks ago when he didn't know I was present. I committed the address to memory. It's 63 Flushing Avenue. Perhaps you don't recall my giving the address to Inspector Conrad when we met him later that day."

"I remember something about a warehouse in Brooklyn, but didn't remember the address. What a memory you have!"

The sky had turned an **ominous** shade of gray as they drove across the East River and took in the majesty of the historic span which linked lower Manhattan to the neighborhood of Brooklyn Heights. The lower Manhattan skyline was **effulgent** against the cloud darkened **firmament**. As their car reached the bridge's **zenith**, it was **buffeted** by the forceful spring **zephyrs** that seemed to **propel** them across the river.

"We've simply got to get to a telephone, or a police station," Ellen shouted, above the traffic's **din**.

Luckily, a police substation stood like a **sentinel**, near the eastern end of the bridge.

Ken pulled his roadster up in front and the two ran inside. The desk sergeant  sat **impassively** behind an **ornate** antique desk, a **dour** expression on his face, a copy of *Doc Savage Magazine* in his hands.

"Excuse us, sergeant, but we'd like to report a kidnapping."

"A kidnapping, you say? Now, who would it be that's been kidnapped? Your dog?"

"No, sergeant, his name is Klaus Mueller and he's the **proprietor** of a bookstore in Stratford, Connecticut. Ken, here, works for him."

"That's right, sergeant. He's been kidnapped by some **fifth columnists** and taken, we believe, to a warehouse at 63 Flushing Avenue. We followed the truck from Morningside Heights, but we don't dare take on these men by ourselves. They're armed and dangerous," Ken added.

"Well, I should say! Is there someone who can **corroborate** your story?"

"Yes, call Chief Inspector Conrad of the F.B.I. Here's his card."

Taking the card in his hands, the sergeant, still **dubious**, put *Doc Savage* down and dialed the number.

"This is Sergeant Muldoon at the Poplar Street police station in Brooklyn. I have two young people here who claim they're witnesses to a kidnapping. They tell me that Chief Inspector Conrad can **corroborate** their story."

"What are your names?"

"Ellen Anderson and Ken Swenson," Ellen replied.

"Ellen Anderson and Ken Swenson," repeated the sergeant. "Yep, sounds like they're from a Swedish detective agency, if you ask me," he continued, with an impish grin on his face.

"Here. The Inspector wants to talk to you."

Sergeant Muldoon handed the phone to Ellen who explained their situation to the Inspector:

"You've got to get over here right away, Inspector Conrad," Ellen shouted.

"We lost sight of the delivery truck not more than five minutes ago. Mr. Mueller has been kidnapped and packed in a wooden crate. He may suffocate if we don't find him soon. We're certain they were originally headed to the Hudson River docks, but they abandoned their plans when they saw us following them, and now they're headed for the auto warehouse at 63 Flushing Avenue. However, two of their associates jumped out of the truck near the City Hall subway station at the west end of the Brooklyn Bridge. We think they may have the plans of the Corsair with them."

"Don't wait for me. You must get over to the warehouse right away," urged Inspector Conrad. "Let me talk to the sergeant."

"Sergeant Muldoon, here."

"Sergeant, these young people are telling you the truth. You've got to get over to the auto warehouse as soon as possible. A man's life is at stake. My men and I won't be there for about ten minutes, so your response will be critical."

"O.K. I'll put out a call to all our officers in the vicinity to **converge** on the warehouse. We'll be waiting for you."

Poking his head around the corner, Sergeant Muldoon called out to the officers in the rear office.

"Kidnapping case. I need you men right now. Toracelli, you'll have to take over desk duty in my absence."

Sergeant Muldoon and two patrolmen climbed into the police car, **beckoning** Ken and Ellen to join them.

"I'm bringing you along to identify the kidnapping victim, but I must caution you to keep out of harm's way. There's no telling what we might encounter. I don't want you caught in the crossfire."

"We appreciate that. Let's hope we're not too late," Ellen exclaimed.

The auto warehouse on 63 Flushing Avenue was roughly a mile from the police substation. Flushing Avenue was **adjacent** to the mammoth Brooklyn Navy Yard, one of the leading shipbuilding facilities in the United States. When they arrived, however, there

was no sign of the truck they had pursued all the way from Morningside Heights. Instead, they encountered a **redoubtable**, but **ostensibly** abandoned, six-story building with limestone **façade**, above which hung a large faded wooden sign reading: "Brooklyn Auto Warehouse." Sergeant Muldoon instructed Ken and Ellen to remain in the squad car while he and his men approached the building. The mood on the street was **eerily** quiet as they examined two possible entrances: a normal-sized steel door and a garage door large enough to accommodate the largest vehicles. The only windows were on the upper stories. At that moment, two additional squad cars pulled up in front of the building and four officers emerged to lend support. Drawing his service revolver, Sergeant Muldoon pounded on the smaller door.

"Police! I advise you to come out with your hands up!"

There was no answer. Subsequent attempts to rouse the occupants were to no avail.

"Baldelli! Bring me a crow bar," shouted Muldoon. "Men, be ready to follow me in as soon as we've gained entry."

Inserting the crow bar into the door jam, Sergeant Muldoon, after some effort, was able to force the door open. He and four of the officers rushed into the building, their service revolvers drawn. The **cavernous** space was enveloped by a deathly silence. Except for some oil drums and refuse however, the building was, to all intents and purposes, abandoned. The officers scattered to look for any signs of the kidnappers. A few minutes later, they reported back.

"Sergeant Muldoon, we've been hoodwinked. They might have come in by way of Flushing Avenue, but the **deception** allowed them to escape by way of the rear alleyway. There's a rear door for trucks and it's wide open. A **wily** bit of **legerdemain** on their part. Who knows where they've gone to by now."

Ken and Ellen, who had been waiting patiently on the sidewalk across the street, watched as Sergeant Muldoon and the other officers emerged **dejectedly** from the warehouse. At that very moment, a blue sedan pulled up with Chief Inspector Conrad and two of his men inside.

"I'm afraid they've given us the slip," explained Sergeant Muldoon. "The warehouse provides ample means of **egress** on the other side of the building. These people aren't stupid. They used this **ruse** to put several minutes of daylight between them and us. That could prove critical."

"Then, you must put in an all points bulletin on the truck," Ellen urged. "It's a New York plate, number FSX1278."

Sergeant Muldoon returned to his squad car and reported back to police headquarters: "Put out an all points bulletin on a black delivery truck, New York license number FSX1278. I suggest cars be assigned to each of the Hudson River docks."

A few seconds later, a report came across the squad car's radio:

> *Calling all cars! Calling all cars! Be on the lookout for a black delivery truck, New York license number FSX1278. Believed headed for the Hudson River docks, from the Battery to 88th Street. Possible kidnapping in progress. All cars must report in for their dock assignments.*

"I'll put in a call to the New York Port Authority," said Inspector Conrad. "We'll have them alert the Coast Guard to delay the departure of any passenger vessels until we've had an opportunity to examine their cargo and passenger **manifests**. No ships are going to leave New York Harbor until they've been cleared by the F.B.I."

"That was mighty fortunate you got the license number. I'd like you two to accompany us over to the Hudson River docks. You may be able to identify the truck on sight from the West Side Highway," the sergeant urged.

Ken and Ellen were now passengers in the back seat of the squad car which was crossing the Brooklyn Bridge on its way to the southern tip of Manhattan Island. After crossing the bridge, they were soon back at the same subway station into which two of the men had disappeared less than an hour before. And looming near the southern tip of City Hall Park was the towering Woolworth Building, whose impressive **gothic** exterior was a testament to the financial success of the five and ten cent store. They continued speeding in the direction of the West Side Highway and the Hudson River docks via Park Row and Vesey Street.

Starting just north of Battery Park, Ken and Ellen strained their eyes for any sign of the black delivery truck along the waterfront. Ten minutes later, having passed Gansevoort Street, with Pier 52 approaching on their left, a call came in on the squad car's radio:

"Vehicle with license plate FSX1278 has been spotted at Pier 97 of the Swedish-American Line. All cars in the area are ordered to converge on Pier 97."

"I hope that's it," Ellen cried. "And I hope we're not too late."

Chapter 20

Trapped at Pier 97

In less than five minutes, Sergeant Muldoon and five other squad cars had **converged** on the entrance to Pier 97 at 57th Street, **precluding** any means of escape for the black delivery truck and its occupants who were already inside the terminal building.

"Stay right here until I call for you. We know these men are armed and dangerous."

"That's the truck all right. And the license plate is a match," said Ken.

"Ken, that's the Drottningholm. My parents sailed on her in 1936 when they made their first trip to Sweden. It normally sails between New York and Gothenburg, Sweden. But why would the Drottningholm be **implicated** with Nazis? After all, unlike its **subjugated** neighbors, Sweden is a **neutral** country," Ellen explained.

"I have no idea, but here comes Chief Inspector Conrad. Perhaps he can **enlighten** us."

"Ellen, Ken, I just got off the phone with the Port Authority. The Drottningholm was scheduled to depart at 4:00. We got here with just twenty minutes to spare."

"But why the Drottningholm, Inspector?"

"Because the United States, British and French governments recently chartered her to exchange diplomats and prisoners of war. We're also using it to **deport** and **repatriate** dangerous German and Italian nationals living in this country. No doubt, the members of the spy ring learned of this and thought it their best hope of getting back to Europe **unimpeded**. We've **cordoned** off the area, however, and will be conducting an inspection of the cargo and passengers. I'm going to need your help in identifying the members of the gang from among the passengers."

"Of course. But has the cargo been loaded?" Ken inquired.

"Yes, they just lowered it into the hold."

"Then it's critical that we open the crates immediately. Mr. Mueller is in one of them. We can only pray that he's still alive. Who can guide us into the hold?"

"That looks like the captain now," Ellen exclaimed.

"I am Captain Larsson. May I be of assistance?"

"Yes, Captain, would you please guide us to the hold," Ken replied. "There's an elderly man **languishing** at this very moment in one of those crates."

"My word! Yes! Follow me, quickly!"

Captain Larsson led Ken, Ellen and Inspector Conrad and his men up the gangplank and down four flights of interior stairs to the cargo hold. Several F.B.I. agents were already there, awaiting instructions. Ken and Ellen rushed frantically among the rows of cargo looking for the stampings that would identify the crates in question.

"Here they are!" cried Ken. "Central European Books and Imports. There's one...two...three...four...five...I think that's it. Who's got a crowbar?"

"Right here," shouted one of the crew. Ken took it and started prying open the crates. The first two yielded up books and files of correspondence.

"Now, this one," shouted Ellen. The lid was swiftly removed.

"There's a body in this one," cried one of the crew members.

Ellen knelt down next to the now opened crate. It was Mr. Mueller all right, but was he still alive? His **pallid** complexion and **emaciated** frame seemed to suggest otherwise. Taking his wrist in her hand, she quickly felt for a pulse.

"Yes! Yes! He is alive! Thank God we found him in time! Mr. Mueller, can you hear me?"

Mr. Mueller's **wizened countenance** looked up at Ellen with a **languid** expression. Momentarily **inarticulate**, and unable to **emote**, he simply nodded. Thankfully, the **infusion** of some fresh air into his lungs, a drink of water, and the sound of Ellen's voice seemed to have a **palliative** effect on his condition. The **nadir** of his life's experience had finally come to an end.

"You're going to be all right, Mr. Mueller. Your nightmare is all over."

"Peterson. You and Hallstrom bring a stretcher," instructed Captain Larsson.

"I'm sure he'll be more **lucid** once the fresh air has revived him," said Chief Inspector Conrad.

"I was afraid someone would be delivering an **elegy** over his lifeless body," Ellen suggested.

Having suffered such **horrific abasement** from his captors, Mr. Mueller was brought out of the cargo hold and the remaining two crates were opened for inspection. One contained a variety of books, letters, and documents, like the others. The last **ostensibly** contained a variety of **objets d'art**, chiefly porcelain vases and statuary. When Ellen reached down to examine them more carefully, however, she detected that there was a **discrepancy**, in that the space devoted to these items did not extend to the full depth of the crate. She correctly suspected that a false bottom concealed another layer beneath. Removing the objects with care, she placed them on an outstretched tarp. Then, taking the crow bar, she used the **implement** to carefully pry open the wooden panel which separated the two compartments. Two leather pouches lay inside.

"Inspector, I believe this is what we have been looking for," Ellen suggested.

She opened the two pouches. There, just as she had suspected, were the detailed plans of the Corsair aircraft and the film can containing movie footage of its test flights. The fruits of months of military **espionage** on behalf of the Third Reich were now **effaced** through the timely **intervention** of the F.B.I. and the New York City Police Department.

Ellen and Ken joined Chief Inspector Conrad and the rest of the **constabulary** on deck, where the assembled passengers were being lined up for questioning.

"Inspector, we caught these two men attempting to escape down the anchor chain," reported one of the **federal** agents.

Ellen promptly recognized Gerard Koch and Helmut Kuhn, now in **fetters**.

"Those are the two men who ran the Stratford operation—Helmut Kuhn and Gerard Koch. Now, we just have to find those **perfidious** associates of theirs," Ellen advised.

Chief Inspector Conrad led Ellen and Ken to the passengers, now lined up on the main deck—more than 300 in all. As they passed down the line, they carefully paused at each male passenger and studied his face. They had gotten through perhaps a third of the assembled **throng** when Ellen looked ahead and spotted Heinrich, whose **pockmarked visage** revealed an **impudent** look of **irreverence**.

"There's the **linchpin** of this operation—Rupert Heinrich, a **truculent** personality if I ever saw one. I could never forget that face."

A little further down the line, she spotted three others.

"Here's another—Biermann, I believe, is his name. He's the one who **assaulted** me in the bookshop and tied me up. And I think those two are Keller and Fischer. Now, we need to find Geyer. He's the one with the microfilm."

"We found this one hiding in one of the staterooms," shouted one of Chief Inspector Conrad's associates.

"That's him, that's Geyer," Ellen replied. "Search his pockets and luggage. I'm sure you'll find the microfilm concealed on his person or in his shaving kit."

The book store clerk, Ernest Dollmeier, discovered hiding in the ship's boiler room, was the last one taken into custody. All were handcuffed and led to waiting squad cars.

"Inspector, there are five more **accomplices** in Connecticut who should be taken into custody immediately: John Schlechter, the New Haven accountant and treasurer of the local Bund movement, and at least four employees of the United Aircraft plant in Stratford: Otto Reisling, Kurt Janning, Eric Miller, Fred Weisfogle. I promised Mr. Mueller that we would make every effort to prevent any of them from communicating with their contacts in Germany who can threaten his relatives there," she explained.

"We'll certainly do our best. And I'm confident that those files will yield up many more names of Nazi agents and sympathizers on the East Coast and around the country," the Inspector added. "There's enough **epistolary** evidence here to convict the entire network, wherever they may be hiding. It's unlikely the military court will treat them with **leniency**. Your **perspicacity** has really paid off, young lady."

By the time Ken and Ellen stepped off the Drottningholm's gangplank, word of their heroics was already being **disseminated** by the local newswires. A **throng** of New York reporters and photographers was waiting for them as they **disembarked**.

"You two, follow me," commanded Chief Inspector Conrad. We'll **truncate** these potential interviews before they can even get started. I told Sergeant

Muldoon I'd get you two
back to the Brooklyn police
station and your car before
you're pestered by these
newshounds. Once I
turn on my siren and hit
the gas, we'll leave them
in the dust."

Summa
Cum Laude

Ellen
Anderson

Chapter 21

A Stratford Welcome

By the time Ken and Ellen **navigated** their way back to the Connecticut border, the dark storm clouds that had loomed so **ominously** at midday had **dissipated** and the late day sun was casting an **iridescent** glow across a sky reflecting a full **palette** of colors. Ellen was overcome with a feeling of **exhilaration** whose full import would probably not be fully **manifest** for some time. For the first time in weeks, Ellen **contemplated** what life would be like without a mystery to investigate or **contemplate**. Instead, she would have to focus her attention on more **mundane** matters, like homework, research papers, and final exams.

By late afternoon, Ellen's mother was already aware that something **momentous** had transpired. Earlier in the day, she had answered a call from the office of the assistant principal inquiring about Ellen's unexplained absence from school. And later that afternoon, calls from newspapers and radio stations began streaming in, asking for interviews with the girl who had broken a major Nazi spy ring. The Friday evening editions of the Stratford and Bridgeport newspapers ran front-page stories about the Stratford-based spy network and the Stratford High School students who had exposed them. In Stratford, the arrest of several United Aircraft employees by the F.B.I. had plant management scurrying about trying to assure **federal** officials that the security **breach** was contained and that the plant was **implementing** a **comprehensive** review of its personnel and security procedures.

Ellen's father first heard the news while working at his drafting table at the shop. Norm Nelson, one his co-workers, heard a late afternoon news bulletin on one of the New York radio stations and was soon spreading the news. Before long, the entire office was in a state of **euphoria**. Overflowing with excitement, Ellen's father left work early and stopped by the local Bridgeport newsstand to pick up copies of all the local and out-of-town newspapers, each of which contained **laudatory** articles **lavishing** praise on his daughter and her boyfriend. By the time he got home, a half dozen reporters were camped outside the Anderson residence seeking interviews with the pair who had broken the spy network.

When Ken and Ellen pulled into Stratford, their first thought was to check in on Mrs. Mueller. They drove immediately to the Dusty Corner Book Shop, only to find a "Closed" sign hanging on the front door. Hurriedly, they drove to the Mueller home on King Street. When they knocked on the front door, however, they were met by a Stratford police officer.

"May we please see Mrs. Mueller?"

"Mrs. Mueller is resting. May I help you?"

"Yes, I'm Ellen Anderson and this is Ken Swenson. We wanted to tell Mrs. Mueller that..." Suddenly, the front door was opened wide.

"Oh, please come in," said Mrs. Mueller. "I'm so glad to see you. I've been so worried about Klaus. He told me not to call the police when he drove off with those men this morning, but I was beside myself with fear for his safety. I've just been listening to the radio reports. Officer, these are the two young people who rescued my Klaus."

"He's going to be fine, Mrs. Mueller," Ellen advised. "He's had a stressful day, but he's now resting comfortably at the New York Presbyterian Hospital. They expect to release him soon. The F.B.I. arrested what we believe are all the members of the spy network. They won't be communicating with anyone, least of all their contacts in Germany."

"I'm so relieved. It's like the nightmare is finally over for us. We are so grateful to the both of you."

"You're welcome, Mrs. Mueller. Well, we'd better be on our way. Our parents are, no doubt, worried and anxious to see us. We'll be back tomorrow to check in on you."

Freeman Avenue hadn't seen such a flurry of activity since Ellen's neighbor, Amy McGuire, won the national Little Orphan Annie Grand Prize Sweepstakes in 1939. As they approached the Anderson home, Ellen and Ken were surprised to see cars and news vans parked along both sides of the street, and a host of reporters standing outside her front door.

"Can we get a statement, Miss Anderson?" shouted one of the reporters.

"Let me speak to my parents first. Then, we'll be happy to answer all your questions."

As they entered the front door, Ellen could see that look on her father's face. It was **reminiscent** of the one he had after Ellen put her handprints in their next-door neighbor's freshly-poured concrete driveway at the age of five.

"I know what you're going to say, Dad. I had no business involving myself in this dangerous business. I could have been killed. This is no business for girls. And, if anything happened to me, who would bake your favorite chocolate raspberry bars? Did I leave anything out?"

"Nothing of importance. But we're just thankful you're safe. And, of course, mighty proud of what you've done for your country. We just hope you don't plan on making a habit of this."

"Your father bought all the local newspapers and as many out-of-town papers as he could lay his hands on," Ellen's mother added. "But don't forget. We eat promptly at 6:00."

Ellen had to laugh. No matter what she had been through, there was an **inexorable** regularity to the family's dinner schedule. It was that Swedish **punctuality**—Holmgren style.

"Yes, Mother, but let us not keep the press waiting any longer."

Stepping out on the front steps, Ellen and Ken fielded questions from what now amounted to more than a dozen **clamoring** reporters, while photographers snapped their photos.

"Miss Anderson. How did a **novice** like you get involved with Nazi spies, and how did you discover that they were operating in Stratford in the first place?"

"It started slowly, in mid-April, with only **nascent** suspicions on my part. Naturally, the case was **vexing** at first, but it's been **gratifying** that my initial suspicions have been **vindicated**. And it was completely **fortuitous** how it evolved. It began with strange lights in an abandoned house on the Housatonic, a house tied up in a **probate** battle. The fact that the house should have been unoccupied fueled my suspicions and led to my investigation. That's when we discovered that it was a den of **fifth columnists** whose chief aim was stealing the plans of the Corsair from the United Aircraft plant. One of the **litigants** in that **probate** battle is now behind bars, along with the rest of the network."

For the next hour, Ellen and Ken answered a multitude of questions from the **inquisitive** reporters, and posed for photographs, both singly and together. It was a heady experience for two high school students who had grown up in Stratford and now found themselves the subject of national press coverage.

~~~~~~~~~~~~~~~

From the moment they walked into Stratford High School on Monday, Ellen and Ken were **besieged** by fellow students and showered with **myriad** congratulations and **compliments**. When Ellen entered her Latin class that morning, she was immediately greeted by the words "*Summa cum laude, Ellen Anderson!*" written boldly across the blackboard. This was followed by a chorus of *Gaudeamus Igatur* (Let us therefore rejoice), led by Mr. DeLeurere:

> *Gaudeamus igitur,*
> *Juvenes dum sumus;*
> *Gaudeamus igitur,*
> *Juvenes dum sumus;*
> *Post icundum iuventutem,*
> *Post molestam senectutem*
> *Nos habebit humus.*
> *Nos habebit humus.*

Miss Satterfield's American history class was given over to a discussion of Ellen and Ken's adventure, with a steady stream of questions from her **awestruck** classmates. Miss Satterfield concluded the discussion with a review of the quotation she had introduced to the class the previous Thursday:

> *Great nations rise and fall. The people go from **bondage** to spiritual truth, to great courage, from courage to liberty, from liberty to **abundance**, from **abundance** to selfishness, from selfishness to **complacency**, from **complacency** to **apathy**, from **apathy** to dependence, from dependence back again to **bondage**.*

"Class, there's nothing **inevitable** about the predictions in that quotation. What we've witnessed this week is why this nation will not **inevitably** fall into **complacency** and **bondage**. You have two classmates who discovered that liberty was endangered and stepped forward to defend it against its enemies. It's not only our soldiers in the field who do the work of preserving liberty, but civilians of **indomitable** spirit who step forward to meet challenges on the home front. Not all are **indolent**. Sometimes, extraordinary challenges summon extraordinary responses from the bravest among us," she explained. "I trust Ellen and Ken's example will be a lesson to us all."

~~~~~~~~~~~~~~~~~

Ellen had little **respite** that week from the media and public attention. When it wasn't local radio stations **rhapsodizing** about her and Ken's exploits, it was neighborhood children knocking at the door and asking for her autograph. Trying her best to remain **stoic** in the face of all this **acclaim** was definitely a challenge. Nevertheless, she made every effort to **jettison** any distractions even remotely **tangential** to her studies.

On Sunday morning, after church, Ellen's father announced that they were going on a little drive, but did not say where. Their destination did not become apparent until, after driving south on Main Street, they had reached the Stratford-Bridgeport Airport and heard a band playing in the distance. Ellen recognized the tune. It was John Philip Sousa's *Semper Fidelis*. As they parked their car in the parking lot and began walking in the direction of the assembled **throng**, Ellen spotted Ken standing on a reviewing platform that was decked out **resplendently** in red, white and blue **buntings**. It was at that moment that she realized what it was all about, and a **surfeit** of **ineffable** emotion swelled up inside her.

As the band played an **encore**, an officer of the Stratford Police Department approached Ellen and escorted her to Ken's side, while her parents joined the assembled **throng** seated in front of the airport's massive hanger. Joining Ellen and Ken on the platform were town manager Bill Shea, Chief Inspector Conrad of the New York City F.B.I. office, Rex Beisel, chief engineer of United Aircraft, Stratford police chief George Stratton, and Mr. Bernard Copley, representing the Roosevelt administration. The pride Ellen felt was almost overwhelming.

Ellen's father had been in on the planning from the beginning. Getting Ellen to the airport at noon was his responsibility. It was a ceremony honoring Stratford's two young heroes. Each of the assembled dignitaries gave **florid** speeches laced with **felicitous** phrases and periodic expressions of **grandiloquence**. Although the event was a bit **grandiose**, the speeches were relatively **succinct**, and the speakers lapsed only occasionally into the kind of **hackneyed** and **trite** phrases typical on such occasions. Ellen was humbled by the experience and sincerely appreciated the **ingenuous** sentiments **extolling** her and Ken's heroics.

From her seat on the platform, Ellen could observe her family and friends sitting in the front row of the audience. Her parents and grandparents, aunts and uncles, cousins and friends, the employees of the E.V. Anderson Company were all there to share the day with her. Ken's parents and, **presumably**, his relatives and friends, were there as well. She also spotted her friends Betsy Dalrymple and Linnea Matthews, as well as Christine Applegate, wearing one of Ellen's dresses, Christine's mother, brother Billy, and **scores** of her high school classmates. She also spotted Abby Wexler, Tommy McCauley, the Muellers, and all of her high school teachers, including Mr. DeLeurere and Miss Satterfield.

After an invocation by Rev. Sellick, pastor of the First Congregational Church, President Roosevelt's representative, Mr. Bernard Copley, stepped up to the microphone and addressed the crowd:

> *Today, we honor two of the finest examples of American and Stratford youth. Their **exemplary** bravery, intelligence, determination, and sense of patriotism at a time of national peril have exposed a significant threat to the cause for which we now fight. Without their **resolute intervention**, agents of the Third Reich would have succeeded in stealing the secrets of the Corsair aircraft which the workers of this city are toiling tirelessly to produce. At this moment in our history, we cannot afford to **equivocate** on matters of national security until our foes have been **vanquished**. Faced with the **pertinacious** and **scurrilous assaults** of our enemies, we must remain **vigilant** in defense of our country. Ellen Anderson and Ken Swenson are two young citizens who, on their own initiative, and with **equanimity**, heeded that call to serve. On behalf of President Franklin*

Delano Roosevelt, and the United States of America, I hereby present to Ellen Anderson and Ken Swenson the Air Force Civilian Award for Valor in recognition of their extraordinary contributions in defense of their country.

Summoning Ellen and Ken to his side, Mr. Copley presented the two with personally inscribed medals and engraved plaques. In response to **solicitous entreaties** from members of the press, and amid handshakes from dozens of grateful Stratford residents, they posed for photographs with Mr. Copley.

As the band struck up another Sousa march, and the formal ceremony concluded, a United States Marine Corps pilot escorted Ken and Ellen to a Vought F4U Corsair parked on the **tarmac**. There, next to the famed fighter aircraft whose plans they had protected from the **espionage** efforts of Nazi agents, they posed for more photographs. Before the event was over, Ellen and Ken had been congratulated by literally hundreds of well-wishers.

Chapter 22

An Evening to Remember

When they got home, Ellen collapsed in her father's Queen Anne wing chair and put her feet up on the matching ottoman. A few minutes later, her mother went into the front hall closet and removed a large box from Caruthers' Department Store in New Haven. Ellen had never known her mother to shop at Caruthers', particularly since she had worked at Howland's in Bridgeport before she was married and continued to give them most of her business.

"What's this? Caruthers? When did you shop at Caruthers', Mother?" Ellen rested the box on her knees and removed the lid. Peeling back the tissue paper inside, she removed an elegant dress and held it up to the light. She immediately realized that it was the very one she had admired in the Caruthers' store window the day she and Ken were in New Haven. It was a combination of midnight blue taffeta and matching velvet, featuring an embroidered bolero jacket over a floor length taffeta skirt, with velvet corselet waistband. Standing in front of the living room mirror, Ellen held it against her body and imagined herself wearing it to the prom. Also in the box was a **luxuriant** pair of silk stockings, an accessory not generally available in wartime.

"I don't believe it. How did you know?" Ellen exclaimed.

"Ken told us about it," Ellen's mother replied. "He said he remembered how you fell in love with it on your trip to New Haven, and filed the information away in his memory bank. You know, Ellen, I think he's a keeper."

~~~~~~~~~~~~~~~

Prom night—June 6, 1942—came before she knew it. And the day was notable for more than the end-of-year formal dance for the Stratford High junior class. The United States had scored an impressive victory over Japan at the tiny Pacific **atoll** of Midway Island. After four consecutive unsuccessful air attacks on Japan's naval **armada**, a fifth bombing raid sank three Japanese aircraft carriers, bringing its total losses to four aircraft carriers, one cruiser, and 332 planes. It was a **devastating** blow to Japan's Pacific ambitions and gave a much-needed boost to American morale.

The prom itself was like a dream come true, and Ellen's first formal dance. Ken went out of his way to decorate his roadster with red, white and blue ribbons for the occasion. When he met Ellen at the Anderson's front door, his eyes lit up. She looked radiant in her stylish taffeta and velvet gown, her hair done up in an elegant braided **coiffeur** he had never seen on her before. The corsage of pink orchids he gave her earned him a kiss on the cheek. Paying his respects to Ellen's parents, the two were off to Quilty's.

Quilty's Colonial Ballroom, occupying the second and third floors of Bridgeport's Bijou Theater building on Fairfield Avenue, had been a local institution since 1909. Dance master and ballroom operator Dan Quilty had taught several generations of Bridgeporters to dance, including Hollywood musical comedy star Eleanor Powell, who had grown up on Barnum Avenue in Stratford. **Navigating** their way up  the wide, steep steps from street level, Ken and Ellen were met by an enthusiastic and sustained round of applause from the members of the junior class who ringed the perimeter of the elegant ballroom. Smartly decorated by members of the prom committee, the ballroom featured a canopy of blue stars accented by patriotic red and white streamers, creating a magical and **ethereal** effect.

Soon, it was time for the Grand March, which Ken and Ellen had been invited to lead. Taking their places at the head of the 128-couple procession, they led off to the strains of Richard Wagner's *Entrance of the Guests at the Wartburg*, from his opera *Tannhauser*, played by Bert Keeling and His Orchestra.

It was an **auspicious** start to a glorious evening. For more than three hours, the class members danced to the music of the younger generation: Benny Goodman, Glenn Miller, Tommy and Jimmy Dorsey, Ozzie Nelson, Kay Kayser,

Tony Pastor, Artie Shaw, Duke Ellington, Sammy Kaye, Jerome Kern and George Gershwin. Swing tunes, waltzes, and fox trots, punctuated by an occasional tango and rumba, echoed throughout the ballroom and to the street below. Ken never let Ellen out of his sight. She felt so comfortable in his arms, and he so comfortable with her in them. They danced together the entire evening.

Finally, as midnight approached, Bert Keeling announced the **penultimate** dance of the evening: Jerome Kern's *The Way You Look Tonight*, after which the couple climbed the stairway to the third floor balcony overlooking the dance floor.

Ellen and Ken were coming of age in an unsettled world. As they gazed down upon their classmates on the dance floor and listened to the strains of the evening's final number—*There'll Be Bluebirds Over the White Cliffs of Dover*—they couldn't help imagining what their futures might hold. But for now, for them, time was suspended. Ken took Ellen's hands in his, then, pulling her close, looked into her eyes and kissed her. She rested her head against his chest and felt a warm glow course through her body. Her mother was right. He was "a keeper."

Glossary

Glossary of SAT Vocabulary Words

A

abase *(v.)* to humiliate, degrade

abate *(v.)* to lessen, to reduce

abdicate *(v.)* to give up a position, usually one of leadership

abduct *(v.)* to kidnap, take by force

aberration *(n.)* something out of the norm

abet/abetting *(v.)* to aid, help, encourage

abhor *(v.)* to hate, detest

abide *(v.)* to put up with; to remain

abject *(adj.)* wretched, pitiful

abjure *(v.)* to reject, to renounce

abnegation *(n.)* denial of comfort to oneself

abort *(v.)* to give up on a half-finished project or effort

abrasions *(n.)* wounds consisting of superficial damage to the skin

abridge *(v.)* to cut down, shorten; *(adj.)* shorten

abrogate *(v.)* to abolish or reject, usually by authority

abscond *(v.)* to sneak away and hide

absolution *(n.)* freedom from blame, guilt, sin

abstain *(v.)* to freely choose not to commit an action

abstemious *(adj.)* eating and drinking sparingly

abstract *(adj.)* conceived apart from matter and from special cases; theoretical

abstruse *(adj.)* hard to comprehend

absurd *(adj.)* unreasonable. nonsensical, foolish

abundance *(n.)* a large amount, more than sufficient, plenty

accede *(v.)* to agree to their request

accelerate *(v.)* to increase in speed; to cause faster or greater activity, development, progress, advancement, etc.

acceleration *(n.)* the rate of change of velocity with respect to time

accentuate *(v.)* to stress, highlight

accessible *(adj.)* obtainable, reachable

acclaim *(n.)* high praise

accolade *(n.)* high praise, special distinction

accommodating *(adj.)* helpful, obliging, polite

accomplices *(n.)* those who knowingly aid another in committing a crime

accord *(n.)* an agreement

accost *(v.)* to confront verbally or physically

accretion *(n.)* slow growth in size or amount

acerbic *(adj.)* biting, bitter in tone or taste

acquiesce *(v.)* to agree without protesting

acquisition *(n.)* something acquired or owned

acquisitive *(adj.)* tending or seeking to acquire and own, often greedily; eager to gain wealth or possessions

acrid *(adj.)* harsh, burning, or biting to the touch, taste or smell

acrimony *(n.)* bitterness, discord

acumen *(n.)* keen insight

acute *(adj.)* sharp, severe; *(adj.)* having keen insight

adage *(n.)* an old saying; a maxim or proverb

adamant *(adj.)* impervious, immovable, unyielding

adept *(adj.)* extremely skilled

adhere *(n.)* to stick to something; *(n.)* to follow devoutly

adjacent *(adj.)* close by; lying near, but not necessarily in direct contact with

adjunct *(n.)* something added to another thing, but not necessarily a part of it; an assistant, often in a military capacity

admonish *(v.)* to caution, criticize, reprove

adorn *(v.)* to decorate

adroit *(adj.)* skillful, dexterous

adulation *(n.)* extreme praise

adversary, ies *(n.)* a person, group, or country one fights against; an enemy

adverse *(adj.)* antagonistic, unfavorable, dangerous

adversity *(n.)* misfortune, hardship, great difficulty or trouble

advocate *(v.)* to argue in favor of something; *(n.)* a person who argues in favor of something

aerial *(adj.)* somehow related to the air

aesthetic *(adj.)* artistic, related to the appreciation of beauty

affable *(adj.)* friendly, amiable

affinity *(n.)* a spontaneous feeling of closeness

afflicted *(v.)* to suffer grievous physical or mental suffering

affluent *(adj.)* rich, wealthy

affront *(n.)* an insult

agents *(n.)* a person or business authorized to act on another's behalf

aggrandize *(v.)* to increase or make greater

aggregate *(n.)* a whole or total*); (v.)* to gather into a mass

aggrieved *(adj.)* distressed, wronged, injured

agile *(adj.)* quick, nimble

agnostic *(adj.)* one who questions the existence of God

agricultural *(adj.)* of or relating to farming

aisle *(n.)* a passageway between rows of seats

alacrity *(n.)* eagerness, speed

alias *(n.)* a false name or identity

allay *(v.)* to soothe, ease

allege/allegedly *(v. or adv.)* to assert, usually without proof

alleviate *(v.)* to relieve, make more bearable

allocate *(v.)* to distribute, set aside

allotted *(adj.)* assigned as a portion, set apart

alluded *(v.)* to refer to indirectly, to mention casually

alluring *(adj.)* highly attractive, tempting, charming

aloof *(adj.)* reserved, distant

altercation *(n.)* a dispute, fight

altruism *(n.)* unselfishly concerned with or interested in the welfare of others

amalgamate *(v.)* to bring together, unite

ambiguous *(adj.)* uncertain, variably interpretable

ambivalent *(adj.)* having opposing feelings

ameliorate *(v.)* to improve

amenable *(adj.)* willing, compliant

amenity *(n.)* an item that increases comfort

amiable *(adj.)* friendly

amicable *(adj.)* friendly

amorous *(adj.)* showing love, particularly sexual

amorphous *(adj.)* without definite shape or type

anachronistic *(adj.)* being out of correct chronological order

analgesic *(n.)* something that reduces pain

analogous *(adj.)* similar to, so that an analogy can be drawn

anarchy *(n.)* a state of society without government or law; political and social disorder due to absence of governmental control

anathema *(n.)* a cursed, detested person

anecdote *(n.)* a short, humorous account

anguish *(n.)* extreme sadness, torment

animated *(adj.)* lively

annex *(v.)* to incorporate territory or space; *(n.)* a room attached to a larger room or space

annul *(v.)* to make void or invalid

anomaly *(n.)* something that does not fit into the normal order

antagonism *(n.)* hostility

antecedent *(n.)* something that came before

antediluvian *(adj.)* ancient; lit. before the biblical flood

anteroom (n.) an outer room that leads to another room and that is often used as a waiting room

anthology *(n.)* a selected collection of writings, songs, etc

antipathy *(n.)* a strong dislike, repugnance

antiquarian (adj.) relating to persons who study or deal in antiques or antiquities

antiquated *(adj.)* old, out of date

anti-Semitic *(adj.)* prejudice against or hostility towards Jews often rooted in hatred of their ethnic background, culture, and/or religion

antiseptic *(adj.)* clean, sterile

antithesis *(n.)* the absolute opposite

anxiety *(n.)* intense uneasiness

apathy *(n.)* lack of feeling or emotion, interest or concern; indifferent

apocryphal *(adj.)* fictitious, false, wrong

appalling *(adj.)* inspiring shock, horror, disgust

appease *(v.)* to calm, satisfy

appraise *(v.)* to assess the worth or value of; to evaluate

apprehend *(v.)* to seize, arrest; *(v.)* to perceive, understand, grasp

approbation *(n.)* praise

aptitude *(n.)* skill, expertise, ability

aquatic *(adj.)* relating to water

arable *(adj.)* suitable for growing crops

arbiter *(n.)* one who can resolve a dispute, make a decision

arbitrary *(adj.)* based on factors that appear random

arbitration *(n.)* the process or act of resolving a dispute

arboreal *(adj.)* of or relating to trees **AT Vocabulary**

arcane *(adj.)* obscure, secret, known only by a few

archaic *(adj.)* of or relating to an earlier period in time, outdated

archetypal *(adj.)* the most representative or typical example of something

ardor *(n.)* extreme vigor, energy, enthusiasm

arid *(adj.)* excessively dry

armada *(n.)* a fleet of warships

arrogate *(v.)* to take without justification

artifact *(n.)* a remaining piece from an extinct culture or place

artisan *(n.)* a craftsman

ascendancy *(n.)* state of being in the ascendant; governing or controlling influence; domination

ascertain *(v.)* to perceive, learn

ascetic *(adj.)* practicing restraint as a means of self-discipline, usually religious

ascribe *(v.)* to assign, credit, attribute to

aspersion *(n.)* a curse, expression of ill-will

aspire *(v.)* to long for, aim toward

assail *(v.)* to attack

assault *(n.)* an attack, an unlawful physical attack upon another with or without a case of battery

assess *(v.)* to evaluate

assets *(n.)* the entire property of a person, association, corporation

assiduous *(adj.)* hard-working, diligent

assuage *(v.)* to ease, pacify

astute *(adj.)* very clever, crafty

asylum *(n.)* a place of refuge, protection, a sanctuary; *(n.)* an institution in which the insane are kept

atoll *(n.)* a ring-shaped coral reef or a string of closely spaced small coral islands, enclosing or nearly enclosing a shallow lagoon

atrophy *(v.)* to wither away, decay

attain *(v.)* to achieve, arrive at

attribute *(v.)* to credit, assign; *(n.)* a facet or trait

atypical *(adj.)* not typical, unusual

audacious *(adj.)* excessively bold

audible *(adj.)* able to be heard

augment *(v.)* to add to, expand

auspicious *(adj.)* favorable, indicative of good things

austere *(adj.)* very bare, bleak

authoritarian *(adj.)* of, relating to, or favoring a concentration of power in a leader or an elite not constitutionally responsible to the people; dictatorial

avarice *(n.)* excessive greed

avenge *(v.)* to seek revenge

aversion *(n.)* a particular dislike for something

avid *(adj.)* marked by active interest and enthusiasm

avuncular *(adj.)* suggestive of an uncle, especially in kindliness or geniality

awestruck *(v.)* impressed or struck with awe.

B

balk *(v.)* to stop, block abruptly

ballad *(n.)* a poem or song narrating a story in short stanzas, often of folk origin

banal *(adj.)* dull, commonplace

bane *(n.)* a burden

banter *(n.)* playfully teasing language, good-natured raillery

bard *(n.)* a poet, often a singer as well

bashful *(adj.)* shy, excessively timid

battery *(n.)* a device that supplies power *(n.)* assault, beating

beckon *(v.)* to signal, summon or direct; to lure

beguile *(v.)* to charm or divert; or to trick, deceive

behemoth *(n.)* something of tremendous power or size

belligerent *(adj.)* inclined or eager to fight; hostile or aggressive, including in war; *(n.)* a person or country engaged in fighting or war

benediction *(n.)* a short invocation for divine help, blessing and guidance, usually at the end of worship service

beneficiary *(n.)* a person who receives a benefit, especially an inheritance

benevolent *(adj.)* marked by goodness or doing good

benign *(adj.)* favorable, not threatening, mild

bequeath *(v.)* to pass on, give

berate *(v.)* to scold vehemently

bereft *(adj.)* devoid of, without

beseech *(v.)* to beg, plead, implore

besiege *(v.)* to crowd around; hem in

bias *(n.)* a tendency, inclination, prejudice

bibliophile *(n.)* a lover of books, a book collector

bilk *(v.)* cheat, defraud

blandish *(v.)* to coax by using flattery

blemish *(n.)* an imperfection, flaw

blight *(n.)* a plague, disease; *(n.)* something that destroys hope

boisterous *(adj.)* loud and full of energy

bombastic *(adj.)* excessively confident, pompous

boon *(n.)* a gift or blessing

bondage *(n.)* the state of one who is bound as a slave or serf

bourgeoisie *(n.)* the middle- or propertied class, capitalist

brackish *(adj.)* slightly salt; having a salty or briny flavor

brazen *(adj.)* excessively bold

breach *(n.)* a break or opening in something; a failure to do what is required by a law an agreement or a duty

brusque *(adj.)* short, abrupt, dismissive

brutes *(n.)* brutal, insensitive, or crude persons

buffet *(v.)* to strike with force; *(n.)* an arrangement of food set out on a table

buntings *(n.)* a coarse, open fabric of worsted used for flags, signals, etc.; flags

burgeoning *(adj.)* growing or developing quickly

burnish *(v.)* to polish, shine

buttress *(v.)* to support, hold up; *(n.)* something that offers support

ℂ

cabal *(n.)* a conspiratorial group of plotters or intriguers; a group of persons involved in a plot, such as to overthrow a government

cacophony *(n.)* tremendous noise, disharmonious sound

cadence *(n.)* a rhythm, progression of sound

cajole *(v.)* to urge, coax

calamity *(n.)* an event with disastrous consequences

calibrate *(v.)* to set, standardize

calisthenics *(n.)* exercises for the muscles for the purpose of improving health, strength, and grace of form and movement

callous *(adj.)* harsh, cold, unfeeling

calumny *(n.)* an attempt to spoil someone else's reputation by spreading lies

camouflage *(n.)* the art of disguising things to deceive the enemy, deception

camaraderie *(n.)* brotherhood, jovial unity

candor *(n.)* honesty, frankness

canny *(adj.)* shrewd, careful

canvas *(n.)* a piece of cloth on which an artist paints; *(v.)* to cover, inspect

capacious *(adj.)* very spacious

capitulate *(v.)* to surrender, to give up, give in

capricious *(adj.)* subject to whim, fickle

captivate *(v.)* to get the attention of, hold

carouse *(v.)* to party, celebrate

carp *(v.)* to annoy, pester

catalog *(v.)* to list, enter into a list; *(n.)* a list or collection

catalyze *(v.)* to charge, inspire

catastrophic *(adj.)* involving or pertaining to a great disaster, terrible misfortune or total failure

caucus *(n.)* a meeting usually held by people working toward the same goal

caustic *(adj.)* bitter, biting, acidic

cavernous *(adj.)* deep-set; containing caverns

cavort *(v.)* to leap about, behave boisterously

cease and desist *(v.)* an order or request to halt an activity (cease) and not to take it up again later (desist)

censorship *(n.)* the act suppressing speech or other communication which may be considered objectionable, harmful, sensitive, or inconvenient

censure *(n.)* harsh criticism; *(v.)* to rebuke formally

cerebral *(adj.)* related to the intellect

chafe *(v.)* to irritate or annoy; to wear or abrade by rubbing

chancery *(n.)* the proceedings and practice of a court of chancery; equity

chaos *(n.)* absolute disorder

chastise *(v.)* to criticize severely

cherish *(v.)* to feel or show affection toward something

chide *(v.)* to voice disapproval

choreography *(n.)* the arrangement of dances

chronicle *(n.)* a written history; *(v.)* to write a history

chronological *(adj.)* arranged in order of time

circuitous *(adj.)* roundabout, indirect

circumlocution *(n.)* indirect and wordy language

circumscribed *(adj.)* marked off, bounded

circumspect *(adj.)* cautious

circumvent *(v.)* to get around

clairvoyant *(adj.)* able to perceive things that normal people cannot

clamoring *(adj.)* insist loudly

clandestine *(adj.)* secret, not disclosed

claustrophobic *(adj.)* afraid of being in a small or enclosed space

clemency *(n.)* mercy, forgiveness

clergy *(n.)* members of Christian holy orders

clientele *(n.)* customers or patrons collectively

clique *(n.)* a small set or group , usually one that is snobbishly exclusive

cloying *(adj.)* sickeningly sweet

coagulate *(v.)* to thicken, clot

coalesce *(v.)* to fuse into a whole

cobbler *(n.)* a person who makes or repairs shoes

codger *(n.)* an odd or peculiar person,

coerce *(v.)* to make somebody do something by force or threat

cogent *(adj.)* intellectually convincing

cogitations *(n.)* concerted thought or reflection; meditation; contemplation

cognitive *(adj.)* knowing, conscious

cognizant *(adj.)* aware, mindful

coherent *(adj.)* logically consistent, intelligible

coiffure *(n.)* a hairstyle, typically an elaborate one for a special occasion

coincidentally *(adv.)* characterized the occurrence of two or more events at one time, apparently by mere change

collateral *(adj.)* secondary; *(n.)* security for a debt

collectivism *(n.)* a political or economic theory advocating collective control especially over production and distribution; emphasis on collective rather than individual action or identity

collectivization *(n.)* the forced consolidation of privately held farms into group enterprises in a failed attempt to boost agricultural production, such as in the former Soviet Union

colloquial *(adj.)* characteristic of informal conversation

collusion *(n.)* secret agreement, conspiracy

colossus *(n.)* a gigantic statue or thing

combustion *(n.)* the act or process of burning

comeuppance *(n.)* a deserved rebuke or penalty, usually unpleasant

commendation *(n.)* a notice of approval or recognition

commensurate *(adj.)* corresponding in size or amount

commodious *(adj.)* roomy

communism *(n.)* a theory or system of social organization in which all property is held in common or by the state

communist *(adj.)* a member of a Marxist-Leninist party; a supporter of such a party or movement; a radical viewed as a subversive or revolutionary

compelling *(adj.)* forceful, demanding attention

compensate *(v.)* to make an appropriate payment for something

compile *(v.)* to gather from different sources and put together in an orderly form; to organize

complacency *(n.)* self-satisfied ignorance of danger

complement *(v.)* to complete, make perfect

compliant *(adj.)* ready to adapt oneself to another's wishes

complicit *(adj.)* being an accomplice in a wrongful act

compliment *(n.)* an expression of esteem or approval

component *(n.)* a constituent part; element; ingredient

compound *(v.)* to combine parts; *(n.)* a combination of different parts; *(n.)* a walled area containing a group of buildings

comprehensive *(adj.)* including everything, complete

compress *(v.)* to apply pressure, squeeze together

compunction *(n.)* distress caused by feeling guilty

concede *(v.)* yield; admit; accept

conciliatory *(adj.)* friendly, agreeable

concise *(adj.)* brief and direct in expression

concoct *(v.)* to fabricate, make up

concomitant *(adj.)* accompanying in a subordinate fashion

concord *(n.)* harmonious agreement

condolence *(n.)* an expression of sympathy in sorrow

condone *(v.)* to pardon, deliberately overlook

conduit *(n.)* a pipe or channel through which something passes

confection *(n.)* a sweet, fancy food

confidant *(n.)* a person entrusted with secrets

conflagration *(n.)* great fire

confluence *(n.)* a gathering together

conformist *(n.)* one who behaves the same as others

confound *(v.)* to frustrate, confuse

confronted *(v.)* to come up against, to come face to face with, especially with defiance or hostility

congeal *(v.)* to thicken into a solid

congenial *(adj.)* pleasantly agreeable

congregants *(n.)* members of a congregation

congregation *(n.)* a gathering of people, especially for religious services

congruity *(n.)* the quality of being in agreement

conjugations *(n.)* the regular arrangement of the forms of the verb in the various voices

conjured *(v.)* to affect or influence as if by or spell

connive *(v.)* to plot, scheme

conscientious *(adj.)* according to conscience, scrupulous, showing thought and care

consecrate *(v.)* to dedicate something to a holy purpose

consensus *(n.)* a general agreement or understanding

consign *(v.)* to give something over to another's care

consolation *(n.)* an act of comforting

console *(n.)* a floor model radio cabinet; *(v.)* to comfort, to alleviate grief or sorrow

consonant *(adj.)* in harmony

conspicuous *(adj.)* obvious, easy to see

conspiracy *(n.)* a planning and acting together secretly, esp. for an unlawful or harmful purpose, such as murder or treason

constabulary *(n.)* the police force of a particular area; an armed police force organized on military lines but distinct from the regular army

constituent *(n.)* an essential part

constrain *(v.)* to forcibly restrict

construe *(v.)* to interpret

consummate *(v.)* to complete a deal; to bring to completion or perfection

consumption *(n.)* the act of consuming

contemplate *(v.)* observe thoughtfully, reflect upon

contemporaneous *(adj.)* existing during the same time

contentious *(adj.)* having a tendency to quarrel or dispute

context *(n.)* the words that are used with a certain word or phrase and that help to explain its meaning

continuum *(n.)* a coherent whole characterized as a collection, sequence, or progression of values or elements varying by minute degrees

contradiction *(n.)* a logical incompatibility between two or more propositions; assertion of the contrary or opposite; denial, inconsistency

contravene *(v.)* to contradict, oppose, violate

contrite *(adj.)* penitent, eager to be forgiven

contusion *(n.)* bruise, injury, where the skin is not broken

conundrum *(n.)* puzzle, problem

convene *(v.)* to call together

convention *(n.)* an assembly of people; *(n.)* a rule, custom

converge *(v.)* to move toward one point and join together; to come together and meet

convivial *(adj.)* characterized by feasting, drinking, merriment

convoluted *(adj.)* intricate, complicated

copious *(adj.)* profuse, abundant

cordial *(adj.)* warm, affectionate

cordoned *(tr. v.)* to form a cordon around (an area) to prevent movement in or out

coronation *(n.)* the act of crowning

corpulent *(adj.)* extreme fatness

corroborate *(v.)* to support with evidence

corrosive *(adj.)* having the tendency to erode or eat away

cosmopolitan *(adj.)* sophisticated, worldly

countenance *(n.)* look, expression

counteract *(v.)* to neutralize, make ineffective

coup *(n.)* a brilliant, unexpected act; *(n.)* the overthrow of a government and assumption of authority

covet *(v.)* to desire enviously

covert *(adj.)* secretly engaged in

credulity *(n.)* readiness to believe

crescendo *(n.)* a steady increase in intensity or volume

criteria *(n.)* standards by which something is judged

cryptology *(n.)* science concerned with data communication and storage in secure and usually secret form, or secret codes

culinary *(adj.)* of or relating to the kitchen or cookery

culmination *(n.)* the climax toward which something progresses

culpable *(adj.)* deserving blame

cultivate *(v.)* to nurture, improve, refine

cumulative *(adj.)* increasing, building upon itself

cunning *(adj.)* sly, clever at being deceitful

cupidity *(n.)* greed, strong desire

cursory *(adj.)* brief to the point of being superficial

curt *(adj.)* abruptly and rudely short

curtail *(v.)* to lessen, reduce

Ⓓ

dappled *(adj.)* having spots of a different shade, tone, or color from the background; mottled

dastardly *(adj.)* cowardly and malicious; base.

daunting *(adj.)* intimidating, causing one to lose courage

davenport *(n.)* a large sofa, especially a formal one, often convertible into a bed

dearth *(n.)* a lack, scarcity

debacle *(n.)* a disastrous failure, disruption

debase *(v.)* to lower the quality or esteem of something

debauchery *(n.)* extreme indulgence in sensuality; bad or immoral behavior

debunk *(v.)* to expose the falseness of something

deceased *(adj.)* dead, no longer living

deception *(n.)* the act of deceiving or tricking, duplicity

deciphering *(v.)* to change from code into ordinary language, to translate

declensions *(n.)* in certain languages, the inflection of nouns, pronouns, and adjectives in categories such as case, number, and gender

decorum *(n.)* the conventions of polite behavior that shows respect and good manners; literary and dramatic propriety

decried *(v.)* condemned openly; expressing a strong disapproval of

deface *(v.)* to ruin or injure something's appearance

defamatory *(adj.)* harmful toward another's reputation

defer *(v.)* to postpone something; to yield to another's wisdom

deference *(n.)* courteous regard for people's feelings

deferential *(adj.)* showing respect for another's authority

defile *(v.)* to make unclean, impure

deft *(adj.)* skillful, capable

defunct *(adj.)* no longer used or existing

dejectedly *(adv.)* being in low spirits; depressed

delegate *(v.)* to hand over responsibility for something

deleterious *(adj.)* harmful

deliberate *(adj.)* intentional, reflecting careful consideration

deliberations *(n.)* discussion and consideration of all sides of an issue: careful consideration before decision

delineate *(v.)* to describe, outline, shed light on

demagogue *(n.)* a leader who employs emotion to appeals to a people's prejudices

demarcation *(n.)* the marking of boundaries or categories

demean *(v.)* to lower the status or stature of something

demeanor *(n.)* conduct, behavior

demure *(adj.)* quiet, modest, reserved

denigrate *(v.)* to belittle, diminish the opinion of

denounce *(v.)* to criticize publicly

deplore *(v.)* to feel or express sorrow, disapproval

deport *(v.)* to expel a person or group of people from a place or country

deposition *(n.)* a testimony generally taken under oath; a formal statement that is made before a trial by a witness who will not be present at the trial

depravity *(n.)* wickedness

deprecate *(v.)* to belittle, depreciate

derelict *(adj.)* abandoned, run-down

deride *(v.)* to laugh at mockingly, scorn

derivative *(adj.)* taken directly from a source, unoriginal

desecrate *(v.)* to violate the sacredness of a thing or place

desiccated *(adj.)* dried up, dehydrated

desolate *(adj.)* deserted, dreary, lifeless

despicable *(adj.)* deserving to be despised; contemptible

despondent *(adj.)* feeling depressed, discouraged, hopeless

despot *(n.)* one who has total power and rules brutally

destitute *(adj.)* impoverished, utterly lacking

deter *(v.)* to discourage, prevent from doing

detonator *(n.)* a device, such as a fuse or percussion cap, used to set off an explosive charge

devastate *(v.)* to bring to ruin or desolation by violent action; to reduce to chaos and disorder, as by war or natural disaster

devious *(adj.)* not straightforward, deceitful

devoid *(adj.)* empty, void, or destitute; lacking

dialect *(n.)* a variation of a language

diaphanous *(adj.)* light, airy, transparent

dictator *(n.)* a ruler who assumes sole and absolute power (sometimes but not always with military control

diction *(n.)* choice of words especially with regard to correctness, clearness, or effectiveness; vocal expression, enunciation

didactic *(adj.)* intended to instruct; *(adj.)* overly moralistic

diffident *(adj.)* shy, quiet, modest

diffuse *(v.)* to scatter, thin out, break up; *(adj.)* not concentrated, scattered, disorganized

dilapidated *(adj.)* falling to pieces, broken down, in disrepair

dilatory *(adj.)* tending to delay, causing delay

dilemma *(n.)* a situation in which none must choose between equally unpleasant or unfavorable options

diligence *(n.)* constant and earnest effort to accomplish what is undertaken; persistent exertion of body or mind

diligent *(adj.)* showing care in doing one's work

diminutive *(adj.)* small or miniature

din *(n.)* continuous, loud or annoying sound or uproar

dire *(adj.)* causing or involving great fear or suffering; dreadful; terrible

directive *(n.)* an order or instruction, especially from an authority

dirge *(n.)* a mournful song, especially for a funeral

disaffected *(adj.)* rebellious, resentful of authority

disavow *(v.)* to deny knowledge of or responsibility for

discern *(v.)* to perceive, detect

disclose *(v.)* to reveal, make public

discomfit *(v.)* to thwart, baffle

discordant *(adj.)* not agreeing, not in harmony with

discourse *(n.)* conversation, formal or orderly speech

discreet *(adj.)* cautious in one's speech or actions, tactful

discrepancy *(n.)* difference, failure of things to correspond

discretion *(n.)* the quality of being reserved in speech or action; good judgment

disdain *(v.)* to scorn, hold in low esteem; *(n.)* scorn, low esteem

disembark *(v.)* to go ashore from a ship; to leave an aircraft or other vehicle

disgruntled *(adj.)* upset, not content

disheartened *(adj.)* feeling a loss of spirit or morale

disheveled *(adj.)* hanging loosely or in disorder; unkempt

disparage *(v.)* to criticize or speak ill of

disparate *(adj.)* sharply differing, containing sharply contrasting elements

dispatch *(v.)* to send off to accomplish a duty

dispel *(v.)* to drive away, scatter, dismiss

disperse *(v.)* to scatter, cause to scatter

dispute *(n.)* a conflict or controversy; a conflict of claims or rights

disrepute *(n.)* a state of being held in low regard

disseminate *(v.)* to spread widely

dissent *(v.)* to disagree; *(n.)* the act of disagreeing

dissipate *(v.)* to disappear, cause to disappear; *(v.)* to waste

dissonance *(n.)* lack of harmony or consistency

dissuade *(v.)* to persuade someone not to do something

distend *(v.)* to swell out

distress *(n.)* anxiety or mental suffering

dither *(v.)* to be indecisive

divine *(adj.)* godly, exceedingly wonderful

divisive *(adj.)* causing dissent, discord

divulge *(v.)* to reveal something secret

docile *(adj.)* easily managed or handled

doctorate *(n.)* the highest degree awarded by a university

doctrine *(n.)* a theory or set of principles actively taught and promoted by those who believe it

documentation *(n.)* the provision of documents or published information as proof or evidence

dogged *(adj.)* refusing to give up despite difficulties

dogmatic *(adj.)* aggressively and arrogantly certain about unproved principles

domestic *(adj.)* pertaining to the home, the household, or the family; of, relating to, or originating within a country and especially one's own country

domination *(n.)* supremacy or preeminence over another; exercise of mastery or ruling power

dormant *(adj.)* sleeping, temporarily inactive

dour *(adj.)* stern, joyless

dry goods *(n.)* textile fabrics and related articles of trade, in distinction from groceries, hardware, etc.

dubious *(adj.)* doubtful, of uncertain quality

dumbfounded *(v.)* as if struck dumb with astonishment and surprise

duress *(n.)* hardship, threat

dynamic *(adj.)* actively changing

E

ebullient *(adj.)* extremely lively, enthusiastic

eccentric (adj.) deviating from conventional or accepted usage or conduct especially in odd or whimsical ways

eclectic *(adj.)* consisting of a diverse variety of elements

ecstatic *(adj.)* intensely and overpoweringly happy

edict *(n.)* an order, decree

edifice *(n.)* building, especially a large or elaborate on

edifying *(adj.)* morally, spiritually or educationally instructive

eerily *(adv.)* inspiring inexplicable fear, dread, or uneasiness; frightening

efface *(v.)* to wipe out, obliterate, rub away

effectuate *(v.)* to bring about, to cause to happen; effect; accomplish

effervescence *(n.)* liveliness, enthusiasm; bubbling, sparkling

effrontery *(n.)* impudence, nerve, insolence

effulgent *(adj.)* radiant, splendorous

egotistical *(adj.)* full of an exaggerated sense of self-importance; conceited

egregious *(adj.)* extremely bad

egress *(n.)* a place or means of going out

elaborate *(adj.)* complex, detailed, intricate

elegant *(adj.)* tasteful in dress, style, or design; dignified and graceful in appearance, behavior, etc.

elegy *(n.)* a speech given in honor of a dead person

elicit *(v.)* to bring forth, draw out, evoke

elite (n.) the choice or best part of a body or class of persons

eloquent *(adj.)* expressive, articulate, moving

elucidate *(v.)* to clarify, explain

elude *(v.)* to evade, escape

emaciated *(adj.)* very thin, enfeebled looking

emanate *(v.)* to come or send forth, as from a source

embellish *(v.)* to decorate, adorn; *(v.)* to add details to, enhance

embezzle *(v.)* to steal money by falsifying records

emend *(v.)* to correct or revise a written text

eminent *(adj.)* distinguished, prominent, famous; *(adj.)* conspicuous

emollient *(adj.)* soothing

emote *(v.)* to express emotion

empathy *(n.)* sensitivity to another's feelings as if they were one's own

empirical *(adj.)* based on observation or experience; *(adj.)* capable of being proved or disproved by experiment

emulate *(v.)* to imitate

enamor *(v.)* to fill with love, fascinate, usually used in passive form followed by "of" or "with"

encore *(n.)* the audience's demand for a repeat performance; also the artist's performance in response to that demand

encumber *(v.)* to weigh down, burden

encyclopedic *(adj.)* relating to all branches of knowledge

endeavor *(v.)* to make a serious attempt or effort

endorse *(v.)* to support, to give one's approval of

enervate *(v.)* to weaken, exhaust

enfranchise *(v.)* to grant the vote to

engender *(v.)* to bring about, create, generate

engrossed *(adj.)* to have absorbed the complete attention or interest of, fascinated

enigmatic *(adj.)* mystifying, cryptic

enlighten *(v.)* to make the truth or nature of something clear; to free from ignorance or prejudice; to educate

enmity *(n.)* ill will, hatred, hostility

ennui *(n.)* boredom, weariness

ensued *(v.)* to follow in order, to come afterward

entail *(v.)* to include as a necessary step

enthrall *(v.)* to charm, hold spellbound

entreaties *(n.)* earnest or urgent request; appeal for help; plural of entreaty

enumerate *(v.)* to list one after another, court off, name individually

ephemeral *(adj.)* short-lived, fleeting

epic *(adj.)* significant, consequential; pertaining to or having the qualities of a long, poem, novel or play, usually written in a dignified or elevated style, celebrating heroes and heroic deeds

epistolary *(adj.)* relating to or contained in letters

epitome *(n.)* a perfect example, embodiment

equanimity *(n.)* composure

equivocate *(v.)* evade, mislead

eradicate *(tr. v.)* to get rid of as if by tearing up by the roots

erratic *(adj.)* not regular or consistent, odd or peculiar

erudite *(adj.)* learned

eschew *(v.)* to shun, avoid

eschatological *(adj.)* having to do with any system of doctrines concerning last, or final, matters, as death, the Judgment, the future state, etc.

esoteric *(adj.)* understood by only a select few, profound

espionage *(n.)* the practice of spying on others, the systematic use of spies by a government to discover secrets of other nations

espouse *(v.)* to take up as a cause, support

essence *(n.)* the basic, real, and invariable nature of a thing or its significant individual feature or features

estimable *(adj.)* deserving of esteem; admirable

ethereal *(adj.)* heavenly, exceptionally delicate or refined

ethos *(n.)* the distinguishing character, sentiment, moral nature, or guiding beliefs of a person, group, or institution

etymology *(n.)* the history of words, their origin and development

euphoria *(n.)* a feeling of great happiness, elation, well-being

evanescent *(adj.)* fleeting, momentary

evasive *(adj.)* meaning to evade, not forthright, indirect, intentionally vague

evince *(v.)* to show, reveal

exacerbate *(v.)* to make more violent, intense

exalt *(v.)* to glorify, praise

exasperate *(v.)* to irritate, irk

excavate *(v.)* to dig out of the ground and remove

exceptional *(adj.)* extraordinary, outstanding

excise taxes *(n.)* an internal tax levied on the manufacture, sale, or consumption of a commodity; any of various taxes on privileges often assessed in the form of a license or fee

exclusive *(adj.)* admitting only certain people as friends, associates, or members, a select group

exculpate *(v.)* to free from guilt or blame, exonerate

excursion *(n.)* a trip or outing

execrable *(adj.)* loathsome, detestable

exemplary *(adj.)* worthy to serve as a model

exert *(v.)* to put forth or bring to bear, to bring pressure

exhort *(v.)* to urge, prod, spur

exhilaration *(n.)* the feeling or the state of being exhilarated, joyous, animated

exonerate *(v.)* to free from guilt or blame, exculpate

exorbitant *(adj.)* excessive

exotic *(adj.)* unfamiliar, strikingly different, from faraway places of the world, alien

expanse *(n.)* a wide and open space

expatriate *(n.)* a person temporarily or permanently residing in a country and culture other than that of the person's upbringing

expedient *(adj.)* advisable, advantageous, serving one's self-interest

expertise *(n.)* specialized skill or knowledge

expiate *(v.)* to make amends for, atone

explication *(n.)* the act of explicating; an explanation; interpretation

explicit *(adj.)* clearly defined, definite, precise

exploit *(v.)* to use productively or to greatest advantage; *(n.)* deed, act; especially a notable or heroic act

exposé *(n.)* a formal statement of facts; an exposure of something discreditable

expound *(v.)* to explain by giving detail, to express a point of view

expunge *(v.)* to obliterate, eradicate

expurgate *(v.)* to remove offensive or incorrect parts, usually of a book

expurgated *(adj.)* to amend by removing words, passages, etc., deemed offensive or objectionable

extant *(adj.)* existing, not destroyed or lost

extol *(v.)* to praise, revere

extract *(v.)* to remove with effort, to obtain despite resistance

extraction *(n.)* descent or lineage

extracurricular *(adj.)* not part of the regular course of study of a school or college

extraneous *(adj.)* irrelevant, extra, not necessary

extravagant *(adj.)* excessive, immoderate, extremely wasteful

extricate *(v.)* to disentangle; to free or remove from an entanglement or difficulty

exult *(v.)* to rejoice

F

fabricate *(v.)* to make up, invent

façade *(n.)* the wall of a building; a deceptive appearance or attitude

facetious *(adj.)* meant to be funny or playfully disrespectful

facile *(adj.)* easy, requiring little effort; *(adj.)* superficial, achieved with minimal thought or care, insincere

facilitate *(v.)* to make easier, to help cause

faculties *(n.)* powers or capabilities of the mind or body, either natural or acquired

fallacious *(adj.)* incorrect, misleading

fanatical *(adj.)* excessively enthusiastic or devoted

fascism *(n.)* a governmental system where all political and economic power is centralized in the state and no dissent is tolerated

fascist *(n.)* a form of radical left-wing authoritarian nationalism that came to prominence in early 20th-century Europe

fastidious *(adj.)* meticulous, demanding, having high and often unattainable or unreachable standards

fatherland *(n.)* the nation of one's "fathers", "forefathers" or "patriarchs." It can be viewed as a nationalist concept, insofar as it relates to nations

fathom *(v.)* to understand, comprehend

fatuous *(adj.)* silly, foolish

fecund *(adj.)* fruitful, fertile

federal *(adj.)* pertaining to, or of the nature of, a union of states under a central government; pertaining to such a central government

federalism *(n.)* a system of the government in which sovereignty is constitutionally divided between a central governing authority and constituent political units (like states or provinces)

feign *(v.)* pretend, fake, make believe

felicitous *(adj.)* well suited, apt; *(adj.)* delightful, pleasing

feral *(adj.)* wild, savage

fertile *(adj.)* productive, able to produce offspring, seeds, fruit, etc.

fervent *(adj.)* ardent, passionate

festooned *(adj.)* decorated with strings or chains of flowers, foliage, ribbon, etc.

fetid *(adj.)* having a foul odor

fetter *(v.)* to chain, restrain; also *(n.)* a chain or restraint

fiasco *(n.)* a total and ignominious failure

fickle *(adj.)* shifting in character, inconstant

fidelity *(n.)* loyalty, devotion

fiduciary *(n.)* a person who is under an obligation to act in another's interest to the exclusion of the fiduciary's own interest, a relationship based on faith

figurative *(adj.)* symbolic

filigree *(n.)* an intricate, delicate, or fanciful ornamentation

finagle *(v.)* to trick, swindle, or cheat; to get or achieve something by guile, trickery, or manipulation

firmament *(n.)* the expanse of the sky; heavens

fiscal *(adj.)* of or relating to taxation, public revenues, or public debt; of or relating to financial matters

flabbergasted *(adj.)* astounded

flaccid *(adj.)* limp, not firm or strong

flagrant *(adj.)* offensive, egregious

flirtatious *(adj.)* feeling or showing a sexual attraction for someone that is usually not meant to be taken seriously

florid *(adj.)* flowery, ornate

flout *(v.)* to disregard or disobey openly

foil *(v.)* to thwart, frustrate, defeat

folio *(n.)* a sheet of paper folded once to make two leaves, or four pages, of a book or manuscript; a volume having pages of the largest size, formerly made from such a sheet

foment *(v.)* to promote the growth or development of

foolhardy *(adj.)* bold in a foolish and reckless manner

forage *(v.)* to graze, rummage for food

forbearance *(n.)* patience, restraint, toleration

forbidding *(adj.)* grim, sinister, menacing

foreclose *(v.)* to hinder or prevent

forestall *(v.)* to prevent, thwart, delay

forgery *(n.)* the act or legal offense of imitating or counterfeiting documents, signatures, works of art, etc. to deceive

forlorn *(adj.)* lonely, abandoned, hopeless

formidable *(adj.)* inspiring fear, dread or amazement; awesome

forsake *(v.)* to give up, renounce

forthright *(adj.)* going straight to the point without hesitation

fortitude *(n.)* strength, guts

fortuitous *(adj.)* happening by chance, often lucky or fortunate

forum *(n.)* a medium for lecture or discussion

foster *(v.)* to stimulate, promote, encourage

fractious *(adj.)* troublesome or irritable

fraught *(adj.)* filled or accompanied with

free market *(n.)* economic activity governed by the laws of supply and demand, not restrained by government interference, regulation or subsidy.

frenetic *(adj.)* frenzied, hectic, frantic

frivolous *(adj.)* of little importance, trifling

frugal *(adj.)* thrifty, economical

fruitless *(adj.)* unsuccessful, useless, producing nothing

full bore *(adv.)* with maximum effort or speed

fumigating *(v.)* to completely fill an area with gaseous pesticides to suffocate or poison the pests within

furtive *(adj.)* secretive, sly
fuselage *(n.)* the framework of the body of an airplane
futile *(adj.)* of no use, ineffective, pointless

G

gallivanting *(v.)* to travel around for pleasure; to travel around with no purpose except enjoyment
galvanize *(v.)* to rouse to action, excite
garish *(adj.)* gaudy, in bad taste
garrulous *(adj.)* talkative, wordy
gauntlet *(n.)* an open challenge (as to combat); a glove worn with medieval armor
genial *(adj.)* friendly, affable
genocidal *(adj.)* characterized by the deliberate and systematic destruction, in whole or in part, of an ethnic, racial, religious, or national group
genre *(n.)* genus, sort, kind, style
genteel *(adj.)* elegant, courteous, refined
girth *(n.)* a measure around something, esp. a person's waist, circumference
glean *(v.)* to gather information or material bit by bit
glum *(adj.)* gloomy, moody, dejected
gluttony *(n.)* overindulgence in food or drink
goad *(v.)* to urge, spur, incite to action
gourmand *(n.)* someone fond of eating and drinking
graffiti *(n.)* unauthorized writing or drawing on a public surface
gramophone *(n.)* a phonograph, device that was most commonly used for playing sound recordings
grandeur *(n.)* magnificence, splendor
grandiloquence *(n.)* lofty, pompous language
grandiose *(adj.)* on a magnificent or exaggerated scale
grapple *(v.)* to engage in a struggle at close quarters, wrestle, vie
gratify *(v.)* to please or satisfy; to give what is desired to; indulge
gratuitous *(adj.)* uncalled for, unwarranted
gregarious *(adj.)* drawn to the company of others, sociable
grievous *(adj.)* injurious, hurtful; serious or grave in nature
grisly *(adj.)* inspiring horror or intense fear, disgust or distaste
guile *(n.)* deceitful, cunning, sly behavior

H

hackneyed *(adj.)* unoriginal, trite
hallowed *(adj.)* revered, consecrated
hapless *(adj.)* unlucky
harangue *(n.)* a ranting speech; *(v.)* to give such a speech
hardy *(adj.)* robust, capable of surviving through adverse conditions
harrowing *(adj.)* greatly distressing, vexing
haughty *(adj.)* disdainfully proud

hegemony *(n.)* domination over others

heinous *(adj.)* shockingly wicked, repugnant

heterogeneous *(adj.)* varied, diverse in character

hiatus *(n.)* a break or gap in duration or continuity

hibernation *(n.)* passing the winter in a sleeping or inactive condition

hierarchy *(n.)* a system with ranked groups, usually according to social, economic, or professional status

hoax *(n.)* a trick or fraud, esp. one meant as a practical joke

horrific *(adj.)* causing horror, awful

hubristic *(adj.)* exhibiting excessive pride or arrogance

hydraulic *(adj.)* operated by or employing water or some other liquid

hyperbolic *(adj.)* having the nature of hyperbole; exaggerated

hyperventilating *(v.)* breathing abnormally fast or deeply, usually from excitement or anxiety

hypocrisy *(n.)* pretending to believe what one does not believe

hypothetical *(adj.)* supposed or assumed true, but unproven

I

iconoclast *(n.)* one who attacks common beliefs or institutions

ideology *(n.)* a body of doctrine, myth and symbols of a social movement, institution, or political philosophy

idiosyncratic *(adj.)* peculiar to one person; highly individualized

idolatrous *(adj.)* excessively worshipping one object or person

ignominious *(adj.)* humiliating, disgracing

illicit *(adj.)* forbidden, not permitted

immerse *(v.)* to absorb, deeply involve, engross

imminent *(adj.)* about to happen, impending

immutable *(adj.)* not changeable

impassive *(adj.)* stoic, not susceptible to suffering

impeccable *(adj.)* exemplary, flawless

impecunious *(adj.)* poor

imperative *(adj.)* necessary, pressing; *(n.)* a rule, command, or order

imperious *(adj.)* commanding, domineering

impertinent *(adj.)* rude, insolent

impervious *(adj.)* impenetrable, incapable of being affected

impetuous *(adj.)* rash; hastily done

impinge *(v.)* to impact, affect, make an impression; *(v.)* to encroach, infringe

implacable *(adj.)* incapable of being appeased or mitigated

implement *(n.)* an instrument, utensil, tool; *(v.)* to put into effect, to institute

implicate *(v.)* to involve in an incriminating way, incriminate

implicit *(adj.)* understood but not outwardly obvious, implied

import *(n.)* importance, significance; a product brought into a country

impoverished (adj.) without money or resources

impregnable *(adj.)* resistant to capture or penetration

impudent *(adj.)* casually rude, insolent, impertinent

impulsive *(adj.)* actuated or swayed by emotional or involuntary impulses

impute *(v.)* to attribute or ascribe often something dishonest or dishonorable

inane *(adj.)* silly and meaningless

inarticulate *(adj.)* incapable of expressing oneself clearly through speech

incarnate *(adj.)* existing in the flesh, embodied; *(v.)* to give human form to

incendiary *(n.)* a person who agitates; *(adj.)* inflammatory, causing combustion

incessant *(adj.)* unending

inchoate *(adj.)* unformed or formless, in a beginning stage

incisive *(adj.)* clear, sharp, direct

inclination *(n.)* a tendency, propensity

inconspicuous (adj.) not easily noticeable, not obvious

incontrovertible *(adj.)* indisputable

incorrigible *(adj.)* incapable of correction, delinquent

increment *(n.)* something gained or added; an addition or increase

incumbent *(n.)* one who holds an office; *(adj.)* obligatory or required

incursion *(n.)* a hostile entrance into or invasion of a place or territory, especially a sudden one; a raid

indefatigable *(adj.)* incapable of defeat, failure, decay

indigenous *(adj.)* originating in a region

indigent *(adj.)* very poor, impoverished

indignation *(n.)* anger sparked by something unjust or unfair

indispensable *(adj.)* absolutely necessary

indolent *(adj.)* lazy

indomitable *(adj.)* not capable of being conquered

induce *(v.)* to bring about, stimulate

industrious *(adj.)* hardworking, persevering

ineffable *(adj.)* unspeakable, incapable of being expressed through words

inept *(adj.)* not suitable or capable, unqualified

inevitable *(adj.)* impossible to avoid or prevent; predictable

inexorable *(adj.)* unyielding or unalterable; incapable of being persuaded

inextricable *(adj.)* hopelessly tangled or entangled

infamous *(adj.)* having a reputation of the worst kind; notoriously evil

infamy *(n.)* notoriety, extreme ill repute

infatuated *(v.)* having a fascination or intense liking for something

infusion *(n.)* an injection of one substance into another; the permeation of one substance by another

ingenious *(adj.)* clever, resourceful

ingenuous *(adj.)* not devious; innocent and candid

inhibit *(v.)* to prevent, restrain, stop

iniquity *(n.)* wickedness or sin

injunction *(n.)* an order of official warning

innate *(adj.)* inborn, native, inherent

innocuous *(adj.)* harmless, inoffensive

innovate *(v.)* to do something in an unprecedented way

innuendo *(n.)* an insinuation

inoculate *(v.)* to introduce a microorganism, serum, or vaccine into an organism in order to increase immunity to illness; to vaccinate

inquisitive *(adj.)* given to inquiry or research; desirous of or eager for knowledge

inquisitor *(n.)* one who inquires, especially in a hostile manner

insatiable *(adj.)* incapable of being satisfied

insidious *(adj.)* appealing but imperceptibly harmful, seductive

insinuate *(v.)* to suggest indirectly or subtly

insipid *(adj.)* dull, boring

insolent *(adj.)* rude, arrogant, overbearing

insomnia *(n.)* inability to obtain sufficient sleep; difficulty in falling or staying asleep; sleeplessness

instigate *(v.)* to urge, goad

instinctively *(adv.)* as a matter of instinct; arising from impulse; spontaneous and unthinking

insular *(adj.)* separated and narrow-minded; tight-knit, closed off

insurgent *(n.)* one who rebels

integral *(adj.)* necessary for completeness

integrity *(n.)* adherence to moral and ethical principles; soundness of moral character; honesty

intellectual *(adj.)* possessing or showing intellect or mental capacity; *(n.)* those who use intelligence and critical or analytical reasoning in either a professional or a personal capacity

intelligible *(adj.)* capable of being understood or comprehended

interject *(v.)* to insert between other things

interlocutor *(n.)* someone who participates in a dialogue or conversation

intermediary *(n.)* a go-between or mediator; a person who acts as a mediator or agent between parties

interminable *(adj.)* without possibility of end

intermittent *(adj.)* alternately ceasing and beginning again

internment *(n.)* the imprisonment or confinement of people, commonly in large groups, without trial, and within the limits of country or place

interred *(v.)* to place in a grave or tomb; bury

interrogation *(n.)* an examination by questioning

intervene *(v.)* to come between, interfere

intervention *(n.)* the act of coming between, or interfering in, the affairs of another party, such as a person or country.

intestate *(n.)* the description of a person who dies having made no valid will

intimate *(v.)* to hint, suggest

intimidating *(adj.)* discouraging through fear in the face of superior display of power, wealth, talent, etc.

intimidation *(n.)* is intentional behavior that would cause a person of ordinary sensibilities fear of injury or harm

intolerance *(n.)* unwillingness to accept or respect the beliefs or practices of others

intoxicating *(adj.)* exciting or pleasing (someone) in a way that suggests the effect of alcohol or a drug

intractable *(adj.)* difficult to manipulate, unmanageable

intransigent *(adj.)* refusing to compromise, often on an extreme opinion

intrepid *(adj.)* brave in the face of danger

intricacy *(n.)* something detailed, complicated, complex, entangled or involved

intricately *(adv.)* characterized by complexly arranged elements; elaborate

intrinsic *(adj.)* belonging to the essential nature of a thing

intuition *(n.)* the faculty of knowing instinctively, without conscious reasoning

inundate *(v.)* to flood with abundance

inure *(v.)* to cause someone or something to become accustomed to a situation

invaluable (adj.) valuable beyond what can be reasonably estimated, priceless

invective *(n.)* an angry verbal attack

inveterate *(adj.)* stubbornly established by habit

invigorate *(v.) to* give strength and energy to

inviolable *(adj.)* secure from assault

irascible *(adj.)* easily angered

iridescent *(adj.)* showing rainbow colors

ironic *(adj.)* Interestingly contrary to what was expected or intended

irony *(n.)* a figure of speech in which the literal meaning of a locution is the opposite of that intended

irreverence *(n.)* disrespect

irrevocable *(adj.)* incapable of being taken back

J

jeopardize *(v.)* to expose to loss or injury; imperil

jettison *(v.)* to throw away; abandon; to throw overboard

jubilant *(adj.)* extremely joyful, happy

judicious *(adj.)* having or exercising sound judgment

juncture *(n.)* a point of time; especially one made critical by a concurrence of circumstances

juxtaposition *(n.)* the act of placing two things next to each other for implicit comparison

K

keen *(adj.)* intellectually sharp, characterized by strength and distinctiveness of perception, having great mental penetration

kindle *(v.)* to ignite or light; to sir up or excite

knell *(n.)* the solemn sound of a bell, often indicating a death

kudos *(n.)* praise for an achievement

L

labyrinth *(n.)* a maze, an intricate combination of passages making it difficult to find the exit

laceration *(n.)* a cut, tear

lackluster *(adj.)* without brilliance or sheen, dull

laconic *(adj.)* terse in speech or writing

languid *(adj.)* sluggish from fatigue or weakness

languishing *(adj.)* losing strength or health, becoming weak

larceny *(n.)* obtaining another's property by theft or trickery

largesse *(n.)* the generous giving of lavish gifts

latent *(adj.)* hidden, but capable of being exposed

laudatory *(adj.)* expressing admiration or praise

lavish *(adj.)* given without limits; *(v.)* to give without limits

left-wing *(adj.)* members of a socialistic or fascistic political party or movement; embracing a variety of big government policies, ranging from welfare state socialism and paternalism to government ownership of the means of production

legerdemain *(n.)* deception, slight-of-hand

legitimate *(adj.)* lawful; according to established norms

leniency *(n.)* tolerance, mercy, gentleness

lethal *(adj.)* deadly, fatal

lethargic *(adj.)* in a state of sluggishness or apathy

leverage *(n.)* the increase in force gained by using a lever; influence or power used to achieve a desired result

levity *(n.)* joking or gaiety, especially at inappropriate moments

liability *(n.)* something for which one is legally responsible, usually involving a disadvantage or risk; *(n.)* a handicap, burden

liberation *(n.)* the act of liberating; the state of being liberated; freed from control

libertarian *(adj.)* advocating principles of liberty and free will

licentious *(adj.)* displaying a lack of moral or legal restraints

limbo *(n.)* an intermediate, transitional, or midway state or place

limpid *(adj.)* clear, transparent

linchpin *(n.)* something that holds separate parts together

lingerie *(n.)* women's intimate apparel or nightclothes

listless *(adj.)* lacking spirit, energy, or interest

litany *(n.)* a lengthy recitation or enumeration

lithe *(adj.)* graceful, flexible, supple

litigant *(n.)* someone engaged in a lawsuit

loquacious *(adj.)* talkative

lucid *(adj.)* clear, easily understandable

ludicrous *(adj.)* provoking laughter, scorn, or ridicule

luminous *(adj.)* brightly shining

lurid *(adj.)* ghastly, sensational

luxuriant *(adj.)* rich, fancy or elaborate

lyrics *(n.)* a set of words that make up a song

Ⓜ

maelstrom *(n.)* a destructive whirlpool which rapidly sucks in objects

magnanimous *(adj.)* noble, generous

malediction *(n.)* a curse

malevolent *(adj.)* wanting harm to befall others

malleable *(adj.)* capable of being shaped or transformed

mandate *(n.)* an authoritative command

maneuver *(v.)* a skillful moving or proceding; *(n.)* planned and regulated movements of troops, war vessels, etc.

maneuverability *(n.)* capable of being steered or directed; easy to control

manifest *(adj. or n.)* easily understandable, obvious; *(v.)* to show plainly; *(n.)* a list of cargo or passengers carried on a ship or plane

manifestation *(n.)* one of the forms that something has when it appears or occurs

manifold *(adj.)* diverse, varied

maritime *(adj.)* connected with the sea or navigation

maudlin *(adj.)* weakly sentimental

mausoleum *(n.)* a large tomb or a building that houses many tombs

maverick *(n.)* an independent, nonconformist person

mawkish *(adj.)* characterized by sick sentimentality

maxim *(n.)* a common saying expressing a principle of conduct

meager *(adj.)* deficient in size or quality

meander *(v.)* to follow a winding or intricate course

medley *(n.)* a mixture of differing things

mien *(n.)* air, bearing, or demeanor, as showing character, feeling, etc.

mellifluous *(adj.)* flowing with sweetness or honey; smooth

mendacious *(adj.)* having a lying, false character

mental capacity *(n.)* sufficient understanding and memory to comprehend in a general way the situation in which one finds oneself and the nature, purpose, and consequence of any act or transaction into which one proposes to enter

mercilessly *(adv.)* without mercy, cruel

mercurial *(adj.)* characterized by rapid change of temperament

meritorious *(adj.)* worthy of esteem or reward

mesmerized *(v.)* hypnotized; visually captivated

metamorphosis *(n.)* the change of form, shape, substance

meted *(v.)* to allot; distribute; apportion

methodically *(adv.)* characterized by ordered and systematic habits or behavior

meticulous *(adj.)* extremely careful with

milieu *(n.)* the physical or social setting in which something occurs or develops

miscreant *(n.)* a vicious or depraved person; villain

mitigate *(v.)* to make less violent, alleviate

mobilization *(n.)* the act of putting armed services into readiness for active service; to organize or adapt industries for service to the government in time of war

mocking *(v.)* to mimic, as in sport or derision

moderate *(adj.)* not extreme; *(n.)* one who expresses moderate opinions

modicum *(n.)* a small amount of something

modulate *(v.)* to pass from one state to another, especially in music

mollify *(v.)* to soften in temper; to appease

momentous *(adj.)* of utmost importance; of outstanding significance or consequence

monarchy *(n.)* a state or nation in which the supreme power is actually or nominally lodged in a single person, whether absolute or limited

monosyllabic *(adj.)* having only one syllable; brief, terse

morass *(n.)* a wet swampy bog; figuratively, something that traps and confuses

mores *(n.)* the moral attitudes and fixed customs of a group of people.

morose *(adj.)* gloomy or sullen

multifarious *(adj.)* having great diversity or variety

mundane *(adj.)* concerned with the world rather than with heaven, commonplace

municipality *(n.)* an administrative division composed of a defined territory and population; a local government entity serving a specific political unit such as a town or city

munificence *(n.)* generosity in giving

musings *(n.)* contemplations, thoughts

mutable *(adj.)* able to change

myriad *(adj.)* consisting of a very great number

N

nadir *(n.)* the lowest point of something

nascent *(adj.)* in the process of being born or coming into existence

naught *(n.)* nothing, zero, complete failure, ruin, destruction

nautical *(adj.)* of or pertaining to sailors, ships, or navigation

navigate *(v.)* to follow a planned course on, across, or through: navigate a stream

navigator *(n.)* one who navigates or practices the skill of navigation, whether of ships, planes, or other vehicles

nebulous *(adj.)* vaguely defined, cloudy

nefarious *(adj.)* heinously villainous

negligent *(adj.)* habitually careless, neglectful

neophyte *(n.)* someone who is young or inexperienced

neutral *(adj.)* not taking part or giving assistance in a dispute or war between others

neutralize *(v.)* to render ineffective, counteract; to put out of action

newshounds *(n.)* newspaper reporters, or journalists, especially those who are energetic and aggressive

niche *(n.)* a place or situation especially suited to a person or thing, a recess in a wall

nocturnal *(adj.)* relating to or occurring during the night

nomadic *(adj.)* wandering from place to place

nominal *(adj.)* trifling, insignificant

nonchalant *(adj.)* having a lack of concern, indifference

nondescript *(adj.)* lacking a distinctive character

nonplused *(adj.)* full of difficulty, confusion or bewilderment

notorious *(adj.)* widely and unfavorably known

novice *(n.)* a beginner, someone without training or experience

noxious *(adj.)* harmful, unwholesome
nuance *(n.)* a slight variation in meaning, tone, expression
nurture *(v.)* to assist the development of

Ⓞ

obdurate *(adj.)* unyielding to persuasion or moral influences
obfuscate *(v.)* to render incomprehensible
objets d'art *(n.)* an article of some artistic value
oblique *(adj.)* diverging from a straight line or course, not straightforward
oblivious *(adj.)* lacking consciousness or awareness of something
obscure *(adj.)* unclear, partially hidden
obscured *(adj.)* not clearly seen or easily distinguished
obsequious *(adj.)* excessively compliant or submissive
obsolete *(adj.)* no longer used, out of date
obstinate *(adj.)* not yielding easily, stubborn
obstreperous *(adj.)* noisy, unruly
obtuse *(adj.)* lacking quickness of sensibility or intellect
odious *(adj.)* instilling hatred or intense displeasure
officious *(adj.)* offering one's services when they are neither wanted nor needed
ominous *(adj.)* foreboding or foreshadowing evil
onerous *(adj.)* burdensome
operative *(n.)* a worker; a detective, secret agent, or spy
oppressive *(adj.)* burdensome, unjustly harsh, or tyrannical
opulent *(adj.)* characterized by rich abundance verging on ostentation
oration *(n.)* a speech delivered in a formal or ceremonious manner
ornate *(adj.)* highly elaborate, excessively decorated
orthodox *(adj.)* conventional, conforming to established protocol
oscillate *(v.)* to sway from one side to the other
ostensible/bly *(adj.)* appearing as such, seemingly
ostentatious *(adj.)* excessively showy, glitzy
ostracize *(v.)* to exclude from a group
oust *(v.)* remove, or expel from a place or position
overtly *(adv.)* openly, publicly

Ⓟ

pacific *(adj.)* soothing
palatable *(adj.)* agreeable to the taste or sensibilities
palate *(n.)* the roof of the mouth separating the mouth from the nasal cavity; the sense of taste
palette *(adj.)* a range of colors or qualities
palliative *(adj.)* soothing, calming, reducing the severity of symptoms
pallid *(adj.)* lacking color
panacea *(n.)* a remedy for all ills or difficulties

panoply *(n.)* a wide-ranging and impressive array or display

panoramic *(adj.)* an unbroken view of an entire surrounding area

paradigm *(n.)* an example that is a perfect pattern or model

paradox *(n.)* an apparently contradictory statement that is perhaps true

paragon *(n.)* a model of excellence or perfection

paramilitary *(adj.)* a group of civilians trained and organized in a military fashion, or working alongside the regular military

paramount *(adj.)* greatest in importance, rank, character

pariah *(n.)* an outcast

parody *(n.)* a satirical imitation

parsimonious *(adj.)* frugal, stingy

partisan *(n.)* a follower, adherent

patent *(adj.)* readily seen or understood, clear; patent leather: a hard glossy smooth leather, usually finished in black

pathology *(n.)* a deviation from the normal

pathos *(n.)* an emotion of sympathy

patronize *(v.)* to favor with one's trade; to treat in a condescending way

paucity *(adj.)* small in quantity

pedagogical *(adj.)* of, relating to, or befitting a teacher or education

pedometer *(n.)* an instrument for recording the number of steps taken in walking

pejorative *(adj.)* derogatory, uncomplimentary

pellucid *(adj.)* easily intelligible, clear

penchant *(n.)* a tendency, partiality, preference

peninsula *(n.)* a piece of land bordered on three sides by water; literally, almost an island

penitent *(adj.)* remorseful, regretful

penultimate *(adj.)* next to last

penurious *(adj.)* miserly, stingy

perennial *(n.)* lasting through many years, enduring

perfidious *(adj.)* disloyal, unfaithful

perfunctory *(adj.)* showing little interest or enthusiasm

periphery *(n.)* the outermost boundary of an area

permeate *(v.)* to spread throughout, saturate

pernicious *(adj.)* extremely destructive or harmful

perpetrate *(v.)* to perform an act, usually with a negative connotation

perplex *(v.)* to confuse

perseverance *(n.)* steady persistence in a course of action, especially in spite of difficulties, obstacles, or discouragement

personification *(n.)* a person or thing that typifies or represents some quality, idea

perspicacious *(adj.)* having a powerful and penetrating mind, quick to see and understand

perspicacity *(adj.)* shrewdness, perceptiveness

pert *(adj.)* flippant, bold

pertinacious *(adj.)* stubbornly persistent

perusal *(n.)* a careful examination, review

perusing (v.) reading or examining, typically with great care hroughout

pervade *(v.)* to be present throughout; permeate

pervasive *(adj.)* having the tendency to spread t

petulant *(adj.)* rude, irritable

philanthropic *(adj.)* charitable, giving

phlegmatic *(adj.)* uninterested, unresponsive

picturesque *(adj.)* of a character as to suggest a picture, strikingly interesting or colorful

pillage *(v.)* to seize or plunder, especially in war

pinnacle *(n.)* the highest point

pithy *(adj.)* concisely meaningful

pittance *(n.)* a very small amount, especially relating to money

placate *(v.)* to ease the anger of, soothe

placid *(adj.)* calm, peaceful

plagiarist *(n.)* one who copies or imitates the language, ideas, or thoughts of another and passes them off as his own

platitude *(n.)* a trite, dull, or obvious remark or statement; a commonplace

platonic *(adj.)* transcending physical desire and tending toward the purely spiritual or ideal

plaudits *(n.)* enthusiastic approval, applause

plenitude *(n.)* an abundance

plethora *(n.)* an abundance, excess

pliable *(adj.)* flexible

pockmarked *(adj.)* a mark, pit, or depressed scar caused by smallpox or acne; an imperfection or depression like a pockmark

poignant *(adj.)* deeply affecting, moving

poised *(v.)* state of balance or equilibrium; composure, self-possession.

polemic *(n.)* an aggressive argument against a specific opinion

ponder *(v.)* to consider deeply, meditate, to weigh carefully in the mind

portent *(n.)* an omen

potable *(adj.)* suitable for drinking

potentate *(n.)* one who has great power, a ruler

power of attorney *(n.)* an authorization to act on someone else's behalf in a legal or business matter

pragmatic *(adj.)* practical

precaution *(n.)* care taken in advance; a measure taken beforehand to prevent harm or secure good

precision *(n.)* the quality or state of being precise, accurate

preclude *(v.)* to prevent

precocious *(adj.)* advanced, developing ahead of time

predicament *(n.)* a difficult, perplexing, or trying situation

predilection *(n.)* a preference or inclination for something

predominantly *(adv.)* in greater strength, influence or number; most frequent or common

pregnant *(adj.)* being with child; fraught, filled

prejudice *(n.)* an unfavorable opinion or feeling formed beforehand, often irrationally

prematurely *(adv.)* occurring too soon, overhasty

preoccupation *(n.)* the state of being focused on and engrossed in something

preoccupied *(v.)* completely engrossed in thought; absorbed

preponderance *(adj.)* superiority in importance or quantity

prepossessing *(adj.)* occupying the mind to the exclusion of other thoughts or feelings

presage *(n.)* an omen

prescient *(adj.)* to have foreknowledge of events

prescribe *(v.)* to lay down a rule

presumably *(adv.)* by reasonable assumption

presumptuous *(adj.)* disrespectfully bold

pretense *(n.)* an appearance or action intended to deceive

pretext *(n.)* a purpose or motive alleged or an appearance assumed in order to cloak the real intention or state of affairs

primeval *(adj.)* original, ancient

pristine *(adj.)* something that is still in its original condition or still pure

privation *(n.)* lacking basic necessities

probity *(n.)* virtue, integrity

probate *(n.)* the legal process of administering the estate of a deceased person by resolving all claims and distributing the deceased person's property under the valid will

proclivity *(n.)* a strong inclination toward something

procrastinate *(v.)* to postpone taking action until a later time

procure *(v.)* to obtain, acquire

prodigious *(adj.)* huge, enormous, monumental, extraordinary

profanity *(n.)* language, gestures or actions that are considered as insulting, rude, vulgar, obscene, obnoxious, foul

proficient *(adj.)* highly capable, expert, skilled

profligate *(adj.)* dissolute, extravagant

profound *(adj.)* intense, extreme

profuse *(adj.)* plentiful, abundant

proletariat *(n.)* the working class, or wage earners in general

promulgate *(v.)* to proclaim, make known

prone *(adj.)* lying with the front of one's body facing downward

propaganda *(n.)* ideas, facts, or allegations spread deliberately to further one's cause or to damage an opposing cause

propagate *(v.)* to multiply, spread out

propel *(v.)* to drive, or cause to move forward; to urge onward

propensity *(n.)* an inclination, preference

propitious *(adj.)* favorable

proprietor/proprietress *(n.)* one who owns or owns and manages a business or other such establishment

propriety *(n.)* the quality or state of being proper, decent
prosaic *(adj.)* plain, lacking liveliness
prototype *(n.)* the original or model after which anything is formed
protracted *(adj.)* to draw out or lengthen in time, extend the duration of
provenance *(n.)* the origin or source of something
prow *(n.)* the bow of a ship; a pointed projecting front part
prowess *(n.)* extraordinary ability
proximity *(n.)* nearness in place, time, order, occurrence, or relation
prudence *(n.)* cautious, circumspect
prurient *(adj.)* eliciting or possessing an extraordinary interest in sex
pseudonym *(n.)* a fictitious name assumed to conceal identity
puerile *(adj.)* juvenile, immature
pugnacious *(adj.)* quarrelsome, combative
pulchritude *(n.)* physical beauty
punctilious *(adj.)* eager to follow rules or conventions
punctuality *(n.)* the quality or state of being on time
pungent *(adj.)* having a pointed, sharp quality—often used to describe smells
punitive *(adj.)* involving punishment
purloin *(v.)* stolen, often in a violation of trust; to commit theft
purported *(adj.)* said to be true or real but not definitely true or real
putative (adj.) commonly regarded as such, reputed, supposed
putrid *(adj.)* rotten, foul

ⓠ

quagmire *(n.)* a difficult situation
quaint *(adj.)* charmingly old-fashioned
quandary *(n.)* a perplexed, unresolvable state
quell *(v.)* to control or diffuse a potentially explosive situation
querulous *(adj.)* whiny, complaining
quiescent (adj.) quiet, still, motionless
quixotic *(adj.)* idealistic, impractical
quotidian *(adj.)* daily

ⓡ

racist *(n.)* one who believes that race is the primary determinant of human traits
  and capacities and that racial differences produce an inherent superiority of a
  particular race
radical *(n.)* extreme, going to the root or origin, one who follows extreme principles
rail *(v.)* to scold, protest
rancid *(adj.)* having a terrible taste or smell
rancor *(n.)* deep, bitter resentment
rapport *(n.)* mutual understanding and harmony
rash *(adj.)* hasty, incautious

rationale *(n.)* the fundamental reasoning behind a decision or something

rationalize *(v.)* to think about or describe something in a way that explains it and makes it seem proper, more attractive, etc.

raucous *(adj.)* loud, boisterous

ravenous *(adj.)* extremely hungry; famished; voracious; greedy

raze *(v.)* to demolish, level

rebuke *(v.)* to scold, criticize

recalcitrant *(adj.)* defiant, unapologetic

recapitulate *(v.)* to sum up, repeat

recede *(v.)* to go or move away; retreat; withdraw

reciprocate *(v.)* to give in return

recluse *(n.)* a person who shuns society, a loner

reconcile *(v.)* to settle or resolve; to make consistent with existing ideas

reconnaissance *(n.)* a preliminary survey to gain information, especially an exploratory military survey of enemy territory

rectitude *(n.)* uprightness, extreme morality

recuperating *(v.)* to recover from injury, illness or fatigue

redoubtable *(adj.)* formidable; *(adj.)* commanding respect

refract *(v.)* to distort, change

refurbish *(v.)* to restore

regale *(v.)* to entertain sumptuously; to give pleasure or amusement to

regime *(n.)* a form of government, a government in power

regimen *(n.)* a regulated course of diet, exercise or manner of living

regimentation *(n.)* systematic order; systematic; uniformity and rigid order a regulated course of diet, exercise or manner of living

regurgitate *(v.)* to throw back exactly; to give back or repeat, esp. something not fully understood or assimilated; to vomit

relegate *(v.)* to assign to the proper place; *(v.)* to assign to an inferior place

relish *(v.)* to enjoy

remedial *(adj.)* intended to repair gaps in students' basic knowledge

reminiscent (adj.) tending to remind or remember

remiss *(adj.)* negligent, failing to take care

rendered *(v.)* made or caused, performed, furnished

rendezvous *(n.)* an appointment or engagement between two or more persons to meet

renounce *(v.)* to refuse to follow, obey, or recognize any further; to give up (a title, for example), especially by formal announcement

renovate *(v.)* restore, return to original state; *(v.)* to enlarge and make prettier, especially a house

renown *(n.)* honor, acclaim

reparations *(n.)* the making of amends for wrong or injury done

repatriate *(v.)* to restore or return to the country of origin, allegiance, or citizenship

repentance *(n.)* regret, guilt, sorrow

replete *(adj.)* full, abundant

repose *(v.)* to rest, lie down

reprehensible *(adj.)* deserving rebuke

reprieve *(n.)* a temporary delay of punishment

reproach *(v.)* to scold, disapprove

reprobate *(adj.)* evil, unprincipled

reprove *(v.)* to scold, rebuke

republic *(n.)* a form of government in which power is held by the people and representatives they elect

repudiate *(v.)* to reject, refuse to accept

repulse *(v.)* to disgust; *(v.)* to push back

reputable *(adj.)* of good reputation

requisition *(n.)* a demand for goods, usually made by an authority

rescind *(v.)* to take back, repeal, revoke

reservoir *(n.)* reserves, large supply; an artificial lake where water is collected and kept in quantity for use

resilient *(adj.)* able to recover from misfortune; able to withstand adversity

resolute *(adj.)* firm, determined

resolve *(v.)* to find a solution; *(v.)* to firmly decide

respite *(n.)* a break, rest

resplendently *(adj.)* in an impressively beautiful manner

restitution *(n.)* restoration to the rightful owner

restive *(adj.)* resistant, stubborn, impatient

restraints *(n.)* something that holds one back, bonds, self-control,

reticent *(adj.)* disposed to be silent, reserved

retract *(v.)* withdraw

retrospect *(n.)* the consideration or analysis of past events

revel *(v.)* to enjoy intensely

revelations *(n.)* something revealed or disclosed

revere *(v.)* to esteem, show deference, venerate

revoke *(v.)* to take back

rhapsodize *(v.)* to engage in excessive enthusiasm

rhetoric *(n.)* the skillful and persuasive use of language; overblown or intellectually empty language

ribald *(adj.)* coarsely, crudely humorous

ridicule *(n.)* speech or action intended to cause contemptuous laughter at a person or thing; derision

rife *(adj.)* abundant

ruminate *(v.)* to contemplate, reflect

ruse *(n.)* a trick

ruthless *(adj.)* showing no pity or compassion; cruel, merciless

S

sabotage *(n.)* malicious injury to work, tools, machinery, or any underhand interference with production by enemy agents during wartime

saboteur *(n.)* one who commits or practices sabotage

saccharine *(adj.)* sickeningly sweet

sacrosanct *(adj.)* holy, something that should not be criticized

sagacity *(n.)* shrewdness, soundness of perspective

salient *(adj.)* significant, conspicuous

salutation *(n.)* a greeting

salve *(n.)* a soothing balm

sanctimonious *(adj.)* giving a hypocritical appearance of piety

sanguine *(adj.)* optimistic, cheery

satiate *(v.)* to satisfy excessively

satirist *(n.)* one who uses irony, sarcasm, ridicule, or the like, to expose, denounce, or deride vice, folly, evil, etc.

scapegoat *(n.)* one who is made to bear the blame for others or suffer in their place

scathing *(adj.)* sharp, critical, hurtful

scenario *(n.)* an outline of the plot of a dramatic work

scintillating *(adj.)* sparkling

score *(n.)* twenty

scoundrel *(n.)* an unprincipled, dishonorable man, a villain

scrupulous *(adj.)* painstaking, careful

scurrilous *(adj.)* vulgar, coarse

secluded *(adj.)* isolated, hidden, removed

sedentary *(adj.)* sitting, settled

seemingly *(adv.)* to appearances; apparently

semaphore *(n.)* a system used for sending signals by using two flags that are held in one's hands

seminal *(adj.)* original, important, creating a field

sensual *(adj.)* involving sensory gratification, usually related to sex

sensuous *(adj.)* of or pertaining to the senses; readily afffected through the senses

sentimentality *(n.)* the expression of tender feelings, sometimes to excess

sentinel *(n.)* a sentry; guard

serendipity *(n.)* luck, finding good things without looking for them

serene *(adj.)* calm, untroubled

servile *(adj.)* very obedient and trying too hard to please someone; subservient

shellacking *(n.)* to cover with varnish; a sound thrashing; an utter defeat

shrouded *(adj.)* shut off from sight or light, hidden, concealed

shun *(v.)* to keep away from deliberately, avoid consistently

simultaneously *(adv.)* existing, occurring or operating at the same time

sinister *(adj.)* threatening or portending evil, ominous

sinuous *(adj.)* lithe, serpentine

skeptical *(adj.)* tending to question or doubt, disbelieving

skullduggerist *(n.)* one who engages in dishonesty, trickery, or hishonest activity

sleuthing *(n.)* investigation, carrying out a search or investigation in the manner of a detective

smattering *(n.)* handful: a small number or amount

smoke screen *(n.)* a screen of smoke to hinder enemy observation of a military force, area, or activity; something designed to obscure, confuse, or mislead

sobriety *(n.)* the state of being sober; sedate, calm

socialist *(n.)* one who advocates the community ownership and control of the means of production, capital, land, etc.; a statist

sodden *(adj.)* soaked with liquid or moisture; saturated

soffit *(n.)* the underside of a part or member of a building, as of an overhang or staircase

solicitous *(adj.)* concerned, attentive

solipsistic *(adj.)* believing that oneself is all that exists

soluble *(adj.)* able to dissolve

solvent *(n.)* a substance that can dissolve other substances; able to pay all just debts

somnolent *(adj.)* sleepy, drowsy

sophistication *(n.)* the state of being poised, cultured, refined, knowledgeable and worldly-wise

sophomoric *(adj.)* immature, uninformed

sovereign *(adj.)* having absolute authority in a certain realm

speculation *(n.)* opinion, guesswork, not based in fact

spire *(n.)* a tapering conical or pyramidal structure on the top of a building, particularly a church tower

spurious *(adj.)* false but designed to seem plausible

stagnant *(adj.)* inactive, not developed, not flowing

staid *(adj.)* sedate, serious, self-restrained

staple *(n.)* a basic or principal element or feature; principal, main

stereotypical *(adj.)* something or someone that conforms to a fixed pattern

stingy *(adj.)* not generous, not inclined to spend or give

stoic *(adj.)* unaffected by passion or feeling

stolid *(adj.)* expressing little sensibility, unemotional

strategic *(adj.)* important or essential in relation to a plan of action

strenuous *(adj.)* requiring tremendous energy or stamina

strident *(adj.)* harsh, loud

stupefy *(v.)* to astonish, make insensible

subjugate *(v.)* to bring under control, subdue

sublime *(adj.)* lofty, grand, exalted

submissive *(adj.)* easily yielding to authority

subordinates *(n.)* occupying an inferior position, rank or class; secondary, minor

subside *(v.)* to become quiet or less active

subterranean *(adj.)* existing below the surface of the earth, underground

subvert *(v.)* to overturn or overthrow, destroy, ruin

succinct *(adj.)* marked by compact precision

succulent *(adj.)* full of juice; moist and tasty

succumb *(v.)* to submit to an overpowering force or yield to an overwhelming desire; give up or give in

summa cum laude (Latin) with the highest honor or praise

supercilious *(adj.)* looking down on or treating others in a proudly superior way

superficial *(adj.)* concerned only with the surface, shallow

superfluous *(adj.)* exceeding what is necessary

suppress *(v.)* to hold back or stifle

surfeit *(n.)* an overabundant supply or indulgence

surmise *(v.)* to infer with little evidence

surreptitious *(adj.)* done in a secret way; stealthy

surrogate *(n.)* one acting in place of another

surveillance *(n.)* the monitoring of the behavior, activities, or other changing information, usually of people and often in a surreptitious manner

swarthy *(adj.)* of dark color or complexion

sycophant *(n.)* one who flatters for self-gain

T

tacit *(adj.)* expressed without words

taciturn *(adj.)* not inclined to talk

tangential *(adj.)* incidental, peripheral, divergent

tantamount *(adj.)* equivalent in value or significance

tardiness *(n.)* lateness, the state of being delayed

tarmac *(n.)* (short for tarmacadam, or tar-penetration macadam) a type of road surfacing material patented by Edgar Purnell Hooley in 1901.

tattered (adj.) ragged, torn, shredded

tedious *(adj.)* dull, boring

temerity *(n.)* audacity, recklessness

temperance *(n.)* moderation in action or thought

tenable *(adj.)* able to be defended or maintained

tenuous *(adj.)* having little substance or strength

testamentary capacity *(n.)* the legal term used to describe a person's legal and mental ability to make or alter a valid will

tethered *(v.)* to fasten or restrict with a rope, chain, or similar restraint

theoretical *(adj.)* pertaining or consisting only in theory, not practical, hypothetical

threadbare *(adj.)* so frayed that the threads show, old and worn out

throng *(n.)* a host of people, a crowd, multitude

tiara *(n.)* a jeweled, ornamental coronet worn by women

timorous *(adj.)* timid, fearful

tirade *(n.)* a long speech marked by harsh or biting language

toady *(n.)* one who flatters in the hope of gaining favors

tome *(n.)* a large book

torpid *(adj.)* lethargic, dormant, lacking motion

torrid *(adj.)* giving off intense heat, passionate

tortuous *(adj.)* winding

totalitarian *(adj.)* characterized by a government in which the political authority exercises absolute and centralized control and the people have virtually no power

tract *(n.)* A leaflet or pamphlet containing a declaration or appeal, especially one put out by a religious or political group

tractable *(adj.)* easily controlled

tranquil *(adj.)* calm

transfixed *(adj.)* to make motionless with amazement, terror, etc.

transgress *(v.)* to violate, go over a limit

transient *(adj.)* passing through briefly; passing into and out of existence

transmute *(v.)* to change or alter in form

treacherous *(adj.)* disloyal, betraying trust; unstable

tremulous *(adj.)* fearful

trenchant *(adj.)* effective, articulate, clear-cut

trepidation *(n.)* fear, apprehension

trite *(adj.)* not original, overused

troubadour *(n.)* any wandering singer or minstrel; originally one of a class of medieval lyric poets who flourished principally in southern France from the 11th to 13th centuries

truculent *(adj.)* disposed to fight; pugnacious; expressing bitter opposition; scathingly harsh, vitriolic

truncate *(v.)* to shorten by cutting off

turgid *(adj.)* swollen, excessively embellished in style or language

turpitude *(n.)* depravity, moral corruption

U

ubiquitous *(adj.)* existing everywhere, widespread

umbrage *(n.)* resentment, offense

unabridged *(adj.)* complete, having nothing removed, or the most complete of its type

unanimous *(adj.)* having the agreement of all

uncanny *(adj.)* of supernatural character or origin

unconstitutional *(adj.)* not constitutional; unauthorized by or inconsistent with the constitution, as of a country

unctuous *(adj.)* smooth or greasy in texture, appearance, manner

undaunted *(adj.)* fearless and determined, not discouraged

underpinnings *(n.)* something that serves as a foundation; also women's undergarments

undulate *(v.)* to move in waves

unforeseen *(adj.)* not felt or realized beforehand; unexpected

uniformly *(adv.)* identically, consistently

unimpeded *(adj.)* not impeded; unhindered; not slowed or prevented

unkempt *(adj.)* messy, untidy

unobtrusive *(adj.)* not attracting attention in a way that bothers you; inconspicuous

unorthodox *(adj.)* not customary, unusual

unsavory *(adj.)* undesirable, objectionable morally offensive

unscathed *(adj.)* unharmed, uninjured, undamaged

unscrupulous *(adj.)* without conscience, unprincipled, unrestrained by scruples

upbraid *(v.)* to criticize or scold severely

usurp *(v.)* to seize by force, take possession of without right

utilitarian *(adj.)* relating to or aiming at usefulness, practical

utopia *(n.)* an imaginary and remote place of perfection

V

vacillate *(v.)* to fluctuate, hesitate

vacuous *(adj.)* lack of content or ideas, stupid

valedictorian *(n.)* the student who generally ranks highest in scholarship and delivers the farewell oration at a graduation ceremony

valedictory *(n.)* a bidding farewell, a farewell address or oration

validate *(v.)* to confirm, support, corroborate

vandalism *(n.)* willful or malicious destruction of property

vanquished *(adj.)* defeated, subdued, conquered, overcome

vantage point *(n.)* a position which gives one an advantage or favorable place for action or defense

vapid *(adj.)* lacking flavor or liveliness, dull, bland

variegated *(adj.)* diversified, distinctly marked

vaunted *(adj.)* highly or widely praised or boasted about

vehemently *(adv.)* marked by intense force or emotion

veneer *(n.)* a superficial or deceptively attractive appearance, façade

venerable *(adj.)* deserving of respect because of age or achievement

venerate *(v.)* to regard with respect or to honor

veracity *(n.)* truthfulness, accuracy

verbatim *(adj.)* in the exact words; word for word

verbose *(adj.)* wordy, impaired by wordiness

verdant *(adj.)* green in tint or color

verify *(v.)* to prove the truth or accuracy of

verisimilitude *(n.)* the appearance or semblance of truth; likelihood; probability

veritable *(adj.)* being in fact the thing named and not false, unreal, or imaginary

vestibule *(n.)* a small entrance hall or anteroom; lobby

vestige *(n.)* a mark or trace of something lost or vanished

vex *(v.)* to confuse or annoy

viable *(adj.)* capable of working, functioning, or developing; capable of living or of developing into a living thing

viaduct *(n.)* a bridge, esp. for carrying a road or railway across a valley, etc.

vicarious *(adj.)* experiencing through another

vicissitude *(n.)* event that occurs by

vigilant *(adj.)* watchful, alert

vile *(adj.)* morally despicable or abhorrent; evil or immoral; physically repulsive

vilify *(v.)* to lower in importance, defame

vindicate *(v.)* to clear from a charge or suspicion; to ascert, maintain, or defend against opposition

vindictive *(adj.)* vengeful

vipers *(n.)* venomous snakes

virtuoso *(n.)* one who excels in an art; a highly skilled musical performer

virulent *(adj.)* marked by a rapid, severe, and destructive course

visage *(n.)* the face, countenance, or appearance of a person or sometimes an animal; aspect, appearance

viscous *(adj.)* not free flowing, syrupy

vitriolic *(adj.)* having a caustic quality

vituperate *(v.)* to berate

vivacious *(adj.)* lively, sprightly

vocation *(n.)* the work in which someone is employed, profession

vociferous *(adj.)* loud, boisterous

volition *(n.)* the power to make your own choices or decisions

voracious *(adj.)* having a huge appetite, ravenous, excessively eager

vulgar *(adj.)* without refinement or taste, course, crude, gross

vulnerable *(adj.)* susceptible to being injured or wounded, open to attack

W

wafting *(v.)* born or carried through the air or water

wallow *(v.)* to roll oneself about in a lazy, relaxed, or ungainly manner, such as hogs wallowing in the mud; to come or remain helpless

wane *(v.)* to decrease in size, dwindle

wanton *(adj.)* undisciplined, lewd, lustful

wary *(adj.)* watchful and cautious, leery, suspicious

weathered *(adj.)* faded or altered by exposure to the weather

weigh *(v.)* to balance in the mind in order to make a choice; ponder or evaluate

whimsical *(adj.)* fanciful, full of whims

wily *(adj.)* crafty, sly

winsome *(adj.)* charming, pleasing

wistful *(adj.)* full of yearning; musingly sad

witticism *(n.)* a witty, clever remark or sentence

wizened *(adj.)* dry, shrunken, wrinkle

wrath *(n.)* vengeful anger, punishment

wreak *(v.)* to inflict or bring about

writhe *(v.)* to turn or twist, as in pain

Y

yoke *(n.)* a contrivance for joining together a pair of draft animals, such as oxen; an emblem or token of subjection, servitude, or slavery, etc.

Z

zealous *(adj.)* fervent, filled with eagerness in pursuit of something

zenith *(n.)* the highest point, culminating point

zephyr *(n.)* a gentle breeze

zoning *(n.)* the regulation of the use of land and structures within a particular geographic area

Other noteworthy references

Art Deco. An eclectic artistic and design style which had its origins in Paris in the first decades of the 20th century.

Axis. The alliance of Germany and Italy in 1936, and later Japan and other nations, that opposed the Allies in World War II.

bandeau. A simply shaped brassiere, usually of a soft fabric and delicate trimmings providing little support or shaping

Björling, Jussi (1911-1960). Swedish operatic tenor considered by many to be the greatest singer of the 20th century. He made his debut at the Swedish Royal Opera in 1930, at the age of 19, and, except for the war years, was the leading tenor at the Metropolitan Opera from 1938 to 1960.

Bolsheviks. The more radical majority of the Russian Social Democratic Party that advocated the abrupt and violent seizure of power by the proletariat (workers).

Brownshirts. Members of the SA (Assault Section), Hitler's violent unofficial military organization known for the color of their shirts; also known as stormtroopers.

brownstone. A building made of reddish-brown sandstone.

Chamberlain, Neville (1869-1940). Conservative politician and British prime minister from 1937-1940, known chiefly for his appeasement of Adolf Hitler at Munich in 1938.

Civil Air Patrol. A Congressionally chartered, federally supported, non-profit corporation that serves as the official civilian auxiliary of the United States Air Force (USAF).

Communist Manifesto. A short, but highly influential political tract written by Karl Marx and Friedrich Engels that presents an analytical approach to the class struggle, both historical and present, and the problems of capitalism.

Crimean Peninsula. A peninsula in the southern Ukraine on the Black Sea that has been controlled by various powers over its long history. It became part of the Russian Empire in the 18th and into the 20th centuries. Except for the period when the forces of Nazi Germany gained control during World War II (1941-1944), the Russian Soviet Federative Socialist Republic and Soviet Union controlled the Crimea for most of the 20th century. It became part of independent Ukraine with the breakup of the Soviet Union in 1991.

crystal set *(n.)* a very simple radio receiver, popular in the early days of radio (1920s).

Damocles, Sword of. A Greek legend in which an obsequious courtier named Damocles is given the opportunity to switch places with the tyrant Dionysius, but with a giant sword held by a single hair of a horse's tail hanging over his head. The moral of the legend is that with great power and wealth come great peril and anxiety.

dry goods. Textile fabrics and related articles of trade, in distinction from groceries, hardware, etc.

excise taxes. An internal tax levied on the manufacture, sale, or consumption of a commodity; any of various taxes on privileges often assessed in the form of a license or fee.

Fifth Columnists. Persons residing in a country who are sympathetic to its enemies and serving their interests.

free market. Economic activity governed by the laws of supply and demand, not restrained by government interference, regulation or subsidy.

German American Bund. An American Nazi organization established in 1936 to succeed the Friends of New Germany. Its primary goal was to promote a favorable view of Nazi German and encourage ethnic solidarity.

Gothic. A style of architecture originating in France and spreading over western

Page 255

Europe from the 12th to the 16th centuries, and characterized by soaring heights, pointed arches, ribbed vaulting, and flying buttresses.

Goy. The standard biblical term for a "nation," including the "great nation" of Israel. The term was also used pejoratively to describe those not of Jewish descent. Long before Roman times, it had also acquired the meaning of "gentile," which is also its meaning in Yiddish.

gramophone. The trademark of an early phonograph player; an instrument for reproducing sounds by means of the vibration of a stylus or needle following a spiral groove on a revolving disc or a cylinder.

Hitler, Adolf (1889-1945). Austrian-born German politician and leader of the National Socialist German Workers Party (commonly known as the Nazi Party). He was Chancellor of Germany from 1933 to 1945, and served as head of state as *Führer und Reichskanzler* from 1934 to 1945.

hyper-inflation. Extremely rapid or out-of-control inflation. Hyperinflation is a situation characterized by price increases so rapid that a country's currency quickly becomes worthless.

Jews. A nation and ethno-religious group originating in the Israelites or Hebrews of the Ancient Near East, the Hebrew or Jewish people; members of the tribe of Judah.

Kristallnacht (German). Literally "Crystal night," or the Night of Broken Glass, this was an anti-Jewish pogrom, or violent riot, in Nazi Germany and Austria on November 9-10, 1938.

Lenin (Vladimir Ilyich Ulyanov) (1870-1924). Russian Marxist revolutionary and communist politician who led the October Revolution of 1917 and ruled Russia until his death in 1924.

lingonberry. A Swedish berry similar to the cranberry.

National Socialism. The name used for political ideologies which merge nationalism and socialism, as was realized by the Nazi Party in Germany.

Nazi. A member of the National Socialist German Workers' party, which in 1933, under Adolf Hitler, seized political control of the country, suppressing all opposition and establishing a dictatorship over all cultural, economic, and political activities of the people, and promulgated belief in the supremacy of Hitler as Führer, the natural supremacy of the German people, aggressive anti-Semitism, and the establishment of Germany by superior force as a dominant world power. The party was officially abolished in 1945 at the conclusion of World War II.

Nelson, Ozzie (1906-1975). Popular American entertainer and band leader who originated and starred in *The Adventures of Ozzie and Harriet* radio and television series.

Nietzsche, Friedrich (1844-1900). German philosopher, essayist and cultural critic who advanced the concept of self-aggrandizement or the will to power as the chief motivating force of both the individual and society. He questioned both the religious and philosophical traditions of the West.

objets d'art. Literally, art objects (from the French); an article of some artistic value.

power of attorney. An authorization to act on someone else's behalf in a legal or business matter.

Queen Anne (1665-1714). Queen of England from 1702-1714; *(adj.)* elegant architectural style that emerged in the United States in the 1870s and was characterized by rich ornamentation, including gables, and wrap-around porches.

Roerich, Nicholas (1874-1947). Russian-born artist and mystic noted for his prolific depictions of the Himalayan landscape, which were suffused with symbolism. Settling in New York City in 1920, he inspired a coterie of followers who built the Master Apartments in 1928-29 as a combined museum, cultural center, and residential apartment building.

Romanesque. Noting or pertaining to an architectural style that predominated in southern and western Europe from the late 10th to the 12 and 13th centuries, and was widely copied in later centuries in the United States.

Roosevelt, Franklin D. (1882-1945). The 33rd President of the United States who led the country through the Great Depression and World War II. His administration, which greatly expanded the powers of the federal government, was called the New Deal.

rumble seat. An upholstered exterior seat which hinges or otherwise opens out from the rear deck of a pre-World War II automobile, and seats one or more passengers.

Russian Revolution. The Russian Revolution is the collective term for a series of revolutions in Russia in 1917, which dismantled the rule of the Tsar and led to the creation of the Russian SFSR, or the Russian Soviet Federative Socialist Republic.

Stalin, Joseph (1878-1953). One of the Bolshevik revolutionaries who took control of the Soviet Union in 1917, and ruled it from the mid-1920s until his death in 1953. Stalin was one of the 20th century's most ruthless and murderous dictators.

step-ins. Panties with wide legs; also an undergarment combining a camisole and panties; term used from the late 1920s to the 1940s.

Stormtroopers. Members of a private Nazi army under Adolf Hitler notorious for aggressiveness, violence, and brutality. Also known as brownshirts.

testamentary capacity. The legal term used to describe a person's legal and mental ability to make or alter a valid will.

Third Reich. Nazi Germany, or the Third Reich, is the common name for the country of Germany while governed by Adolf Hitler and his National Socialist German Workers' Party (NSDAP) from 1933 to 1945. It was preceded by the Holy Roman Empire of the German nation (962-1806) which constituted the First Reich; and the German Empire (1871-1918) which constituted the Second Reich.

U-boat. A military submarine; the anglicized version of the German word *U-Boot*.

undue influence. An equitable doctrine that involves one person taking advantage of a position of power over another, and where free will to bargain is not possible.

USO. United Service Organization. A nonprofit organization that provides programs, services and live entertainment to United States troops and their families.

Victorian. Of or pertaining to Queen Victoria or the period of her reign; noting or pertaining to the architecture, furnishings, and decoration of English-speaking countries between c1840 and c1900, characterized by rapid changes of style and changes of fashion, by the frequent presence of ostentatious ornament, by the presence of heavy carved ornament, elaborate moldings, etc.

Victory Garden. Also called war gardens or food gardens for defense, these were vegetable, fruit and herb gardens planted at private residences and public parks in United States, United Kingdom, and Canada during World Wars I and II to reduce the pressure on the public food supply.

War Production Board. Established by President Roosevelt on January 16, 1942, this U.S. government agency supervised war production during World War II. The WPB directed conversion of industries from peacetime work to wartime production, allocated scarce materials, established priorities in the distribution of materials and services, and prohibited nonessential production. It rationed such things as gasoline, heating oil, metals, rubber, paper and plastics. It was dissolved shortly after the defeat of Japan in 1945, and was replaced by the Civilian Production Administration in late 1945.

Wehrmacht. The German armed forces.

Bibliography

Austin, Paul Britten. *On Being Swedish*. Coral Gables, FL: University of Miami Press, 1968.

Breuer, William. *Nazi Spies in America: Hitler's Undercover War*. New York; St. Martin's Press, 1989.

Breuer, William B. *Undercover Tales of World War II*. New York: John Wiley & Sons, 1999.

Burns, Ric, James Sanders and Lisa Ades. *New York: An Illustrated History*. New York: Alfred A. Knopf, 1999.

Calhoun, John D., Lewis G. Knapp and Carol W. Lovell, for the Stratford Historical Society. *Stratford (Images of America)*. Charleston, SC: Arcadia Publishing, 1999.

Calhoun, John D. and Lewis G. Knapp, for the Stratford Historical Society. *Stratford (Postcard History Series)*. Charleston, SC: Arcadia Publishing, 2004.

Churchill, Winston S. *The Second World War*. 6 vols. Boston: Houghton Mifflin, 1950.

Dunning, John. *On the Air: The Encyclopedia of Old-Time Radio*. New York: Oxford University Press, 1998.

Eisner, Will. *The Plot: The Secret Story of The Protocols of the Elders of Zion*. New York: W. W. Norton & Co., 2005.

Gimpel, Erich. *Agent 146: The True Story of a Nazi Spy in America*. New York: St. Martin's Press, 2003.

Groom, Winston. *1942: The Year That Tried Men's Souls*. New York: Grove Press, 2005.

Guyton, Boone T. *Whistling Death: The Test Pilot's Story of the F4U Corsair*. Atglen, PA: Schiffer Publishing, 1994.

Hastings, Max. *Inferno: The World at War, 1939-1945*. New York: Alfred A. Knopf, 2011.

Hirsch, E.D. *Cultural Literacy: What Every American Ought to Know*. New York: Vintage, 1988.

Hirsch, E.D. *The Knowledge Deficit: Closing the Shocking Education Gap for American Children*. New York: Mariner Books, 2007.

Hirsch, E. D., Joseph F. Kett and James Trefil. *The New Dictionary of Cultural Literacy: What Every American Needs to Know*. Houghton Mifflin Harcourt, 2002.

Hirsch, E.D. *The Schools We Need: And Why We Don't Have Them*. New York: Anchor Books, 1999.

Knapp, Lewis G. *In Pursuit of Paradise: History of Stratford, Connecticut*. Kennebunk, ME: Phoenix Publishing, 1989.

Lorenzen, Lilly. *Of Swedish Ways*. New York: Barnes and Noble Books, 1964.

Roth, David M. *Connecticut: A Bicentennial History*. New York: W. W. Norton & Co., 1979.

Schweikart, Larry and Michael Allen. *A Patriot's History of the United States: From Columbus's Great Discovery to the War on Terror*. New York, Sentinel, 2004.

Sikorsky, Sergei I. *The Sikorsky Legacy (Images of Aviation)*. Charleston, SC: Arcadia Publishing, 2007.

U.S. Works Progress Administration. Federal Writers Project. *Connecticut: A Guide to its Roads, Lore and People*. Boston: Houghton Mifflin Company, 1938.

West, Diana. *American Betrayal*. New York: St. Martin's Press, 2013.

Wilcoxson, William Howard. *History of Stratford, Connecticut: 1639-1939*. Stratford, CT: The Stratford Tercentenary Commission, 1939.

Biographies

A native of Gary, Indiana, and graduate of Emerson High School, Kendall Svengalis received his B.A. in English literature (1970) and M.A. in American history (1973) from Purdue University in West Lafayette. His M.A. thesis was entitled *Progressive Education in Indiana: William A. Wirt and the Gary Schools, 1906-1920*. In 1975, he received his M.L.S. from the University of Rhode Island's Graduate School of Library and Information Studies. He has also done graduate work in American history at Brown University. In 1976, Ken joined the staff of the Rhode Island State Law Library, and was appointed State Law Librarian in 1982, a position he held until his retirement in 2002. From 1985-2002, he also served as an Adjunct Professor of Library and Information Studies at the University of Rhode Island. A nationally renowned expert in cost-effective law library acquisitions, he has published the *Legal Information Buyer's Guide & Reference Manual* annually since 1996 and for which he received the prestigious Joseph L. Andrews Bibliographical Award from the American Association of Law Libraries. He is currently President of New England LawPress/Duneland Press.

In 2006, Ken published *Gary, Indiana: A Centennial Celebration* to honor the city of his birth. He is currently working on a history of Emerson High School, which was the flagship school of Superintendent William A. Wirt's world famous 'Work-Study-Play' system of education. Ken is also President of the Rhode Island Swedish Heritage Association, and Vice-President of the Jussi Björling Society - USA, which honors the career and legacy of the 20th century's greatest operatic tenor. *Conspiracy on the Housatonic* is his first work of historical fiction, and the first installment in the Ellen Anderson mystery series.

Ellen Haffling Svengalis is a native of Stratford, Connecticut, and the inspiration for the novel's heroine. A graduate of Bunnell High School in Stratford and Norwalk State Technical College, she has been employed as computer programmer and analyst for a number of business concerns, including the NASDAQ. She is currently editor of *Musiktidning*, the national newspaper of the American Union of Swedish Singers (AUSS); as well as the organization's webmaster. She performs multiple roles for New England LawPress/Duneland Press, including those of editor, graphic designer, and webmaster.

Ken and Ellen reside in the rolling hills of Connecticut and spend their leisure time as a vocal and instrumental duo performing Swedish folk music at Swedish and Scandinavian folk festivals in the Northeast. In 2004, they were featured soloists on the AUSS Grand Concert program in Dearborn, Michigan, and, in 2005, on a 17-day American Union of Swedish Singers' chorus tour of Sweden. Ken's ancestry is Swedish and Lithuanian, while Ellen's is 100% Swedish.